BISH[OP]
PAWN

*Amy —
Happily Ever After
Guaranteed* ♥

Suzanne Halliday

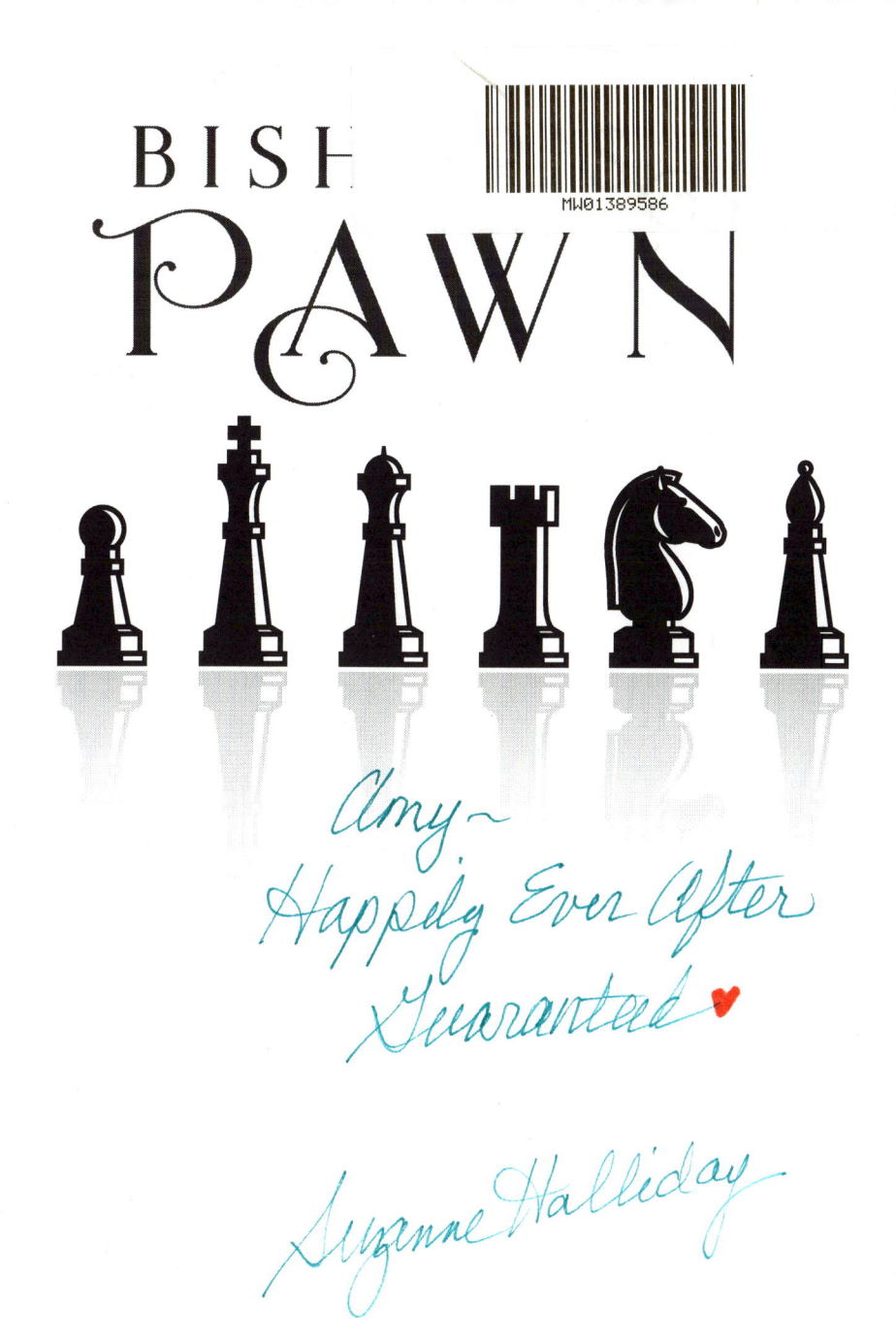

SUZANNE HALLIDAY

Copyright © 2017 by Suzanne Halliday
Bishop's Pawn

ISBN-13:978-1544083223
ISBN-10:154408322X

All Rights Reserved. No part of this book may be reproduced or transmitted in any form or by an means, electronic or mechanical, including photocopying, recording, or by any information storage and retrieval system without the written permission of the author, except where permitted by law.

*This book is meant for mature readers who are 18+.
It contains explicit language, and graphic sexual content.*

Edited by Gemma Rowlands
Book Cover Design by Sommer Stein of Perfect Pear
Cover Photo by Sara Eirew
Formatting By Champagne Formats

Dedication

Semper Fi

Chapter One

The plane whisking him from Arizona to New York City reached cruising altitude before Roman glanced up from the report in his lap. He had little more than eight hours to decide the best way to explain what he'd learned to his employer, along with a reasonable plan for how to go forward. And damn; this thing had more branches than he or his boss, Liam Ashforth, expected.

Turning his head, he gazed out the window. All he saw was miles of empty blue sky and puffs of white clouds. The five-hour flight with nothing else to do except think was going to serve him well if he had any hope of doing what Liam expected, which was to show up prepared with a plan and be ready for pretty much anything, because that's what his life was like now.

A slow smile crept onto his face. Ready for anything. Yep. Perfectly summed up the whirlwind that Rhiann Wilde brought to Liam Ashforth's previously starchy, uptight world.

Liam was easy to like. They had more in common than anyone realized. Loss, regret and resolve are powerful forces. He understood what drove Liam, and in their time together the two became friends.

Their relationship might look like the classic bodyguard and client arrangement, but Roman was essentially being paid an ass-load of money to be Liam's guy friend and Jiminy Cricket with the occasional dodging-a-bullet thing thrown in for shits and grins.

And then, of course, there's Rhiann. His smile grew bigger when he thought about the vivacious young woman who turned Liam's life upside down without lifting a finger. Love has a way of making a man do strange things. Like trade in his tailored suit for jeans and a button down shirt—even if it was only for one day each week.

On paper, Liam and Rhiann were mismatched sentences in search of a paragraph. She smoothed his sharp edges, and he gave her someone to focus her energy on. A quick snorting chuckle rose from his chest. The two were the poster kids for couples yin and yang.

He was happy for them. Really, really happy. Being around their joy almost renewed his severely damaged faith and hope. Almost.

But none of that was about him. Not really. As Liam's friend and an unabashed admirer of Rhiann's, it was up to him to put as much positive energy into the ether around them as possible. They deserved a break.

"Excuse me, sir?"

His head rolled on the seat back, and he looked at the first-class attendant. She was a very neat and efficient looking woman with a happy smile. He wondered what it was like to do her job. It couldn't be easy. Not dealing with the public when most people behaved like belligerent assholes.

"Would you like a beverage?"

"Yes, thank you," he replied. "Coffee, black." Offering a business-like smile, he mentally dismissed her without a second look.

This was new. Having zero interest in any of the women crossing his path. He wasn't sure why and wasn't planning on picking it apart…it just was.

Gathering up the papers and files on his lap, he made a neat stack and slid it into the briefcase bag on the seat next to him. Two thoughts were front and center in his mind.

First was the oddity of reverting to older forms of exchanging sensitive information. With being hacked as commonplace these days as the weather was unpredictable, there were times when not leaving a digital trail was essential. This classified situation with Liam's sister was one.

The second was the extra seat he reserved for the single reason that he didn't want to engage in perfunctory human-to-human contact with a stranger. Luckily, Liam didn't give a flying fuck what was on his expense report. He was awesome that way, and truly didn't care how much of his max-millions Roman spent, or on what. If he wanted to drop a wad of cash on lap dances and hotel room porn, Liam would just snicker and sign off.

Coffee in hand he went back to analyzing his current assignment of tracking down Liam's half-sister. Discovering he had a younger sibling had shaken the man's world.

He hadn't seen Liam or Rhiann in over a month. After hanging around Pennsylvania and New York following the summer arrival of Rhiann's newborn niece, they took off to London for a planned business trip that, Roman was thrilled to learn, included the two making their relationship official. Rhiann sent him a barrage of comical selfies from Liam's over-the-top formal proposal. Roman especially approved of the thoughtfulness and attention to detail, things that didn't surprise him about Liam. Not where his lady was concerned.

As he expected of his boss, the guy went right past taking it to an eleven and brought enough damn cowbell to send the dial off the charts. Knowing she was a writer at heart, he'd taken full advantage of being across the pond and found a charming bed and breakfast in the English countryside near Stratford-Upon-Avon. The fact that they weren't in a five-star hotel was a huge concession, but because it's Liam Ashforth after all, the man booked the entire B&B for the duration of their stay and turned it into a romantic's fantasy nirvana.

The happy couple were arriving in New York City a few hours after him, and he honestly couldn't wait to see them. They'd been through a lot, the three of them, not the least of which was Rhiann very nearly getting killed by Liam's crazy ex-business partner. No joke. They were all lucky to be alive.

How would he go about telling Liam all that he'd discovered? Having the Justice Agency and particularly Cameron Justice involved in the data gathering gave him an unusually thorough picture of what was going on. Cam was a tracking savant. He could find anybody, anywhere. But the bonus of uncovering the mother's background filled in a lot of blanks.

Roman detested Adam Ward almost as much as Liam did. It rankled the shit out of him how big a cold-blooded motherfucker the man was. He'd done Carolyn Ashforth dirty and in a particularly sleazy way. Using an employee, a secretary, as a sexual plaything and then kicking her to the curb after knocking her up was in his mind a heinous and despicable way to behave.

Learning the dick had a second bastard offspring by yet another secretary turned his stomach.

Kelly Anne James.

The attendant sauntered by and took away the empty coffee cup. She approached with an expectant look—a signal he read loud and clear. With an impatient sigh, he barely managed to be civil when she asked if he needed anything else.

Was trolling the first class cabin hoping to catch a guy a thing? He spent the fraction of a second considering the difficulty scale he'd face getting into her pants and just as quickly nixed the idea. Blowing off sexual steam with a bit of Jane Doe strangely held zero appeal. Avoiding eye contact made her dismissal easy. He was relieved when she left him alone and he could return to his thoughts.

Staring blindly out the window, he worked out a plan worthy of Liam's consideration. It might be a bit unorthodox but so the fuck what. This whole situation was irregular and fraught with problems.

Liam would see the advantages to Roman's plan. It kept the number of people who knew anything to a minimum and put not just eyes on the subject but feet on the ground.

He was less worried about a young twenty-something holed

up in a rural community a hundred miles off anyone's beaten path than he was about keeping the whole matter quiet. If things went as planned, he'd target Kelly Anne James, get every single scintilla of information about her that he could, and then hand it over to Liam.

He was feeling pent up and overly restless so dicking around with a twenty-three-year-old country girl one second more than was necessary just wasn't going to happen.

Maybe when this is over, he thought, I'll think about taking some time off. Plan an actual vacation. Someplace on the water where he could find some frickin' Zen and reset.

Seeing the whole pack of Justice Brothers married and with growing families shook him up more than he wanted to admit. Once upon a very long time ago that had been him.

But that was then, and this is now, and in his current reality, shit like marriage, kids, and a happy home life were things meant for other guys. He'd had his shot and enjoyed the sweetness until evil swept it all away.

He was content with his predictable life where a smooth brandy, a good cigar, a stack of philosophy books and Rachmaninoff on the sound system was enough.

"You motherfucker," she grumbled through gritted teeth and a clenched jaw. Applying all of her body weight, Kelly dug one foot into the dirt as a brace and put the other on the crooked bumper of her ancient but still road-worthy truck named Blue Bandit. A violent push-pull yank on the wrench finally got results even if she ended up losing her balance and dropping like a stone onto her ass with a thud.

Yelping because a rock digging into her butt triggered a sharp stinging pain, she rolled to her knees and struggled back on her feet.

"Kiss my bruised ass, Bandit," she snickered in triumph with a slap on the hood of the quirky blue vehicle. Tossing the wrench into her toolbox, she flinched slightly as the loud bang of metal hitting metal rang out.

Swiping her hands down jean covered thighs, she sidled up to the open truck window, reached inside the cab and grabbed her thermos bottle for a quick slug of sweetened coffee. She hated the bitter brew and ended up dumping way too much sugar into the vile necessity. Some days it seemed that without copious quantities of caffeine, she'd be screwed. Shuddering after another healthy swallow from the thermos, she gave the metal canister's lid a last turn and put it back on the truck's seat.

Overhead, the sky was an ominous gray, signaling another shit-tacular weather system was moving in. She could feel the deep furrows on her forehead when a frown settled. Mother Nature was at the top of her enemies list because nothing messed with her composure more than pretty much anything that made her already hard life even more difficult.

Just past twenty-three, Kelly Anne James knew more about life's cruel bitch side than most.

Lugging the old, rusty toolbox across the yard to the tool shed, she kicked with a rough-sounding grunt and opened the door. Her nose was instantly assailed with the musty smell of the small, cramped building.

Half the crap shoved into the shed was stuff from another era left there by her mother's family and forgotten. Just like the twenty-five acres she called home that decades ago had been a small farm tucked away in the woods and rolling mountains of Oklahoma.

"Forgotten should be my middle name," she groused faintly.

Hurrying away from the dilapidated shed, she made straight for the steps of the porch she proudly rebuilt. When the original wood rotted away, she'd made a project of tearing down the old structure and replacing it with simple planks. It might not be perfect, but it was functional and safe – good enough in her book.

The minute she stepped through the door her senses filled with the sights, scents and sounds of the little home she inherited when her mother passed. It wasn't much, but it was hers.

As the faint sound of classical music coming from the back of the house and the familiar smell of wood smoke settled around her like a warm hug she pulled on the neck of a hoodie acquired for two dollars in a thrift store and lifted it over her head. Quickly hanging it on a stubby wooden peg, she rubbed her hands together briskly and hurried to the fireplace.

While whisking stray ash off the brick hearth, she listened for telltale sounds from the bedroom at the nearest end of the hallway. Hearing nothing, she tended to the fire, scooping paddles full of glowing red and gold embers into a pile before adding a layer of wood chunks topped with a hefty log.

It was almost lunch, time to pay attention to mundane domestic chores such as the bread dough rising in two large stoneware bowls placed in a warming niche set into the red bricks next to the chimney. Say what you will about the rigors of rural living, but she rather liked the practical little touches from another century that gave her world its quirky definition.

Snatching an apron she'd made from a remnant of sturdy fabric, Kelly tied it behind her neck and wound the long ties around her waist twice, securing them with a firm tug.

Shoving a biscuit slathered with honey and drizzled with hot sauce down her throat, she injected some speed to her chores. With luck, she just might be able to get the bread ready for the oven before Matty woke up from his mid-morning snooze.

Without thinking, the steps she'd performed twice a week since she could remember played out. Living in the middle of nowhere at the intersection of Forgotten and Ignored, luxuries like fancy grocery stores and home delivery were unheard of. On her more and more frequent trips into Fairley, a real city about sixty miles away, sometimes she'd splurge on a loaf of bread from the shiny, overstocked grocery store. The convenience was cool, but she wasn't overly fond of the bland, tasteless product.

"I'll make my own bread thank you very much," she muttered

into the silence, wiping her hands on a dishtowel.

Cracking open the oven door she peered inside at the thermometer hanging on the middle rack. Perfect. Just as she slid the last loaf onto the rack, a small voice called out. "Kiki?"

"I'm in the kitchen, Matty," she answered. "Making lunch. Go potty and then come here."

"Okay."

She smiled. Matthew James had to be the coolest almost-four-year-old on the entire planet. Not only was he self-regulating and capable, the kid had an old soul quality that meshed well with her in-the-moment, getting-shit-done approach to living.

They were an awesome team.

At the stove, she lifted the lid on a pot of meatballs in bubbling sauce, scooped out two and put them in a dish to cool. It was lunch, and her rule that milk was always on the menu for the midday meal meant she needed Matty's favorite cup. Finding it in the rack with the other breakfast dishes she'd yet to put away, Kelly retrieved the blue plastic cup with the green dinosaur tail for the handle and placed it on the kitchen table.

Matty loved the stupid cup. They found it last year at a flea market and paid a whopping nickel to bring it home. It was the dinosaur that sealed the deal. From the time he was old enough to be interested in something, the kid was a full-on junior paleontologist.

"Is it gonna snow?" he asked after turning up two inches behind her butt. She was used to the soundless way he moved but it still startled her.

"Soon, I think. Winter is almost here." Stooping, she kissed him on the nose. "Did you wash?"

Proudly grinning, he nodded eagerly and did a hand flip display and then cupped both hands near his nose. He made one of those noisy exaggerated kid inhales and delightfully exclaimed, "Strawberry soap, Kiki!"

Ruffling his dirty blonde hair, she snickered softly and drawled, "You're welcome."

Smelly soap was another of Matty's favorite things. There was something about getting clean with a delicious smelling simple luxury that took some of the ache out of their hard-scrabble life in rural Oklahoma. Smelly soap, however, wasn't easy to come by or cost efficient. But then a snippet of random information she picked up during a friendly chat with the woman behind the counter at her favorite thrift store changed how she approached trying to solve the problem. For a two-dollar investment, she picked up three large bottles of no-brand strawberry shampoo and one of those pump soap things that turns water and soap into foam. Matty thought they were living high on the hog now with their fancy fruit foam. The bonus was that she ended up with enough shampoo to mix up a year's worth and still have enough left over for countless hair washes.

"Okay, Mr. James. Grab the milk and plant your bottom on the bench while I get lunch. You want s'ghetti noodles or elbows with your meatballs?"

"S'ghetti, Kiki! And can I have bacon too?"

She cracked up laughing and slapped her hands to her waist. "Eww. Bacon spaghetti and meatballs? Yuk."

"But I like Sam's bacon. He says he smokes it with magic powder."

Joining him at the table, she pushed a bowl of spaghetti and meatballs close and gestured at the napkin. "Manners, young man."

"Aw," he grumbled while slapping a cotton square onto his lap. "No bacon?"

"Matthew James," she teased with laughter. "You are becoming a ravenous carnivore."

"I know both words," he proudly crowed. "The Megaraptor is a carnivore."

"Was," she reminded him. "We don't have dinosaurs anymore."

He shrugged off her reasoning like any kid would. "But we have books and pictures. Can I watch Jurassic World?"

"No!" she barked. "Enough with the dinosaurs. Eat your lunch, and then you can help me find a tree for Christmas."

My god. Jurassic World? No way. She watched it one night on

a shitty DVD one of the guys at Shorty's had to hand over when she beat his stupid raggedy ass at a game of pool. The movie scared the snot from her nose and gave her nightmares.

Although… that guy, the actor, Chris what's-his-name. He was kind of hot—if it mattered. Not that it did. She didn't have time for messing around. Not with a wood pile that needed stacking or the small matter of the broken window and pane on the second floor that absolutely had to be fixed before winter set in—the result of a tree limb crashing into the house during a violent spring storm.

Matty's mention of their friend Sam, the butcher, reminded her of the occasional forays into town and visits to Shorty's Bar that were requirements if she wanted to continue flying under the radar. A lesson her foolish mother never learned. Her refusal to interact with the folks spread out around their small town only made people whisper and talk more.

By the time Kelly was a young teenager, she was in charge of socially interacting with the neighbors. She made the dump runs to get rid of their trash, picked up the mail, dealt with the only local store and generally represented their notoriously private family, the product of Debbie James' boneheaded and absolute refusal to be part of the world.

As Matty chowed down on lunch, she picked at hers and glanced around. Restless eyes spied the calendar hung by the back door.

December second. Ugh. Another year was coming to an end. A thousand details cramming into one month exploded in her head. She had orders to finish and mail to go out next week, and with some luck there'd be more interest in her work from people in the gift-giving mood.

Thank god for the satellite dish they installed with the surprise inheritance she and Matty discovered after Debbie breathed her final breath. Plugging into the outside world changed everything for them. The ironic punch to the gut she felt was because her mother's avoidance of human contact left them cut them off from life – a situation that ended the second they learned of the financial windfall.

Thanks, Mom.

Twenty-five thousand dollars might be nothing more than a drop in the ocean to people of privilege and means. But to a country girl raised on home canned food, who bought her clothes second-hand and who took the annual maximum on her hunting license, that kind of money was a life changer.

Once the window was cracked and the Internet blew a hole in their off-the-beaten-path bubble, all things became possible. The breath of fresh air gave strength to her artistic flights of fancy, and she found an instant niche with her stained glass knick-knacks, nature jewelry and the quirky watercolors she used in her brand advertising and packaging.

That's right. K.A. James was a brand. Take that, life! She had plans. Plans for her and Matty that someday soon would mean they could leave Providence behind and strike out on their own into the big world. The world where she and Matty weren't the illegitimate spawn of the man who destroyed their mother's life and doomed them to an anonymous, forgotten hell. A new world where the past didn't define the future.

But pulling off such a monumental life change was all on her. This wasn't the time to fake-make. Nope. The coming new year held nothing but hopes and dreams. If her mother had taught her anything, it was one simple fact. Never rely on anyone else for anything. People were undependable and mercurial. Today's friend could easily become tomorrow's foe. If she expected to succeed, then she had to put her back into it. Everything depended on her.

An uncomfortable twinge, like a flutter, made her tummy quiver. Lately, her dreams of taking Matty and leaving had become curious and confusing. There were shadows of a person who she sometimes ran toward, and at other times ran from. It was weird and so unlike her. But one thing these dreams had in common was the feel of his hand and a deeply masculine voice saying, "Thank God I found you."

She didn't know what it meant, but she did know that the

dream-like sensation of sliding her small hand into his changed her in some way.

"Hey, Kik," Matty mumbled through a mouthful of meatball. "Did you get Bandit started?"

She chuckled and made a face. "Darn tooting, I did!"

He clapped excitedly and wiggled in his seat. "Yay! Then can we go to Fairy? I like the library."

"First young man, no talking with your mouth full. Remember? Talking at meals is important, but we have to mind our manners, okay?"

Matty's eyes glinted with impish delight. He was a good kid but had his moments like any preschooler.

"And it's Fairley. With an L. Fair…lee," she enunciated with care.

"Fairley," he crowed. Her little brother's happy giggle made Kelly smile. "Let's look for a Franklin book at the library."

She nodded with a wink to let him know it was a good idea and thought of the wrapped Christmas present shoved in the back of her closet. Along with Internet access came the wide, wonderful world of Amazon. The mailbox at a UPS Store in the city that she used for K.A. James gave her easy access to package delivery. After scouring used book sites, she decided on a pile of hard copy story books. Matty was going to go bananas. Next to dinosaurs, his second great passion was books. The kid loved a good story. Something she knew well, since she'd been weaving fantastic bedtime tales for him since he was still in diapers. Verbal stories were fine but oh my lord. When she read to him from a book? He was mesmerized, so she made sure to get a story about a kid naming his dinosaurs.

Her thoughts drifted as Matty chattered on. Once he got started, it was hard to reel him in. But only with her. When strangers were around, he went silent. She often wondered where he picked up the odd quirk. Maybe their mother? She wasn't what you'd consider talkative.

Not that Matty would know that about her. Or remember her very much. After all, he was a toddler when she died. And it wasn't like Debbie had given two shits or a fart for her son. Or her daughter. No, that distinction was held by a single person. The nameless, faceless piece of dog dirt who fathered them.

"And he said that's the bestest spot to look. We have good trees, Kik!"

What the hell was he chattering on about?

"Sam says our gran let him cut his tree from anywhere on the mountain. He says Gran was a hooter. What's a hooter?"

Good grief. She had no idea. Sam was full of sayings and phrases that made no sense. Probably why Matty was drawn to the sweet old coot who was more grandfather than neighbor.

Before she could respond, Matty changed the subject and off he went on another tangent leaving her to return in her silent musings to the sperm donor responsible for her and Matty.

She wasn't completely sure they shared the same DNA, but all the signs were there. Their coloring was different, but they had similar eyes, and there were other things. Clues left by their mother like a cringe-worthy breadcrumb trail that led to only one conclusion.

Twice a year, Debbie would disappear for a handful of days. Like clockwork, Sam and his wife Ginny would either flat-out babysit her or, once she was old enough, keep an eye on things while her mom did whatever the hell it was that she did.

Right about the time Kelly turned thirteen, her young teenage mind noticed a pattern. Every May and November Debbie became an anxious mess. Then she'd disappear for a few days. When she returned, there was never any explanation, but there was other stuff. Things like her mom's new outfit and a haircut.

And cash. There was always a pile of cash after one of these disappearing acts.

Something ugly and painful swirled in her gut. Not because of the money. Who was she to judge if her mother was whoring herself out? Whatever it took to survive was sort of the family motto. What got her stomach roiling was the timing. Her birthday was in May. May eleventh to be exact. But she had not one memory of anything remotely birthday-like because Debbie was simply absent on the day.

There was no way to explain how she knew this but she was certain that the man her mother spent a lifetime trying to make love her, the man who came before everything else, controlled Debbie James. And that control had strings. Strings the cruel son-of-a-bitch pulled to separate mother and daughter on the one day they were meant to share. It was like he made Debbie choose, over and over and over between his bi-annual attention and the daughter he disavowed.

Asshole.

Bitch.

Determined to transform her birthday from a tragic slap in the face to something, anything, a bit more positive, on her nineteenth birthday she spent the day in Fairley at the old library taking her high school diploma exam. By then she was beyond sick and tired of the woods, the lack of a future and her mother's poor pitiful unloved me bullshit. Figuring out how to grab the bull's horn and take some control turned out to be easy. Knowledge was key. So was ability and she had a shit ton of the latter.

She remembered the day with crystal clarity. Just because her mother was content to be used for some man's sick, twisted pleasure didn't mean she intended to walk the same path. Confident that she'd aced the test, Kelly drove Bandit through a McDonald's for a happy meal she'd scraped enough change together to buy. The meal was nothing short of disgusting but the symbolic act made her feel normal and was a little reminder that she wasn't totally without means.

Life on the mountain was about working hard and getting the most out of what you had even if that meant making do with a whole lot of nothing. So while Debbie hid away in a fantasy world, Kelly did what she always did. Stepped up and in a big way.

By the time she was old enough to count as fast as a grown-up, she'd been a regular at the farmer's markets, church sales and seasonal fairs taking place all around Providence. If she could make it, bake it, can it, craft or draw it, she did, earning enough cash to help keep them afloat.

Confident that she'd pulled off the high school equivalency test and full of carefully thought out plans she was certain her best days were just around the bend.

Six weeks later she got her high school certificate in the mail.

Three weeks after that, Debbie announced she was pregnant, and Kelly's bright dreams instantly dimmed.

Glancing at Matty, she felt instant soul-crushing guilt at remembering how angry and horrified she'd been before he arrived. At the time, all she knew was that her pathetic mother's fucked up life choices once more required cleaning up.

She hadn't known then that managing her mother's trail of stupidity would be a life-long job. Being presented with a little brother at the same time she was leaving her teens behind ended up being a godsend.

The sound of a wood stool dragging on the floor brought her back from the musings running around in her brain. A small chuckle rolled in her throat as she watched her favorite guy clear the table and take their dishes to the sink.

They were a good team, and not just because he was incredibly self-regulating for so young a kid. Matthew James was the Yin to her Yang. Or maybe it was the other way around. She shrugged. Whatever. Specifics didn't matter. It was the point, not the semantics.

When she was frazzled or worried, he was calm and pragmatic. And when he was upset or frightened, she rode in on her dragon-stead and slew his demons.

Getting them out of the woods in time for Matty to start school in another year was the fuel to her fire these days. Everything she did, every plan she made, all of it was with just one thing in mind. She was going to do right by the little boy and give him a real life out in the world where he'd make wishes and dreams that were actually achievable.

The woods and mountains where she grew up were where wishes and dreams went to die a slow, painful death. She didn't want that for him.

Which is where the dirty money they inherited came into the picture. It was Sam's wife Ginny who filled in the blanks after Debbie suddenly dropped from a stroke and died on the spot. Yes, the money was from the man her mother refused to abandon. No, Ginny didn't know his name. All she knew was that Debbie went to great lengths to keep her whereabouts a secret and that the twice-a-year trysts took place in New Orleans. She traveled by bus under a different name and was careful not to leave clues.

The man was a wealthy businessman—which explained the money. The ultimate fuck off directed at Kelly by defiling her mother with clockwork precision on her actual birthday was all either of them needed to know when it came to judging the man's character.

She also divulged that the man was unaware of Matty's birth. Debbie had traveled to meet him when six months pregnant, but something had happened in his life that changed things. Ginny wasn't sure exactly what, but she got the impression from the way Debbie fretted that the man had been brought down by someone. Someone Debbie seemed a little afraid of.

The visits ended after that and triggered her mother's supersonic descent into poor health and becoming even more isolated if that were even possible.

When Matty was sixteen months old, Debbie James went to meet her maker. From that moment on, Kelly was the only family and caregiver for her little brother.

Matthew James. She couldn't love him more if she tried.

"Can we go find our Christmas tree now, Kiki?"

Stooping to his level, she wrapped the man of the house in a warm hug, enjoyed the way he hugged her back and then kissed his cheek.

"Thank you for doing the dishes," she drawled while ruffling his hair. "And yes to the tree. I think we need a little Christmas magic don't you?"

He laughed. "Oh, Kik. You're funny. You know if dinosaurs aren't for real then magic isn't either."

Damn. He was too smart sometimes.

"Do you see real dinosaurs in here?" she asked with a tap on his head.

His answering nod and kid-snicker were so him.

"Well, I see magic in my head so…" she hesitated for emphasis, "real enough."

He looked at her long and hard, searching her expression with his wise, old soul gaze. "I want your magic to be real."

"And I want you to see a real dinosaur."

They smiled at each other and broke out the fist bump, shimmy, wiggle that was their private ritual.

Christmas and New Year were careening toward them at high speed and she couldn't be more thrilled. Certain that next year would change everything, she pushed aside the lingering heavy thoughts and concentrated on the future.

Kelly and Matty James were on a roll. Look out world, 'cause here we fucking come.

Chapter Two

"I don't know why you're so surprised. You know how he is, Roman. Better than anyone."

He brought her in closer by moving the arm she held fast to and maneuvered them through the crowds moving swiftly along the city sidewalk. Rhiann Baron-Wilde was his favorite person-of-the-moment. He marveled at her unflagging do-gooder spirit, and thanked his lucky stars for Liam Ashforth's unrequited passion for the wickedly charming young woman.

She'd changed everything just by being Rhiann. Changed Liam's life and Roman's too.

Covering her gloved hand with his big paw, he pressed on her fingers and sighed. "Deliberating is one thing, Rhi," he murmured.

She smiled at his use of the nickname reserved only for those she held closest. He was honored to be in that singular group.

"But the hemming and hawing is ridiculous. It isn't what I expected at all."

She dragged them to the edge of the walk and turned to examine a window display. In the reflection of the large glass panes, Roman saw a slight frown marring her lovely face.

"It's complicated." She hugged his arm tighter and laid her head on his shoulder.

He didn't have to wonder what she meant. Liam Ashforth's relationship with the concept of family was tenuous on his best day. Denied by his father, all he ever knew were protective urges for his betrayed mother. When Carolyn Ashforth died, he'd been driven to seek revenge against Adam Ward. Not for himself, but for his wronged mom.

And he'd succeeded without breaking a sweat. With barely any effort Liam anonymously broke apart and bought up parts of the man's business empire until he owned him lock, stock and whiskey barrel. Everything that happened after that was karma and gave the old bastard a master class in getting what he deserved.

The shocking discovery not all that long ago about the possibility of a half-sibling rocked Liam's well-ordered world and came during a time when life seemed stuck in crisis mode.

"He did okay at Thanksgiving. Don't tell him I said this, but I was proud of how he handled the whole thing." Roman wasn't kidding either. Liam surprised the fuck out of him.

Being dragged along to the Baron-Wilde traditional Thanksgiving was a direct result of his part in saving Rhiann's life earlier in the year. There was nothing like a crazy employee going off the rails when it came to heart-pounding excitement. Stalking the boss's girlfriend like she wrote the manual had only been the beginning. It took him, Liam and an entire SWAT team to resolve the matter. It wasn't just Rhi who was lucky to be alive.

Overnight, he and Liam became heroes to Rhi's family, so he'd tagged along because Rhiann's grandmother, the quirky matriarch of the clan Bryanna Charles, had insisted. And when a Broadway legend insists and does it with tremendous panache and flair, there isn't enough wiggle room to decline.

Thanksgiving with the Baron-Wildes turned out to be not just a good time but an occasion when a smart guy like him could clearly see the life changes coming everyone's way. He'd thought a lot about that night and everything he learned just by paying attention. It was his training as an interrogator.

Liam's respect and admiration for Rhiann's dad, the hilariously irreverent Professor Robert Wilde, was an eye-opener. In all the years he'd spent with Liam on a daily basis he'd never seen him defer to any other man. Ever. It was a trait Roman understood since he shared the same one. But when it came to the scholarly professor, his boss was almost on his knees like a drooling fanboy.

The good Professor's robust acceptance of Liam and Rhiann's romantic relationship sealed the deal.

Then there were the Baron-Wilde sisters and their men, and holy god what a crew they turned out to be. Not that he was terribly surprised. Rhiann was one-of-a-kind, so meeting her equally original siblings was like being introduced to a cast of characters as memorable as any book he'd ever read.

First was big sister Brynn and her husband, Jax. On the outside, they looked like any newlyweds who were also juggling a young baby. Devoted. Slightly gobsmacked by the whole being parents thing, and clearly in love. The baby, a little girl, named Bryanna Katherine Merrill was quite a beauty and had been passed endlessly from person to person in a never-ending cavalcade of love.

Discovering that Jax was a war veteran made him view the guy through different eyes. He remembered Rhi mentioning PTSD in his background. Watching him and Brynn with their baby tugged at Roman's heart. If Jax Merrill could survive a ton of fucked up shit and find a normal life, then maybe all wasn't lost.

Thoughts of his Justice Brother friends flashed in his head. He always figured they'd be like him with a bad case of lone wolf and the unspoken belief that family and shit like that was for other people. But he'd been wrong about them. All three were happily married and making babies.

It was just Roman doing the same old same old while treading water and holding fast in the same old spot.

Rhiann's younger sister was an amusing piece of work who

redefined the hippie chick vibe. Charlize, or Charlie as she preferred to be called, was a card-carrying fairy-child draped in crystal jewelry. She had a laugh capable of stopping a speeding train and an infectious sparkle to her personality that he found charming.

Her boyfriend Caleb turned out to be Jax Merrill's brother, and because that wasn't weird enough, after a random tip Roman passed along back in the spring, the brother took the lead on a construction project in the Justice compound. And from what he'd learned through his conversations with Cameron Justice when they met to go over the information on Liam's sister, the Justice wives thought Charlie was an artistic genius.

In a surreal sort of way, Roman found different parts of his life morphing together. By chance or providence? Time would tell, but for now, the re-invigorated connection he kept with the Justice Brothers and their acclaimed security agency doing the tango with this unusual assemblage of people introduced into his life by Liam's involvement with the Baron-Wildes was bizarre enough.

So Thanksgiving unfolded in strange, weird, eye-opening and unusual ways. Liam held his own, and that's what mattered. Rhi's loving influence was slowly chipping away at the man's impenetrable reserve, and nothing could please him more. Having friends he could always turn to had saved Roman's life when things were darker than dark. Liam deserved the same.

The tale of the romantic proposal Liam pulled off while he and Rhi were in Europe was pretty much a guaranteed coup de grace, after which he'd gotten sucked into to the brother-in-law dynamic with glee.

Roman wasn't even a tiny bit surprised when Liam, Jax, Caleb and both their fathers—because the Merrills were also at the Thanksgiving table—ended the evening with the outline of a business project already being put in motion. He'd been impressed by the ease with which the group of men exchanged ideas and admitted their scheme of buying property to build clusters of mini cottages— slightly bigger than a tiny home—was fucking brilliant.

So what did all this mean in the bigger picture? Nothing less than a real, live, warm-blooded, family unit had taken Liam Ashforth in and given the driven loner a place bypassing. Saying it's complicated was only part of it.

"The devil is in the details," Rhiann murmured. "This was his first holiday with my family. He had to get it right."

Roman's cheek moved on Rhiann's head when he nodded his understanding. Success and failure balanced on a razor's edge in Liam's mind. There wasn't any middle ground. Maybe as time went on and Rhi loosened him up some more, but right now shit was still black and white.

"Dealing with everything you found out, right after we got back from London, well…he chose to invoke the Goddess Ignora as Charlie would say and push it all aside until after the holidays."

The people moving by bumped against them. Instinct made him block Rhiann from further contact. His protective nature was more than reflex, more than training. If anything happened to her, he wouldn't be able to live with himself.

"Easy, Rambo," she drawled. Her hand rubbed between his shoulder blades. "I'm pretty sure a sidewalk threat assessment is a bit much."

"I'm starting to hate the city," he grumbled. "Too goddamn many people."

Turning his back on the teeming throng, he whirled around and checked to be sure Rhi was okay. When she pulled off her glove so she could fix her hair, Roman growled and snatched the glove from her hand.

"What did I tell you about flashing that ring?"

She made no effort to hide the fact that she was laughing at him as he struggled to push her hand back into the glove. Shivering from the biting cold, she gave him a cheeky grin and elbowed his side.

"You'll lose your GTA privileges if I'm returned to your overlord with frostbite."

Slinging an arm around her neck as she yowled her displeasure, he dragged her close in an overly protective big brother way and marched them straight to the edge of the sidewalk where he quickly flagged down a cab.

"Have I expressed to you how fucked up it is that you dragged his overachieving ass into the realm of video gaming? Not nice, Ms. Wilde. Not nice at all."

She was cackling with laughter when he pushed her into the backseat of the shitty cab. Scooting out of his way when he claimed most of the seat with a bold man-spread, she smacked him on the arm in protest.

Barking their destination at the driver, he sat back and grabbed his assaulted arm. "Watch it, lady. You're flirting with workman's comp injury or maybe even a trip to BPG's human resources for a good talking to about abusing the help."

"Abusing the help!" she shrieked with hysterical glee. "Roman Bishop," she taunted, "you are a fraud."

"How so?" he asked, shocked by her words.

"I realize you get a paycheck from Black Phoenix Group. I did too once upon a fucked up time. But calling yourself the help is a joke."

Boom. That one landed with neat precision straight in his heart. He knew what she was getting at and came back with some humor so she'd know he was just messing around.

"Hey. It's not my fault. I've all but begged that uptight fuck stick to adopt me. Make our relationship official," he snickered. "But he insists on pretending I'm his bodyguard instead of…"

"His butt buddy?"

"Jesus H Christ, Rhiann! Butt buddy? You know what that means, right?"

"Yes, I do," she simpered with a goofy expression and a hair toss. "It means you're my fiancée's blood-brother. Sworn to protect me against all threats foreign and domestic."

The driver chuckled and then coughed to hide the fact that he was listening.

"I'm cool with the blood-brother thing but seriously, Rhi. Ask someone to explain what butt buddy means and then please god, use the term sparingly."

He could see by the glimmer in her eyes that she knew exactly what the words meant and was deliberately rattling his cage. This was a new wrinkle in his life. Having a female friend. A for real friend. Not someone he secretly wanted to shag. His affection and regard for Rhiann were the genuine article. In some convoluted way, she was a lot like the men he called comrades. Fiercely loyal, smart, and about the bravest badass female motherfucker he'd ever come across.

That's right. Rhiann Baron-Wilde, soon to be Ashforth, earned 'badass motherfucker' status and did it with equally as much if not more panache and flair than her Broadway legend grandmother.

With a sharp tug the gloves keeping her hands warm came off, and she jammed them into her pocket. His and Liam's edict that she not flash her ever increasing collection of expensive bling while in public was proving to be harder than anyone imagined. Rhi was one of the girliest girls he'd had the pleasure to encounter. Shoes and accessories were her not-so-secret guilty pleasures. It didn't seem in any way unusual to find her in the kitchen on a sunrise coffee run wearing nothing but Liam's shirt with a pair of outrageous bedroom slippers with Lucite heels and pink marabou feathers. The look was so Rhiann, as was the snarky humor because she named the slippers her bedroom hooker heels.

And nine times out of eleven she'd also be sporting something from the vast assortment of fabulous necklaces, earrings, bracelets and anklets that Liam was showering her with.

In Roman's opinion, the engagement ring only made things worse. Liam's knee-jerk default setting was to immediately go for whatever was the best. The most expensive. For him, details were irrelevant. Until Rhiann set him straight. As a result, he took a dog's age to find the perfect ring. During the long process, a representative from every high-end jeweler from Bahrain to Los Angeles came and went from the executive suite of BPG's offices in Manhattan.

Roman sat in on a few of these meetings and did his very best not to laugh in Liam's face. Watching the coldly polite, cutthroat businessman with shark-like instincts and a shrewd eye for value struggling to get in touch with his inner romantic was funny as shit. He wondered at those times whether Rhi fully appreciated how her love had changed Liam's life.

Pfft. Changed? Fuck. Try transformed.

In the end, Liam settled on a custom design. If the man could have mined the damn diamond himself he would have, but in the end he chose a classic three stone ring with pretty side-profile pavé-set diamonds set in platinum. It was a stunner and hard to miss. In today's fucked-up world, having eyes in the back of your head was necessary if you planned to wear something like that out in public.

And since Rhi was blissfully unaware when it came to situational awareness, they'd lowered the boom and demanded she cover up or take it off. Not long after, an assortment of gloves appeared in her wardrobe because no fucking way was she taking that ring off now that Liam finally balled up and proposed.

"I can hear your brain churning."

Raising his gaze to her expression hoping to find a clue, his brow shot up at her knowing smirk.

"Is this like a guy thing? You know," she chided playfully. "Say three sentences and then drift away in silence? What's going on inside that thick skull of yours?"

He chuckled and returned her smirk. "Sorry. Occupational hazard bolstered by a bad habit. My inner dialogue is strong."

"Well, I get that Mr. Bishop. But maybe you try a little more of this," she said in a soft voice as her fingers touched his heart, "and a little less of this?" Her gentle tap on his forehead felt like a shot straight to his heart.

Silence was his only defense against her keen observation. Convinced she had empathic powers, sometimes he meditated on Rhiann's unusual ability to go straight to the heart of something—completely by-passing or ignoring barriers and warning signs. The quality gave her a quiet, sure wisdom he rarely found in others.

"It's a new year Roman, full of chance and possibility, not just a date on a calendar."

She scooted up against him and clutched his arm as she rested her head on his shoulder. After a long sigh, she hugged him tight for a moment and then relaxed.

"Charlie would profoundly declare that Liam and I found our happily ever after at the exact moment things seemed the bleakest. I'd like to think our destiny was a bit more certain than that."

Her head moved on his shoulder, and she looked up at his profile. "I think we would have found our way back to each other eventually no matter what circumstance."

He nodded and patted her hand. True. There were some things that were just meant to be. Liam and Rhiann was one of those things.

She let out a sigh that sounded concerned and settled against him once more.

"But you've got a different situation."

Her voice was soft, almost a whisper. She was treading into the murky waters surrounding the foul swamp where fear and failure lived inside him.

"For you, there is no finding your way back. I get that. But there is a chance to let go of the past."

When he bristled, she kept right on speaking, using a soft but firm tone. "And maybe if you can't let it go there's a way to move it to the side. Respectfully, of course," she added.

Shit.

Fuck.

He didn't want to think about Vanessa and the child that would never be. Didn't want the glaring reminder of his failure to keep his loved ones safe. Rhi was exposing a raw nerve, and he wasn't sure he could keep it together.

"Please don't close the door, Roman. That's all I'm saying, okay? A little more heart and a little less mental. Promise me, and I'll shut up. Promise," she growled with a firm tug on his arm.

Dammit. He didn't have it in him to deny her, and he wasn't the type who could lie just to shut her up.

Patting her hand once more, he dipped his head and rubbed his cheek on her hair. "Doorstop in place, you bossy wench."

Her head popped up and very nearly clocked him in the jaw. The beaming smile evident in her eyes made him all sorts of twitchy.

"Really? How wide?"

Jesus fuck me Christ. Only Rhiann would have the balls to demand specifications.

"Inches. Less than a foot. And only because you asked nicely."

"That'll do," she crowed happily, and then with all the cheeky mock smugness she could round up, she extended her hand like a royal princess and cooed, "You may kiss the ring."

He dropped his best sardonic smirk onto his face and drawled, "Yeah, no." When her eyes widened he snickered and added, "If it's all the same to you, I'll wait till there's a wedding band."

Her laughter ricocheted off the walls of the cab as they pulled up to the massive Manhattan tower holding the corporate offices for Liam's Black Phoenix Group.

Swiftly paying the driver and leaving a hefty tip, he scurried after his wayward charge as she nonchalantly made her way through the lobby to the bank of elevators.

They'd left the apartment and gone out to window shop. Hopefully to clear their heads, too, but he was no more certain of how to move forward in the matter of Kelly Anne James than when they set out. Liam's uncharacteristically extended deliberation was getting on his nerves. He wanted the matter settled and off his plate.

In the crowded elevator, his hand shot out and stabbed at the button for the executive floor. The guy next to him shrank back – a small reminder to Roman that he needed to dial back the take-no-shit-or-prisoners persona he'd been overly aggressively rocking lately. Rhiann's telltale snicker-cough indicated she was thinking the same thing.

When the door opened to the main lobby of the BPG offices, he waved her on but followed closely behind, his eyes swinging corner to corner and up and down as Rhiann put on a little show for Liam's adoring minions.

"Hi Tammy," she cried with a friendly wave at someone milling around.

The tap-tap-tap of her shoes—a pair of suede pumps she called her 'daytime Choo's'—marked their progress. Everyone looked up. Liam had always been a good boss. He could certainly attest to that. But once Rhiann happened, he became a caring boss, and everyone knew how and why. For BPG, Rhiann Wilde was a fairy princess in real life come to break the spell of loneliness trapping the man-genius they worked for and transform him into the boss of the year.

"Ms. Wilde!"

Roman stayed back and watched as Liam's longtime personal secretary, Marjorie Gardner, pulled Rhiann into a hug.

"You look wonderful as always, my dear."

"Aww, thanks, Marjorie. Do you think this looks Duchess Catherine enough?"

He chuckled when Rhi pirouetted in front of Gardner's desk like a high fashion model on the runway in Milan.

"Dear lord," Gardner sniped. "Please tell me he didn't ask you to…"

"Good heavens, no!" Rhiann chirped in an amused giggle. "Come on now. He wouldn't know the difference between Stella McCartney and Stella D'Oro."

Both ladies cracked up, and he had to hand it to Rhi because the snarky observation was really funny.

"Is he busy? Can I go right in or do you have to make an announcement?"

That was it. Roman didn't have time for any of Liam's high and mighty bullshit. "Fuck that," he drawled and blew right past both of them, flinging wide the two massive doors guarding BPG's inner sanctum against mere mortals.

Gardner tried scrambling in front of him, but he anticipated the move and quickly sidestepped the block, earning Rhiann's amused cackle.

Framed by the enormous wall of glass that offered a spectacular view, Liam stood at one corner of a massive wood desk wearing an immaculately cut three-piece suit and his usual frown.

"Gardner," Liam grumbled. "What have I told you about letting this shithead in without proper warning?"

Executing a courtly bow punctuated with a middle finger salutation, Roman did his very best to play the fool to Liam's god-on-a-pedestal act. "I bring you the fair maiden, Lady Rhiann of Baron-Wilde."

The instant Rhiann swept into the cavernous office the man's face and mood lightened. So did his common sense. Lighten that is because for some insane reason he didn't bother to lower his voice and asked, "Did you talk to her?"

"Ah, shit," Roman grunted. He totally forgot.

"Talk to me about what?" Rhi asked.

Glaring at Liam for steering them into a ditch, he made a lame attempt to clam up, only to have Rhiann explode as Gardner stood by and snickered knowingly before scurrying away, closing the door behind her as she went.

"What part of his dirty work did he try to force on you, Roman?"

She'd stopped an arm's length short of Liam and slapped her hands on her waist in that wide-legged stance a woman deployed when she wanted to scare the snot out of a man.

"Honey," Liam stammered with his hands up in supplication.

"Zip it Ashforth. This is between me and your butt buddy."

"What?" Liam's icy stink eye was hella' funny.

Roman groaned and put a hand on his forehead. Being in the middle of these two wasn't all that different from dodging enemy incoming. He never knew where or when something potentially explosive would get tossed.

With a growl, he drawled, "She means blood brother, right Ms. Wilde? The look he shot her way bounced off the smug sneer that made him chuckle.

"If you say so, Mr. Bishop. Now tell me what nonsense he has formulating in that overactive mind. What exactly is he too much of a wuss to say to my face?"

"Jesus, Rhiann," he pleaded. "You do realize he's standing right there."

"Then I guess you better talk fast," she replied. When Liam took a step forward, her hand went up to keep him at a distance.

"Not even a hello kiss?" Liam asked sulkily.

"Only if you're prepared to kiss my ass in front of Roman," was her snippy reply.

Liam's reaction to her deliberate taunt let Roman know he had seconds before all hell broke loose. Best to lay it out there. "He thinks you were too friendly with your London security. Braedon I think his name was. Some shit about tea and scones or maybe it was fish and chips, I don't remember." He shrugged. "The point being, he wants me to wag a finger in your face and remind you that security is no laughing matter. Oh," he quickly added after catching his breath, "and he wants you to remember who you are."

"For Christ's sake, Bishop. Really?"

"Well, that is what you said, right? Don't fraternize with the bodyguard—no matter how hunky he is."

It was Liam's turn to groan and cover his eyes.

"And take the security seriously. You're the wife of a prominent man."

Rhiann gasped and folded her arms with an indignant huff. "No, he did not!"

With a scathing sneer, Liam growled, "I fucking hate you."

Roman was openly laughing now.

"Give him a raise," she demanded in a tight-lipped, stern nanny voice.

Liam looked like his brain was short-circuiting. "Excuse me?"

"A raise. I want you to give Roman a raise. Ten percent."

"He just got an annual raise."

"Did this annual increase address the fact that you expect him to do your relationship dirty work?"

"Rhiann," Liam begged. "Come on."

"As the wife of a prominent man," she said with a biting sneer, "I should get a say in his annual review. I want an additional ten percent on top of whatever he was already getting."

It was evident she had no fucking idea just how much Liam shelled out for his services, extended and all-encompassing as they were, because tacking on ten percent to the already exorbitant remuneration felt like taking candy from a baby.

Cracking a joke seemed like a clever maneuver, so he tossed out a good one.

"Hey," he told Liam with mock gravity. "It's like I keep saying. Be a lot cheaper to adopt my ass. Put me in the will. You do that, and I'll happily call you Daddy."

Then he looked at Rhi with a shaking head. "But no fucking way am I calling you Mommy."

Ten seconds of stone-cold silence dragged by and then all three of them exploded with gales of laughter and several exuberant high fives. Eventually, Rhiann pushed Liam into his penis-envy executive chair, the one so big it was visible from space, and climbed on his lap. Pulling a seat to the side of the desk, Roman ignored the all-too-familiar make-out session happening feet away and plopped down with an audible grunt.

"Ten more seconds and then I throw a glass of water onto you two."

It wasn't Liam who ended the kiss. Rhiann giggled and pushed him away as she sat up and wiped the corners of her mouth. Clapping her hands for their attention she eyed them both and said, "Gentlemen, no more fucking around. What's the plan? I've got a wedding to plan and a niece to spoil rotten. It would be nice to know if I also have a sister-in-law."

The expression on Liam's face when she referred to Kelly Anne James as her sister-in-law was all he needed. Suddenly the long agonizing deliberation made sense. Liam was afraid. Afraid to want something. Afraid that one more thing associated with the scum who fathered him would be a disappointment.

He didn't care at that moment what Liam's decision was because he intended to do everything in his power to see to it that brother and sister were reunited in a positive way. He wanted that for his boss-friend.

Rhiann caressed the side of Liam's face and smiled at him. "It's time, love. Just say what's in your heart, and we'll figure out the rest."

Roman swallowed a lump of emotion that sprang from nowhere and lodged painfully in his throat. Rhiann Wilde was an extraordinary woman.

Liam reached for her hand and kissed it, then closed his fingers around hers. When he swung his head and met Roman's curious gaze, the eyes meeting his were clear and focused. His voice was strong and confident.

"I want you to handle this personally, Roman. No one else. And I want things old school. No emails, no digital trail. Go to Oklahoma and check things out. Find out everything there is to know about my sister…Kelly," he said in a halting voice.

"Do you want her to be told or is this seek and find a general thing?"

Liam stared unblinking as he considered what Roman was really asking, then replied somewhat unsurely, "We're assuming she knows nothing but you know what they say about assumptions. Until we're sure, the connection should remain anonymous."

Anonymous.

Hmm.

That meant blending into the scenery in a place where a stranger asking questions might set off alarms. He'd already done some research and had half a plan ready to go in just this instance.

"Instead of trying to play incognito games, I'll just be someone passing through. Might take some time, though. Her being off grid from a traditional standpoint complicates things. No digital trail whatsoever—no email, bank accounts, credit cards, et cetera."

"I hope she's okay," Rhi whispered.

Liam rubbed her back. He seemed about to say something but didn't.

"What do you need Roman? Just tell Gardner, and she'll take care of accounts. Anything at all."

The sad hopefulness edging Liam's voice doubled Roman's resolve. Either Kelly Anne James was in for one hell of a surprise or his friend was going to get another painful life lesson.

He was sincerely pulling for the surprise scenario.

Chapter Three

Closing the book on his lap, Roman inhaled deeply, enjoying the way his favorite chair to read in rose up around him like an embrace. The modern version of a high back Queen Anne Chesterfield, upholstered in soft gray velvet, was angled to afford him warmth from the fireplace and a great view out the oversized windows of his Tribeca home.

How damn lucky was he that a guy like him was able to pay cash for a New York City loft apartment? In the right place at the perfect time, he'd snapped up the old two-bedroom unit for next to nothing when the original owner's family decided to sell and sell quickly.

Back then the place was a disaster, but he hadn't cared one bit. For him, the thrill came from the process. Buying the property, pinning down an architect and designer, and then bringing his vision to life.

Putting his book on the small round table beside him, he hiked his feet onto the round ottoman and sank into the chair so he could study the large room in comfort.

The muted grayness outside signaled yet another dreary city day. Typical winter weather tended to be damp and sometimes snowy but more than that, what grabbed on and held fast was bitter, unshakeable cold.

A log popped and crackled on its way to becoming ash. His eyes swung to the fireplace with its marble hearth and mantle. He loved having a wood fire in his home. It was so much better than one of those gas-powered fakeplaces. Luckily, his loft was accessible by a key elevator opening directly into the foyer. If not for that he'd be lugging wood up three flights of stairs.

Mahogany panels rose dramatically to the thirteen-foot ceiling above the fireplace. Several of the panels cleverly concealed a flat screen TV. The bold masculine vibe of the wood and the surrounding exposed red brick walls complemented his nature.

So did the ceiling to floor bookcases flanking either side of the fireplace. He almost made love to his designer on the spot when she added moveable, decorative cast iron ladders for easy access.

He glanced at the rack of antlers hung in the top third of the mahogany wall and snickered. They were a new addition and a tongue-in-cheek affectation that cost him a fucking bundle. Courtesy of Rhiann and her sometimes nauseating optimism.

After giving her the grand tour one afternoon she went off like she had a tendency to do. And because Rhi never encountered a point she couldn't make better through imagery, they ended up watching some fucking Disney movie. *Beauty and the Beast*. Because, she quipped, he reminded her of a character. Gaston. Gaston who could kick anyone's ass and who decorated with antlers.

The next thing he knew, Roman was on a fervent search for the perfect wall hanging.

Antlers. Jeez.

Using the control pad sitting on the small side table next to the chair, he turned on the sound system. His annoyingly restless and antsy feelings were back. Maybe music would soothe the beast inside.

Flipping through the eclectic assortment of playlists he'd meticulously programmed, he stopped and scrolled back to an oldie but goodie. A Rachmaninov symphony, number two, third movement. It was the perfect accompaniment to a fidgety Sunday morning.

As the composition filled the air he thanked the heavens for the wondrous magic of music. The soundtrack of his life was as random and varied as the experiences he carried like baggage. He flashed on the endless war soundtrack in his head full of AC/DC, Rage Against the Machine, Metallica, and his all-time favorite, Drowning Pool's *Let the Bodies Hit the Floor*. Not exactly what you'd expect of a Rhodes Scholar with a Master's in Philosophy.

He ran a hand through his hair and rubbed the lazy beard on his jaw. The crackling pops from the fireplace receded into the background as he let the music fill the emptiness inside.

Putting his head on the back of the chair, he stared at the ceiling and willed the demons and unruly troublemakers lurking inside him to ease off. It was his usual to be a right royal prick at the beginning of every year. Part of him hated the constant passage of time because in his case, instead of making things better, each new year only reminded him of the moment, frozen in time, when he lost everything. Including the future.

"Fuck this," he muttered in an irritated growl. Hauling up from the chair he stomped on bare feet into the kitchen and yanked open the refrigerator. Protein. That's what he needed. A big old pile of protein and one of his throw-together raw juice drinks.

Maneuvering around the two parallel counters in the galley kitchen he helped design, it took no time at all to broil a steak and juice up his secret recipe of raw fruits and veggies. At the last second he added a serving spoon loaded with hash browns to the plate and carried it behind the living room's sofa to the long rectangular pedestal table serving as a dining space.

From his seat, he could see out the windows and also enjoy the exposed brick walls that made his home so distinctive. He was drawn to the melding of styles and time periods throughout the apartment. The refined next to the rustic struck him as some sort of allegory. Unsure of the hidden meaning but aware that there was one, he slugged down half the glass of juice and focused on more important matters.

Like the eye-opening tidbit of insider information he pulled out of Liam after the man dropped a clue in Rhiann's presence. Remembering to circle back and find out what the fuck Liam wasn't telling him, he finally got him to drop the stoic reserve long enough to share.

Even though he hadn't been involved when Liam Ashforth went on his slash and burn crusade to destroy the man who fathered him, Roman was quietly aware of what went down. Most of it.

Liam's dogged persistence and steely focus built and powered a global enterprise of staggering wealth and influence. In his spare time, he meticulously and painstakingly poked, prodded, chipped away at, taunted, and finally annihilated Adam Ward.

And because the guy deserved it for the shitty way he treated the guy's mother, it seemed right to give Liam all the space and privacy he needed to deal with his demons. Roman was a seasoned veteran of the demon-inside wars and understood all too well what that kind of shit made a man capable of. From his place on the inside, however, Roman did some digging of his own, maintaining loose tabs on the situation and keeping an active dossier. He didn't want his friend walking into anything.

So he was aware of Liam's final death blow to Ward Industries. Knew of the face-to-face coup de grace involving handing the scumbag swimming in his gene pool the exact amount of pay off the old fucker had given to Liam's mom. But not until after he'd bankrupted him of course.

A backhanded 'fuck you one more time' in the form of detailed reports about her husband's lechery couriered to Adam Ward's wife had Liam's fingerprints in jet black indelible ink on all of it. She left Ward's sorry ass, thank god, and got the last laugh too. It ended up that while Adam was screwing every available hole attached to a pulse, his wife had been humping the family's lawyer for a decade or more. When Ward's sleazy shit hit the fan, she simply packed, left, and moved on up to a much better situation. Adam, on the other hand, found a condo outside Boca Raton in a halfway acceptable but right on the edge of society neighborhood.

It was just a random fluke when Roman stumbled on the dirty little secret that made Ward an even bigger douche. Discovering a half-sister was lurking out there had taken the whole wild fucked up saga to an eleven. Maybe a twelve.

Time wasn't much of a consideration though until Liam's bombshell. It turned out that Ward was on his way out. Some sort of cancer. Stage four. Roman didn't doubt Liam probably had the man's blood counts in a secure file—that's how close a watch he kept. The tension when he gave up this new wrinkle in the Ward saga gave Roman a sense of urgency. Locating Kelly James and figuring out what the fuck her story is was now time sensitive. It was glaringly evident Liam needed this thing wrapped up before the old fucker took a permanent dirt nap.

The steak was history along with the hash browns, and he was still ruminating over a thousand details when his phone pinged. Fishing it from the deep pocket of his Sunday morning sweats, he gave it a glance and instantly smiled.

It was Rhiann.

Have decided on blush pink for my bridesmaids.
Soon as you meet her let me know if pink is a good color.
Hugs Big Guy ~ be safe ~ miss you already
Xoxo Rhi
P.S. Your stand-in is a dud. Can't you train these guys to smile?

He snickered and shook his head. Damn straight the substitute bodyguard was a dud. Liam had enough problems with Rhiann. After the way he overreacted to their European team being too friendly, well…he wasn't a numb skull. Liam had his limits. All men do.

To avoid more problems, he'd hooked them up with an ex-cop who was the Terminator's doppelganger in appearance and attitude. Liam loved the guy. Rhiann? Not so much.

He'd thought about pulling her aside for a little lecture but after careful consideration nixed the idea. It wasn't necessary. Most of Rhi's fuckery was deliberate. Liam needed her enthusiasm, wit, and zest for life. She might come off as a spoiled, over energetic handful but it was an act. When it came to looking out for and after Liam Ashforth, he and Rhiann were on the same page. She'd walk into a hail of gunfire without flinching if it meant saving his life.

Her loyalty was unimpeachable, rock steady, and impressive.

The thought triggered an uncomfortable tightening in his chest that turned to a slow burn. Women with those traits were hard to find. He would know because once upon a long time ago there was a girl who tried…

Angrily shaking his head to chase away the memory, he stood up and shoved the chair out of the way with his foot. This wasn't about him. He had no personal life to speak of and intended to keep it that way.

Putting his plate and glass into the deep sink, he made quick work of cleaning up while examining the cold hard facts of his non-professional life.

When he needed sex, he got it. Uncomplicated hook-ups, nearly always with experienced women who shared or weren't adverse to his particular kink. He liked to fuck. And when he did, he fucked hard and with no apologies.

He'd done the Hallmark relationship. The one with sappy cards and over-the-top gestures. But that was then and this is now. Things change. People die. Circumstances evolve.

On his way down the brick-walled hallway to his bedroom, he considered getting his freak on before heading out to Oklahoma. Maybe letting off some of the steam powering his control-dominated engine was a smart move.

By the time he peeled of his sweats and turned on the shower the idea was relegated to the dustbin. Indulging in some pleasantly diverting dungeon play with someone who knew the score did not appeal to him in any way at the moment.

Under the steady stream of warm water he scrubbed shampoo into his hair and blamed the feisty Rhiann and lovesick Liam for his change in attitude.

Not content to place all his ire in one spot, he also included those Justice fucknuts and their perfect desert family.

Jesus Christ, he thought. Even Cam, bitter, anti-social Cam, had a gorgeous wife, a kid and another rugrat on the way.

Why was it just him whacking off in the shower when what he'd really like is a hot-blooded woman with a ballsy attitude who'd enjoy spending a lazy Sunday morning sucking his dick and going for a ride? A guy didn't need a wedding ring or a house in the suburbs for that. Didn't seem fair.

Suds rinsed away, he grabbed a body wash, squirted a glob into his hand and then smirked ruefully at the half-a-hard-on taunting him.

"Aw, come on," he grumbled.

Determined to master his baser urges, Roman exercised the control he was known for and finished the shower in record time.

With a towel slung low on his hips he walked around his closet tossing things into a pile for his trip to rural Oklahoma. Preferring order to chaos and systems to mayhem, he focused on the section where he kept the clothes he'd consider outdoorsy and rugged. None of his expensive tailored suits would be needed this time.

His mind ticked off a thousand details. He was flying into Amarillo first where he'd pick up the truck Gardner arranged for him.

From there the plan was to head southeast to a remote corner of Oklahoma where a set of GPS coordinates and nothing else would be all he had to locate and then pin down Kelly James.

He'd researched the hole in the woods town called Providence that was closest to her family's property. Far as he could tell it was a five street mish mosh of businesses and shitty houses that melted into the surrounding woods.

One of his Justice contacts led him to the only bar in town, a rundown saloon called Shorty's. Because all things were separated by those famed six degrees, it turned out Shorty's owner was an ex-Marine. And since Marines sticking together was the way shit worked, the owner, Jimmy gladly offered him a room above the saloon where

Roman could set up camp.

If Jimmy turned out to be a long-time local, Roman hoped he'd have useful information or point him in the right direction so he could get this show on the road and move things along.

The sooner and easier the better as far as he was concerned. And then maybe when this matter was wrapped up and Rhi's June wedding was over, he could step back and maybe take a real vacation. Sit in the sun and get his damn priorities straight. Decide what the fuck he wanted to do with his life now that he was a bona fide grown up.

Kelly glanced at Matty in his spot near the fireplace as he scooted around the rug building a rather impressive structure out of the oversized bin of second-hand Lincoln Logs she'd scored for ten bucks. When he saw the massive assortment tucked under the Christmas tree with a tag from Santa, his adorably cute face simply lit up with joy. Who said you needed expensive tech toys and batteries to have fun?

Kneading the ache in her lower back, she shifted in her seat to wake up muscles turned sluggish from her long sit at the kitchen table. The monthly paperwork for KA James and a stack of bills were spread out around her. She might be a shitty housekeeper with a bad habit for attracting clutter, but when it came to accounts and stuff like that? Well, she thought with a bit of pride. *I've got that shit covered in spades.*

Taking the number off the handheld solar calculator she got for free at the bank in Fairley, Kelly migrated the figure to an accounting sheet where she recorded every sale, expense and debt for her fledgling business venture.

The numbers weren't all that bad. Her stained glass trinket boxes were a big hit before the holidays, and the silver snowflake earrings were selling fast enough to be a seasonal favorite. It wasn't a lot, but her hard work and perseverance paid off. They'd turned the corner a few months ago, and she could now say with some assurance that their modest, thrifty household took in more than went out.

Balancing the books and making a nest egg for the future drove her hard. She was determined not to tap any more of the twenty-five grand her mother stashed in a duffle bag. They'd always lived hand-to-mouth, but she was smart and determined. Not everyone had the wherewithal to use what little he or she had to build a ladder out of despair. But she did, and that ladder was going to be strong because getting Matty out of the woods and into the real world was all that mattered and what she thought about twenty-four seven.

She had one year. One year to achieve the near impossible. He'd be four in February. Once he hit five, they needed to be settled someplace. She didn't dream about bright lights and big cities. Fame, fortune, and acclaim were not on her to-do list.

Nope, for her, ordinary and normal was the goalposts she ran toward. Being isolated and forgotten may have served her mother's purposes but all it meant to her was struggle. And she was sick and freakin' tired of struggling.

"Kik, look!" Matty squealed with childish delight. "I made you a fortress. And it has a real garage."

A fortress with a garage. Hmmm. The kid might be on to something.

Abandoning the monthly busywork, she hurried to his side and sank onto the rug. Playtime with Matty was as important as staying on budget. His refusal to speak around strangers was a real problem, but rather than focus on something she couldn't change and didn't understand, she devoted herself to verbalizing with him at every opportunity. Building his vocabulary and giving him confidence would serve him well eventually.

"This is the door," he proudly proclaimed. As he flopped onto his belly, she watched him with a smile lighting up her heart. She might only be twenty-three and have no real world experience, but she'd been a damn fine parent so far.

Virgin parent, her brain tittered.

Her chin tilted defiantly upward. There wasn't a single thing that she had to explain or apologize for. Not that anyone was asking her to, or paying attention to them in any way.

"What's this?" she asked, pointing to a stack of logs situated next to the fortress door.

With his chin resting in one hand and his feet waving in the air behind them, he explained in great detail how he saw things.

"They're for your garden, Kik. Right outside the door, so you don't have to walk so far. These logs," he explained while lining them up in a row, "will be the fence. No deer," he murmured.

She chuckled. Even at such a young age he already knew what a pain in the ass the wildlife could be and the toll their grazing ways took on their food supply.

"I like the way you think," she teased. "And what's this over here?" Side-by-side short towers stood at the rear of the fortress. The placement didn't seem haphazard, so she asked for clarification.

"Oh," he mumbled. His feet lowered, and he leaned on his forearms as a pensive look appeared on his face. "Sam says he'll come to wherever we are and build me a swing set."

Her heart did that little two-step thump she was intimately acquainted with. It happened every time she heard that small, yearning quaver in his voice. Lately, those times were happening more and more frequently.

She knew what moved him. Knew what he yearned for even if he was too young to put it into words.

They were okay, the two of them. A great team. But the world was big and had much to offer. To an old soul like Matty, the longing to break free was part of his first breath. She might not be in a position to personally explore all of the planet's seven wonders with him, but goddammit she was going to put him in a regular school where education would open the doors in his mind. After that, anything was possible.

"I think a real swing set with a sliding board would be nice.

Much better than our old tire swing."

His beautiful eyes crinkled at the corners when he smiled.

Overcome with sudden emotion, she scooted closer and grabbed him up into a fierce hug. "Matty, I promise. When we leave here, you can have a swing set and a bike and enough books of your own to make a library."

It almost killed her when he put his little hands on her face and gushed with love. "I'm man of the house, and I'll look out for you Kiki. Nobody is ever gonna make you sad again."

Her mind flashed on the memory of that butt-fuck from town, Burton Dulb. He and his old man had been after her to sell the land the moment Debbie died. To them. For an absolute pittance. Her old house, shed and half-barn might not be worth anything but twenty plus acres that included a stream and a pond was nothing to sneeze at. Maybe not this year or in the next five, but someday the James property would be worth something and she planned to hold onto it no matter what as something she could hand down to Matty.

Burton was an asshole of the highest order. Five years her senior he'd been giving her shit for years. When she was fourteen he tracked her in the woods, discovered her hidden tree stand and tried to bully her into sharing. She kicked him in the shins. He smacked her so hard she fell to the ground.

That moment marked her immediate growing up. Maybe her mother was okay with being treated like shit, but she was having none of Burt's crap. Scrambling to her feet she spied a perfect tree switch on the ground, grabbed it, and proceeded to beat the holy shit out of him while chasing the smarmy fuck to the edges of the property.

He'd been out to get her ever since. Having a fourteen-year-old whip your ass with a branch while you ran for cover was Burt's secret humiliation.

Believing she was at her most vulnerable following Debbie's shocking death, he moved in for the kill. She'd been frightened at first. He threatened to contaminate their well if she wouldn't sell the property, to cut the power lines, and anything else he could think of to make her life hell.

Those days were known as her funk time. She'd been sad and a whole lot more. But then she found the duffel bag of money. From despair came hope. Fighting back was her natural setting. The Dulbs were fucking insane if they thought she was going to be intimidated. So she got them back in her own way. Subtle 'fuck you's that almost dared them to come after her. Even if they threw the worst at her, she could shrug it off if she had to. She wasn't a runner. Sticking to her guns and standing her ground was much more her style so that's what she did. But it was still comforting to know if they had to bolt, they could.

"Oh Matty," she cried, holding him tight. "You're all I need little man. We're a team, remember? As long as we have each other, we'll always be all right."

Chapter Four

The vibration and thud as his booted feet struck the wood table made a stack of magazines slump to the side, and the two glasses of cheap whiskey next to them jiggle. An ear-splitting belch shot from his mouth, which in turn triggered a symphony of bellowing cackles from his drinking companion.

Waving his hand back and forth to clear the stench from the air, his host and temporary landlord, Jimmy Alton, lost no time piling on a mountain of shit. "Fuck man. Is that how they do at Oxford? Cam swore you're a…what did he call it? Oh, yeah. A scholar. Ha! Nice to know y'all scholarly types do the burp and fart chorus like the rest of us."

Roman smirked. "It's what you deserve for feeding me that slop or whatever the hell you called it."

"Ah, you big pussy. Fried catfish doesn't qualify for slop."

"Yeah? Well, fuck you because fried mashed potato and cheddar bacon bombs are on no sane person's healthy foods list. That belch was nothing. Hope your plumbing can take a hit."

He was enjoying himself. Jimmy turned out to be one fucking hilarious guy with a wry sense of humor wrapped in an appreciation of the absurd. Planting his butt in a room above the small town's only watering hole was a brilliant tactical maneuver. So was being a veteran. Not a lot of folks around a place like Providence were going to question a war hero, and hooking up from the get go with Jimmy made his presence a non-event.

Reaching for his glass of whiskey, Jimmy sniggered and held it aloft in salute. "I hear what you're saying but dude. A word of warning. My lady will kick your ass if she has to march up here with a plunger and unclog the john."

Slapping his stomach, he rubbed back and forth to relieve the burning in his gut. "I'm grounded," he chuckle-sneered with a wave at his glass. "Put that thing in my hand would you?"

"Lazy cockstucker."

A nanosecond of frozen silence ensued, and then they cracked up.

"Oh my god," Jimmy snorted with laughter. "Did I just brainfart a new word? Cockstucker?"

Laughing along with his new bud, he took a healthy swallow of whiskey and made a joke at the other guy's expense. "Firewater makes you smart, my friend. Or so they say."

Jimmy arched a brow and looked at him. "What?" he drawled. "You think some fancy degree that means exactly shit around here says you can spout bullshit and pretend to make sense?"

"Busted," Roman cackled. "Dude, I had no idea what that meant either."

Deciding to give up acting civilized, he deftly undid the buckle on his belt, unsnapped his jeans and let some of the over-stuffed feeling have space. "Ahh. That's better. Maybe I can think clearer now."

They relaxed and sipped in silence. From time to time he glanced around the surprisingly comfortable room tucked away on the second floor of Shorty's where Jimmy had an office.

It didn't have a king size bed with Egyptian cotton sheets or a flat screen TV. The pathetic thought made him wince. When had he gotten soft? Simple answer. About fifteen minutes after leaving the

Middle East behind. That's when. The occasional unease he felt about the luxuries in his life was entirely the result of the lingering feeling that being tired, thirsty, hot, stressed and hunkered down so your head didn't get blasted off was the only shit that mattered. Filtered water, one hundred and seventy satellite channels and a concierge service seemed like overkill until he remembered he earned every bit of the remarkable life he'd made.

"Turns out," Jimmy murmured after a long silence, "that my lady has all sorts of useful information on what you've been asking about. Or rather, who."

Roman's eyes shifted without his head moving. "What would that be?"

"She does most of her business clear across the county in Fairley. The butcher on Main Street? Name's Sam. He hooked her up with a booth at the farmer's market. Last time Kelly was in, she mentioned to Lil that she was selling crafts and not just eggs and stuff."

Really? Hmm. The girl has ambition. He liked that. Until he got to town, all Jimmy knew from Justice was that he needed a place to stay while he worked. When he started asking questions about the James family, the energy shifted.

Jimmy wasn't stupid. He wouldn't pry, and he'd keep his mouth shut. A mission was a mission was a mission, even in the civilian world.

"I'm curious about the mother. Debbie, right? What do you know about her?"

"Geez," he drawled. "Didn't you know? Deb James died, oh," he shrugged and stared at his hands a minute, "I don't know, almost two years ago. Right after I took over Shorty's. The folks living in the hills don't exactly put out newsletters, but I remember the talk at the time was that she just dropped one day. Aneurysm, heart attack, lightning strike, a zombie attack. Dunno. Dead is dead around here. Not much interest in the particulars."

Nothing chased off a cheap whiskey buzz like a thunderbolt of relevant intelligence. Sitting up, he took his feet down and ditched the ends of his drink on a side table.

"So the girl lives by herself?"

Jimmy's amused laughter cut through the air. "Seriously? She's an Okie. Believe me. N-B-D."

"Fuck yeah it's a big deal," he snarled. Unsure why this piece of information bothered him so much, Roman struggled to shake off the effects of heavy eating and drinking so he could think better.

Feeling an even greater urgency than before, he knew there wasn't time to lay out a plan. Adam Ward was flirting with death, and now the girl's mother turned out to already be gone. Liam wasn't going to like this. Not at all. Too many loose ends.

"Okay," he growled. "So the go-slow plan just got shot to hell. New focus."

Jimmy sat up and gave him all his attention.

"I need to see this girl in person. Meet her. How do I make that happen?"

A slow, wily grin marched across Jimmy's expression. "Dude," he chuckled. "You open your wallet, and I can totally make that happen."

"How?"

"Kelly James is a goddamn pool shark. Ain't nobody in their right mind around here these days who'll play against her, she's that good. I'd say it's a safe bet that the first annual buck fifty winner takes all Shorty's Eight Ball Tournament will draw her butt into town."

"You'd do that?" Roman asked with a wry chuckle. "Fuck, man. Pool tournaments attract barroom brawls faster than flies to shit."

"Yeah, well you just make sure my ass doesn't get beat, and I'll handle the rest."

Well, hot damn. This might be easier than he thought. Fuck wandering around dirt roads with a GPS. The clearest directions Jimmy could find for the old James farm was down the back road to the split and then take the third dirt path up the mountain. He'd need a fucking experienced Sherpa to figure out where the hell this girl was hiding. And since wandering the hills and woods was a surefire way to get his ass shot for trespassing, he had a bit of a problem.

"Tell you what. I'll pony up the buck fifty to the winner and tip the bar two hundred. And if there are any damages at the end of the night, I'll take care of it."

They shook hands and made a couple of lame jokes. As Jimmy made for the door, he turned at the last minute. "I don't know what this is all about, but I wanna say one thing, okay?"

He nodded. "Go on."

"Living in the woods, in the hills, well it's a tough life. Nobody around here butts in but that don't mean they forget about looking after their own. She keeps to herself and don't cause trouble. People won't take kindly to you fucking with her—not if she gets hurt."

"I'm not here to fuck with her. Look, I can't go into details, but Justice has my back on this. I hope that's enough for you to trust me."

"Point taken," he replied firmly. "I owe a lot to those guys."

And with that Jimmy left and Roman immediately got out his iPad and started to make notes. There was a lot to share with Liam, and he wanted to keep it all straight.

"Thanks, Ginny. I appreciate you keeping Matty overnight. These things can go late and I'd rather he wasn't alone."

"No problem, hon," the smiling woman assured with a warm squeeze on Kelly's arm. "You know how much we love having Matty over. My Sam loves the boy as if he's a grandson. You too, Kelly."

She threw her arms around the kindly grandmother surrogate she'd known all her life.

Ginny's wry grimace matched her words. "I feel bad for saying this, but you've changed for the better since your ma died. It's almost like her passing was a good thing."

She watched Ginny Martin bite her lip and make a sheepish face. "Not a good Christian woman thing to say."

"It's okay," she assured her. "We'll keep it between us 'cause I feel the same way. Debbie was always so…"

"Unhappy?"

"Yeah. And detached." She added a shrug and wrinkled her nose. "Not everyone is cut out to be a mother. I guess you could say as a parent she did what she could but only because she had to."

"She was a complicated, flawed sinner. Like the rest of us. I'm sorry she lived an unhappy life and glad she's in a better place so you and Matthew can get on with it."

Talking about Debbie's life and failings was on Kelly's least favorites list, so she took Ginny's last few words and turned them into a subject change.

With a smirky chuckle, she elbowed the older woman. "Well, tonight getting on with it involves taking pool cue candy from a baby. I'll be coming home with a hundred and fifty dollars in my pocket!"

Ginny shook her head and gave a comical eye roll. "Always so dang sure, Kiki! Hope Shorty's isn't setting you up with a ringer."

"*Pfft.* As if! And it doesn't matter who's lining up against me. Not only do I have a magic pool cue, if the going gets dicey," she said with a laugh, "all I have to do is flick open a few buttons, flash some boobs and bam. Victory."

With the perfect accent of droll, Ginny replied, "Men."

"Exactly."

Kissing the woman and giving her a shove to the door, she said, "Get moving old woman. It's cold as a witch's tit out there, and I'm sure Matty has already talked Sam's ear off while they waited for you."

"There's a storm coming in. I can smell it."

Both of them looked at the sky when they stepped down off the porch. At the end of the walkway, Sam's drool-worthy F-250 growled deep and low as it idled in the brutally cold temperature.

There was already a layer of old snow, not much—but enough to cover the ground. She made a quick mental bullet note to restock the wood stack by the back door just in case they got more.

"Now you be careful in town, young lady. No drinking! And whatever you do, don't instigate a bar fight."

The thought was outrageously funny enough to make Kelly laugh as she waved like a goofball at Matty who had his nose pressed against the rear cab window.

Bar fight? Who? Her?

Get real.

"Oh, fuck my daddy's wife," some drunk moron shouted, earning the shithead a malevolent glare from Roman.

"Did you see that?" the guy roared. "That girl knows how to fill a hole."

The room erupted in groans and rough laughter. He felt the clench in his jaw and mentally willed it to release before the unrelenting pressure cracked his teeth.

In the center of this assemblage of down home good ol' boys was his quarry. The mysterious Kelly Anne James. He glanced her way and clenched his jaw harder. She wasn't anything like he expected.

The minute she walked through the door all kinds of shit started happening inside him. Jimmy's nodding heads up when she arrived got his heart thumping with pent up anticipation, but once he laid eyes on her the thumping went from slow and steady to a racing rhythm that forced him to suck in air.

She was a smaller, dark-haired version of her older half-brother. The resemblance was a little weird—all things considered.

For the first ten or fifteen minutes, he'd managed to convince himself that he was just going through the basics. He was supposed to watch and observe, right?

The way too intimate full body assessment made whatever professional decorum he imagined turn to dust.

Pale skin and black as night hair that reflected the overhead lights gave her an unusual aura. Kelly James in her natural state was quite a sight.

If he had to guess he'd bet on five five. A little on the short side he supposed, although put her in a pair of heels and...yeah. That's where his mind went.

Wearing the uniform of her environment, she had on old jeans with a blue flannel tucked into the waist. When she came through the door, her hair hung loose, falling beautifully across her shoulders. But once the playing started, she'd pulled the whole mass into a high ponytail that for some unknown reason made his dick wake up. Watching her roll the flannel sleeves up to her elbow, he'd been more than a little fascinated how she trapped the cue between her legs to keep it standing upright as she fussed with her hair and sleeves. The sight of the red elastic band clutched in her teeth waiting to be put to use did more strange things to his dick.

Until those first moments the hysterically laughing sardonic commentary going on in his head had been largely quiet. He was too much the spit shine and organized type for random flights of fancy that led nowhere. But his visceral response to Kelly Anne James in the flesh set off an explosion inside him.

It was something Roman couldn't explain. Or wrap his mind around. She was a girl for Christ's sake. Barely in her twenties. Didn't he know better than to let his control off the leash around someone so clearly not for him?

Shit.

What the fuck was going on?

For the first ninety minutes, he kept to himself. Stayed almost hidden in a corner, observing his quarry while making assessments of the locals and her standing with them.

Not for the first time in his life, he nursed a beer and considered how unfriendly women could be to each other. Years of being a watcher gave him a unique insight into these things. Like right now, he could point out three females who gave the impression of social friendliness but who, when thinking no one was paying attention, snarled and rolled their eyes.

One, in particular, a tall bottle blonde with an attitude three miles wide, showed a particular disdain for Kelly.

Roman knew a set of surgically purchased tits when he saw them and even from across the room he could tell Miss Backwoods was rocking the Dolly Parton special.

Sneering into his drink, he took a short swallow. Fake tits were a weird universal truth. They showed up everywhere. In boardrooms, suburban bedrooms, and out-of-the-way hamlets in the middle of nowhere.

He wondered if the blonde disliked Kelly because her boob to body ratio fell in salivating range and were Grade A Prime and obviously God given.

Women. Go figure.

The men were a different story. He knew these guys without really knowing them. Most turned out were ex-military. Not a lot of opportunity in places like this where there was no real industry to speak of, so a stint in the service was almost a lifestyle. They worked hard and loved America. He silently tipped his hat to each and every one.

They also drank hard, and he knew what letting off steam on the weekend and an ass load of alcohol did to the social dynamic. Throw in a pool room challenge plus the lure of easy money, and a recipe for shit-fuckery was in the making.

Oh, and where Kelly was concerned, the men gave her a pretty wide berth. He wasn't close enough to hear the banter between her and the guys she played against, but body language told him a lot.

His general assessment at this point was garden-variety basic. She was one of them but not. And she might be young but the lady put off a prison warden air. Messing with her would not end well for the unlucky fool taking a chance.

He liked that. Another reminder of Liam, only in his boss-friend's case substitute warden for commander in chief and add a double measure of iron will. Maybe there really was something in the power of a single thread of DNA, because the half siblings were remarkably alike.

A round of shouts, catcalls and high fives around the three pool tables in the space wedged between the bar and tiny dining room rang out. He followed Kelly with his eyes. She milled around in a corner, pretending to fiddle with her cue. The way she turned her back to the room was the loudest fuck off he'd heard in a long time.

Jimmy sauntered by with an armload of empties collected from a circuit through the room. Like a seasoned operative with an understanding of tradecraft, he wiped off a round top behind Roman while juggling the bottles and calmly spoke. Anyone looking wouldn't notice their communication.

"Food break. About a half hour. Roast beef sandwiches at the bar if you're interested. She's ahead—no surprise. But a couple of the young wang whackers are starting to bitch."

Roman didn't nod or react. His eyes swung around the room. A ruckus at the bar had everyone's attention. Good.

"What's she driving?"

With a final swipe of the table, Jimmy straightened. "Blue truck. Ford. Seventy-one. Difficult to miss."

"One last question. Any of these meatheads a friend? She have history with someone?"

Jimmy juggled his burden again and moved closer to answer. "If she does, it's a well-kept secret. Nobody pays much attention. Although someone's gotta have her number."

"How come?"

The friendly saloon keeper snorted. "I figured you knew. She's got a kid, and I'm pretty sure there ain't a lot of virgin births going on around here."

The expression 'almost swallowed his tongue' had new meaning when he all but choked to death from shock. "Say again? A kid? What the fuck, man. You never mentioned a kid."

"Seriously. Thought you knew. Couple of people have seen him. Lil says she saw them once talking to Sam the butcher. But she never brings the kid into town and you know how that goes. Country folk. They keep to themselves. No big," he added with a growl.

Fuck.

Shit.

Goddammit.

This changed everything. A kid?

Jimmy walked away leaving Roman to struggle with this new piece of information.

From nowhere, a slow burn started in his gut. A dozen unsavory scenarios crowded his mind. All of them cast Kelly James as a victim. The idea that some man used her and left a kid for her to contend with made him physically sick. His earlier thought about how young she was only compounded the growing anger.

An instinct, old and primal, took root inside him. He needed to protect this woman. It infuriated him that someone, anyone, messed with her. A simmering pot of raw anger fired up and complicated how he viewed this assignment.

Finding Liam's sister was one thing. He'd done that. Shit. They were sharing the same oxygen. Mission accomplished.

Then, a powerful wave of emotion washed into his soul when a schism unexpectedly cracked open deep inside. He hadn't felt anything quite like it in a very long time. Perhaps ever.

Though his conscience flashed a neon warning that this was Liam's blood sister, he completely ignored the consequences of his reaction and concentrated solely on the impulses driving him.

The space separating them vanished in his mind's eye. He felt drawn. Pulled toward her. Compelled by forces he scarcely understood, Roman discarded the beer bottle and let his internal guidance system lead him straight to her.

Carefully maneuvering through the crowd without drawing attention, he was at the edge of the pool table she was hiding behind when he heard her voice for the first time.

Two things happened in the same instant.

The tinge of female huskiness in her voice made his dick rock hard, and he flew into a near blind rage upon discovering a male buck trying to corner her.

"Oh fuck off Burt," she growled with a snark-filled bite in her delivery. "Find a different tree to bark up before another switch falls on your delicate arse and makes you cry."

She was glaring up at a fat, greasy looking piece of nothing wearing a fake leather jacket.

Roman was stopped dead by the whiney, high pitched squeal, completely lacking in testosterone, coming out of the guy's mouth.

"You won't win Kelly. My dad says the land shoulda' been his and that you and your kind are nothing but a bunch of squatters. Bastards the whole lot of you."

It would take no effort at all to squash the fucker like a bug, but before he got the chance, the dark-haired beauty gave back as good as she got. And then some.

Holding up a fist, she used her other hand to imitate a turning crank that made her middle finger unfold. When it was at full attention she said, "Oops," covered her mouth in mock apology, and then proceeded to crank in reverse till the implied fuck you was lowered.

"You're fucking with the wrong people," her antagonizer spat out.

"Yeah, yeah," she smirked. Waving her hand in the air, she brushed him off. "Wah, wah. Go home to Daddy."

With that he marched off, muttering under his breath. Roman caught a heartbeat long flash of uncertainty in her eyes and marveled at the bravado it took for her to stand her ground.

Continuing to ignore the warning bells clanging in his head he walked right up to her and drawled, "That guy's a dick."

Her surprised blinks and the silence following his blunt observation suggested he might have miscalculated the right approach.

Apparently social niceties were not on the menu. Before he could introduce himself, she took a determined step backward, crossed her arms and cocked a hip. The body language dared him to step over the line.

It took a shit-ton of effort not to smile.

"You're not from around here."

A statement, not a question.

He wondered what would come next, only to end up stupi-fucking-fied when she ground out, "Go away."

Wow. From zero to complete dismissal in under fifteen seconds. He must be losing his touch.

"My name's Roman. Roman Bishop," he told her with a hand extended in friendly greeting.

She just stared at him. He tried the old stick-to-your-guns tactic and decided to wait her out with his hand hanging in mid-air between them. In his experience, the most common response was embarrassment for the display of bad manners. But not her!

"I don't give a rat's ass who you are. Go. Away."

Ah. He liked her spunkiness. She had real fire. Not pretend smoke and mirrors.

"You're Kelly, right? Kelly Anne James."

She shut down and froze so fast he felt an arctic chill flutter across his balls. Before he knew what happened, she was out the fucking door. He'd literally never seen anything happen so quickly before in all his years. One minute she was defending her territory and the next thing she was gone. G-O-N-E, gone.

That's when the shit hit the fan. When the undisputed pool champ up and ditches a game in progress, a game with a cash prize, all sorts of shit gets unleashed.

In no time at all, the entire event became ugly. Accusations got hurled. A chair flew through the air. Everything went downhill from there. As a full out brawl built to a drunk weekend crescendo, Roman had plenty of time to consider what the fuck just happened with Kelly as he fended off and laid down his share of punches.

Getting his ass beat hadn't been on the evening's agenda, but once the warrior inside caught the rumbling, clarion call of the alpha, well, what's a guy to do?

"What the holy fuck, Jimmy!"

Roman lifted his head off the throbbing hand, holding it up in time to see his new friend's self-declared 'old lady' toss an ice pack at the guy's face a split second before one also sailed in his direction. He plucked it out of the air with his working hand and pressed the welcome cold against his cheek.

"Did you two share a cup of stupid?" Lil snarled. With a snappy head shake and some seriously pursed lips, she glared at them through her glasses.

"Aw, now come on baby. It was a good night, right Roman?" Jimmy replied with a hopeful, pleading look. "Made buck and cleared the place out with a bar fight."

"You got your asses kicked," she muttered.

Roman gave a slight nod. Yeah. But totally in a good way. "Sorry little lady," he chuckled. "But I have to side with my buddy. The bank gets a nice fat deposit, and y'all closed up early after the boys and us blew off a little steam."

"Oh geez," Lil snapped in her cute Okie twang. "Zip it ride or die. He don't need none of your Marine back up bullshit swagger."

Jimmy was nodding his head and smirking while a devilish glint lit up his eyes. "Marine back up bullshit swagger. I like how that sounds."

Lil threw back her head and laughed. "Give it a rest, Jimmy. You barely know what it means."

"Because it barely makes sense you little witch."

They stuck their tongues out at each other. "Nyah, nyah!"

He had to admit it. These two offered another insightful peek inside an honest relationship. It was as if the universe wouldn't let up with this one thing. The happy couple reminders.

Jimmy and Lil were hilarious. He enjoyed how they swatted comments back and forth like Wimbledon champs. They were also very much a team. A unit. The concept held surprising appeal.

"I've got closing out to do in the bar," she said with a thumb pointed over her shoulder. "You gentlemen need anything?"

Jimmy shook his head no and quickly colored when his lady bent over and whispered something. Roman knew the look and chuckled quietly.

After she left and shut the office door, Jimmy offered a half shrug and a self-deprecating laugh. "Please explain how a woman goes from you're a stupid ass to…well, you know."

"There is no other explanation than this one my friend. The women you describe? They're the ones you keep."

"Got my Lil on lockdown," Jimmy sniggered. "So let's get back to your problem. What the hell happened man?"

Anger and concern knotted inside him. "I have no fucking idea."

"Why did she take off?"

The silence grew until it became awkward. Jimmy arched a brow and waited.

"I spooked her," he admitted.

"Meaning?"

Good question, Roman thought. He wasn't sure what caused her immediate withdrawal. So he started at the beginning.

"On approach, I overhear her giving a load of grief to some jerk named Burt. Hear the idiot give her back the same load. It wasn't friendly and-or pretty."

Jimmy nodded. "Burton Dulb. Daddy's boy. Hates everyone."

"Tell me something," Roman said, making no attempt to hide his confusion. "What did he mean when he said her land should have belonged to his dad and that her people were squatters?"

"Aw, god. Really? Is that what he said?" Jimmy sighed heavily and muttered. "What a fucking dick."

"Do you know what he's talking about?"

"Yeah. It's an old feud. The James family has farmed that land for generations. Back in the late sixties when things around here started going south, one of the daughters had a kid that she gave up. Fast-forward a couple of decades and one by one the family dies off until the last one standing is the daughter. She didn't have other kids so when she passed on, the property went to the one she gave away.

Enter Deb James. She turns up out of the blue with a bunch of legal documents supporting her claim. Not much to say after that. She was a recluse and, frankly, a fucknut from what people say. She was close to Sam the butcher and his wife but mostly she avoided Providence and kept to herself."

"And another local family thinks the land is theirs?"

Jimmy let out a hooting laugh. "Jesus. Burt Dulb's old man was doing old lady James. He figured his dick gave him rights to her land when she croaked. He's a redneck son-of-a-bitch with a mean streak. Hell, everyone hates him. Drew Dulb is a prick."

Roman laughed. "Hold up. Drew Dulb?" he was barely keeping from falling over with laughter.

"I know, right?" Jimmy snickered.

"Dude," Roman growled after a hearty chuckle. "This shit gets more complicated by the minute. Any other family secrets or mountain feuds I should know about? Like who's the father of her kid? By the way," he thought to ask. "Got an age range on said offspring?"

"Lil said she wasn't sure but if she had to guess, maybe four?"

The math made him angrier than before. A teenage mom. A now dead and once reclusive mother. A land feud. Ugh. Liam was going to have a shit fit.

"What did you say to spook her?"

"Fuck if I know," he muttered. "Introduced myself. That's all."

"Gotta be more to it than that. Are you sure you didn't say anything else?"

Roman shrugged. "Just her name. I said her name and before I could blink she was gone."

The knot in his stomach firmed up and got damn painful. She probably needed the money. After all, that's what they used to lure her out of the hills. But because of something he did, she chose to run rather than collect.

Fuck. His conscience got all kinds of twitchy.

"What are you gonna' do?" Jimmy asked.

"I'm going to take the back road to the split and hope I don't drive off the side of a fucking mountain."

"Better do it quick then. Storm's coming. The weather service threw up an alert. Looks like we're gonna get snow slammed when that massive winter front moves in from the north."

Standing up, he tossed aside the wilting ice pack and grabbed Jimmy's wrist to yank him from the chair. They walked out of the office and made for the stairs to his room while shooting the shit and having a good laugh about the night's antics.

Later, when he was alone, he considered calling Liam with an update but decided against it. The time difference was a factor plus he didn't know much that was definite at the moment except what she looked like.

Tomorrow would bring more answers. All he had to do was go on a blind hunt in the woods with no real guide and hope he wasn't walking into any more surprises.

Chapter Five

THE FREEZING COLD SHOWER DID NOTHING TO HELP HER DAY get started. Neither did the break-of-dawn bucket of day old coffee she reheated and drank because there was no other choice.

Trudging from the chicken coop to the goat pen, she took care of the early chores while keeping a wary eye on the thickening cloud cover. By the time she lugged and arranged enough logs to over-stack the porch pile, her arms were on fire, and her stomach was growling. And it was only nine in the morning.

Stomping the dirt off her boots at the back door, Kelly rubbed ice-cold hands briskly on her jeans-covered thighs, hoping to generate some heat. Shaking off the old denim jacket big enough that she wore a bulky sweatshirt beneath, she was hanging it on a peg at the door when the phone rang. The jarring, unexpected sound made her jump.

Nobody ever called, so it had to be Sam or Ginny. Hurrying to the phone on the wall, she yanked it against her ear and barked an unintentionally unfriendly hello.

"Oh dear," a concerned voice murmured. "Should I assume from your tone that last night didn't go as planned?"

It was Ginny. Kelly heaved a pained sigh. What would she do without the older woman's calm gentleness? She counted on it more than she probably should.

"I should have stayed home, that's how much good going into town was." Throwing a bit of steel into her voice, she immediately declared perhaps a bit too forcefully, "Men ruin everything."

Ginny snicker laughed. "Boys will be boys, I suppose. Does your morning grumble have anything to do with the brawl that broke out at Shorty's? Sam called just now. Said the first thing on everyone's mind this morning was the beer soaked fracas. Did you start a fight, honey?"

"What? No! Not a single punch got thrown while I was there. What are you talking about?" Her mind broke into a fast sprint gathering every impression from last night searching for who or what might trigger a slugfest.

A long, awkward pause ended when Ginny asked, "What aren't you saying, dear?"

Two things, separate and distinct from each other, stood out in her mind.

"The Dulbs are losing their shit. That idiot Burt tried to school me. Apparently, and I quote him here, I'm messing with the wrong people." Her snorting dismissal showed what she thought of the whole thing.

"They're threatening you now? What the blue blazes is wrong with Drew for egging Burt on? This is ridiculous."

Kelly couldn't agree more. "I'm not disagreeing," she scoffed.

"And?" Ginny quietly inquired.

"How do you know there's an 'and'?"

"Because you can handle Burton Dulb in your sleep."

"Oh," she murmured, chuckling softly. "You have a point. Yes, well. Um…"

"Kelly?"

"There was a stranger."

"What kind of stranger?"

What kind? Sheesh. Kelly shivered remembering. The kind of stranger who was big and dangerous. The kind of stranger who talked and looked all citified. The kind of stranger who made her boots shake from how bad her legs quivered when he was near. The kind of stranger who…

"He knew my name, Ginny. My full name," she said with emphasis.

Everything in her life shifted at that exact moment. She wasn't sure what that meant, but she felt the fluctuation when it happened due to the abrupt change in Ginny's tone and demeanor.

In a no-nonsense voice, Ginny demanded, "What name exactly?"

A warning bell clanged inside her head. That was an odd question, right?

"Uh," she stammered. "My name. You know. Kelly Anne. Kelly Anne James."

An anxiety bomb exploded in her stomach when Ginny's unmistakable sigh of relief came through the phone line. Something wasn't right. She was sure of it when her proxy granny spat out questions, strange questions, in short, clipped bursts.

"Did he approach you?"

"Did you see him before he spoke?"

"What was he wearing?"

Kelly blinked at each interrogative question. Sensing the importance to Ginny's line of inquiry she answered straight away.

"He appeared out of nowhere at the exact moment Burt slithered away. Called him a dick. And no, until he was in my face I wasn't aware of him. He was wearing black. Lots of black. Why?"

"Have a bad feeling about this," Ginny muttered.

"Look, I knew something wasn't right. Told him from the start to go away. He's the persistent type if you know what I mean."

"Go on."

"Well, he didn't. Go away. And then he um," she hesitated while her mind recreated the encounter. "Then he introduced himself. I told him to fuck off. That's when he said my name."

"So a man you didn't know fell from the sky, and you basically gave him the finger. Something he ignores. When you don't play, he throws down with your full name. Have I got this right?"

"Pretty much, yeah."

"And what did you do?"

A blast of wind rattled the windows. She glanced out the frosted panes above the sink and despite being inside felt the arctic chill. The full body quiver moving from head to toe, however, had everything to do with the stranger and nothing at all to do with the weather.

"I uh…ran. When go away didn't work, I chose the low road."

"You ran as in mid-sentence booked for the door?"

"Uh, yeah. Again. Pretty much."

"Oh Kelly," Ginny groaned.

"What? What did I do? Ginny, I mean shoot! A stranger walks up to me in Shorty's. A stranger in Providence. Like that's not weird enough. He got what they all get. Not interested and a direct back the eff off. I knew the second my name came out of his mouth I had to get out of there. So I did. End of story."

Kelly had a new understanding of the word unsettled. The way Ginny was reacting made the hair on her neck stand up. She knew her imagination was operating in overdrive when the only thing she could come up with was a witness protection arrangement because she was sure of one thing. Ginny knew something that Kelly didn't. And whatever that thing was, well, it was mighty important.

"Look. I've got a dozen things to do before the weather turns and I'm sure you didn't call to chat about strangers. Is Matty okay? Are you bringing him home?"

"Actually dear," Ginny murmured. Kelly could hear the concern in her voice but now was not the time for a heart-to-heart. Life in the woods didn't wait while folks worked through their issues. "We thought keeping him here was best. The storm is going to slam hard. Sam only went into town this morning so people could get their supplies ready. They say we might be on our own for days."

"I know. Dumb luck, huh? Like we need a foot of snow. Send it to California."

"Is that okay with you? One less thing to worry about for you, and you know Matty and Sam. They'll turn it into a fireplace campout."

As much as she needed Matty close by for her own selfish, fearful reasons, Ginny was right. He'd be better off with them. They had a fancy generator and could easily ride out a storm. Unlike her. The stack of logs she hauled earlier made the argument for her. If the storm got really bad, it'd be a far sight easier and safer to have just herself to worry about.

"Can I talk to him?"

"I hope that's a yes to him staying."

"Of course it is. We love you guys. You're family—you and Sam. Matty likes being spoiled, so thanks. But I want to talk to him."

"Oh, of course, dear! Of course. He's anxious to tell you about last night. He and Sam made a Lego castle. He's obsessed with building a castle for Kiki. But he's out back with Sam. They're marching along the back fence in the yard as we speak," she chuckled. "That's why I called now. A little adult talk minus the three-year-old."

"Almost four," she chided softly. "Whatever ya' do, don't call him a three-year-old!"

They laughed together and her heart filled with joy. She and Matty weren't the isolated loners they started life as. If nothing else, they had Sam and Ginny.

Arrangements made for an early evening call, they hung up, and she instantly switched to high gear. Her eyes ticked methodically around the kitchen and living room. Everything was in place to ride out a heavy snowfall. There were even two sturdy shovels propped right next to the door for her to dig a path to the animals. It really was a help to have Matty safely cared for. One less thing to worry about.

A quickly thrown together overstuffed bologna sandwich went down smooth with a half glass of ice cold milk. She had just enough time to trudge along the crooked path up behind the house to a spot where she was sure to find a small animal wandering her woods. A quick hunt she could use to restock the meat supply would keep her busy if the storm hung on.

Stuffed once again into the denim jacket, she wound a scarf around her neck, crammed a pair of heavy gloves into a pocket, slid a paper sack with an oatcake and some raisins inside the jacket, and headed out. Stopping at the Blue Bandit, she pulled open the passenger door and took a rifle off the gun rack. Spying a red wool cap on the seat, she pulled it on and impatiently shoved stray hair under the rim. She already had her hunting knife strapped on. The backpack stuffed behind the cab's bench seat had everything else she'd need.

Setting off, she made the arduous hike in fast time. With any luck, she'd bag something small and be home before the storm hit.

Three hours later she had some quail strung together. What started as a light freezing drizzle turned to a steady snow shower by the time she was ready to head out. Impatient and tired as can be, she hurried when she should've been cautious. A foolish move but she knew every tree and rock in the woods and counted on that knowledge to see her through.

Mother Nature, however, either had on her bitch panties or was having a bit of a giggle at her expense. That's the way she rationalized the Olympic effort it took to stay on her feet. The deepening snow covered dangerous ice patches, and she found herself with flailing arms and wobbly legs as she skated along unable to gain any traction. A bumpy ice covered mound was her undoing.

With gravity and shitty luck in control, she launched off the mound, tumbling awkwardly to the other side only to skate down the steep hill on her butt. She tried to dig in and stop her fall, but the layer of hard ice beneath the white blanket made that impossible.

Once or twice she slowed down and was able to make the icy descent more controlled.

At a dip wide enough to stop her downward roll, Kelly caught her breath. Shaking her head vigorously to get rid of the snow clinging to her cap, she didn't pause for long. Every minute that went by made the conditions worse. Getting her bumped and probably bruised ass safely home was priority one.

Climbing out of the ditch wasn't easy, but somehow she managed to slide, roll to her knees and then get up by clinging to a tree. Picking her way with slow, careful steps she stayed upright, propelling from tree to tree all the way down the last part of the rolling hill to a treacherous spot just a few hundred yards from the bend behind the house.

Tossing her backpack and the chain holding the birds over an embankment onto the snow-covered dirt road, she was making good progress inching her way around the embankment when she lost her footing.

Figuring it was easier to go with the fall and hope she could roll out of it, the last thing Kelly expected was the sound of brakes locking up and the unexpected shine of headlights glowing through the heavy snowfall.

A dull thud hit her elbow and hip. The energy from this contact sent her flying over the road into a mound of snow-laden bushes and ground cover.

Dull pain shot through her when she tried to move. On her back, she looked up at the gray sky and waterfall of snow. Flakes clung to her eyelashes and cheeks.

In this grey-white tableau, a face appeared, looming over her. A dark scowl contradicted the concern she found in the eyes boring into hers.

"Are you all right?"

The voice barking in her face sounded familiar but laying on her back in a snow pile was a more immediate concern.

A hand touched her shoulder and slid down the arm of her jacket until instant reflex made her kick out and whomp her foot on his calf.

"Get your hands off me," she growled. He didn't, so she angrily swatted at his insistent fingers as they touched her everywhere. Determined to put up a fight she got heated and struggled twice as hard to haul herself off the ground.

Standing up on unsteady feet, she swiped snow from her face and glared at the do-gooding trespasser. Prepared to rip him a new one, her words died when she realized why the voice sounded familiar.

No.

Oh god, no.

Roman Bishop.

Mumbling dark oaths as he drove at a snail's pace through the thick snowfall, Roman questioned his sanity for doing this when the weather reports preached caution. He just figured they always blew stuff up for ratings.

"Why does this have to be the one time the weather guys are right?"

The wipers arced back and forth at intervals, pushing snow around the windshield. He was pretty much guessing where the road was from the trees lining each side. Harrowing didn't come close to describing the situation in which he found himself.

Unsettled by what he'd learned so far, he abruptly abandoned his original go slow and earn her trust plan. Fuck that. In his mind, things were more critical than he or Liam imagined. Discovering she lived alone, and with a kid to take care of, changed everything. The land feud and asshole threats simply topped off this recipe for problems.

One thing he was sure of though was that she had no idea that for all intents and purposes she was going to end up with quite a pile of money someday. Knowing that day loomed sooner than later, he felt the push to get this thing done before Adam Ward died. Not for her so much, but for Liam.

Peering intently through the snowy windshield, he kept a close eye out for the road bend leading to the James farm. A gust of icy wind slammed his truck. Gripping the wheel tighter, he squinted at the roadway when movement on his right caught Roman's attention. All of a sudden a boulder of snow hurtled toward a ledge next to the road.

Standing on the brakes, he heard the anti-lock systems engage as the vehicle came to a lurching, sliding stop. The chunk of snow hit the fender and bounced across the road. Rolling his window down, he peered through the curtain of white and froze.

Holy fuck. Giant chunks of snow do not wear red hats. Reacting instantly, he pushed open the truck door and slip-slid across the road to the fallen snowball.

A body lay motionless in a pile of white along the side of the narrow road. He bent to get a closer look and nearly shit his pants.

Oh god, no. It was her, and she was groaning slightly.

In a voice that sounded unnecessarily harsh, he barked, "Are you alright?"

She blinked but didn't react. Emergency triage being just one of his many unique skills, he began a swift physical assessment. When he touched her shoulder and moved his hand down her arm, she reacted like an outraged royal virgin being manhandled by a servant.

Grunting when she landed a vicious kick to his leg, he ignored the pushback and continued his assessment.

Her voice was thick and husky when she angrily growled, "Get your hands off me."

There was a frantic quality to the way she avoided being touched. As she struggled to her feet, he stepped back and admired her grit. This girl wasn't going to take anyone's shit. Not even his.

She wobbled and swayed like a flag at the mercy of a windstorm. When her shoulders went back and she defiantly pushed snow off her face Roman was seized with an attack of primal lust so hot and heavy that he let out an involuntary grunt.

The withering glare she shot his way instantly died when they were face-to-face. He saw the recognition light up in her eyes. Whatever verbal shot she was preparing to fire got lodged in the chamber when their eyes met.

"Aw, shit."

He shared her reaction.

Sensing she was undoubtedly going to be one hundred percent resistant to an offer of help, he sidestepped the whole thing and simply took control. And besides, he could see she was in distress. They didn't have time for any of her fuck off and die nonsense.

"It's good to see you again too," he snarled between gritted teeth. Crowding her with his body, he forced her to go where he wanted. "Now get in the truck. Gotta keep moving or we'll be stuck right here."

She didn't resist and she didn't comply. He stared down into her shocked face and willed some of the fierce scowl he was sure he wore to soften.

"You can trust me," he said softly.

Her caustic snort revealed what she thought of his unsolicited declaration. "Yeah, whatever."

Shifting away from him she walked away and began kicking the snow behind the truck.

"What are you doing?" he asked.

"I'm not going anywhere without my stuff."

"What stuff?"

"Ah, here we go," she declared from twenty feet away. Cradling her elbow, she bent and grabbed hold of something.

"Don't just stand there, fancy man. Lend me a hand would you? Sheesh."

I don't believe I've ever been called a fancy man before, he mused as he snapped to attention and did as she demanded. Handing him an old backpack, she wrapped her fist around a chain and pulled a chain of quail out of the bushes.

He couldn't tell if she was hurt or not. At times she favored one arm but it wasn't consistent.

She was peering intently through the heavily falling snow at the hilly tier of woods that she fell from rising above the road. Suddenly turning away, he heard a softly muttered oath, "Balls."

"What's wrong?"

"Nothing," she replied with brusque coolness.

He was irked by the undisguised annoyance directed at him. His jaw clenched tighter. She turned away and swept past him as if he was invisible, marched to the rear of the truck and flung the dead birds onto the snow-covered bed.

For whatever reason he didn't move at all, just stood there holding the ratty old backpack as thick snow clung to his clothing, and stared at her.

Yanking on the passenger door, she pulled it open and then whirled back to glare at him with a mocking look that triggered a very unwelcome sexual response.

"Okay, look," she sneered with cold impatience. "You're not trespassing on a private road that put you in spitting distance of where I live for no reason. So cut the astonished act. I'm not buying it. Hill folk ain't stupid," she drawled.

Time out, time out, his brain hollered. Pay attention man because there was a mega-tonnage of information and clues in what just came out of her mouth. That last part? The sarcastic dig about mountain folk? Yeah. Totally a twangy approximation of the local drawl. But everything else? Absolutely no accent whatsoever. As a matter of fact, her speech resembled the patois of a New Englander.

His face remained blank but inwardly his eyebrows were arched high enough to blend into his hairline. Fascinating.

"You want something. From me. Bad call by the way, but hey, that's on you. Now unless I'm missing something," she continued with a heavy dose of sarcasm, "you just ran me over with your vehicle. A moving violation, yes? And a blizzard has settled overhead so either get in this truck and take me home or throw it in reverse and drive your unwelcome ass outta here." She glanced at the sky. "But put up or shut up, mister. I don't have all day."

Kelly Anne James was, in actuality, cleverly disguised kryptonite. Had to be. That's the only way to explain the burst of raunchy vignettes crowding his mind. Shit. For half a nanosecond he considered ripping her jeans off and throwing her onto her ass in a snowdrift so he could fuck her into oblivion.

No. Seriously. That just happened.

This snip of a girl with an attitude begging to be tamed overrode decades of the practiced control he was known for. He glared at her, frowning. This was an assignment. She was Liam's sister. And way too fucking young and unworldly for the likes of him. None of those thoughts belonged in the same narrative but there ya' have it. If he could be any more uncomfortable, it'd be a first.

"Get in the fucking truck," he snapped in an angry snarl.

His brain was in chaos. Bewildered by his reaction he stomped up to the driver's door, the one he left open allowing snow to blow inside, stowed her pack in the extended cab and then wiped the layer of white off his seat with an indignant huff.

She all but melted into the passenger seat in an apparent effort to stay as far from him as she could so they drove in silence until, with an impatient hand gesture, she pointed out where to turn. After that, it was a few more minutes of ear-splitting dead air before the small house came into view.

"Don't block bandit," she grumbled as he maneuvered the bumpy drive.

Assuming bandit was the name of her truck, he didn't just pull alongside but went through the process of backing in. "Make it easier to get moving once the snow stops."

His words bounced off her like a basketball hitting the rim. When it came to completely ignoring him, she was the winner by a mile. Not only didn't she give any indication whatsoever that he spoke, the cold-shoulder defensive strategy he had to kind of, sort of admire, left him tongue-tied.

So instead of talking, he observed.

She was on the small side. Not overly so, but next to his size and brawn the size difference between them was glaringly obvious.

When he'd seen her at Shorty's, the atmosphere had been what you'd expect from a bar. The lighting sucked, half of everyone there openly smoked like chimneys, and he wasn't just referring to cigarettes. The hazy and dim view from that night didn't prepare him for how beautiful she was up close. With the red knit hat covering her hair he could only see her face but holy hell what a face.

Her naturally arched dark brows drew attention to her eyes. Not unlike Liam's, they were an unusual color, misty gray with touches of deep blue framed by thick, dark eyelashes. The family resemblance was strong.

Annoyance popped and snapped inside him as cherry bombs went off in his conscience. She's Liam's sister. Get your fucking priorities straight.

About to say he was sorry they were meeting under such bizarre circumstances, he sucked the words back into his throat when the passenger door was furiously kicked open and she slid out.

So much for taking a stab at civility. Dismissing him like an overcharging cab driver, she marched to the truck bed, retrieved her birds and then continued a tight ass march away from the truck toward the tiny house. He quickly exited the vehicle but remained where he was.

She stomped her feet and kicked snow off the steps leading to the front door. At the last second, she looked straight at him. Her expression charted midway between scathing and withering.

The thunder-jolt of primitive, crude lust landing in his groin made Roman tighten. It was a wonder his jeans didn't combust and melt right off him. What the hell was it about this girl's snide dismissal that got him so unusually riled up?

Was it his natural instinct for taming her fire?

Or was it a more disturbing impulse? Something deeper, more elemental. A response that went lightyears beyond simple, biological sexual urges.

"If you're coming, bring my pack. If you're leaving, and please don't let me stop you, drop it next to the path."

Dismissal achieved, she shrugged and then disappeared into the house.

He glanced around. The amount of snowfall was intense. For once the Weather Channel wouldn't be exaggerating if they were calling this the blizzard of the century.

By rote, his mind attacked the situation. Shit in the form of uncontrollable Mother Nature was about to get real.

Grasping the straps of her pack, he pulled it from the cab, shut the door and pocketed the keys. While it was still light and he was able to see at least a short distance, he surveyed the physical surroundings around his vehicle, noting where the snow-covered access road broke through the thick trees. It's always good to keep your bearings. Situational awareness was practically his middle name.

Tromping through the building accumulation he slowed, giving the house a quick inspection as he approached the small porch. Though quite small, the one story dwelling had a portico covering the front door with two windows to the right. A chimney rose from the shingled roof. Barely visible from this angle and even more obscured by limited visibility, he spied a satellite dish behind the chimney.

Kicking snow off his boots, he stepped onto the small porch beneath the peaked portico. Though the house was obviously old, he could see the siding had been recently painted. And the little porch. New wood. Nicely done too. The front door was also new. A multi-colored curtain covered the glass center pane.

For no reason whatsoever, a sleeping demon he kept on a short chain deep inside him woke up and started to growl. New porch. Fresh paint. A front door perfectly hung. He breathed heavily, his senses on high alert. All these things indicated the presence of a man.

Another male to contend with wasn't something he'd taken into account. Jimmy made it pretty clear that even with a kid on the scene there wasn't any evidence of Kelly having an involved baby daddy.

He didn't like the idea of there being a rival of any sort. Not one bit.

With a final kick to clear his boots, he opened the front door and followed her inside. Making sure to step carefully onto the door mat, he wiped his feet, looked up, and stumbled to a halt.

My god. He'd stepped into an Americana exhibit. The interior of the modest home was tidy enough, he supposed. It was a little hard to tell though from the sheer preponderance of stuff the little place harbored. Every place he looked his gaze fell on something. There wasn't an inch or a crannied nook left untouched.

For a neat freak like him, the overwhelming visual was both horrifying and sweetly endearing.

Noise across the small living room caught his attention. A kitchen table just inside the door sat at the end of an L-shaped kitchen. She stood at the sink. He watched her in profile. She knew he was there but continued to ignore him.

A fire crackled in the fireplace at the far side of the living room. The mantle was cluttered with mismatched knick-knacks and on the wall above it hung a cheaply framed painting depicting a lighthouse and cottage on a rocky coastline. Basic, blunt, colorful.

On the far wall, splitting the space evenly, was a darkened hallway.

Quirky and small, like its owner, the little house struck him in an entirely unexpected and sentimental way.

She moved around and threw him some not-at-all subtle shade before stomping out of the tiny kitchen. Curious where she went, he dropped the backpack on the table, took off his leather jacket, hung it on a chair to dry, and then tracked her path. He found her in a small cramped mud room behind the kitchen. A door leading to what he assumed was the backyard and an old washer and dryer took up most of the space. At a relatively new looking utility sink, the cheap kind the home improvement stores put on sale all the time, Kelly had her sleeves rolled up as she attacked a task her angle prevented him from seeing.

"Do you always stand around like there's nothing to do?"

He almost smiled. Almost. There was defiance in her voice and a sneering challenge.

Challenges were cool with him. He responded to any contest whether physical or cerebral.

"Sorry," he sniggered. "Thought I chipped a nail coming through the door. Stopped to check my manicure."

She whipped around, tilted her chin defiantly, balled her fists, and placed them on her waist. The look on her face suggested she almost fell for his light tease. Almost.

She boldly met his gaze. He caught the slight movement when she swallowed, but mostly he just stared her down. Every second ticking by in which she didn't capitulate fueled the inferno of his unfortunate desire.

He found the way she held fast to her ground humorous. The bluster delighted him. She was trying ridiculously hard to make it seem like she wore the pants in every situation. Oh my god, he thought with a laugh. There was no fucking way she'd ever known a man like him.

"While we wait for your pithy retort, how about you tell me what needs doing? I noticed the copper tub beside the fireplace only has two logs. Point me to the log pile."

She sputtered, and color bloomed on her cheeks. It was all kinds of fun to meet her death rays with practiced indifference. Mostly due to the obvious fact that his laid-back vibe was driving her nuts.

He snapped his fingers twice. "Come on lady. I realize my fancy pants scramble your brain, but it's like you said. Shit to do."

If she could have gotten away with ripping his throat open she probably would have, at least that's the story her eyes told. Using her words against her was a stroke of finger-poking brilliance.

He bared his teeth in a cheeky grin and topped things off with a wink. Her gray eyes turned stormy. Heaven help them if he ever forgot who he was. Who she was. Who they both were.

Showing all the prowess of an outmaneuvered battlefield commander, he marveled at the neat, clean way she shifted focus. Marshaling her defenses for a better time was a smart move.

His eyes narrowed as he viewed her anew. Kelly James country gal wasn't at all who she was at the heart of things. It was an act. A performance born of experience, only he was certain she wouldn't see it that way. He wondered what she'd be like in the real world. Imagining Kelly going toe-to-toe with her belligerent older brother triggered an involuntary bark of laughter to erupt from his mouth. This girl was trouble with a bold faced capital T.

She stiffened so fast and so rigidly his guffaw cut short mid-note. Uh oh. Roman recognized a hard limit when he saw one.

A sharp head flick sent a ponytail of black hair over her shoulder. His warrior's brain, trained to notice externals, deciphered the movement one way but his primitive testosterone driven brain read a different challenge in her gutsy insolence.

Recognizing the authoritative, home field advantage in her delivery, he gave her a gentlemanly pass with a brief nod.

"Don't patronize me, Mr. Bishop."

One eyebrow shot up without any help from him. He knew it was a mistake when her withering expression hardened.

"What? Surprised you're not the only one with five dollar words?"

"Touché," he replied with a barely concealed smirk.

There was a nearly indiscernible quiver at the corner of her mouth. She liked sparring with him! Holy shit. Ignoring every single warning bell clanging discordantly in his head, he pushed aside all reason, abandoned his fucking sanity and stepped into the game.

"Well shee-it, honey," he drawled with mocking glee. "Being snowed in with a harpie didn't hold much appeal." His voice dropped a gazillion octaves until he found the smoky, innuendo-laden tone he wanted. "But a fast-paced volley of bourgeois taunts? Yeah. That's what I'm talking about."

She burst out laughing. Not what he expected, but hey. As long as she wasn't thinking about neutering him with the menacing knife balancing on the edge of the utility tub, he was good.

"I can't with you," she scoffed after a thirty-second pause to catch her breath. "Just go out back and haul in some logs, okay? Fill the bucket and stack a few more to the side. Won't be long now," she muttered heavily with a dark glance at the overhead lights, "before the power goes out. Wet snow weighs down the lines. Best to be prepared."

And then she dismissed him. Turning away, she went back to processing her birds. He marveled at the way she met the conditions life sent her way. He watched her wield the heavy knife. In that second the tremendous disparity between the life she led now and the one about to overtake her made him uneasy. It wasn't always a good thing to interfere.

Liam and Roman existed in a world of five-star living. Though not exactly foodies in the classic sense, they shared an appreciation for a restaurant on the lower east side with a remarkable pheasant pate and a braised rabbit main that rivaled the chef's award-winning bison steak in taste and originality.

He'd done a lot of stuff in his life, but hunting and dressing a bird meant for the dinner table? Not so much.

Suddenly her fancy man taunt wasn't so funny.

Stepping into the backyard, he made quick work of moving two-dozen good size logs to the back door. He also managed to end up cold, wet and pissy. Outside the cocoon of Kelly's tiny house, there was nothing but cold, treacherous white. Darkness had fallen. The dim bulb above the door flickered.

Picking up the pace, he got the wood arranged by the fireplace and was sweeping up the mess he made while glancing here and there to ascertain where the hell she was. And where the hell the kid was.

Sitting on booted feet, he rested his hands on his thighs and swept the room for clues. The coffee table next to him was cluttered with crap. An ancient Magic 8 ball became a paperweight on a stack of crossword puzzle pages that appeared ripped from magazines. Next to that was an old coffee mug with a broken handle holding assorted pens and pencils. Taught to notice extraneous detail, the logo of Cheers, the bar in Boston from the classic TV show stuck out.

A distinctly northeastern dialect, the lighthouse painting and now a souvenir mug.

Also on the table was a remote control with a length of duct tape wound around the bottom to keep the battery door in place. He looked across the tiny room to the out-of-place-looking flat screen television. Next to the television was a built-in with books haphazardly crammed onto four shelves.

Anne of Green Gables.

David Copperfield.

Joseph Campbell's *The Power of Myth.*

Really? Now he was really intrigued.

The Alchemist by Paulo Coehlo. Wow. He wanted to curl up by the fire with a snifter of brandy and talk to her about the main character's search for the meaning of life.

The faint but unmistakable sound of a toilet flushing solved the mystery of where she was hiding. Before he turned away from the shelves full of interesting reading materials, he noted that the bottom compartment was overflowing with kids' books.

So there really was a kid. His gaze swept quickly around the entire space. A plastic bowl full of crayons teetered on the edge of a side table. A small plastic dinosaur was wedged between a recliner and the table beside it. On the pegs at the front door hung a child's jacket and scarf.

Clues, yeah, but the lack of pictures mystified him. A small frame on the mantle held a picture of a harried-looking young woman awkwardly cradling a swaddled baby.

Deb Jenkins? Debbie James?

Everything made sense, and none of it made sense. How could that be?

Chapter Six

Kelly snapped the elastic band one last time and tugged her tail of hair before stuffing the thick mass into the neckline of her hoodie. Wiggling and flexing her fingers and wrist, she scowled when a twinge of pain shot into her elbow.

"Frickin' fuck." The harshly muttered expletive was necessary for this instance. Annoyed that she had more checkmarks in the disadvantage column now than when the day started, her mood grew gloomy and irritated.

Her hand hurt like a mother. The significant snowfall had a *Day After Tomorrow* quality to it. She dropped her favorite rifle when she tumbled into the road and thanks to the weather would never locate it now. Why the hell not?

It was no use pretending the biggest check mark wasn't messing with her in a big way. A quick peek in the old bathroom mirror showed lips thinned by tension.

Roman Bishop.

Ugh.

He didn't scare her, but she was fairly sure he'd get off on it if he did. That didn't mean that she wasn't on full alert. Knowing who she was gave him an advantage that made her teeth clench. If he hadn't taken a verbal shot at Burt the other night, she'd suspect he was a lawyer or some other official type hired by the Dulbs to rattle her cage. It was a reach, yeah, but what the hell else could explain his presence? Providence was hardly a stop on a touristy trail of quaint little towns.

But here he was, and now she was stuck with him and his hidden agenda thanks to that sneaky bitch, Mother Nature. Nothing like inviting the enemy to hang out during a snowstorm for fun times to ensue.

She stared at her reflection. What she saw was a rather unremarkable, harried looking female wearing a worried frown.

Glaring at the bathroom door, she walked toward it and sighed. He was on the other side, and though she tried every way in the book to ignore his ass, her attempts were laughably inadequate. Refusing to look at him or engage on any level didn't stop all of her senses from being drawn to him anyway.

Him getting a laugh out of her shocked Kelly. She'd been trying overly hard to be glib and dismissive, so the involuntary guffaw made her uneasy. Nobody ever wiggled around her defenses.

Until now.

Her stomach growled. Before leaving the kitchen, she put a pot of chili on a low flame and tossed a bunch of aluminum foil-wrapped cornbread squares into the oven to warm. There was plenty of food in the cupboards and fridge—enough for a week at least. If the power went out, she didn't want to open the freezer at all, so she did a swift mental inventory of supplies on hand to make sure all the bases were covered.

Hand on the doorknob, she straightened her shoulders. Hating that her mother so easily played the victim card, Kelly preferred a more feel-free-to-suck-my-balls attitude. In the end, it didn't matter what Roman Bishop had up his sleeve. He was wasting his time. She wasn't interested in whatever the hell he was selling. Matty, KA James, and getting as far from this place as she could manage was all she should large. Everything else was background noise.

Shoving her hands into the front pouch of a stretched out hoodie, it only took a few steps before she was standing in the living room staring eyeball to eyeball with her problematic visitor.

Crouched by the glowing fire, he reminded her of a jaguar in a documentary about big cats she and Matty watched. All her mind could process was how he looked. Swallowing became difficult. So was admitting she liked what she saw. He had a square jaw covered in several days' growth of a beard. In her world, the men were either bald, had long hair, or fell back on the sharply groomed guise favored by law enforcement and military types. This guy fell in the last category.

Dark hair, dark eyes, dark clothes. Conservative, maybe. Dangerous, definitely.

"Filled the bucket."

Um, huh? She blinked. His mouth moved, and words came out, but for some reason her brain scrambled, and all she noticed were his lips and how his neck looked like a meal.

"Is that chili?" His nose was in the air, sniffing. He rose slowly and ran his hands down his jeans. An adjustment? She supposed he sort of had to with thighs shaped like tree trunks.

Not at all confident that her voice wouldn't betray her thoughts, she nodded and hurried away from him. Making herself busy at the stove, she lifted the heavy lid from the chili pot to give the mixture a stir when he moved in close from behind and hung over her shoulder.

The urge to send an elbow backward was hard to tamp down when he invaded her body space. She didn't like being crowded. Usually, it felt like an unfair power play made possible by her less than terrifying size, but this… this was different somehow.

"Mmm," he groaned close to her ear. "You're killing me, Smalls. Stop stirring and start dishing."

She felt his warm breath on her neck and trembled. "Grab bowls from the cupboard. There's silverware in the dish drainer."

He chuckled then stood at attention, saluting her. "Yes, ma'am."

"And don't call me small," she snidely bit out when he moved away. "It's rude."

He opened every cupboard before finding the dishes. She rolled her eyes. Juggling two stoneware bowls, he snagged a couple of spoons from next to the sink.

"I didn't say you were small," he drawled with annoying charm. "I called you Smalls. There's a difference."

She answered his comeback with a shrug. "Tell me something. Does this seem like a reference I would get?"

He reacted with a jolt and frowned. "You're right. Sorry. My bad. It's from a movie."

She froze when his penetrating gaze swept her head to toe. "And for the record. Small is in the eye of the observer." For a brief second his eyes rested on her chest. "As the observer of the moment, I'd say you're perfect."

Were her eyes blinking? That's what it felt like, but she wasn't sure. Her mind went blank when he looked at her like she was Miss America or something. Was he blind? Stupid? Joking?

"I think we need to start over 'cause this isn't working."

Another blink. Followed by some swallowing and a sniff. She didn't know what else to do. The instinct to shut him down before anything else came out of his mouth hit her hard.

"Better idea," she ground out. Kelly almost winced at the defensive tone in her voice. "Let's not, but say we did, hmmm?"

He let loose with a low, rumbling laugh that triggered a seismic shift inside her. "Now, come on," he smirked. "You know damn well that's not how this is going to go. Can't you try on nice and see if it fits?"

Denting his thick skull with the wood ladle seemed like way too good an idea. Did he actually think that shit would work with her? No man was ever going to tell her how to behave.

Dropping the ladle being sized up for weaponization, she slammed the lid back on the pot, crossed her arms and snarled, "You know what a hat trick is, right? As a sports reference, it's amazing. In a character assessment, not so much."

His answering arm cross put them bully chest to bully chest. To be accurate, it was more like his chest in her face and her chest in his belly.

"Meaning?"

The ominous tone he used activated a flash memory. She was ten or so and curled up on the rug by the fireplace, reading an ancient copy of a Nancy Drew story that once belonged to her grandmother. Her mother was having a heated debate with Sam and Ginny. There was yelling and crying, as usual, courtesy of Debbie. Poor pitiful Debbie. The last thing clinging to this memory was Ginny's voice. "Stop making it about you, Deb. It's Kelly who will pay the price if this continues."

Anger bubbled up inside her. Goddammit. Secrets and lies. Enough!

"That tone will get you nowhere," she scoffed.

Liar, liar, pants on fire!

Shut up, conscience. This isn't the time to weigh in.

"And my meaning is obvious. So far you've patronized and been rude. That's two of the three you need for the shit-monger trophy. Since you haven't bothered with fair, and by that I mean letting me in on the secret, I've got a couple more in my ammo clip that are worthy of consideration." She pursed her lips and plowed on. "Hidden agendas being what they are, you've also pulled off a public ambush and some questionable stalking. On private property. You realize I could put a hole in you with a bullet and you'd be the one getting arrested. We don't like trespassers round here."

"Jesus," he muttered when she finished. "I don't even know where to start. You've got this all wrong."

"And you're full of shit for thinking I'm stupid. You *have* patronized and been rude." She was shouting and didn't care. "You *did* ambush me at Shorty's. Your truck *was* on my property when you ran me down. What part have I gotten wrong?" Her hands were waving like a windmill by the end.

Fifty different things flashed on his face. Good. She hoped some of her accusations stuck. Until he told her what the hell was going on, he could expect more of the same. If he was waiting for her to beg, he'd be waiting a long time. She friggin' hated secrets. Hated the power of a secret and the damage when revealed.

"The only reason you're standing in front of me and not hanging like a gutted deer from a tree in the backyard is because I have a fucking conscience. Something I see little evidence of coming from you Mr. Bishop. Asking for a reset because it's somehow convenient—for you—only makes my point."

Ladling chili into the bowls, she dismissed him with an angry grunt.

Whatever. He was playing her, and she wasn't having it. And she wasn't joking about the gutted deer. She could easily have shot him. He was on her property. Property marked with trespassing markers.

The thing making her uncomfortable was pretending a saintlike, above-it-all persona. It might have been possible to dart off into the woods she knew like the lines on her palm, leaving him to drive aimlessly in a storm of snow blind proportions. But that's not what went down, and if she was honest, him hovering over her with the snow falling all around them and the intensity of his eyes boring into hers…

A sensual jolt snaked along her spine causing an involuntary quivering of her neck and shoulders. She put a hand up to protect the vulnerable stretch of skin.

It took a few minutes, and a couple of back and forth trips before they were sitting in thorny silence at the kitchen table. He'd been quiet following her accusatory outburst, and she assumed he was plotting his next move.

Annoyed, she stabbed at the thick chili with her spoon and shifted restlessly in her chair.

"Good cornbread," he mumbled.

Rubbing some fingers across her frowning forehead, she offered a tepid smile, such as it was, and accepted the compliment.

"Thanks. Family recipe."

His expression when she answered in a civil tone struck her as eager to the point of hungry. The way he looked at her was scrambling Kelly's brain. Momentarily dropping the uncooperative reins, she blurted out a bit too eagerly, "Try it with honey butter and hot sauce."

He blinked in slow motion. So did she. Then he scooped up a wad of the sweet spread and slathered it on half a hunk of bread. The hot sauce was next. He picked it up off the lazy Susan in the middle of the table where she kept the salt and pepper along with a stack of colorful napkins, and checked out the label.

"*Cholula*," he chuckled. "My god. I remember we went through sampler packs of this stuff like a kid plows through M&Ms."

"We?"

Holding the bottle's distinctive wood cap in one hand, he liberally applied the hot sauce to the cornbread. With a sardonic grin, he drawled, "Semper Fi."

No further explanation was necessary, she thought with a quick smile. She eyed him with a fresh perspective. An ex-Marine. Of course. That would explain the neat haircut and superhero-looking brawn.

"Pardon the crude language but fuck yeah this is good," he exclaimed. The whole piece of cornbread was gone in two enormous bites.

My word. How much fuel does an engine like his need?

"Family recipes are the best," he murmured.

She watched in breathless silence as his tongue swept crumbs from lips that made her think of things she'd rather not.

"Uh, yeah. My mom. She had the cooking from scratch thing nailed down."

He asked a series of casual sounding questions as they dug into the chili. The chit chat was calm, courteous, laid back.

"You mentioned your mom. Does she live here?"

The enormous spoonful of chili going into her mouth gave her a few moments to delay answering. He was fishing. If he knew her full name, he had to know Debbie was dead. Who was this guy?

She wasn't one to play word games. Not enough practice, she supposed. A byproduct of living isolated from the rest of the world. "In a manner of speaking. She's buried in the family plot."

He nodded and shoveled more chili into his mouth. "And your son. The dinosaur lover. Where is he?"

How she kept chewing without choking to death was a miracle. Her son? Well, well, well. Mr. Roman Bishop didn't know shit. It seemed to her like all he had was her full name and some town gossip.

She carefully swatted the question back his way. Instead of acknowledging Matty's parentage, she asked, "Dinosaur lover?"

He gave a friendly enough smirk. "Dinosaur cup in the dish drainer and a T-Rex toy under a chair in the living room."

The smile was natural. She couldn't help it. He was an awesome kid. Sister? Mother? She was both.

"Ah, yes. Were you into dinosaurs as a kid, Mr. Bishop?" She was deliberately keeping her answer cheerful and light. "In this house, the prehistoric beasts share top billing with baseball."

His eyes shone with amusement, and she wished she had the strength to look away.

"Would you believe that I was all about the stars? Dinosaurs were cool, but outer space rocked my boat. NASA and the shuttle was my thing."

"How does a junior astronaut end up a Marine?"

"It's worse than you imagine," he offered. His chuckle was without mirth. "Rhodes Scholar, I'm afraid. All highbrow stuff. Fancy degree in philosophy."

"Oh," she snickered. "So you're like the guys around here."

"How so?"

She shrugged and chewed a chunky mouthful before reaching for a napkin to wipe her mouth.

"Not a lot of opportunity in these parts. Sometimes going into the service is the only option." She speared him with a look. "Can't imagine there'd be many job openings for philosophers."

He didn't bite, but he did circle to an earlier question.

"You never said where the boy is."

"Matthew," she told him. "Matty for short. He's riding out the storm with friends."

"And his father?"

He was kidding, right? Did he actually imagine she was going to offer up chapter and verse like a hypnosis volunteer?

"Not in the picture. And it's none of your business."

"Easy, luv. It was just a question."

She sat back, crossed her legs and fixed him with a heated glare. Let's see how much he likes being cross-examined.

"How old are you?"

"Thirty-six."

"Married?"

She noted his slight squirm.

"No."

"Kids?"

Another squirm.

"None."

"Who do you work for?"

Dead silence.

A niggling thought, one she kept carefully tethered in a private area inside her head, broke free. Searing cold danced along her spine. Was this man in black with the unusual mannerisms and speech connected to her father?

All her fears, each and every one, cascaded from her soul in a torrential rush. She'd worried almost from the moment of her mother's untimely passing that the mysterious figure she was certain fathered her and Matty would wonder when Deb didn't turn up at their disgusting liaisons. Would he send out feelers? Was Roman Bishop her father's lackey?

The only thing keeping her in her seat was knowing Matty's real situation was flying under the radar.

Oh, she knew the busybodies in Providence all assumed that when a baby turned up at the James farm, it was hers. Only Sam and Ginny knew the truth. And since Deb rarely if ever ventured into town and Kelly had long ago driven fifty miles in the other direction to take care of business, what the hell did anyone know?

It was a great thing, a really, really, really great thing that the asshole responsible for spawning her and Matty didn't know the truth. And she planned to keep it that way.

She eyed the man across from her. The arrogance rolling off him hit her like a tsunami wave. Who the hell did he think he was? She rescued him from a storm. Made him a meal for fuck's sake. And what had he done? Almost killed her and then showed off his interrogation skills. Asshole.

Oh! And the son-of-a-bitch didn't have the balls to answer her last question. Seriously? She might be young, a measly female, short, and vastly inexperienced in real world situations, but cheese and crackers! She wasn't a potted plant with no clue.

What. A. Dick.

"I believe the question you left hanging in mid-air was who the hell do you work for, Mr. Bishop?" Fuck him if he thought she was too young and silly to hit back and not back down.

"How do you know I work for anybody?"

Oh for heaven's sake. This guy was unreal.

"I'm here in Providence to check out some property for sale. That's all," he said with a dismissive shrug.

"Points for quick thinking but give it a rest would you?"

Score one for the home team, she sniggered when he did a double take and his eyes widened from her overly stern tone.

A good five to eight minutes of intense eyeball combat ensued. She finished her chili and brushed crumbs from her placemat while never looking away. He was crazy nuts for challenging her, something she was sure he came to understand by the time she stood up. Stomping her feet so her jeans would relax she shoved both hands in the hoodie pouch.

Canting her head in the direction of the door she spoke in a calm firm voice. "Have animals to tend. You're on clean-up duty."

The way he leaped from his seat and his vehement, "Let me help," didn't get the reaction he expected when she put up her hand to stop him.

"Look. I would suggest that you fuck off and die but since that's just wishful thinking and I'm stuck with you—for now," she snarled heavily, "make yourself useful and stay out of my way."

His hurt little boy expression reminded her of Matty. "But I can help. With the animals."

She sighed heavily. "Is that so? When was the last time you fed chickens and goats?"

"Well, never," he mumbled. "But you can't do that by yourself, and I'm…"

She cut him off with a ferocious hoot of laughing outrage. "News flash. I do everything by myself. Shall we revisit the do not patronize me part of our fascinating conversation or can you just accept that's what you're doing and get the hell out of my way."

"Wow." He was smirking. She wanted to wipe the masculine leer off his face. "I get that there's a lot you have to do. By yourself. But there are some things that most definitely require two people."

Oh no he didn't!

Did he?

Shit. She didn't know, wasn't sure. Innuendo and flirty talk wasn't her thing.

"Shut up."

He smirked some more.

Stomping away like Matty did when he didn't get his way, Kelly grabbed a knit scarf and hat off the pegs by the door and fished some gloves from the pocket of a hanging jacket.

She wanted to fire back at him with all she had but bit her tongue. Holding her own against someone so much older and more knowledgeable was difficult enough. It would be suicide to give him more ammunition.

On her way to the back door, she turned suddenly and caught him staring at her ass. Whatever she thought to say melted on her tongue.

"Um, tea would be nice when I get back."

And then she bolted, grabbing the snow shovel stowed outside so she could clear a path across the backyard to the animal pens. The snow was coming down so fast she could barely see. The dim bulb above the back door lent an odd glow to the scenery.

With a final look at the house, she pushed Roman Bishop and his murky reasons for invading her life into the background. Life in these hills had a way of being unforgiving, and she didn't have the luxury of time or opportunity to do anything other than survive.

He felt trapped. By his own weakness, because that's the only way he could explain his getting messier by the second feelings for a girl he was supposed to be handling in a professional capacity.

Unfortunately, handling her drool worthy ass was neither professional nor something that should even remotely exist in a realm of possibility.

But, that's exactly where his thoughts dragged him.

Clearing their dishes from the table, he took them to the kitchen and stared blindly out the window above the sink. The snow was insane. It bothered the crap out of him that she was out there doing fuck knows what while he sat on the sidelines.

Part of him, a big part, had a hard time accepting that this was Kelly's life. His assumptions hadn't adequately prepared him for the reality. Especially not when he thought of Liam's life of privilege. Sure, the luxury came from a shit ton of hard work, but still. His friend wasn't going to like learning the blunt truth about his sister's existence.

He could imagine Liam's outrage. 'And what did you do while

she battled the snow to feed chickens?'

Roman grimaced. "What did I do? Well, hell. I did the dishes and made tea."

Ugh. Is this what being a pussy feels like?

Wiping off his hands, he tossed the dishtowel on the counter and reached into his pocket. It took less than five seconds to realize he had zero signal and no chance of making a call from his current location. Dammit. He wanted Liam's input. Conditions here were much different from anything they imagined. The sooner they got her away from here—her and the kid—the better.

When she asked who he worked for, he considered playing all his cards in one hand. Telling her the truth seemed the best way forward, but that wasn't his call to make.

Frustrated, he shoved the phone back in his pocket, crossed his arms and leaned against the counter. Not sure what to do next, he ran some options in his head but came up empty.

He had questions, lots of them. Like how the hell she stayed off radar. If Cam hadn't stumbled on the name change courtesy of Kelly's mother he'd still be spinning his wheels searching for a person who no longer existed. Kelly James was very real, but from a digital footprint standpoint? She was a ghost. No school records. No social security. No driver's license. How the fuck was that even possible? Shit. Not even witness protection was so shrouded in secrecy.

Matthew James. That's the kid's name, right? He nodded and glanced around. This time he saw plenty of evidence that there was a child in the house. Shoes by the door. A handful of crayon drawings hung with magnets on the refrigerator. A plastic shoebox overflowing with chunky building blocks sat on the kitchen counter.

Frankly, the visual stimulation was off the charts in this house. There was stuff everywhere. On the walls, every flat surface, you name it. He thought of his well-ordered life. Shit, man. He was so anal at times that lining up pens on his desk was something he did on the regular.

No need to instigate a psychological profile why. The military might be in the past, but the habits he picked up during that time continued to inform his life. Order was his baseline. His old Justice comrades at their compound in the Arizona desert understood this mindset. They called it the control switch. It grew out of some very fucked up times when enemy kills and shit-stomp-kicking the hell out of every day was their norm. Throwing the switch was part of what saved his life when the dark times came. Not being able to flip the switch put him at a disadvantage. Without control and order, he was flying blind.

Maybe that explained why his dick was hard.

Dude, his conscience scolded. This girl is a babe in the woods. Having a kid as a teenager doesn't make her experienced. Back down. She's too damn young and you? You're one of those shades of fucked up people, only in your case it's more like a thousand shades. And some fresh-faced kid, no matter how hot a piece of ass, wouldn't survive ten minutes in the face of your particular brand of fucking.

Ouch.

Making a valiant effort to hold his confusion and unease at bay, he turned his attention to the task of making tea. She would continue to bristle and snarl unless he gave her something to think about. He didn't want to lie but without the all clear from Liam, he didn't have much choice.

But what if he went with a half truth? Debbie Jenkins, aka Debbie James, was the connector piece. Kelly's lack of an Oklahoma twang, the references to a completely different area of the country, and especially the off radar factoid. That certainly wasn't something a little kid could start. Her mother was the author of their invisible footprint.

He wondered what or how much Kelly knew about her mother's background and made the decision to go down that road of questioning when she returned. If pressed, and he knew she intended to, he'd go so far as to offer up what he knew about Deb Jenkins James and Adam Ward.

A wayward random thought flashed in his head. He wanted to meet the kid. Matty. Kids were kind of cool and this one intrigued him. How old did Lil say he was? Four? That seemed like a good age.

The loud thuds of Kelly stomping her boots by the back door made him swing that way in anticipation. Oh shit. The tea. What the hell was wrong with him that he couldn't produce a hot cup of tea when that was all she asked for?

He cranked the fire under the pot of water and willed it to heat up in a hurry. The sound of the door opening and closing firmly told him he was an epic fail as a tea master.

The failure zinged his pride.

Chapter Seven

Watching from the corner of the doorway, she studied her unwanted trespasser with the hard-to-believe name. Were his parents high when they named him? Roman Bishop. Sheesh.

Her head shook, and she bit her lip at the same time because the arrogant name aside, the man was worth looking at. Why was that? Was it because of how he filled whatever space he occupied? Perhaps the way he moved? Whatever it was, she had a hard time ignoring him.

A tiny swirling nugget of anxiety pierced her center. It became increasingly hard to take in enough oxygen, and her legs tingled from the growing need to start running and not look back. Shifting side-to-side, foot-to-foot, she swallowed hard to keep her panic in check. Not being worldly didn't have anything to do with a person's intuition, and right now her gut was sending bullet messages in rapid-fire succession, none of them were in any way friendly.

Her eyes darted to the kitchen window. The snow was coming down faster now. At this rate, they'd be lucky if the foot and a half predicted didn't turn out to be two feet plus.

Fantastic.

Wiggling the fingers on her sore hand, her mind took off like an athlete at the sound of the starting gun on a mad dash through the thousand problems being snowed in caused—all made more difficult because she'd been a clumsy fool and gotten hurt. Just now, tending to the animals had been difficult. It took her three attempts to grasp the bolt slider on the goat enclosure and push it closed.

The only saving grace was Matty being safe and sound with Sam and Ginny. Knowing how much the little boy liked hanging with them eased any worry. The couple, both entirely comfortable with the term 'old hippies', were surrogate grandparents to her and Matty. Hands down, no hesitation whatsoever, she trusted Ginny and counted on Sam. They'd been close to her mother; something Kelly suspected meant they knew a lot more about Debbie's double life than she did. Knew things about Matty's gene pool, and most likely hers too.

And he talked to them, which was a good thing because in another year he'd be in school, a luxury she'd never experienced, and then he'd have no choice but to talk. And join in. Be social. Make friends. Have peers. All the things absent from her hard-scrabble life. All the things she was working so hard on giving him.

A sound from the stove got her eyes swinging from the unwelcome winter wonderland swirling outside to find Roman Bishop awkwardly juggling a pot. She heard a sharp hiss and sincerely hoped he burned his damn fingers on the hot handle. He might be cultured and polished, but apparently the man knew shit about potholders.

When he finally managed to dump a stream of water into a mug sitting beside him on the counter, she exploded, choking out in strangled outrage, "What the hell are you doing?"

Gesturing at the cup filled with water his attitude suggested the answer was glaringly obvious. "You asked for tea," he stated flatly.

Kelly felt her brow wrinkle from the sudden urge to tear into him for being a dimwitted kitchen klutz. But instead, she marched forward with a huff, grabbed the water-filled mug with her working hand and upended it into the dishpan of suds.

"Move," she growled. All but shoving his stupid ass aside, she returned the pot to the stove and turned up the heat, giving him a double shot of side shade in the process.

"I'm sure where you come from there's some fancy electric tea maker with a digital temperature option, but here we boil water the old fashioned way. In a pot."

An unfortunate and clumsy whack of her already tender wrist against the edge of the counter sent a sharp zinging lance of pain straight to her neck and stole her breath.

She caught him narrowing his eyes and felt a warm tingle as he assessed her with a sweeping gaze. The way his lips thinned made him seem grim and a little dangerous.

Instantly straightening, she snapped to attention and challenged him with her eyes. He had another thing coming if he thought for one second she couldn't take care of herself. Thank you very much. End of story. She didn't need his damn help. Didn't need anyone's help.

Refusing to give him an opening, she hectored on with a dismissive brusqueness that was all an act.

"The operative word, Mr. Bishop, is boil. We boil the water."

"But I did…boil the water," he drawled with air quotes and a chuckle.

Her eyes narrowed, and she stared a hole through his thick skull. Was he stupid or just messing with her?

"Um, no," she grated irritably. "To boil means bubbles roll on the surface. Did you see rolling bubbles?" When he didn't answer right away, she stubbornly persisted. "I didn't think so. A bit of steam and some bubbling snaps on the sides of the pot do not constitute a boil."

"So what you're saying is, the water should be molten lava hot. Not hot tub hot."

"I have no idea what hot tub hot means," she snapped, and then caught herself from launching into a high and mighty tirade when she realized he was teasing—trying to get a rise out of her.

She was raising a preschooler for heaven's sake and had first-hand experience with falling for shit like this. He wanted to play dumb? Fine. She'd give him a lesson in tea basics to prove she had a practical point.

"Unless the water boils, what you'll end up with is a cup of flavored water. Not tea. Tea leaves are delicate but to get the best from them, they require firm handling. Wishy washy makes for bland and boring."

Something moved in his expression. The flash fire burning in his eyes singed her thoughts and made her tremble.

"Understood," he half-growled. His voice was husky. The words deliberate. "You prefer strength to wishy-washy."

"Because the tea is delicate," she persisted in a nonsensical murmur, immediately regretting how lame she sounded.

"Yeah. Got it," he replied.

The weird conversation had an undercurrent that she found confusing. And disturbing. Male-female interactions were not where she did her best work. The guys she knew from taking their money at Shorty's didn't count. Her rep as a pool shark gave her an act to hide behind. The fuzzy eight-ball hanging from Bandit's rear view was a useful prop. Those unremarkable specimens of American manhood didn't see her as a female. They regarded her as a competitor.

So what did that mean as far as how Roman Bishop looked at her?

Rubbing the back of her neck, she tried to ignore the big man sucking all the oxygen out of the small kitchen and set about making the tea. A proper cup of tea. Not whatever the hell he was making.

Reaching into a large ceramic canister adorned with tacky Italian motifs, she pulled out a bag by the tag and dangled it above the mug before draping the thin string over the side.

Angling slightly away from the big man's watchful gaze, she picked up her supply of beverage sugar.

"What's that?" he asked when she turned around holding the enormous glass jar of sugar rocks.

"Rock sugar. From the farmers' market. It's made from beets and molasses. Sweetens but doesn't overpower. Want to try some?"

Carefully putting the breakable container safely on the counter, she motioned with her head for him to uncap the heavy jar and stood aside to give him room.

He laid the cap aside and leaned in for a sniff. "Reminds me of the rock candy we got at the state fair as kids."

"Pop one of the nugs in your mouth and let it dissolve. Better than any candy you'll ever buy."

The pot of water started gently rolling, so she turned off the gas, lifted it with a potholder and deftly poured the steaming fluid into her mug without spilling a drop.

"That's how we do… " she murmured with a short, dismissive shrug. "Boiling water," she drily emphasized, "and rock sugar. Cream when we have some."

"Do you have a favorite tea?"

Scoffing at the absurd question she made a face to punctuate her reply. "Yeah. Whatever's on the shelf at the dollar store."

That certainly shut him up. Wearing a sheepish expression, he backed away so she could maneuver around the small space. When she finished and was satisfied, he grumpily took the steaming mug and moved it onto the kitchen table.

"Sit before you fall down."

With pursed lips she reacted slowly, moving hesitantly to the chair he politely pulled out, annoyed as shit that she was secretly relieved he recognized how close to the edge she was.

"Thank you." A waving arm and harsh gasp followed the perfunctory words as she painfully fell into the chair. She was exhausted.

"Easy does it, Carina. You've got nothing to prove."

His last words were murmured close by her head when he leaned over to push the mug closer to her hand. A sharp, biting put-down clung to the tip of her tongue, but she said nothing.

In the seat across from her, he took up all the space. The effect of his brawny, solid presence filling her field of vision gave her the willies. Feeling small next to his overwhelming superiority rattled her cage.

"What does that mean?" she asked. "Carina? Is it a name?"

His slow smile made her tummy flutter. "Some of the guys I knew in the military will tell you it essentially means I'm fucked."

Her brows bumped together. Sipping the tea, she studied his face. What the hell did that mean?

"But in this instance I believe my intention was observational rather than biographical. Carina. It's Italian. My grandfather loved the word. In the lexicon of my family, it means sweet and pretty. Cute with a nod to size."

She almost aspirated the hot tea, slammed the mug on the wood table and reflexively started spouting. "Are you calling me dinky? 'Cause let me tell you something buster, five feet almost five is enough to kick your six one any day."

"Two," he smirked with a chuckle. "Six two. Two and a half if you want to split hairs."

That was the moment all the oomph left her. She wasn't sure which was worse; the rifle she'd been forced to abandon after sliding off the ice and snow covered path or dropping like a stone in front of a moving vehicle.

She inwardly groused. The specifics didn't matter. What did was the unavoidable fact that she was banged up and out of her comfort zone, plus a total stranger was treating her like a little girl.

Dammit. If her lip started to wobble, that would be it. Hoping that a biting retort would restore her equilibrium, she gave him a snark-filled glare and said, "Only an idiot would compare being short to having a sweet disposition. And you don't come off as an idiot Mr. Bishop."

He laughed. "And you, Carina, do not have a sweet disposition."

She sputtered and made about a dozen different faces, then sat back slowly and regarded the amused stranger with a critical eye.

In a purely physical way, he reminded her of a football player. Big and strong. It was hard to tell from what he had on, but she was sure the beefy arms were hard muscle.

His face had a rugged quality softened somewhat by an air of sophistication that didn't merge believably with his just-another-guy act. There was a hint of mystery and intrigue about him that she found hard to ignore.

It was his eyes though that made her the most nervous—almost twitchy. Dark grey-green in color, she was sure from time to time she saw flecks of gold. They were extraordinary. Like him.

The conservative haircut and square jaw chiseled from granite covered by a week or more of beard gave him a commanding look. She stared at his neck, saw the movement of his Adam's apple when he swallowed, and hastily glanced away.

When he spoke next, his tone was almost tender, and she had to wonder if the bone he threw her was because he knew she was at her limit.

"Drink your tea, and I'll answer your question about who I work for."

Her heart was pounding as the mug lifted to her mouth. She supposed her hand was trembling when she noticed the hot liquid splashing against the sides. That first sip was always her favorite. She drank coffee for fuel. Her tea time, though, represented something else. To her, the entire ritual offered a renewal in every cup. A chance to be who she was—not who circumstance forced her to be.

Fortune cookie babble? Yeah, probably.

The sweetened warmth slid into her throat and spread throughout her body. Without thinking, she yanked the elastic from her hair and shook the messy mane sending the long dark strands dancing around her shoulders. She needed the protective shield.

Her eyes met his. The same expression when she caught him checking out her ass matched the one he wore now, only with a bit more surprise on display. She bit her lip and silently willed her nerves to settle. Then she waited to see what he brought.

"Without a hint of patronization," he began with a determined expression, "You really can trust me. I'm not here to cause you any harm, Kelly."

The battle of restraint raging inside her made appearing impassive a challenge, but she hung on and stayed a blank slate.

"I work for somebody who," he hesitated just a fraction, "knew of your mother's unusual…situation."

Well, that was saying a lot of nothing.

"Mmm hmm," she growled. "This no-name somebody that knew of my mother's sit-u-ation? How is it this know it all wasn't aware that she's dead? Hmm?"

He grunted and sat back in his chair, holding her eyes with his.

"He lost track of her."

She gave him nothing. Nope. He was being a dick with his one-sentence non-answers. He could pound sand. The funny thing was, he didn't seem to know what to do with her silence. Dammit. Biting down on her tongue wasn't enough to keep a smug grin from tugging on her mouth.

He might be all big and bad physically, but fancy pants didn't know shit and was totally off his game when someone else was in control.

Ahahahahahaaaaa!

All of a sudden he grabbed at the back of his neck and laughed. "Jesus Carina. Do you play poker 'cause with that blank shit eating stare you'd clean the fuck up."

A deflection with humor. Nice try, buddy. She calmly volleyed back.

"When they tell our tale in song, I'll be Poker Face, and you'll be Teflon." She delivered this wisecrack with a straight face and a dry tone. He got her message and snickered.

Relaxing in his chair, a leg extended to the side, he dropped a hand onto the table. Tapping his fingers, he cocked his head and looked at her. "One of my dubious learned skills is interrogation." He shrugged like the insider information was no big deal, but she suspected this particular bread crumb led somewhere dark and probably dangerous.

"But nothing I learned prepared me for attempting an information transaction with a stubborn female. You seem to have a superpower."

"Information transaction?" Okay. The laugh wouldn't stay quiet. Did he have any idea whatsoever how absurd he sounded?

He reacted warmly to the crack in her reserve. "Hey." His scoff was real and charming as all get out. "Don't be hatin'. There are whole rooms of smarty pants people who sit around and think this shit up. Operation Cobra Strike? Operation Dragon Hammer? Huh? That crap doesn't happen by itself."

Charming as this break in tension was, she had enough on her plate at the moment.

"Mr. Bishop. I'm tired. My arm is killing me. I don't have time for whatever this is. I've got to get ready for tomorrow. All that snow doesn't signal a day off. And since you'll be leaving in the morning…" her face emphasized the point she was making. "I suggest you get some sleep. You'll be glad when you're digging your way out."

She stood up and marched to the sofa. "You can sleep here. I'll get some blankets. Keep an eye on the fire, please. I'm kind of surprised there's still power, but luck might not be on my side."

He stalked after her and boxed her in with surprising ease. The impulse to shove him away almost got the better of her when he asked a direct question.

"Aren't you even a little bit curious, Carina?"

Was she? No. No, she wasn't. The past can't be changed, and the future belonged to those who take the challenge. There wasn't a single thing this man or anyone could say that would change one simple fact. All she and Matty had was each other and a secret stash of cash courtesy of their dysfunctional mom. They were a team. A damn good one.

Whatever or whoever Roman Bishop represented meant nothing to her. Not really.

"Nope. Can't say that I am. Sorry fancy man but your trip to the woods is wasted time. Matty and I aren't interested."

She marched away with a dismissive wave and nearly stumbled onto her face when she heard him quietly ask, "Even if there's a real good chance you could end up a very wealthy woman?"

What the fuck?

She turned slowly and glared at him.

What. The. FUCK. Oh my god was he ever barking up the wrong tree.

"Mr. Bishop. Let me make myself perfectly clear. I want you and the foul stench you brought off my property at daybreak. You are not welcome here, and no amount of money will change that."

"Kelly…"

"No," she snapped. "I'm not my mother. You can't buy me. Go away."

She was down the hallway and slamming her door with a vengeance before he could speak. Let him figure out the blanket situation. She didn't care.

Filled with a blind rage, she pressed a fist against her mouth to stifle the angry, wounded bellow building in her core.

This was about her father, wasn't it? Hers and Matty's. Had to be. Nothing could infuriate her more. Dangling dollars as if she was a trained animal or a pet up for sale made her physically sick. Being ignored and denied for almost twenty-four years had a way of fucking with a person's head. So did the fact that the miserable piece of garbage who worked Roman Bishop's strings was who destroyed her mother's life.

She already viewed the bonus cash her mom squirreled away as a form of hush money. That was bad enough, but to suggest she'd be susceptible to the suggestion of more? Who were these people that they held such a dim view of others?

Pacing back and forth between the fireplace and the end of the hallway to her bedroom, Roman logged a solid mile while his mind worked overtime.

Kelly Anne James was an uncommon female, that was for damn sure. Feisty, ferociously independent, and possessing more complicated and complex layers than a double batch of his much-loved baklava, she didn't just meet him head on. He'd never seen anyone be quite so consistently in-your-face. In a lot of ways, she called the shots from the second they met. It put him in an unusual position and made him question if he relinquished control or if she just took it.

What was he supposed to make of her immoveable dismissal? "Jesus," he quietly groaned aloud. "What the hell had she been through to make her so hard?"

The answering silence chafed his nuts. Figuring her out wasn't going to be easy. It should be. Considering who the fuck I am, he thought, this whole thing should have been a piece of cake.

He stopped pacing and stared down the short hallway. Despite the closed bedroom door, he sensed her presence. Her agitated presence.

Dammit. He wanted her.

Pinching the bridge of his nose on a long deep inhale he closed his eyes and commanded his usually well-mannered libido to settle down. Letting his feelings muddy the waters wasn't helping.

Stepping away from the temptation of the hallway, he pushed down the urge to kick open her fucking door and force the issue. Now wasn't the time to go cave man.

Kelly Anne James was at the top of the hands-off list.

"Think, ya' dumb shit," he muttered.

He'd made a mess of everything. Instead of playing it cool and laying believable groundwork, he jumped in right away. The hairbrained decision to venture into the hills while a snowstorm loomed wasn't his best move. Add to that the fact that they had the compatibility of oil and water. Or maybe thunder and lightning. He wasn't sure, but one of those was probably accurate.

And it wasn't helping his frame of mind that a twenty-something little girl had him entertaining a whole host of salacious possibilities—the kind that would definitely float his boat but most likely send a youngling like Kelly straight to the exit.

He needed to get his shit together.

A hard glance around the small room brought the flat screen television into clear focus. Earlier, he'd thought it looked out of place.

"Fuck," he muttered. The first clue had been there from the start, but he was too distracted by other things.

His eyes darted around the every inch of the cluttered interior. The lighthouse picture above the fireplace wasn't anywhere near as old as everything else. Walking right up to the painted canvas he inspected the bottom corners until he found what he was looking for.

"K-A-J." Hmph. Kelly Anne James?

Nothing else looked like it came from this century. The furniture was old. A quilt tossed across the back of the sofa was something from another era. Only the painting and the surprising TV were anywhere near new.

He walked into the kitchen. No microwave. Really? How had he not noticed that right away? An old school toaster sat on the counter. Besides that one small appliance, there were no kitchen toys anywhere in sight. Three bins sat side by side along the wall between the kitchen and the table. One held cans and bottles. Another was full of paper. The third was for trash.

Not a single paper towel or box of tissues was evident. The stack of cloth napkins on the table, all the kitchen towels looked like they'd seen better days.

He peered into every cabinet and checked out the pantry. The dishes and equipment screamed 80's yard sale, and the food supply consisted of generic items, and a lot of home jarred things.

How the hell did someone who more or less existed off the grid and didn't waste money on throw away items have a satellite dish and a flat screen?

Things weren't adding up. His gaze swung to the painting once more.

For reassurance, he stuck his head in the mudroom where a

washer and dryer were tucked into a corner and found what he expected. Older model appliances with a pair of pliers next to a missing control knob.

Marching quietly into the hallway he stopped in the bathroom and shut the door firmly behind him. Pink and black tiles from the 1950s livened up the tiny room. The polka dot shower curtain seemed new, but everything else down to the products on the tub ledge left a dollar store impression.

Making use of the immaculate porcelain, he relieved himself and was washing his hands at the sink when a battle broke out in his head.

Don't be a wuss. It's your job to check out everything. That was the rational, highly trained snotbag at the center of his personality weighing in.

He frowned at his reflection in the mirror.

Don't do it, man, a different side to his conscience warned. Haven't you trampled on her privacy enough?

He grimaced at the reflection mouthing "Fuck," and then opened the medicine cabinet behind the mirror.

First aid supplies caught his eye first. He grunted when he saw the little box of powder ampules for pouring on an open wound to stop bleeding. That shit stung and burned like a motherfucker, something he found out first hand on many occasions during his war zone days. It bothered the hell out of him to see it in her supplies.

There wasn't a single prescription, although he did find a small brown envelope with two capsules inside and a ripped sticker on the back. Antibiotics. The kind they handed out at the free clinics.

The toothbrush holder held two. One adult and one child sized.

Also missing from this non-treasure trove of clues was anything male. No razors, shaving cream, deodorant. Nothing. There also wasn't evidence of contraception. No pill pack, diaphragm container, or condoms.

The weird satisfaction he felt did not sit well. He had to wonder what his reaction might have been if he found lube and a butt plug. Jesus. He was losing it.

Switching off the overhead, he peeked into the hallway. Her door remained shut, but a light was evident around the edges. Practically tip-toeing like a cartoon character up to no good, he carefully opened the second bedroom door and slid into the room.

Using his cellphone flashlight, he swept the room and smiled. Posters and pictures taken from magazines covered the walls—mostly of dinosaurs with the occasional appearance of Mickey Mouse.

The bedspread was somewhat new. Prehistoric scenery of course. On the bedside stand was a framed picture. He leaned close for a better look. It was Kelly with a happy kid hoisted on her shoulders. They both wore big smiles. He wondered where they were and who took the picture.

A book on the end of the bed caught his eye. *Sammy and the Dinosaurs.* A pleasant warmth spread slowly in his chest. He bet she read to the kid every night.

Creeping silently from the room, he eyed her closed door one more time and returned to the living room. Crouched at the fire, he stirred the embers and added two hefty logs. Brushing ash off the hearth, he adjusted the safety screen and sat back on his heels.

What had he learned so far? Her truck was older than he was. For a woman with no discernible income except the meager amount her booth at the farmers' market brought, she managed a satellite dish and a TV. The result of her pool sharking efforts? He doubted it. The painting pointed to a creative streak.

The kid was still a mystery, but nothing he'd seen so far indicated their situation was anything more than a young mother pulling a single parent gig. Hell. These days that sort of thing wasn't even unusual.

She was definitely Liam's blood sister. The eyes weren't an accidental coincidence.

He pulled out his phone one more time and silently begged the gods of technology to grant him a little signal. Talking to Liam was imperative. He'd make him see that being overly cautious wasn't what this situation needed. The sooner they brought her up to speed and got her and the kid under the protective wing he and Liam offered, the better.

Still no signal.

Balls.

As if on cue, the tiny house vibrated from the loud, jangling ring of a wall phone. His mouth dropped open. When was the last time he heard the ringing of a land line?

On the second ring, her door flung open with a loud bang, followed by the muffled sound of her feet pounding down the hallway. She blew past him where he stood and completely ignored his presence as she rushed to grab the phone.

"Matty?"

Her happy laugh when the person on the other end spoke made the hair on his neck stand up. The sound was joyous and authentic. He wanted to make her laugh like that. Wanted to lose himself in the sound of her happiness.

"Why aren't you in bed, young man?" she scolded playfully. "Oh no you didn't," she giggled a minute later. "Yep, yep. Two quail!"

Roman's head shook without him being aware that's what he was doing. My god, he thought. What little kid cares about a hunting tally?

His head filled with visions of introducing Kelly to the joys of a shopping trek through Whole Foods. He thought of the oversized box of PG Tips tea leaves in his cupboard that Rhiann brought back from London and mentally wished for a chance to shower her with every awesome tea blend from around the world.

She kept her back to him through the conversation, but that didn't stop him from admiring the view.

She'd taken off her boots and was parading around in a pair of thick pink socks. The jeans were the same, but she'd ditched the hoodie. A thin white t-shirt, neatly tucked into the waistband, clung to her torso. He traced the outline of her bra with his eyes and willed her to turn around.

So far he'd seen her bundled up in a snowstorm and hidden

inside a large sweatshirt. He longed to know if her breasts were the handful he suspected.

When she bent over at the waist to fish something out of the cabinet beneath the sink, he had to count back from one hundred. The sight of the worn jeans molding to her body like a second skin got him hard in seconds. It wasn't difficult to imagine her face pressed into a mattress as she offered herself to him with a beautiful arch in her back.

She chattered on and continued ignoring him. "I love you too. Don't forget to be grateful, okay? Grateful prayers before bed. That's the rule."

He moved in closer. In bare feet, she fit him perfectly. Small and curvy in all the right places.

Did untamed have a smell? Being close enough to pick up her scent, he inhaled and let it fill his senses. The simplicity of soap and toothpaste was more pleasing than a thousand dollar fragrance. She was a combination of the natural world and something else.

She was fresh and wild and…shit. When she suddenly whirled around and found him practically on top of her, she reacted like a cornered animal. Swatting at the center of his chest, she shoved hard and growled, "Back off!"

No. He had no intention of backing off, but he did give her space.

Returning her heated glare, he made a series of rash decisions. She could fight him all she wanted but he was taking her away from this place, and none of her snarling or shin-kicking would make any difference.

That part was for Liam.

The rest was all him because he'd never been surer of anything in his entire life than he was about this female being his for the taking. Knowing it was wrong didn't faze him in the least. He'd deal with Liam man-to-man. The person who was going to object the loudest and be the biggest headache wasn't Liam. Or Rhiann. It was Kelly herself.

Roman felt the satisfied smile before it moved on his face.

Let the game begin.

"Who're you talking to, Kik? Is someone there?"

She gathered every ounce of bad attitude she had and pinned fancy man to an imaginary wall with her eyes. Growling at him when he jumped her from behind had been a stupid move because now Matty would play detective.

Aw, come on. Can nothing ever be easy?

When her trespassing tormentor smiled at her like she was a twenty-ounce steak in an eating contest, she had difficulty swallowing and even more trouble answering.

Before she got a squeak out, Ginny grabbed the phone and said, "Say goodnight." She could hear her directing Sam to take Matty to the bathroom to brush his teeth.

It only took a handful of heartbeats for Ginny to jump down her throat. "What's going on Kelly? Is someone there? Are you okay?"

The near panic in the woman's voice made her nervous. It was so unlike her.

"I'm fine," she assured Ginny with a pointed smirk at the man staring a hole through her. "A, uh, guy from town got stranded by the snow. No need to worry."

"What guy? Stranded where? Should I call for Sam?"

"No, oh my goodness, Ginny. Relax. It's fine. Really."

A worried friend. The plot thickens. "Tell your friend Jimmy can vouch for me."

Kelly flipped Roman the bird but grabbed onto the life vest and repeated his words for Ginny's reassurance.

"He's a friend of Jimmy's. I found him lost in the snow when I came down from the peak. It's not a big deal. I'm all right."

"Let me talk to her," he drawled.

She swatted his hand away when he reached for the phone.

"It's the man from the other night, isn't it? Put him on the phone Kelly."

Was this a joke? How the hell did she end up stuck in the middle? Ginny's terse confrontational tone and Roman's droll approach put her on the defensive with both people.

Covering her mouth and the receiver with one hand, she turned away and murmured, "He knows something about Debbie." She heard Ginny's gasp and quickly added, "But he doesn't know everything."

Roman snapped his fingers and gestured for the phone. She handed it over and crossed her arms. He was crazy if he imagined she intended to back off.

Speaking with grave authority, he announced into the phone, "My name is Roman Bishop. Who am I speaking with?"

She groaned. Good god. He sounded like he'd never been anything but in complete charge.

She watched him listen to what Ginny said. His expression never changed. Finally, he responded, "Miss James is completely safe in my care Mrs. Martin."

He went silent again, and she was sure the ruddy hue on his cheeks was the suggestion of a blush.

"Yes, I do and it's not what you think. He's not a threat. Clearly we need to talk." He didn't say much after that except for the occasional one-word response. When he handed the phone back to her, she noticed right away that something in his attitude had changed.

"Ginny," she murmured into the phone. "What's going on?"

The other woman's long sigh sounded like a harbinger of things she wanted no part of.

"There are things you need to know, Kelly."

"About Deb?"

"Yeah. And um, your uh, father."

"Oh Jesus," she spat. "Please say you're joking. Please."

Ginny sounded on the verge of tears. "I wish I could, hon. You know," she said cautiously, "me and Sam always knew this day would come. Too many secrets and lies. Your mom was a complicated mess. It was inevitable that one day everything would catch up."

"What's everything, Ginny? What else is there?"

"Sweetie," Ginny wailed. "I'm so sorry to do this on the phone, but you need to know. This Roman Bishop? I don't know who he is but he knows about your father, and Kelly, there's another."

"Another what?"

"Another brother. He's also illegitimate."

The world started to spin in front of her eyes. This wasn't happening. Couldn't be happening.

"Honey," Ginny murmured. "Your mom knew, and despite all her crazy thinking, she left you a clue. So you'd know for sure if ever a time came when the whole story came out."

"Oh god," she murmured. "What?"

"Your older brother? His name is Liam."

Matty's homemade birth certificate exploded in her brain. So did the memory of their mother laboring over the hand-lettered document announcing the February birth of Matthew Liam James.

The phone slid from her hand as the kitchen faded to black and she dropped to the floor like a rock.

Chapter Eight

His voice hushed, he spoke into the old school landline as he took a stab at reassuring Liam. "Leave everything to me, boss."

"Shit, Roman. I want her where I can be sure she's okay. Ward will be dead before the week is out, so she has nothing to fear. Bring her here. As soon as you can."

"There's something else," he grumbled.

"Oh for fuck's sake. Now what?"

"There's something up with the kid. The old lady was super cagey about him. I'll learn more tomorrow, but I thought you should know."

Considering Liam's personal understanding of a young, unwed mom's predicament, the anger in his voice wasn't a surprise.

"I want every bit of information you can nail down about the baby daddy. Kelly and her kid must be protected at all costs. No more surprises Roman. You just bring them to me, and I'll take it from there."

He studied the pale-faced girl huddled in the corner of the sofa with a throw blanket clutched around her shoulders. She hadn't uttered a single word since coming to. And she hadn't met his eyes except once, and what he saw in their fiery depths grabbed at his heart.

She was afraid, confused, and worried. He knew all the signs.

"Look, boss. I have to go. She's a mess, and it's still snowing like a mother, but I wanted to touch base and bring you up to speed. Give Rhi my love, and I'll call again when I know more."

He hung the old handset on the wall-mounted phone and kicked the long coiled cord piling on the floor out of the way. His head was spinning. After Kelly hit the floor, the old lady on the other end of the phone ripped into him pretty good, and piled on enough threats to warrant peace negotiations. That's why he broke down and called Liam because honest to Christ he had no idea how to proceed.

Learning that Deb James confided in someone and that those people knew an awful lot about Liam threw him completely. The Ginny person even suggested that Deb and Carolyn Ashforth, Liam's mother, knew each other at one time. That part of the story went over with his boss like a fart in church. Liam was hypersensitive where his mother was concerned.

It wasn't a stretch to wonder if more fuck-fruits from Adam Ward's sexual adventures in his company's secretarial pool were likely.

Approaching warily, he hovered with the coffee table between them. She needed space, and he was determined not to do anything that would further freak her out.

"Kelly?"

He watched her eyes slowly shift his way without moving her head.

"Was that...him?"

"Yes. He's worried about you."

Her expression grew tense. Narrowed eyes concealed thoughts and reactions he needed to understand.

"Cut me a break, okay?"

"I don't know what you mean by that," he replied, and he wasn't just spouting words.

"Worried you say? How nice." The biting sarcasm in her words was hard to ignore. "I guess it's easy," she snarled, "to be worried when you keep secrets. My mother was the secret keeper of all time."

He struggled at the sound of raw anguish in her voice.

"Secrets and lies. That's all I've ever known. And the rest of the damn world? Ginny knew. My sperm donor knew."

Roman cringed at the term she used, and the way it rolled off her tongue like the crudest of all swear words.

"This man in New York who says he's my brother—he knew. You knew. But me?" Her harsh snigger pierced his heart like an arrow. "Why the hell should I know anything? I'm nothing but a pawn. A pawn in a game that totally fucked up my life. And now Matty." She clutched her chest and groaned. "Oh my god. Matty."

Shit. There was so much subtext flying around that he wasn't sure where to start, so he gently tried to bring the conversation around to some of the missing details that were driving him nuts.

"Is taking your son away from here going to present a problem?"

Her head snapped up, and turbulent eyes shot daggers his way. "You can't possibly be that stupid."

Her expression and the disbelief she voiced made him pause. What was he missing?

"Tell me something, Roman Bishop. Why did you automatically assume I was a single mother? Was it because I live in the woods and drive a beat up truck?"

"No," he growled with haste. "Not at all." But inside his head, he was re-evaluating a lot of things. "It's just, oh fuck, I don't know. That's what I heard and…" he shrugged.

"So believing town gossip is how you handle your so-called job? Doesn't whisper down the lane constitute fake news?"

He walked right into that one.

The blanket around her shoulders flung back against the sofa, and she bolted from the room like a jackrabbit on speed. He followed right behind and stumbled to a startled halt in the doorway to her bedroom.

Okay, so maybe bedroom was stretching the truth, because the entire space resembled a workshop with a wide table under a window and a tall bookshelf crammed with baskets and tools. He saw a soldering iron and several colored tiles piled in a basket. An easel with a cover thrown over it was shoved in a corner. His curiosity shot off the charts when an Apple laptop caught his eye.

An old brass bed was against one wall and by the look of things she used the head and foot rails as a clothes closet because literally, shit was draped and hanging everywhere.

Kelly knelt on the floor and pulled an old suitcase from under the bed. He could barely make out the mutters coming from her mouth but was certain they were less-than-friendly.

She popped the case open and rifled through for a minute before pulling out a manila envelope. Tossing it in his direction, she struggled to her feet and met his curious gaze.

"Matty was a home birth."

Ugh, no. He felt sick imagining things he wished he could blank out.

"Not a lot of official paperwork 'round these parts. Debbie made that," she indicated with a dismissive wrist flick.

Roman pried open the metal clasp on the envelope. Every few seconds he would search her face, but she was giving away nothing. A piece of craft vellum slid from the protective wrapping. He dropped the envelope and held the beautifully calligraphed document in both hands. It was a birth announcement.

His eyes searched hers. He didn't like what he saw and found it hard to swallow. Then he focused on the paper as he began to read.

"Out loud," she grunted. "I want to hear you say it."

He cleared his throat. "Born to Deborah Jenkins James on February ninth," his voice trailed off as the shame of his assumption began to eat him up.

Kelly arched an eyebrow and smirked. "Keep reading."

"Seven pounds nine ounces, Matthew Liam James…"

Holy fucking shit.

Holy.

Fucking.

Shit.

"That's right fancy man. Say it again."

"Matthew Liam James."

"We were pawns, the both us. All these years. All the lies. The secrets. And we were nothing but pawns in a game we knew nothing about."

His hands were numb, and a strange buzzing muddied his thoughts. He'd never been so wrong in his whole life. Well, he remembered with pained clarity, that's not entirely true. There was that one other time when he'd been so wrong that his wife and child paid the price.

"He's your brother?"

She looked at him as if he was the dumbest motherfucker that ever lived.

"Liam's brother," he added as an afterthought.

Wrong thing to say, because she ripped the document from his hand and shoved it back into the envelope.

A gust of frigid wind rattled the windows and howled through the trees. What fucked up joke was the universe playing out in this situation? He wished he knew.

"I don't need you or what's his name. Matty is my responsibility, and I've got this, so no harm, no foul. You can toddle on back to the big city and tell your boss."

"He's your brother Kelly."

"I don't care who he is. I'm done being a game piece. You can all go straight to hell in a hand basket. I've got plans. Big plans and they don't include anyone else. Understand?"

"Why are you yelling?"

"Why am I yelling? Are you serious?" she shrieked. "That's it."

Next thing he knew she was physically trying to shove him out the door.

"Go away. Leave me alone. Tell my…brother, I'm not interested."

A feeling of intense panic filled her up. She'd always known whatever lurked in her background was fucked up, but she was unprepared for any of this.

Her hands slammed into the middle of his big chest to push him away, but the tiniest hesitation took over when the heat from his body singed her palms. His large hands covered hers, but instead of shaking her off he pressed her fingers and gave a small shudder.

Some form of instantaneous insanity took her over. The feel of his muscular torso beneath her fingers short-circuited Kelly's common sense. It was enthralling. She'd never touched an adult male beyond the occasional handshake or brief social hug.

He felt hard and soft at the same time. Fascinated, she pressed her whole palm and picked up the steady thumping of his heart. It seemed somehow familiar.

His throat moved when he swallowed. She stared at the column of his neck and failed to stop herself from leaning closer to breathe him in. Her whole being quivered as he filled her senses. She could nearly taste his sexual magnetism.

When their eyes locked, she was shocked by the intensity of his gaze.

"I'm sorry," she muttered. Pushing against him she tried to move away, but he put his hands on her waist and stopped the retreat.

Made helpless by his fierce expression, she stared up at him as soft mewling cries of alarm rolled out of her mouth. A slow burn began in her feet and moved steadily upward until she was engulfed by heat.

The way his jaw clenched and the intense burning in his eyes triggered an uncontrollable response. Rising on her toes, she slid her arms around his neck and pressed her lips to his.

Vaguely aware that this was her first real kiss, she desperately clung to him. Not sure what the hell she was doing, Kelly pursed her lips and smooshed them harder on his.

He moved. She felt his strong hands on her upper arms as he pushed her off. A whimper of disappointment hung in the air.

They locked eyes again. She wasn't sure what was going on, but an inner battle on his part was a definite possibility. Then he grabbed her by the hair and yanked her head back.

"Fuck my life," he growled.

And then he kissed her. For real. The hand in her hair was controlling, but instead of balking at the restraint, she quivered with need. The slow, deep kiss changed quickly. As his mouth moved over hers she felt devoured. When his tongue traced the fullness of her lips, Kelly knew she was lost.

Giving herself freely to the sensual demands of his kiss, she groaned when his tongue explored the recesses of her mouth.

She always thought bone-melting wonder was bullshit made up to sell books and get butts in seats at the movies. Boy, was she wrong.

Needing more, she struggled in his powerful embrace. She wasn't disappointed when Roman doubled down and crushed her against his body. The deep, rumbling grunt of satisfaction that he made inside her mouth nearly buckled her knees.

Shocked by her shameless response, she nonetheless experienced a rush of lusty thrill when his need completely dominated hers. Unglued, untethered, desperate, wildly hot and bothered, Kelly clutched at his face, demanding more even though his lips devoured hers.

The hand in her hair grew forceful. She felt his fingers flex against her scalp. When an ecstatic full-body shudder ripped through her, something inside gave way.

"Roman." She loved the sexy vibe her voice gave. "Make love to me."

Time stopped. Oh my god. Had she truly just said that? The question died a quick death. Her body was calling the shots, and right now nothing mattered except this.

He reacted violently, gripping her upper arms and forcefully separating their bodies. A pained growl made his throat ripple from the vibration. She tried to run her tongue along his neck but he had the upper hand physically and managed to keep space between them.

"Ah god, Kelly. No. Stop. We can't do this."

No, no, no. She needed him. Not understanding why the need was so intense didn't slow her down—not when she was wrecked by greedy excitement. How could she change his refusal and frame things in a way they'd both understand?

Refusing to back off, Kelly's hands mapped his muscular chest. Touching him felt like her destiny. She was sure that connecting with him, like this, was fate.

His halting objection seemed anchored to one thing. A stranger a thousand miles away who somehow held her fate in his hands.

Not on her watch.

"Liam," he ground out. She wasn't interested in some lame explanation and she sure as shit wasn't interested in diddly friggin' squat where that man was concerned.

"Is your damn job that important?"

"You don't understand," he complained. "He's my friend Kelly. The boss thing is mostly bullshit. There are rules about this stuff."

Yeah, whatever. She wasn't unfamiliar with that Semper Fi, bro code, bonded brother, blah-blah-blah talking point guys spouted.

With her hands performing a tactile inspection of his abdomen, she made her objections known.

"Rules mean nothing here, Roman," she demanded in a no-nonsense, take-me-seriously voice.

She had to make him see. Understand. Powerful, unseen forces were deciding her life. After tomorrow everything would change. But right here and now, whatever happened came from decisions she made. About her life and what she wanted.

"Don't you see? This is my last stand. As me. As Kelly James. Country girl. I'm not dumb ya' know. Once Sam and Ginny swoop in, and your boss has a say, I'll be nothing. I've always been nothing. You'll all take over, and," she shrugged to make the point.

"No, darlin'. That won't be happening. This is your life. Yeah, things are going to change, but you're still in control."

Right now she wanted to hold tomorrow at bay as long as she could because, despite his positive words, she knew damn well that there was probably a wagon full of surprises still to happen.

She bit her lip and stroked the well-defined abs she felt beneath his clothes. There was another truth dancing around the edges of her thoughts. What if Roman Bishop was the shadow in her dream? Did he arrive when he did for a reason? Was he the one?

The thought was terrifying, but the pull on her emotions was strong. She felt it from the moment he came up to her at Shorty's. Even if she resisted, Roman Bishop was going to change the course of her life.

Not Liam what's-his-name.

And not some nameless, faceless villain who apparently made a habit of impregnating his employees.

Nope. That stuff was collateral circumstance. The real deal was the animal attraction and the feeling deep in her soul that he was The One.

"This is the last time I get to be me. Just me. And make a decision. Please Roman. Don't push me aside. I," she hesitated to say the rest. Bravery, however, comes at the strangest times. "I need you now. While I'm still me."

Chapter Nine

From the silence came the distinctive click-click-click of an old wall clock counting off the seconds as the hands of the dial tracked time.

The battle raging inside him was taking a toll on his nerves and making it damn hard to remain in control. Losing his shit over a twenty-three-year-old girl was not something he ever thought would happen.

Decades of thinking he was a badass dominant, along with a boat-load of real world experience in that world, crumbled to dust in the face of her blunt desire. She wasn't begging for a quick fuck. Hell. Hadn't she even said 'make love to me'?

He should be tipping his hat and heading for the door. Making love wasn't on his usual to-do list. Matter-of-fact, pretty much anything that smelled of relationship or feelings he kept far at arm's length.

His bottom line had always been that he liked to fuck. And fuck his way. A way that involved more leather restraints than boxes of chocolates and bouquets of flowers.

But the thing was…he wasn't bolting for the exit. In fact, he'd barely moved a muscle due in no small measure to the extraordinary depth of pleasure he got from her tactile exploration.

Did his cock surge when she begged? Of course. The instant visual of sinking his large dick into her tight little body made a different response virtually impossible. He was only human after all.

The thing stopping him was so complicated that he couldn't wrap but a portion of his mind around it.

She was way too young. He was a lot older. And seriously jaded. His sex drive was not rated for the timid.

Liam would most likely kill him.

But she was his in some unexplainable way, and that made Liam's outrage a lot less relevant.

Why was he so strongly affected by this slip of a girl? Was Kelly the breath of fresh air he'd been secretly yearning for?

He stopped rationalizing when she uttered her final words and sealed the plea. She needed him.

Yeah, well he needed her too. Damn the consequences.

The firm grip he had on her arms relaxed, and he let her move closer until she once again settled against his body. With a hand he was surprised to see trembling, Roman smoothed stray wisps of hair away from her pretty face. He brushed a soft kiss on her forehead. Her shaky sigh wrapped around his heart and squeezed.

"Carina," he growled.

"Yes, yes." Her cry was heartfelt. "Oh Roman. Don't you see?"

He got it. The obvious was staring them both in the face. The speed of things and the underlying issues needed reflection, but being logical and thoughtful would have to wait.

Maybe later he'd go over this moment in his head because right now desire was over-riding common sense.

"Are you sure you know what you're asking?" He feathered some fingers down her cheek and caressed the sexy column of her neck.

The grey-blue eyes he was sure could see into his soul became luminous with streaks of gold. She lowered her thick, dark lashes and hid her expression. "I know the specifics," she murmured softly.

Raising her gaze to his, he smiled at the cute way she bit her lip. "But I'm sure a man like you has his own way of doing things."

Roman snickered. She couldn't be more correct.

"We're stepping over a line," he reminded her solemnly.

"I know," she quickly assured him. "But let's leave taboo and bro codes out of this."

The whole house heaved and rattled when a strong gust of wind blew through.

"That's how I feel," she murmured softly. Wiggling against his groin, she gave a little sigh. "All these winds are blowing into my world. You're so strong and big."

He liked the way her small hands stroked his chest.

"I need an anchor, Roman. Someone to have my back. Steady me."

He didn't hold back or hesitate. "I'm your man."

She melted against him, winding her arms possessively around his neck. "Take me."

He put an arm around her waist and one hand under one thigh. "Hop on Carina. Wrap your legs and hold tight."

When her thighs grabbed his side, and she crossed her ankles behind his back, Roman wasted no time. Reclaiming her mouth, he held tight, helped himself to a deliberate caress of her ass, and walked them to the brass bed.

Barely adequate for a guy his size, he nonetheless dropped them onto the firm mattress, devoured her hungry mouth and ground his enflamed cock into the center of her parted thighs. He found it surprisingly hot to feel so aroused when they were still dressed.

She became frenzied in an amazingly short time. Desperate, greedy kisses weren't enough. The small satisfied smile on his face began in his soul. This was why he felt untethered. Because the way she expressed her unbridled passion spoke directly to a part deep inside him that he'd kept locked away.

After pressing hot kisses around her mouth, he traced her jaw from ear to ear and nipped at an earlobe. Kelly was making soft whimpering sounds. Experience told him she wasn't acting. There was an intensely natural, slightly innocent urgency to her response. For him, the response was like a V.I.P. ticket to heaven.

Burying his face in her neck, he breathed her in. He smelled sweetness and a fierce wildness. Was it physically possible to be more turned on?

Surprising him at every turn, she kept her legs wrapped around his waist and wiggled non-stop. Her growing desperation fueled the fire building in his groin. When her small hands pressed demandingly on his head as he licked and kissed her neck, he heard the silent plea and sank his teeth into her skin. Hard.

She groaned and tightened her legs. He was conspicuously aware of heat pouring from her center where she ground her pelvis against him.

He bit her again and this time she cried out. "Oh. Yes!" Her body shook, and his cock surged, expanding until he was sure his jeans would tear.

Licking the wildly pulsing hollow at the base of her throat with a rumbling grunt, he rose over her and stared down into eyes smoky with desire.

"Please don't stop," she begged. Roman struggled to hold it together as her hands held his face and the lower half of her body sent a Morse Code message of bumps and grinds straight to his starved libido.

One side of his mouth made a smile-smirk. "Don't stop?" He leaned down and licked her ear. "Carina, love. I haven't even started."

She pulled his face to her lips and kissed him with sweet, hot desperation. He let her have at it and enjoyed the artless seduction. Her tongue, hesitant for the first minute, subjected him to a wonderfully delicious exploration as she devoured his mouth with abandon.

Chuckling as he pulled away, he kissed the tip of her nose and shifted onto his side. "Your passion turns me on, Carina."

She immediately tried to burrow back into his arms. "As much as I enjoy your enthusiasm, love, I want you to hold still while I undress you. Can you do that?" He kissed the corner of her mouth. "What's your take on obeying?"

Having no idea how much or how little experience she had, Roman wasn't prepared when she grinned and licked her lips. Not the response he anticipated.

"Is obey the same as submit?" She answered with a sexy playful vibe that went straight to his dick.

Oh my god. He couldn't help it. He laughed and gathered her close. "Jesus Kelly. You're stealing all my best lines."

"I knew it!" she chortled with a cheeky laugh. "You sir, have fifty shades of alpha practically tattooed on your face."

His shocked reaction brought an even cheekier grin to her face. "What am I gonna do with you?" she tut-tutted. "Always the astonishment. We're not completely cut off from civilization up here, ya' know."

He started to laugh. She had him dead to rights.

"On Demand movies. Need I say more?"

Okay. Now he really had to laugh. "That guy is a putz," he drawled.

"Says you." Punctuating the sentiment with a naughty swipe of her hand down his chest, he stopped her before her touch drifted into the danger zone.

"Why Miss James," he smirked. "What am I to think? You got me into bed on false pretenses."

"I did not," she shrieked as a giggle shot from her mouth.

"Yes you did. I believe what you so sweetly begged for was some nice, old fashioned, lovemaking. And now?" He scoffed playfully. "Suddenly you have an internet grasp of things you should know nothing about. Next you'll be pleading for a grey tie."

"Actually," she cooed. "I'm thinking black leather is more your style."

He put two fingers on her lips to silence her. "Shh. Let's not go there, okay?"

The play of emotions on her face and in her eyes fascinated him.

She knew when to back down though—a telling response that let him know she wasn't experienced at all in those sorts of things. He'd be more than happy to broaden her flimsy understanding. Later. Right now, he had other things on his mind.

She beat him to the start. "Aren't you supposed to be taking my clothes off?"

The wanton challenge in her voice was perfect for the moment. There was no disguising her need, so she didn't.

"Before we get started, I want you to know that the pink fuzzy socks? They'll be staying on."

"Think they're sexy, do you?" she snickered.

"You have no idea."

His growling response took away the playfulness from seconds earlier.

Rising onto his knees, he maneuvered around the small bed, removing her shirt and jeans until all she wore were the pink socks, a pair of shockingly arousing plain white panties and a front hook bra that struggled to contain her breasts.

He placed his palms atop hers and twined their fingers together as he pulled her arms above her head. Dropping an urgent, exploratory kiss on her mouth, Roman increased the intensity until she was quivering. Then he took her hands and showed her how to hang onto the brass headboard.

"In lieu of leather ties, I want you to keep your hands there, okay?"

She nodded but said nothing. A glaze of lusty passion made her dark blue eyes sparkle.

The ancient bed creaked and complained when he stood up. Her head turned, and he felt Kelly's eyes on him.

"Ordinarily, you'd be doing this part," he explained in the sexiest most suggestive drawl he could muster. "But I'd much rather have you watch this time."

A sharp gasp preceded her eyes darting to his abdomen when he reached for the hem of his shirt and pulled it over his head.

Her soft groaning, "Oh Roman," when his chest was revealed made him feel like a god. She eyed the tattoo on his forearm but said nothing. Good. The explanation was a story for another day.

Pulling a short, rolling stool from the worktable, he sat down right next to her and began removing his heavy boots. His eyes caressed her body as laces came undone and feet slid from confinement.

She had a curvy fullness to her figure that he liked very much. A small freckle close to her belly button taunted his mouth, challenging him to lick her there. He was in the middle of considering doing exactly that when she moved her leg and stroked his arm with a furry sock covered foot.

With taming her fire not even a remote possibility, he grabbed her ankle and teased with a soft kiss on her inner calf followed immediately with a hearty bite.

"Are you going to tell me to behave?"

He smirked as he stood. "Absolutely not. Your fire excites me, Carina. So similar to my own."

An excited flush brightened her cheeks. She was unconsciously nibbling on her lip. "Hurry," she implored warmly.

Her eyes devoured as she tracked his hands. He undid the heavy leather belt and released the button on his jeans before sliding the zipper down, carefully. The pleasure in her expression as he slowly revealed his body inspired more of a sexy striptease. This feeling of satisfaction from seeing her response was a novel experience.

He wasn't an underwear guy. Whatever his hand found when he reached into the drawer was fine by him. As a matter-of-fact, he had no idea what if anything he wore beneath his jeans. As the denim slid down his muscular thighs, he nearly sighed with relief when a pair of black briefs came into view.

Kelly's nervous giggle once the pants were gone and he stood before her hungry gaze made his cock twitch.

"Those things should be illegal," she sighed as her eyes roamed with lascivious slowness over his thighs.

His immediate thought? *All the better to fuck you with.* He kept the words to himself but the thought fired up his brain in a big way.

The lights flickered once. Then again, and a moment later the room plunged into darkness. The timing was perfect. He was about to ravish the young sister of his friend and employer. She was completely aware how begging him to take her would end. The abrupt blackout framed what they were doing in a time out of time sort of way.

His eyes adjusted to the sudden darkness. A shaft of light from the window courtesy of the blizzard full moon bathed them in an ethereal glow. She looked wild and untamed, writhing on the narrow bed with her hands gripping the brass headboard. Her dark hair and pale skin reminded him of Snow White, a perfectly apropos comparison for this unusual interlude.

A long, slow gasp turned to an earthy moan and he chafed at not being able to read her thoughts. What went through her mind at that moment? She sucked in her stomach and held her breath. He nearly pinned her to the spot right then and there.

"I'm going to touch you now and you're not to hold back, Carina. The darkness, it…blinds me to what brings you pleasure. Do you understand what I'm saying?"

"Yes, Roman. I want your hands on me. Everywhere," she added breathlessly.

He got on the creaking bed, straddled her thighs, and leaned over with his hands close by her head. The dim light made her expressive eyes sparkle in the darkness.

With an earthy grunt he demanded, "Open your mouth." He smiled at how eager she was to obey. The next uncomfortable thought involved her mouth and some other guy, any other guy's cock. Instinct and jealousy raced along his nerves making him growl with displeasure.

It was totally fucked up for him to feel that way. After all, it's not like he was the poster boy for celibacy or restraint where his sex life was involved. She was perfectly entitled to express her sexuality however she wanted. But the part of his brain where support for feminism lived wasn't loud enough to be heard over the rumblings of primitive possession scrambling his thoughts.

Grabbing her chin, he took forceful command and subjected her to a punishing kiss with lips and tongue determined to stake a claim. He was partially aware that her eyes rarely closed. She appeared mesmerized.

Having subdued her momentarily he went back to learning her body with his hands. Like a blind man memorizing his lover's face, he traced her eyebrows and gently kissed each eyelid. The slope of her nose, rounded cheeks and the way her chin tilted. And then, Jesus. And then her pouty lips and lush mouth.

His thumb slid into her mouth. She wasted no time unleashing a good deal of passion on sucking it until he was forced to withdraw or lose his damn mind.

Drawing one hand from her chin and down her neck, he stopped when his whole palm was positioned for the perfect lover's grip. Flames of desire licked at the soles of his feet when she writhed and let out a husky moan.

Her eyes fixed on his. She didn't know how to express this particular feeling—the longing to understand was all over her face. Roman nodded slightly and leered into her sultry gaze. He understood what she was feeling. He was making a bold and very dominant claim. Another woman might react fearfully or with hesitation. Not Kelly. She purred and squirmed under him. Claiming her lips with a gentle, sweeping kiss, he murmured, "Good girl," and waited to gauge her reaction.

She balked, and he was glad because it meant she wasn't just a vessel to be used. Then his joy turned incandescent when she relaxed and melted into his grip with a small, almost smug smile curling her lips.

Well hot damn, he thought. His sexy Carina liked being a good girl. A naughty good girl.

One finger trailed leisurely from the base of her throat into the valley between her breasts. He was a connoisseur of boobs and hers held a delicious promise. The convenient front hooks on her bra made it possible to quickly uncover the glorious mounds.

"Ah, Carina," he growled. "Such lovely tits."

He started slow, carefully cupping each beautiful globe, testing the weight and jiggle. He massaged the satisfying fullness and rolled her turgid little nips between his fingers.

She was making sounds, but he was lost in the sensual delight her gorgeous tits offered.

"What do you need, little one? Tell me."

Her gasp was sharp and desperate. "Oh please Roman. Make the ache stop. I can't…"

He knew what she needed. The second his lips closed around one of her nipples, she let out a wail of pleasure, let go of the brass headboard, and grabbed him. With a loud pop, he disengaged from the fierce suckle and reared back.

"Uh uh," he snarled. "No hands. Obey, remember?"

With a rough, annoyed huff she grabbed hold of the brass once more and told him exactly what she thought of this obey thing by sticking her tongue out. "Fine," she snapped. "But if I have to obey, you have to suck harder."

He had to chuckle. "Harder, you say?"

"Yes," she grunted. "Let's call that the operative word, okay?"

Roman pinched a nipple and smirked. "Is hard your normal setting?" He was just messing with her, so he was surprised by her answer.

"I don't know. Let's find out."

If he had any residual sense of deprivation for not being breast fed as a baby, all of it vanished as he went to town and back on her tits. Proving further just how good a girl she could be, Kelly started quiet but got a whole lot louder and more demanding as he encouraged her to express her pleasure.

In their current position with him straddling her, Roman was fast approaching his limit. Every time she writhed or wiggled and rubbed against him, his cock went wild.

Lifting off, he shimmied in the narrow bed until he was stretched alongside her deliciously quivering body.

"Look at me."

She was trembling uncontrollably when her face shifted and she turned to lock eyes with him. He needed to see her. Gauge her expression; read her signals when he touched her pussy.

Watching her chest heave with excited anticipation, he ran a hand, palm down, from her breastbone, across her tummy, stopping for a swift swirl of her navel before he flattened his caress and slid into her panties.

Her thighs momentarily shut and locked. She bit her lip and looked away. He smiled knowingly and drawled, "Don't be embarrassed, luv."

Her sweet, sexy blush was visible in the dim light.

"Come on Kelly. Open those sweet thighs and show me how wet you are." He leaned closer and whispered against her ear, "The wetter the better."

She still hesitated. God. How cute was that?

"Kelly. Baby," he growled. "Open your legs."

Her thighs slowly parted. She kept her eyes on his.

With one finger he traced her center from ass to clit and let out a deep groan when his finger coated with her desire.

Staring intently into her eyes, he showed his satisfaction as best he could and said, "Now see. I like finding your pussy wet and waiting for me."

Her only reply was a small undulation. He cupped her mound possessively and squeezed gently.

"Carina," he gruffly drawled. "Have we done anything that you don't like?"

There was no surprise on his part when she answered him in the most direct way possible. "I like the kissing. Very much. And I liked what you did to my tits."

Before her next words he chuckled softly and said, "Honey, swear to fucking god. You have no idea how much it pleases me that you didn't fall back on politically correct terms."

"You didn't let me finish," she teased in a husky voice. "As I was saying, the tit action? Very nice. And I'm sure whatever you unleash on my pussy will be, um…memorable."

At her naughty words, he wasted no time and sank one finger into her wet depths. She gasped and writhed.

"Roman." Her voice held a plea, but her eyes demanded a challenge.

"Lift your knees, baby."

She complied and he went to work on her magnificent pussy, inserting two fingers and rubbing her clit until she responded with a flood of need. And she still had her panties on. And those cute pink socks.

Short whimpers, husky grunts and drawn out moans provided the backing soundtrack as he sucked on her nipples and fingered her with ruthless intent until he felt her muscles tighten.

So she didn't wonder, he told her in blunt terms what he wanted.

"I find it sexy as fuck that you cream so beautifully from having your pussy fingered. Think of the possibilities. In the car. An elevator. In public under a dinner table. At a concert."

She moaned and undulated.

"Now let's find out how my Carina orgasms. Seeing you come is the best part," he growled with sexy meaning.

"But I thought," she moaned. The sentence dwindled to silence when he twisted his fingers inside her.

"Oh, don't worry. You'll be coming on my cock too. But first…"

He fingered her with ruthless intent. She gushed and shook. The explosion when it happened took his breath away. Nothing could ever be as staggeringly beautiful to watch as Kelly in the throes of a passionate consummation.

When he was sure there wasn't anything left, he calmly withdrew his fingers and patted her mound through the simple panties.

She looked shell-shocked. He didn't know what sort of man she'd been with before now but he was confident an orgasm like the one he'd just given her had never been on the menu.

Now that she'd come, he could continue. His cock was thick and long. To accommodate his size, the wetter the better.

He vaulted off the bed and made quick work of ditching his briefs. Then he grabbed her white panties and pulled them down her legs. He made a production out of smelling the intimate lingerie infused with her sexy fragrance.

Her hands flew off the headboard when she got a good long look at his hard cock. Seeing the lusty desire etched on her face, he knew only tying her up would keep Kelly's hands from his body.

"Oh, may I touch you? You're so beautiful. I didn't know…"

Even if he could have said no he didn't. The wonder and awe on her face did weird things to his sense of manhood. Sure, it was a cliché, but the awestruck expression and the way her hands moved—as if being drawn to his flesh by a magnet—made him feel like the king of the world. No, fuck that. The world wasn't large enough to contain his emotions. She made him feel like emperor of the fucking galaxy.

Jesus H. Christ, though. His brain exploded when the scrutiny she subjected him to with her small hands pushed him way closer to the edge than he was comfortable with. It only took a few seconds for the oohs and ahhs to turn husky and her fingers to push his buttons.

"Easy, sweetheart," he grunted. She was a little too fascinated with the smooth head of his cock. If she tickled the corona one more time with her nails he wouldn't be responsible for what happened next.

She stopped the tactile exploration and literally sat on her hands with her feet dangling off the side of the bed. Her eyes and the visible tension around her mouth held his attention. That didn't mean he ignored the long tumble of hair falling in a glorious mess around her shoulders, or the way her tasty nipples poked through the dark strands.

Roman counted his heartbeats in the ensuing silence. The strangest sensation, sort of like a slow moving waterfall of warmth, started at the crown of his head and drifted down until he felt engulfed and overtaken. Was he glowing? Sure felt like it.

She softly murmured, "I think I've dreamt about you."

This wasn't serendipity. She wasn't just passing through. There was a certainty about their coming together that shook him up and comforted him at the same time.

"Carina," he murmured softly. He lifted her chin with his fingers and peered intently into her eyes. He paused over the words. Once he allowed light to pour into this particular corner of his heart, he'd either end up destroyed or rebuilt. He took the plunge. "I've dreamt of you, too."

With the grace and beauty of an angel she rose from the bed and joined their naked bodies. Wrapping her arms around him possessively, she rose on tiptoes.

Short puffs of air hit his face when she spoke softly but with quiet determination. "I'm not afraid of this. Of you."

Roman took a deep breath and gathered her closer. The way she fit against him took perfection to a whole new level.

He kissed her and it was unbelievable. Naked bodies, skin on skin, straining for more. To be closer, held tighter, kissed more deeply. That didn't last long, not when the fever driving them demanded their full attention.

He used her long hair as a restraint, something she made no effort to pretend she didn't like very much. It was refreshing. She was a natural.

They rolled around the narrow, noisy bed, touching, kissing, stroking, mauling. It was a perfect symphony of building desire that left them writhing jointly in an agony of desperation.

She was with him the whole way, following where he led. Her eyes intrigued. She rarely looked away and her body was truly a paradise of delights.

When holding back stopped being an option, he started moving her into position for the finale when sense erupted in his brain.

"Oh, fuck," he roared.

"Yes, please," she whimpered.

He almost lost it then and there.

Him leaping off her and darting around the room wasn't quite what she expected in that moment, evidenced by the confusion on her face. He'd be embarrassed about so obviously losing his shit at such a crucial juncture, but he had to find his fucking jeans so he could rifle through his wallet for the condom every guy kept for emergency situations like this.

Stubbing his toe on a table leg in the unfamiliar obstacle course of darkness, he located the pants and extracted the wallet. Fumbling with the confidence of a teenage boy he found the small packet and exhaled with relief.

"Sorry," he grunted with real embarrassment as he displayed the protection in his hand. "My bad."

Her luminous smile wasn't at all what he expected. She snorted with a mixture that sounded amused and relieved. "The uh, condom dance you just performed," she said with obvious delight, "well, come on. Cute doesn't quite cover it, fancy man. "

She shocked the holy crap from him when she snatched the condom from his hand and inspected it like a TSA agent screening carry-on luggage. "Is there an expiration date on these things?" she asked with an amused chuckle. "'Cause this one looks like it's spent considerable time in your back pocket."

There wasn't anything to do except laugh. So he did. The passion of moments ago wasn't gone—it was magnified by great happiness. It didn't seem to matter that they could count the length of their relationship in hours. Some things were right and didn't need picking apart.

That didn't mean however that he wasn't ticking off a list of firsts because he couldn't remember ever having laughter be part of a seduction.

"Actually," he told her with mock sincerity as he took the packet from her hand, "it's worse than that."

She snickered and made an adorable face while she waited for his next words.

"This little baby?" he said while waving it in front of her face. "Won it in an arcade. Spent ten bucks in quarters and all I got was this."

Kelly guffawed like crazy, slapped him on the side of his ass and then fell over in a seizure of giggles, smacking her hand on the bed and begging for him to stop.

"The booty prize," she shrieked with glee. "You got the carnival booty prize. What fun."

Stretching out on the single bed, she crooked her finger and waggled her brows. He completely vapor locked when his sexy paramour spread her legs and pointed. "Insert here?"

She said it like a question but he most certainly did not miss the plea in her voice.

He raked her naked body with his eyes as he ripped the condom from the packet and rolled it on. His poor cock was so ready that he gasped and had to shut his eyes for a second just from handling his hard, swollen shaft.

Covering her body with his, he rejoined her on the bed and reignited the blaze until she was shaking and begging for him to take her. She was beyond wet and more than ready when his cock breached the tight entrance to her lush body.

"Kelly," he groaned. She focused in on his eyes, and with that he gave a mighty thrust and his entire world turned upside down.

She made a soft yelp followed by a deep groan as he sank into her pussy. His brain was misfiring. Had to be, because unless he was having a waking hallucination, he'd just ripped through her virginity and done it without any finesse.

He shook his head to clear away the primitive burst of satisfaction and pleasure engulfing his emotions.

She was mewling softly, and her legs made restless movements like she was trying to get closer. He wasn't sure how much closer they could get without him melting into her body.

Aware of his cock pulsing softly in her hot, wet pussy, he swore the damn thing swelled even more. It was as if a switch was thrown because in the next instant she went from shocked and impaled to over-the-top desperate. The girl's muscle control made the Pilates instructor he banged a few months ago fade to amateurish insignificance.

"I changed my mind," he grunted on a particularly ferocious thrust.

She bucked her hips with increasing fervor.

"You aren't a good girl at all, Carina."

The room started spinning when she didn't respond except to grunt and fiercely fuck him from below.

Did virgins come the first time? He wasn't sure, but goddammit, he was up for finding out.

Shoving both hands beneath her ass, he lifted, forcing her knees back and moved her around until he found the right angle. He knew he was in position when her pussy flooded with wet heat.

Sucking a nipple into his hungry mouth, Roman growled commands.

"Keep those knees back."

"Roll your hips baby. Yeah, like that," he grunted when she made a perfectly perfect circle and moaned like crazy the whole time.

Her arms started to flail. She clutched the sheet under her ass, when he wasn't devouring her mouth or mauling her neck, she rolled her head from side to side and made noises he gathered in his memory.

But holy shit, when her hands found the brass headboard, she grabbed tight and used the anchor as leverage, furiously fucking him back as he pumped in and out with a wildness he'd never known before.

It got more than a little fierce in that damn creaky bed. With the winds howling outside and the whole house in pitch blackness, the thunk, thunk, thunk of the metal banging against the wall with each thrust he delivered only made him harder.

She pulled him to her mouth, he thrust his tongue in unison with his cock. Her fingers dug into his neck and shoulders. He was dimly aware of nails raking his back and the way he bellowed with pleasure.

He never faltered, not even when her tight pussy squeezed his shaft so tight he saw stars. Grunting from the effort of each powerful stroke, he surrendered to her ferocious sexuality and lost himself.

She came. He watched and absorbed the mind-blowing sensation of her pussy exploding with an orgasm.

Waiting like a surfer gauging a massive wave, he let her climax build and then as she hit the top of the pleasure swell, he thundered for home. They were both vocal and loud as the skin prickling consummation rolled them around and finally sucked them under.

Roman was aware in a way he'd not known previously of his cock pulsing and spurting as her luscious cunt claimed its prize. It felt never ending too. He let out a tremendous roar and finished inside her. She was shaking uncontrollably at the end. Fuck, the whole bed shook from the power of the earthquakes overtaking them.

It took forever to come back and the moment when he pulled his cock from her body provided an added shock that made Roman freeze. He didn't need the lights on to know they'd experienced a condom fail. A major condom fail.

Struggling to process what happened left him unprepared when Kelly sat up straight like a marionette whose strings were pulled. She looked at him, her eyes wide and an unreadable expression on her face.

He was still fumbling awkwardly to untangle from the bedding they'd made a mess of when she bolted for the door.

What the god damn fuck was going on?

Frantic, he tugged the corner of a sheet wrapped around his calf and growled angrily. Free at last, he took off after her and found she'd taken refuge in the bathroom.

Not knowing what to do, he paced back and forth in the hallway and picked up the faint sound of water running. Scraping a hand on his head, he scowled at the barrier she'd thrown up with the closed door.

That was the exact moment the power came back on. Glancing down his front, he grimaced at the irrefutable evidence of the debacle his out-of-bounds sexuality created. A condom split in two still hung from his dick and because that wasn't enough to freeze his nuts, there was something else. Something that fucked with his head in a major way.

Straightforward was the only way to say it. The ripped condom wasn't the only shocker. The in-your-face proof of Kelly's virginity was more than evident.

Returning to the bedroom, he disposed of the useless condom and stared at the blood-stained bedding.

Oh dear god. What had he done?

He looked at the doorway. She fled the second she could. He couldn't help imagining her attempting to clean up, by herself, when he should have taken care of her.

Guilt flooded his heart.

So did a primal satisfaction that confused the holy shit from him.

Jamming his feet into his heavy work boots, he stomped from the crowded little room, eyed the still-closed bathroom as he walked by, and made for the back door. He had to give the screen door a vicious kick to push back the foot of snow far enough that he could step out.

Brushing the snow out of the way with a swinging leg, he made it down the steps and marched about fifty feet from the house and then stopped. It was cold but he didn't care. The falling snow clung to his hair. Flakes hitting his sex-warmed body melted instantly.

In the biting cold, his naked body exposed to the elements, the truth barreled into him like a herd of buffalo moving at high speed.

Kelly Anne James was the soft whisper calling out from his soul.

Heaviness seized his heart and he clutched his chest. He'd waited forever to find her, even let himself believe it would never happen. And now that he had, their rash actions might prove his downfall.

For the first time in a very long while he thought of Vanessa and felt at peace. He'd loved her as much as he was capable of back then.

She tried to love him the same. They certainly loved the promise of their child. But when he was honest, and the remorse of finding fault in things that death cut off didn't railroad the reflection, he'd come to admit they would have struggled as a couple. Eventually. But knowing that didn't mean he wouldn't continue to love and honor the family he almost had every day for the rest of his life.

But the gaping hole losing Vanessa and their baby left inside him wasn't there any longer. Had it been there yesterday? Or the day before? He couldn't remember, and that was the whole point. Nothing seemed to exist before the boldly self-assured girl he'd just made devastating love to appeared in his field of vision. Without any effort on her part she filled the void.

And what had he done while she was saving his soul from an empty purgatory?

Throwing his arms wide, Roman turned his face to the sky and howled. Guilt, remorse, and fear that he'd killed another chance for happiness before it had an opportunity to grow fueled the harsh sound.

What the fuck was he supposed to do now?

Chapter Ten

"Okay you silly twit," Kelly mumbled out loud. "Get a grip."

Turning off the shower, she flung the curtain open and grabbed her towel from the hook, wrapping it quickly around her body. The flowered shower cap got tossed in the sink. With a second, smaller towel, she vigorously rubbed from face to toes, wicking away the water clinging to her skin.

Swiping condensation off the mirror above the sink, she pointed to her reflection and continued scolding.

"You are not your mother. Having your world shot full of goose bumps and sparkles won't lead to losing who you are, so snap out of it. It was just sex."

She looked away guiltily and winced. With nothing for comparison, she might be operating at a disadvantage, but Kelly was pretty damn sure what she and Roman did in her crappy, old metal bed was a lot more than just sex.

Without the accusatory finger pointing, she griped to her reflection, "And what the hell with the running away. That was a little melodramatic, don't you think?"

Busted.

Snatching a bottle of body lotion off a shelf, she dropped the toilet seat with a loud clang and sat down. Absent-mindedly pumping far too many squirts into a cupped palm, she energetically set about rubbing the sweet smelling cream onto her legs until none remained. Cupping a few more squirts into her hand, she dropped the towel and smoothed the cold lotion all over her torso.

When her hands drifted over her breasts, she flinched. Roman's mouth did quite a number on her nipples, evidenced by the faint bite marks and chafed tenderness.

Kelly ran her hands beneath her naked breasts and gauged their weight and fullness. She'd been more than a little surprised to discover how sensitive they were and how susceptible to her lover's attention.

Her lover. Wow.

She'd taken a man she knew for less than a day as her first and only lover.

Why did everything feel so right when what she'd done, what they'd done, had probably been so wrong?

A movement outside the bathroom window caught her eye. She used her fist to clear a spot to look through and swept the snowy backyard scene looking for clues.

Her breath caught in her throat when Roman's backside came into view. "What's he doing?" she wondered in the silence.

A naked man in her backyard in the middle of a snowstorm didn't happen every day, but how wrong was it that she tingled with pleasure at the sight? The man was built like a marble statue. Hard and with muscles on top of muscles. He had a backside that needed a Grade A Prime Seal of Approval stamped on one mouth-watering cheek, and those thighs? Holy guacamole. Were those things legal in all fifty states?

She startled and jumped back when he suddenly flung his arms and roared at the sky. The sound came through as if the glass window wasn't there.

Shame shot through every corner of her being. The anguished howl cut her to pieces. This was her fault.

He turned around slowly. His head hung at a dejected angle. The veil of snow covering his head reminded her of a white hat. The symbolism ate away at her composure. Her fancy man lover was one of the white hats. Matty would get the symbolism in a flash.

The tingling turned to a shudder as she watched him slowly shuffle through the deep snow. The front view was even more devastating than the rear. Along with the illegal thighs, his chest had to either be dangerous to one's health or flat out the most gorgeous thing she'd ever seen. How the hell did he get that definition? Was it natural?

And then her eyes caught another slight movement and drifted lower. "You've got to be kidding," she muttered right about the time her nose pressed against the frosty windowpane for a better look.

Swinging in a mighty arc, a priceless work-of-erotic art at the juncture of his thighs melted her brain. She blinked and made a small grunt. He was huge. Like seriously huge, and unless he had magical powers and could maintain an erection while buck naked in a blizzard, what she couldn't tear her eyes from was a cock at rest.

Oh, that tingling shudder? About that. She was going to need a mop to clean up after her if the aching pulse didn't quit.

Feeling lucky, her conscience snorted?

Um, well, yeah. Duh.

Then get your ass out there and explain your damn self. He deserves better than to suffer from Deb's from-the-grave bullshit. Take responsibility Kelly Anne, and claim your man.

His teeth chattering from the bone-chilling cold, Roman quickly pulled on his jeans. The ice-cold metal buckle touching his skin made him suck his stomach in as he slid the belt into place.

He looked around for his wallet, found where he'd tossed it on the floor, stooped and picked it up. With it firmly in his pocket, he flopped onto the side of the bed to put his socks and boots on correctly. The sound of the metal creaking and the mattress bumping the wall reminded him why he was so twisted up in knots.

Making fast work of the boots, he stood up and reached for his shirt. His eyes caught sight of the dark stain on the bed. Pulling the shirt over his head, he got one corner of the front tucked in as he searched around the bed until he located the ripped condom packet.

This whole situation was of his making. He was one hundred percent responsible for everything. Period. When he got the chance, he intended to man up. He'd been a brute and handled her badly—especially considering it was her first time.

That was thing one.

Then there was the Liam thing. It didn't matter that she went into it acknowledging they were crossing a line. He was the man. It was up to him to do the right thing. He was gonna ignore the fact that she'd been right there with him the whole way. Or that she started it. He was an adult for Christ's sake and should have known better.

Right?

"So serious," a gentle voice said. He turned toward the sound and found Kelly leaning casually against the doorframe. Her hair was gathered on top of her head. She wore a pair of stretchy gray pants and a big oversized sweater that hung to mid-thigh. He lowered his gaze to the magnificent breasts he knew lay beneath. She wasn't wearing a bra.

When he met her eyes, he shook his head and did a double take. Wait a minute. What? "Are you making fun of me?"

"A little," she laughed. And then she made a frowning face and added a grunt meant to convey that she was serious.

Feeling like he'd stepped off a whirling merry-go-round and had to catch his balance, he stood completely still and gaped at her. The wounded little virgin he created in his mind that he'd ravished like a wild animal was nowhere in evidence.

Well, shit. Another first. How the fuck much more was he going to get wrong?

Throwing her a hard glance and sounding like a grumpy old man snarling at kids on the lawn, he said, "We need to talk."

"Ya' think?" she replied with some knee-smacking hilarity. "Come on," she added with a jerk of her head. "Let's talk next to the fire. In case you haven't noticed it's freezing in here."

Left foot, right foot. That's all it'd take to start moving, but he stood frozen to the spot. That's how bad it was. She'd stolen his ability to function.

When he didn't move, she sighed heavily and came to him with her hand out. "It's okay, Roman. You didn't do anything wrong. Let's get warm, and you can ask me the hundred questions I hear clanging in your head."

She took his hand and led him from the room like a confused child. He followed along and spent more time than was appropriate wondering if she went commando beneath the stretch pants.

The fluffy pink socks captured his attention. His mind flashed to holding her legs open as he pounded her tight passage, and how her sock covered feet swung with each thrust.

In the living room, she gently guided him to the sofa and stroked his face when he sat.

"The fire looks good for now. I'm going to put the pot on to boil. Would you like some tea? Or coffee? I can make coffee if you'd like."

"Tea's fine," he croaked.

Grabbing his shoulders, she playfully shook him and chuckled. "The power came back. We didn't accidentally kill each other in the dark. I'm taking that as a win."

Who was this girl? Why wasn't she berating him for being a macho pig? How come he wanted to drop her to the floor and do it all over again? What the hell was happening?

"Kelly, I'm out of my depth here. Why aren't you tearing me a new one for what happened?"

"Er, yikes," she muttered. "The hymen thing sorta' freaked you out, huh? Sorry."

"The hymen thing?" His voice could not possibly have sounded more incredulous. He facepalmed and shook his head. Feeling full solidarity with every guy throughout all of human history who found himself dealing with a smart-mouthed female, Rhiann's amused snicker sounded in his head. So did Liam's grumpy 'Welcome to the club.' A sentiment quickly followed up with laughter and fall down finger pointing courtesy of his former Justice brother comrades.

Using the sleeve of her sweater, she covered her hand and rubbed the top of his head. "Don't want you catching a cold from wet hair."

Oh.

My.

Fucking.

God.

She was after-caring him and doing it with an ease and naturalness that blew his mind. Wasn't that his job? Feeling like he'd stepped into an alternate universe, he continued being a clueless idiot with limited powers of speech.

"You know," she kidded, "there's a bottle of Jack tucked away on the top shelf of the pantry. I could drag it down and pour you a drink. I don't think tea will be much help." The way she eyed him and the obvious way she tried not to laugh brought him at least part way to his senses.

Forcing a smile to his face, he arched a brow at the same time. "Mmm," he drawled. "I'm not sure that's a good idea. Adding whiskey on top of what you're doing to my head wouldn't end well."

"I'm not doing anything! That's all on you. I get that the virgin thing probably needed a declaration of some sort but everything after that? Roman," she playfully chided. "Come on. You, me and a bottle of whiskey? It'd end exactly like the picture in your head."

"And how do you know what I'm picturing?"

Her laugh wrapped around his heart. "Oh, good grief. When are you going to stop with the 'but you're just a girl' crap? How do I know what you're picturing? Really?"

She pulled him from the sofa and curled around him like a sexy, clinging vine. For no reason other than it was a knee-jerk reaction, he grabbed her ass and helped himself to a glorious handful. Her sultry smile hit him like a ton of bricks.

"You like to fuck. And you aren't a wimp about it."

"Kelly…"

"Shh, I'm just getting started."

He gulped.

"You feel bad because I took your power away. I'd offer to go over your knee as a penance, but then the tea will never get made."

"Have you ever been properly spanked?"

"Good lord, no. Roman. Get with the picture, would you? I've never anythinged. Never been kissed, fondled, fingered, or fucked." He was aware his eyes narrowed. She kissed his nose and raised up higher. "I don't want nicey nice, and I suspect you don't either. And before you growl or frown some more, no. I don't talk like this normally." She shrugged a shoulder. "This feels very real to me. Careful, polite language doesn't fit."

"I like how blunt you are."

"Good because I'm still answering your question and yeah, I'm going to get vulgar."

"Vulgar has its place."

"I'm glad we agree. Back to what you're picturing. Even though you feel like shit because you think I'm some delicate, innocent flower, the very nice butt grab just now tells me that a little face in the carpet, ass in the air action is a safe bet."

The things he could do, the sounds he'd get out of her in that delicious position, turned him on quicker than flipping on a light.

"So let's stop dancing around the obvious. You want me, and I want you. Is it complicated as all get out? Yeah. Just don't let the complex part of things change what's happening between us."

"But you're so young, and…"

She wasn't taking his shit and cut him off with a ferocious squeeze. "And you're ancient. Whatever." Her annoyed growl made him smile inside. "Look. Stop overthinking. First of all, it isn't fair 'cause I'm not a fool. You know way more about me than I do. You get me, right?"

Oh hell yeah.

"And secondly, can I have some credit, please? Unless I imagined things, what went down earlier? I started it. And knowing whatever the hell else it is that you know didn't stop you from letting me. So the overthinking after-the-fact is a little self-defeating."

"There's something you don't know."

She kissed him so sweetly he wanted to cry. With a small, encouraging smile she nodded. "Okay. Tell me."

"The uh, condom broke," he blurted out.

"What does that mean exactly?"

A thousand random thoughts and emotions shook his previously well-ordered life.

"It means we're getting married."

She shoved him so hard he stepped back. "Married? Why? I don't understand."

He plowed ahead because all of a sudden his mind cleared and he knew what this surreal situation needed.

"To be perfectly blunt," he spelled out with emphasis, "there's something primal sparking between us. Pardon the vulgar directness of this but Carina, when our clothes come off? We fuck like animals. And that energetic fucking left you in a vulnerable spot courtesy of some shitty latex. I'm not clairvoyant, but it's a safe bet that we'll be heading for round two and probably three, possibly four before tomorrow rolls around. And since I'm not fully loaded with protection our options are thin. Pulling out and coming on your tits sounds like fun, but not all the time."

"Oh."

"Yes, oh. And since I'm guessing neither of us intends to back off, the chances of you getting pregnant go up exponentially every minute we're alone together. There have been enough illegitimate kids in your family tree."

"Ouch," she griped. "That was a bit brutal, don't you think?"

"Brutal but true, luv. Your mother, you, Matty, Liam. I don't know what's going on with us, but one thing is sure. You're mine, Kelly. And I think you like the idea."

They looked at each other in silence for a long time.

"God. Now I really need that tea."

That's all she said before making a mad dash into the kitchen. He let her go and allowed the space between them. She needed time to come to grips with everything being thrown her way.

Tomorrow really would be the dawn of a new day, and it was going to take everything he had to keep this whole thing from heading straight into the crapper.

He'd called it when suggesting they'd fuck the night away, and she had not a single regret about any of it. It worried her though how quickly she'd let him into her life. She'd never let anyone in. Ever. Only Sam and Ginny were the exception. And Matty, of course.

"You guys don't seem bothered at all by the snow," she remarked to the brood of Rhode Island Reds. "Bet you're glad now that I insulated this baby, huh?"

She did a bit more upkeep to the chicken coop and made sure her hens had plenty of water. The overnight conditions made ice in their pan, so she had to remind herself to trek out here every few hours and break up any chunks that formed.

On the way across the backyard to the goat shelter she built with her own hands and Matty's questionable assistance, Kelly trudged through the snow, at times breaking a path through thick drifts of the frozen white.

Goats were her mother's brilliant idea, one of the few she brought to the table and miracle of miracles, the little animals turned out to be a very good idea. First, they were better than any lawnmower Sears ever came up with, and to be honest, she liked the milk goats they kept.

Ginny showed her ways to manage a small group of animals and how to get the most bang for her buck. The goat cheese and milk products she sold at the Farmers' Market paid for the annual costs and gave her a free and easy supply of milk.

Chuckling she muttered, "Ah, life in the wild."

A while later the chores were done, and the sun finally came out. They were buried under a foot and a half of snow and some pretty significant drifting piles. The only thing keeping her from jumping out of her skin was knowing Sam would arrive at some point and use his truck plow to clear the bumpy dirt road to the house and help get Bandit dug out. Good thing too, because there was a pile of trash covered with a tarp and ready to go to the dump in the truck's bed.

The rumbling growl from her stomach was all the reminder she needed that food was next on her to-do list. The heated up leftover coffee from yesterday that she held her nose and guzzled earlier had eaten a hole through her empty gut. She needed something substantial before getting on with the rest of the daily grind.

"Shuffle, shuffle, shuffle." Using her booted feet as mini-plows, Kelly kicked snow away from a new path leading from the rear of the big backyard to the door. Half way there she noticed the smoke from the chimney had increased and the porch light was off.

Roman must be up.

She paused. The thought came so easily to her. It was as if he belonged there. Maybe not so much in a literal way, because he was a fish out of water in her world. But everything she felt and all they'd shared seemed like destiny. There was no way two people who just met could generate that much intensity, heat, passion and connection for no goddamn reason.

At the steps, she kicked snow off her boots and then almost flew into the house when the aroma of bacon wafted through the air. She and Matty were a lot alike in their dedication to all things bacon. Sam sold the best smoked pork belly in Oklahoma. Knowing a butcher wasn't exactly a bad thing!

Bursting through the back door, she called out while ditching her hat, scarf, coat and boots in record time. "Is that bacon I smell? You realize of course I will arm wrestle with you over every piece."

She stepped around the corner into the kitchen and stopped dead. Had he become even more head-to-toe yummy in his sleep? My word! Nobody should look that hot or be so distracting this early in the morning.

Following her nose, she sniffed her way next to him at the stove and stood on her toes to try and get a look over his shoulder. "Why, Mr. Bishop. You know your way around a cast iron skillet!"

He snickered and smiled down at her. "The trick is to get the pan screaming hot before adding the bacon. This fancy man has done his share of camp cooking, and I'm not talking about leisurely recreation in a national park."

"Semper Fi?"

"Yup."

Did you kill anybody when you were in the war?"

His jaw clenched so tight she was sure his teeth would crack from the pressure. She pressed a kiss to his shoulder and moved away to let him finish.

"I'm going to wash up. Be right back."

Dashing into the bathroom, she questioned why she felt so perfectly at ease with him. And why she was secretly bummed the storm ended, and the sun came out. She'd have liked another day of it being just the two of them before that other life she could feel pressing urgently against the boundaries of her simple existence came crashing down.

Roman watched her cute, curvy backside march away and sighed. Everything about this was so damn weird. They interacted like an old married couple, banged like porn stars, and verbally sparred better than a point-counterpoint TV show.

Relieved that the things they'd done and said in her old brass bed hadn't destroyed the unusual bond forming, he'd mentally fist pumped his joy when her lips touched his shoulder.

Kelly James was one tough, fierce female. But that didn't mean she was hard. This harsh, unrelentingly difficult life she was placed in by her mother hadn't damaged her heart or her ability to be deeply empathetic. And wise.

He thought of them curled together in the narrow bed as sleep claimed her, and how she burrowed into him murmuring, "Hold me tighter." It had been his pleasure to pull her tight. She'd curled closer like a small child and tucked a hand beneath her chin. It felt so right that some part deep inside him wept tears of happiness.

And then, as dawn broke and he reached for her only to find the bed space beside him empty, his desire to introduce his young love to the sweet relief of morning sex crashed and burned in the face of this life she led.

It amazed him that she showed no frustration or displeasure with the hard realities she so adroitly managed. That amazement tripled because she wasn't bitter. Or full of crazy anger. From where he was sitting, this balls-to-the-wall twenty-three-year-old had more sense and drive than a good many of her peers.

"What were you doing out there?" he asked when she came back. "And why didn't you wake me up?"

"Wake you up?" she said with a half-startled expression. "Whatever for?"

Jesus. She was gonna kill him with this 'I can do anything' shtick. Forking the crispy bacon from the skillet, he dropped the hot strips onto a plate and pushed the hot pan from the burner before facing her.

There were probably a dozen responses vying for air time as he turned, but all of them vanished when they were face-to-face. Sliding an arm around her waist, he pulled Kelly forward and kissed her firmly on the mouth. "Good morning."

Her lovely smile had a lighthearted quality. She melted into him and twined her arms around his neck. "Good morning to you too."

Palming her ass, he relaxed his hips against the counter and kept her plastered to his front. "I could have helped," was all he said. She looked at him quizzically. Didn't she get it?

"But I didn't need any help, Roman." Her shrug was short and to the point.

"But I could have helped," he said again.

"But…I didn't need any help." Her face was a mask of confusion. "Is this a macho thing? Because that's what I'm hearing."

He started to answer, but she kept speaking.

"Does it bother you that I have things under control? By myself?"

Attempting to defend his position he growled, "You shouldn't have to do all this by yourself."

"But I did, and I do, and to be frank with you, I don't know any other way."

She sounded like Liam and the way he described growing up with his mom. She was so damaged by Adam Ward's malevolence that he'd truly been the man of the house while still riding a bicycle. He was starting to see more than just eyes as a similarity in the siblings.

Her stomach growled.

One quick but extremely thorough kiss later he had her at the table, digging into a pile of bacon and a plate of perfectly fluffy eggs while they enjoyed a leisurely breakfast and discussed the world.

"May I ask a few questions?"

Her eyebrow arched. Dropping a strip of bacon on her plate, she wiped her hands on a purple fabric napkin and gave him all of her attention. "Sure."

"Why don't you talk like everyone else around here? It's not my imagination that you show zero southern or country twang. What am I missing?"

"Wow. You went straight to it, didn't you?"

He wasn't even going to pretend he wasn't pleased with her

reaction. That's when it struck him that not many people got this close to her.

"The simplest answer is the truth. Outside of my mother, I wasn't exposed to other people very much. She home schooled me. Sam and Ginny are from the east and don't talk Okie either. So I guess you could say that you hear my mother's background."

Roman nodded and considered the new information. Deb James was the key to so much, and he needed to understand what the fuck had been going on here all these years.

"How did your mother afford all this? I know it's not much, and you pretty much exist off-grid, but there are still expenses."

Her half-smirk was not in any way warm or friendly. "I believe the expression you're searching for is sugar daddy."

His eyes narrowed, and a dangerous surge of anger toward Adam Ward fired off inside. "Are you serious?"

Kelly shrugged again and crossed her legs. The hair flip was intended to be nonchalant as if to suggest she didn't care but he saw through the act. Roman wanted to lash out at everyone who in even the most insignificant of ways had fucked with her life.

"I don't know anything for sure except this. Along with the house and land, part of Deb's inheritance included an escrow account with funds to cover the land taxes for about twenty years. Lucky her, huh?"

The gritty animosity came through loud and clear.

"She insisted there were savings too and that's what paid the meager bills. After she died, those so-called savings took on another form."

Emitting a pained and heavy sigh, she rose and went into the pantry, coming back a minute later carrying two old tin cans from another era. One said Beechnut coffee and the other slightly larger can read Charles Chips. She placed them on the table in between them and sat down.

"Go ahead. Look."

He watched her face in between reaching for a can, prying the lid off and looking inside. Pulling out several plastic storage bags he had a second of complete astonishment at what he found.

"When I found it in an old bag in her closet there was a little over twenty-five thousand dollars. Spent some," she ground out. "There's roughly nineteen thousand four hundred and sixteen dollars left."

Ah. Now he understood so many things. Like having a satellite dish and a flat screen but no microwave.

"And you think this money is from your uh…"

"Father? Pfft, please! I'm not sure he would even qualify as a sperm donor."

"We'll get to him, Carina," he drawled smoothly. "But let's stick to the cash for a minute."

"Well, I'm afraid if you want additional information, you'll have to wait for Ginny. Doesn't take a rocket scientist to figure out she knows way more than I ever imagined."

Hmmm. He considered her wording and manner. Not a deflection. She knew nothing. And despite her clear affection for the older woman, Kelly wasn't pleased about it.

Touchy subject. He got it. Moving on…

"You mentioned home-schooling," he said with a deft subject change. "Is that why you don't show up in official records?"

Her answer was a starchy sniff, hastily crossed arms, some evil eye, and a shaking foot. "Are you legally allowed to stick your nose into anyone's business?"

The smirky grin spread across his face with supersonic speed. "Wanna see my badge?"

She ejected out of her seat with an awkward jerk and stood up with an expression of alarm on her face. "Are you with the government?"

"Easy sweetness," he calmly murmured. Gesturing, he asked her to sit down. "I'm sorry. Let me explain."

"I don't need any trouble, Roman," she spat in a very unambiguous way.

Oh god. His clumsy attempt to be charming and funny did not

get the laugh he expected.

"Cards on the table?" he asked.

"I'm a pool shark. Not a card player. Hard to learn when it's just you."

He reached across the table, took one of her hands and brought it to his mouth for a gentle kiss. He didn't relinquish control though and kept a firm grip.

"Yes, I am licensed to carry. I'm also what the feds will tell you is a highly trained interrogation specialist courtesy of the military. For the past many years I've been doing private security. Security that sometimes includes surveillance."

"And protection?"

"Yes."

"You're my…you're that guy's bodyguard?"

He noticed she went out of her way not to say Liam's name, a quirk he found troubling.

"I prefer Head of Security. And these days it's more like a friend who also takes care of shit."

Her hand got pulled back, he searched her face for why and knew immediately he'd unintentionally put his entire size thirteen foot into his mouth.

"Did you just refer to me as shit?"

"Please don't overreact."

"How 'bout you watch your mouth?"

Heat like what you'd expect if you got too close to a sun flare burst around them. Her fire tempted him in ways that would shock her innocent sensibilities if she knew.

"You get one," he told her. "And that was it. The next time you get bitchy with me the view of the floor will be all you see."

He expected a comeback, but instead she colored like a summer rose coming to bloom. And then his dick started doing the rhumba in his jeans. Her embarrassed, guilty-pleasure silence almost ended with her naked from the waist down and impaled on his cock.

"I was poking around in your father's house of lies when a

surprising tidbit of information came to light. That tidbit led me to you. Liam was dumbfounded. Frankly, so was I. But we couldn't move the information ball downfield at all. Your mother did an excellent job of slamming that door shut." He paused and considered how to say what he knew she had the right to know.

"Kelly Anne James is not your birth name."

All the color leeched from her face. He gulped and prayed she didn't faceplant on the table if she fainted.

"Looking for you was like trying to find the needle in a haystack. Once Debbie brought you here, the leads ran cold. No school records. Social security. Bank accounts. Nothing. How is that, Kelly? What am I missing? Besides Matty."

Chapter Eleven

The muffled buzzing in her head had a strangely cold quality that gave her a shiver.

Not her name. Of course not. Why would it be?

An angry blast of hurt engulfed her soul. Her mother was an even more fucked up unit than she ever imagined. Same for Kelly's biological other who manipulated and destroyed everything—with Deb's complicit consent. The two of them. *Ugh.*

She reached up and threaded shaking fingers through her hair, pushing the whole mess away from her face. He was only asking for the whole story, and she wanted to let it all out. God knows she did. But with every minute she was reminded of how little she knew.

The name thing for instance. An old memory, a conversation with Debbie sprang to life in her head. It was the year she turned sixteen, and all she wanted, all she cared about, was getting a driver's license. Such a simple thing in her young mind but holy crap Deb reacted like a driver's license was a threat to mankind. She'd worn her down and eventually got permission to go through the fuss and bother.

Needing a certificate of some kind to prove who she was, Kelly had been astonished when her mother produced an Oklahoma I.D.

and social security card. Only the name was Kay James. Her explanation at the time was that somehow her initials, K and A, morphed into Kay and became the name on record. As far as the state was concerned, she was Kay James which also explained why she called her brand K.A. James. If Roman or anyone was searching for her as Kelly, they were gonna come up empty.

Everything was such a mess and starting to feel like a boulder picking up speed and damage potential as it hurtled downhill. For the very first time in her life that she could recall, Kelly felt a worrisome tingling in her nose as hot tears gathered in her eyes.

Was this her breaking point? Shit. A week ago she knew who she was, what she faced, and had a plan for the future all mapped out. Now she had a supposed older brother, an unexpected lover, her name wasn't hers, and the unsettling feeling she had never been or would never be anything except a pawn in someone else's game.

"Come here," Roman growled. She was being lifted out of her chair before she knew what was happening. He carried her to the sofa and sat down with her on his lap. "Better?"

Feeling like a kid without their security blanket, she was grateful for his presence and strength. He rubbed her back and shifted until they were both comfortable.

"I know this is hard, Carina."

When he called her by the sweet endearment, she snuggled onto his broad chest and lay her head on a comforting shoulder.

"If you need a trail to follow, try Kay James. Date of birth May 11th."

"But you were born on the twelfth."

That was it. That was the last straw. Unless she was also a virgin birth or had been left in a space capsule by aliens, what the fuck else could possibly be left to scramble her brain even more? The struggle became too much, and a river of hot tears spilled from her eyes.

"Oh my god," she sobbed. "Anything else? How old am I?"

"Shhh. Take a deep breath. You're twenty-three. It's going to be okay, Kelly. I know what your mother was doing, honey. She stayed close to the facts but added a few detours and dead ends. She was hiding you. But that's all done with now. I'm here, and I swear on all that's holy that I'll protect you."

She pushed off his chest and rubbed a hand under her nose. Tears and snot were making a mess on her face. "Why?" she wailed as misery swamped her emotions. "Why all the drama? Roman," she cried. "You don't know what else she did. My birthday, oh my god. How could she?"

He used the end of his sleeve to dry her tears. "What about your birthday?"

It took her a good minute or two to find the composure to respond. "I never spent birthdays with her. She'd take off and be gone for days. Every damn year. It was him," she griped. "Like clockwork—every six months and always, always for my birthday."

"Son of a bitch."

"I think that's where the money came from. Cash. Do you think he used her like a prostitute and then left a wad of bills on the dresser?" It was horrifying to hear her secret shame spoken out loud.

"I'm going to fucking kill that piece of shit," Roman roared.

The soft, warm comfort his body gave transformed to something hard and unyielding.

"Oh my god," she groaned. "He's still alive? I thought he was dead and that's why you're here."

"Liam, your brother," he added for emphasis, "he says the old bastard is half a step from the grave. Him knocking on death's door at the same time that we found you is a coincidence. And so you understand where your brother is coming from, you are his priority, honey. Not that cow turd who fathered you."

"Can we stop talking about him? Please."

"Your father?'

"No. The other. My, uh brother." Choking the word out was all kinds of hard.

"Kelly," he began with a frown and an equally grave sounding tone.

She didn't want to hear it.

"No," she interrupted. "Please Roman. I can only take on so much." Her whole body started to vibrate with anxiety. "I need Matty," she blurted out.

"Okay, easy, love. We've talked enough for now."

He hugged her close and said a bunch of soothing stuff while gently stroking her back. It reminded her of being in his arms last night. She'd never slept better. He'd made her feel safe, something she hadn't known was missing.

"And don't worry about Matty. They're on their way. Sam called while you were outside. He said it'd take a while because he was pretty sure he'd be plowing the whole way."

She sat up at this news and gave him a wobbly smile. He glanced at his watch. "Maybe half an hour?"

"You talked to Sam?" she asked. "How'd that go?"

Roman shook his head at her like she was all kinds of naughty and smirked. "You could have saved some time by telling me Sam and Ginny are like grandparents. Walked face first into him threatening the snot out of me if I harmed a hair on your head."

Kelly ran her fingers along several very visible claw marks on his neck. "Looks to me like you were the one who got harmed."

"Says the wanton virgin who is showing some impressive maul marks of her own."

Slapping her hand on her neck with a wink and a giggle, all the upset of earlier vanished when she turned flirty and suggestively announced, "Oh those? *Pfft.* That's nothing. You should see the dirty pictures your teeth left in hickeys on my boobs."

He teased her by trying to peek through the space between the buttons on her flannel shirt. She playfully slapped him away and laughed.

He acted put out by her refusal. "Aw, come on! No show and tell? You're no fun."

"I'd show you plenty of fun fancy man if not for the fact Sam is plowing his way here. Don't think he'd react well to a replay of our greatest hits."

"Oh. Didn't you get the memo?" he asked. His leering smirk melted her bones. "No nookie for you today little miss."

"What?" she shrieked. "Why? Did I do it wrong?"

"Ah, Carina," he answered in a husky, seductive growl. "You did everything right. And there is so much more I plan to teach you, but this?" he said as his hand slid between her thighs and gently caressed her denim covered mound. "My lady needs a rest. Recovery time, to put it another way. We weren't exactly uh, restrained."

Oh. He was right. She was a little tender down there, but nothing short of a gaping wound or stitches were enough to dampen her desire.

"Don't look so disappointed," Roman snickered. "My cock isn't going anywhere."

Well, thank god. Which reminded her. If he was gonna take intercourse off the menu maybe she could ask for a different kind of lesson. He hadn't allowed much more than some tentative touching last night, and she was eager to explore him in other ways. Other tasty ways.

She didn't want this interlude to end, but it was clear that time wasn't going to be her friend, so she asked one last question and did it fearfully because she wasn't so sure the answer was anything she wanted to hear.

"So…what happens now? What happens after you meet Matty and talk to Sam and Ginny? I'm asking nicely, and you'll never know how hard that is, so please do not Chinese water torture me. Drip, drip, drip will not end well. For you and everyone else."

It took a long time for him to voice an answer. The thoughtfulness was reassuring. He wasn't going to blow her off with a calculated reply. Gosh. She liked him more and more every minute.

"Is it up to me? What happens? Because my answer, in that case, has very little to do with the backstory and everything to do with what we discussed last night. We took it to an eleven, and you know it. That much unprotected sex can lead to consequences."

Kelly examined her conscience. Yeah, they'd been incredibly cavalier about the details. In her case, she was driven by passions and desires that shed practical concerns like a dog shaking off water.

Would she behave the same way and make the same decisions now that the light of a new day calmed the tenacious urges of her previously dormant sex drive? Oh god, yes. And if that made her a bit too uncomfortably like her mother, well…so be it. Whatever the future held she couldn't say she wasn't aware of the fire she played with.

Plucking absently at the buttons on the black, Henley shirt it would be fun to tear off, she attempted one of those flirty pouts all the celebrities and models did. Though it wasn't natural, she didn't miss Roman's immediate response. She felt it on her bottom. The bottom resting on his lap.

Seriously? Her inner voice erupted with laughter. Oh lord, this was priceless. So guys really did lose their shit over some female nonsense? Well, well. Perhaps this was something she should check out.

Was it all kinds of crazy and wrong that she suddenly had no problem wielding this newly discovered talent? Mmm, eh…no. She wasn't a total moron, though. Some flirty pouts and calculated sexiness weren't going to shift the balance of power. He was the m-a-n and hell yeah she was fine with that.

"Not all of that unprotected sex was a problem," she purred.

He fell for it. Of course he did. No way could she remind him of some of the highlights from last night without getting a swift reaction. If they couldn't lose their pants and take a quick walk on the wild side, then she at least wanted some wicked sparring.

He grabbed a fistful of hair and firmly pulled her head back. She liked the zing of excitement she felt each time he played the caveman. Eyes reflecting filthy scenarios that made her tummy quiver stared into hers.

"I saw how much you liked that, Carina." His lusty growl turned her blood to liquid fire. "But you'll have to enlighten me a bit. Was it having my come dripping from your beautiful tits that turned you on, or watching me handle my cock?"

Not answering wasn't even an option. It was exhilarating to feel so free and open with Roman. He was asking so she tried her best to share what she felt.

"Honestly? It was all hot. Watching. Yes. I liked that very much. And the moment when you came?" She shuddered involuntarily from memory. "Seeing what until then I'd only felt while you were inside me? Roman, you have no idea what that does to me, but the best part?"

She paused and searched his face. A slight flush highlighted his cheekbones. He was getting as fired up as she was on this topic, but there was one more thing to add.

"When you pulled out of me and wrapped your hand around it?" His knowing leer made her inwardly sigh. "I was amazed how much wet clung to your cock. That was incredibly hot. And sexy."

"That was all you, love."

"No," she quickly corrected with another smaller pout. "That was what you do to me, fancy man."

Roman chuckled and kissed the end of her nose. "Don't frown. It's a compliment, and I like how wet you get. I like it very much."

Her eyes drifted across the clock on the wall. They really needed to move on to other things or else face the potential embarrassment of being caught in the act.

He was a wicked, wicked man, though—not that she minded in the least—and damn him if he didn't push the envelope.

He let go of her hair and wrapped a hand around the back of her neck. Then he pulled her closer as he met her halfway and began nuzzling her neck. His lips, teeth, and tongue did outrageous things to a few inches of skin and reduced her to a drooling wanton in no time.

Hot breath singed her ear. "Are you wet right now, Carina?"

Through the thickening fog of skin prickling lust he drew from her, she thought about the question for a second and almost laughed. He was kidding, right? She'd been a gooey mess from the first moment her fingers touched his chest. It was a wonder she hadn't completely dehydrated by now.

Did he want an answer? Fine. Let's see where this got her. "Why don't you find out for yourself?"

If she shocked him he didn't show it, but Kelly was pretty certain she surprised him with virtually every word she uttered and every reaction she had. What happened next made her question her sanity.

"Stand up."

Huh? She had no time to react as Roman pushed her off his lap. She barely saved herself from tumbling to the floor and awkwardly struggled to her feet. What the hell?

He sat back on the sofa and got comfortable. The way he moved reminded her of a man who was used to commanding everything in his orbit.

"Now take your jeans off. And do it quickly unless you want to enter the danger zone and drag things out."

Her eyes darted to the front door. The latch was on. Good. But the back door was unlocked. The only saving grace at the moment was knowing they'd hear Sam's truck and the snow plow long before anyone reached either door. Her jeans came off with astonishing speed.

"Leave the panties on. Now come here," he demanded with a crooking finger. Performing a bit of a man spread, his legs slid further apart, and he patted his thigh. "Plant your ass, honey. Straddle me until your knees are on the sofa and spread really wide."

Smacking her hands together with lusty glee, she barked, "Yes!" and did as he instructed. He did nothing to aid her, mostly he just sat there and grinned. When she was settled, and sure she wasn't gonna fall off or end on the floor, she took his hands and put them on her flannel covered boobs. "You were saying?"

She yelped when he tugged quite hard on her nipples right through the shirt. "Sorry babe. No time for play. This is straight pussy action." He pulled up a hand and consulted his watch. "Countdown clock, check." He pushed a button or something and a timer appeared. "Proceed to orgasm."

She was giggling when he grabbed her face and forcefully took her lips in a passionate kiss that left nothing on the table. She was whimpering when he finished.

"Hands on my shoulders and eyes on me."

Swaying from the effects of the ferocious desire he awakened, she did as he asked and almost lost it completely when he wasted no time, running the flat of his hand down her belly, under the elastic of her panties, and went straight to her opening.

"Sweet baby Jesus," he groaned when his fingers found out exactly how wet she was.

She winced just once when his knowing fingers explored the anatomy of her swollen pussy.

"Is this okay?" he asked gently.

"Yes, oh yes." She locked eyes with his and wiggled as the desperate needs he unleashed broke free.

There was something naughty and yet deeply erotic about him reaching into her panties. She understood why he asked her to leave them on.

One thick finger slid into her passage. She gasped, froze, and then undulated on his lap. The finger withdrew. She moaned her need. Two fingers were next, and this time he didn't withdraw. No, this time he pumped her with shallow thrusts, hitting her vulnerable clit with each insertion.

She was losing it in record time and gripped his shoulders with desperate hands. The flood of wet he drew from her body made them both grunt.

"By the way," she heard him growl.

Huh? What? The way he built her excitement pushed her perilously close to the edge in record time.

"This?" he said with a deep thrust for emphasis. Kelly shuddered from head to toe. "This belongs to me."

Was that somehow in doubt? She couldn't think. Ruthlessly calling an orgasm from her body, she was teetering on the edge, bucking her hips into his touch and wondering if this was what falling off the edge of the world felt like.

"Come on, Carina," Roman growled. His expression was possessive, fierce and very pleased. "Show me what ya' got, baby."

She did. Practically on command. With a wild cry, her hips started jerking uncontrollably. His knowing eyes bored into hers as ecstasy ricocheted through her body.

She fell into the seductive, possessive lure of his gaze.

He grunted. "That's it, luv. Come on my fingers. Don't hold back."

So she didn't. It was wild and raunchy, and she wanted to do it again and again and again and…

Shit. The sound of Sam's monster truck interrupted her ravished euphoria. He lifted her off his lap with two fingers still buried in her pussy. Before withdrawing, her fancy man with the knowing leer used his thumb to circle her still throbbing clit. Her fingers dug into his shoulders, and she shook her head, no.

"Mine. If I want you to come again, right now, you will. Don't forget it."

She was trembling like crazy when he finally withdrew. The climax was one thing. The realization that he spoke the truth shook her up a whole lot more.

The possessive way he patted her through the dampened panties sealed her fate. She was his. All this other shit? Background noise.

Kelly slid from his lap and hurriedly grabbed her jeans, wiggling into them with clumsy speed.

"Let me help you."

He tugged the pants into place and zipped them up. With a fast flick, he had the button done too.

She was frantically pushing her hair into some semblance of order when he grabbed her chin and stared her down.

"What do you say when your man gets you off?"

Right then and there she didn't care who walked through the door. With all the insolence she could gather, and with a dollop of in-your-face, she wrinkled her nose and sweetly replied, "Thank you. May I have another?"

Roman's happy laugh made her smile. He kissed her quickly and gave her a once over. "You look fine. Before we get invaded, what are you going to tell Matty? About me."

Her answer was immediate, firm and in no way wishy-washy. "I'll never lie to Matty. Or keep secrets. There's been enough of that already."

"So, that means what, exactly?"

Hmph. Good question. What did she mean?

"Nobody's going to be fooled," he murmured quietly. "Not the adults, anyway."

He was right. Being fully dressed didn't hide the freshly-mauled look they were both giving off. She wasn't an expert on these things by any means, but she knew enough to realize the cat was clawing its way out of the bag.

"And besides, we're getting married," he insisted somewhat belligerently. "Maybe that's the place to start."

She wasn't about to get into a debate with him about the ridiculous notions he had swirling in his head, so she shrugged.

"Jesus Roman. Even Monopoly starts with a first move. He's a boy, not an adult with knowledge and understanding of grown up things. Matty doesn't warm up to people easily. Let me handle him, and you just follow my lead."

Chapter Twelve

Washing Kelly's delicious scent from his hands at the kitchen sink with a sweet smelling strawberry soap, Roman kept one eye on her as she raced around for lord knows what reason. The house was such a cluttered mess, how could she even tell if something was out of place?

A roar of activity outside let them know Sam was having a helluva' time clearing the snow from the driveway. He was grateful for the short respite. Gave him time to get his thundering libido under control. Bringing his sexy little lover to a spellbinding climax with nothing more than his hand in her panties affected him in surprising ways. Controlling his passions was second nature, something he had a damn difficult time doing around her.

Through the kitchen window he saw the truck and plow finally shut down in the parking spot Sam cleared. The passenger door flew open and a small boy scrambled over the woman seated there. He dropped onto the white covered ground and started running for the back door.

His heart started to pound the closer the lad got. A black knit hat tucked into the neck of his winter coat covered his head leaving only a face peeking out. Right away he noted that the kid moved with the same exuberance he saw in Liam.

And then his face came into focus. Holy fucking shit. Matthew Liam James was the spitting image of Kelly only with Liam's coloring, which meant he basically looked like a junior doppelgänger of his older half-brother.

He barely had his surprise back under wraps when the boy bounded up the back stairs hollering, "Kik! I'm home."

Kelly raced across the living room and dashed toward the mudroom with a broad smile on her face.

"Mateo!" she crowed loudly as the back door banged shut. "Cómo estás?"

"Muy bien," a little voice answered.

That sound? It was Roman's jaw hitting the floor. She was teaching the boy languages. He also noticed that just like his sister, Matty had a flawless east coast accent.

Nervousness and worry started bumping uglies inside him. Had he ever before cared what a kid thought of him? Probably not. But this? He was clever enough to realize that only his whole future hung on what happened next—when Kelly introduced them.

He gulped like a cartoon character, quickly tucked in his shirt properly and smoothed his hair. Good god, he thought. You'd think I was meeting the Pope or something. The conversation coming from the mudroom kept him riveted.

"'N Gigi said I could have two cookies because I drank all my milk, Kik!"

"No boots in the house, young man."

Muffled sounds of a jacket being hung and boots taken off made their way into the house. When Kelly spoke again, Roman had to steel himself for what was about to happen.

"Please god, don't let me fuck this up."

"Sam let me steer," Matty proudly announced as they started down the hallway. The second they came into the kitchen and the kid saw him, Roman blanched when Matty's knee jerk reaction was to shield his sister with his little body.

Kelly put her hand on the boy's shoulder and squeezed. She met Roman's eyes but he wasn't able to read her expression.

"It's okay Matty. This is a friend of mine. He has a very cool name. Wanna hear it?"

Roman stopped breathing. Matty's fiercely protective gaze checked him out from head to toe. For a brief moment their eyes met. It was disconcerting to find Liam Junior staring at him.

Finally, after an eternity of waiting, the boy nodded yes and looked up at his sister.

Kelly's gentle smile was filled with love for the boy. Roman wished she'd look at him the same way.

"Get this," she chuckled playfully. "He calls himself Roman Bishop! Awesome, huh?"

Steely grey blue eyes narrowed and then widened as a small smile crept onto the boy's face. Without the hat, Roman saw Matty's hair was the same dirty blonde as Liam's. In many ways the kid was a miniature version of his much older half-brother.

"Roman," she continued. His eyes swung to hers. "This handsome young man is Matthew James."

Uh, fuck. What was he supposed to do? The weirdest thought from out-of-the-blue hit him full on. What Would Major Marquez Do? Odd time to think about his good friend and former commanding officer, but that's where his mind went. He supposed the reason was simple. Alex Marquez was, simply put, the best man he'd ever known besides his own parent and grandfathers. Surely his mentor would know exactly what this situation called for.

Channeling the other man's impeccable manners, he took a knee so he'd be on the boy's level. Alex would call this a gesture of respect. Roman wanted the kid to know he understood Matty's place in Kelly's life. Holding his hand out for some tribal mano-e-mano, he smiled and gave the boy his due.

"I'm pleased to meet you, Matthew James. May I call you Matty?"

The ball is in your court, kid. He waited, his hand hanging in mid-air. Finally, after a long, tense silence, he slotted his tiny hand into Roman's bigger one and confidently declared, "I'm the man of the house."

At that moment a bunch of things happened. Roman watched as Kelly's mouth gaped open and she stared at the boy as if she'd never seen him before. Simultaneously, an older woman appeared in their midst. She too had the same dumbfounded, mouth open expression Kelly had.

The woman spoke quietly to Kelly. "He's talking, Kiki."

Kelly whispered, "I know."

Matty, on the other hand, ignored them both and kept focused on Roman.

"Are you here to take our land?"

Jesus Christ! What? He looked at Kelly for help.

She was already on it. "No, Matty. Oh my god. Honey, no. He's not after the house. I told you. Roman is my friend."

Roman got comfortable on his knees and tried to hide his confusion over the ladies' reaction and wrap his mind around the cross examination card this really young kid was hell bent on playing.

"Are you from the big city?"

This was one of those times when the observation skills he relied on as an interrogator came in super handy. Assured by his sister that Roman wasn't a threat, his segue question revealed a lot.

Once again, he saw glimpses of Liam's quirky curiosity in the boy's manner. If the kid was interested in life beyond a patch of woods, maybe he could use that as an advantage because he was beginning to suspect Kelly was going to dig in her heels and refuse the life waiting for her.

"Why, yes I am, Matthew." He hadn't been given permission to call him by his nickname so he didn't. "I'm from the best city. New York. Ever heard of it?"

"Maybe."

Roman silently applauded the kid's chutzpah. Good for him. Not being a pushover was a worthy trait.

"Are there dinosaurs in New York?"

Kelly let out a small groan. The old lady chuckled. Roman remembered the dinosaur books and toys in the living and smiled. He had him.

"Indeed there are." Matty gasped, and his eyes lit up, going from cloudy and gray to brilliant blue. "At a wonderful pace called the American Museum of Natural History. Have you ever been to a museum?"

No prevarication this time, just a long, grumpy, "Nooo."

Above Matty's head, Kelly sighed and rolled her eyes. The other woman reached out, patted her shoulder and smirked.

"Well, maybe Kelly will take you someday."

Matty stared at him so hard Roman was sure the kid could read his thoughts and probably, without much effort, see into his very soul. He was going to need to stay on his toes around this one.

Roman felt the seismic shift that made Kelly waver where she stood when Matty left his protective blocking position and took two steps toward him. He cocked his head to the left to regard the captivating little man in front of him as Matty tilted his head in the opposite direction. The synchronous movements moved him in an unfamiliar way.

In a kid whisper that was profoundly louder than was necessary, Matty informed him, "I call her Kiki. Kik for short. Know why?"

Roman shook his head. "Nope. Tell me."

"Cuz she's short," the kid whooped with enthusiastic glee. Looking back at his sister for agreement he said, "Right, Kik?"

"Matthew James," Kelly sniffed. "Not nice."

The older woman laughed along with Matty and came toward him with her hand out, "I'm Ginny in case you haven't put that together yet."

He gave her a polite nod, stood up and shook her hand. When they were eyeball to eyeball she subjected him to an impressive ocular pat down. Her eyes narrowed and she turned sharply to Kelly. "Kik, take Matty and go help Sam clear snow off Bandit. There's something

I want to discuss with Mr. Bishop."

"Uh…" That was all Kelly squeaked out before being summarily dismissed.

"Go on now. Do as you're told." Ginny gestured for them to clear out.

He was quite astonished when the woman who pushed back against every fucking word he uttered meekly acceded to the woman's demand. She reacted the way he used to when his grandmother would use that certain tone. The one that suggested all manner of punishment for refusing.

When the room emptied, Roman's confidence evaporated under the woman's wilting glare. *Some badass I am*, he thought.

Ginny stalked him into an actual corner and boxed him in. He'd survived blistering attacks and stealthy ambushes but surviving her onslaught was another thing altogether. Jesus, this lady was good.

"Mr. Bishop," she began in a voice reminiscent of his seventh grade math teacher. The one with the stick up her butt who made his twelve-year-old life bloody hell. "I know we have things to talk about. Important things, but I'm a little distracted at the moment."

She made a bunch of body gestures and hand moves suggesting she was a befuddled old lady. Yeah, right.

While he was distracted by her performance she was loading a mega-ton explosive device into her verbal arsenal. When she aimed and fired, he suffered a direct hit.

"I'm sorry, but I have to ask. Are you okay?"

Man, there was so much in that snarkily asked question that he didn't know where to start. He knew she was centering him in her viewfinder and threw up his hands in defeat. She read the bring-it-on body language and let him have it.

"I have a first-aid kit in the car," she silkily challenged. "I think those scratches on your neck could use some attention. Meet up with a wild animal?"

Boom! Just like that she had his balls firmly in hand. He tried to stare her down but gave in astonishingly fast. With a grumpy frown he thought the government would be better off recruiting baby booming grannies with attitude to get information rather than training a bunch of dudes because, seriously.

Blurting out the first stupid thing that came to his mind he went with, "Ran into some thorns out in the woods."

The arched brow, crossed arms and unforgiving smirk were like an ice water bath.

"Hunting snipe, were you?"

Roman mentally thanked his lucky stars. He knew this obscure reference. His cousin went to college in Philadelphia and one of the fraternity initiations included a fool's errand hunt for the imaginary animal. She was taunting him. He liked her a shit ton more for being such a hard ass. Kelly and Matty were damn lucky to have her as a guardian angel.

With a slight to-the-victor-go-the-spoils head nod, he met her expression and offered a weak smile that he hoped to god she understood.

"Uh, no to the snipe hunting. Out of season and it's not a moonless sky," he chortled. "More like being blinded by a shooting star and tumbling head first into who the hell knows what."

That was the best he could do. It was up to her whether she believed him.

He felt the protective shield surrounding his young lover. Fascinating.

With an edge of caution that captured his attention, she dropped an unprompted nugget of information.

"Matty doesn't talk to strangers. Ever. Only to me and Sam."

That explained Ginny and Kelly's reaction when the boy talked to him.

"He's very protective of her, isn't he?"

She nodded solemnly and he felt the pressure release. No longer seeing him as a threat, she motioned him to the kitchen table and sat down.

Instead of joining her he cleared the table of their abandoned meal. "Sorry. I should have finished what I started," he explained.

"You made breakfast?" she asked on a chuckle ringing with delight. He didn't have to say anything. The question was rhetorical.

Following what he'd seen Kelly do, he carefully put the food scraps in a small covered pail, rinsed the dishes for later washing, and gathered the trash into a sorting bin against the wall. Ginny watched him the whole time.

Once he sat down she wasted no time. "What do you know?"

"Well, I know a lot less than I thought. Beyond the barest of basics, we read this whole situation with a magnifying glass that missed a lot."

She guffawed and slapped her hand on the table. Her amused cackle was infectious, and he smiled even though he didn't know why.

"Is that what you do for a living? Answer questions with a whole lotta nothing wrapped up in some pretty words? I like you Roman Bishop."

Seriously, he wasn't even joking. She made him want to spill his guts about anything she wanted to know. Next time he talked to any of his government or military buddies he was definitely gonna bring up using a bunch of tough old broads for information gathering. But over a bottle of Johnnie Walker, because they would think him daft otherwise.

"I can see this information exchange is a one-way street until you're sure I'm not a threat."

Without missing a beat she nailed him with a pointed look and pithily replied, "It's not necessarily you I'm worried about, although those claw marks suggest something that is more than a little concerning."

His only thought was, damn, she'd have a fucking heart attack if she knew what went on five minutes before she walked in the door.

"Okay." He put his hands on top of the table palms up. "This is everything." He cleared his throat and gave her as much as he knew.

"You know who I am and you know who I work for, but what

you don't know is that when all is said and done, Liam Ashforth is my friend and a good, decent man. Please believe me, Ginny. I didn't come down here to start shit."

"So how did you come to be looking for Kelly in the first place?"

"Honestly? It happened by accident. I was poking around. That poking led me to a lawyer with um, compromising issues he was eager to keep quiet. Hung Adam Ward out to dry in a heartbeat."

"That's his name, then? Adam Ward?"

He nodded gravely and continued. "Did you know that Liam made destroying the man his life's work?"

Ginny sighed heavily. "What I know is Deb's story, only without names. The only reason I know about Liam is because she told me after the boy was born. It was like she knew one day Kelly would need to hear an explanation and by giving Matty the middle name of Liam, all would be made clear. He didn't know," she added. "About the boy. Deb wasn't a twenty-something piece of ass anymore. He made her beg before each rendezvous. It was sickening. She was in her forties, and he had long ago lost interest."

What a piece of work Deb James must have been.

"I knew you'd come one day. Maybe not you precisely but Liam. Once Deb told me about his mother and how the man she was so hopelessly in love with had used and abandoned someone else from their secretarial pool, I knew it was only a matter of time."

"If you know about Liam's mother I'll spare the details except to say she's gone. Died many years ago. Her death triggered Liam's drive to make the man who hurt her pay. And he did. Big time. Took everything, and when the man was at his lowest, only then did he reveal that the bastard son he'd denied had been systematically and doggedly picking apart his business interests and destroying them one by one."

"Whoa. For real?"

"Yeah," he confirmed with a curt nod. "He basically left him with enough to force the man's total humiliation by reducing him to a standard of living that makes this a palace. And then he went for broke and let the guy's wife know what he'd been up to. They divorced. She took whatever was left and…mission accomplished."

"Son of a bitch. I'm glad he rubbed his nose in it."

"Me too," Roman agreed. "The compromised lawyer agreed as well. When he let slip that Liam wasn't the only one, and that there appeared to be another, shit got real. One of my contacts is a guy who I swear to god finds Waldo every time. I asked him to investigate and see what shook loose."

"Are there any others?"

He knew what she was referring to. "Not as far as we know, but we didn't have a clue about Matty. Liam still doesn't know."

They both drifted away, lost in thought for a few moments. It was a lot to take on no matter which side of the story you came from.

"So," he continued. "We were looking for Grace Jenkins."

Ginny's eyebrow shot up again.

"Kept hitting a wall and found nothing but zero. My buddy was able to connect the dots through Deb's convoluted family history. That's how we found Kelly Anne James tucked away in the woods of Oklahoma. With nothing but a name and the land records as a guide, here I am."

"I'm curious," she murmured. "What did you and Liam hope to achieve?"

"At the time there wasn't a game plan beyond finding her and figuring out what she knew about her parentage. I won't bullshit you Ginny. Liam is a powerful man. He had to know if this supposed half-sister was real and if she was, for lack of a better way of putting it, on Adam Ward's payroll."

"I wouldn't say that to Kelly," she informed him with a terse snap.

"Agreed. But you have to admit it was a fair question."

"My god," she muttered darkly. "That horrible man hurt so many people."

"There's more."

"I'm not going to like this, am I?" she asked.

"Probably not." After a short pause he shrugged. "Ward? He's counting his last breaths. We don't know what if anything will happen when he dies, but Liam wants her protected against any potential from-the-grave fuckery. And now that I'm here and have met the boy, I have to agree. Both of them need a shield. A protector."

She looked at him long and hard and then glanced away.

"Liam is a good man, Ginny. Now that you know his last name you can Google him if you want. He can be trusted, I promise."

"And what about you, Roman? I know Kelly. If she's already marked you as hers, I don't see where Liam Ashforth figures into this frankly. She's made a choice whether you're willing to recognize it or not. She isn't going to dance to the tune of someone she doesn't know, no matter what he calls himself. I'd say you have a whole other issue to confront rather than what happens when some miserable old prick dies."

He was actively trying not to think about what she was referring to. The primitive way he claimed Kelly, and the possessive nature of their connection, had the potential to trigger serious upheaval between him and his friend.

Liam's claim was as a half-brother. Roman's was far more intimate, and Kelly's willingness was obvious. Matty shocking his family by immediately gravitating to Roman had to be cosmic validation. His boss and friend didn't know it yet but any decisions about the future were for he and Kelly to decide. Not Liam.

"I'm not disputing your point. Any guidance you could offer would be great."

"You don't need me, " she scoffed. "You got the Matty James seal of approval the minute he started talking. They're a package deal, ya' know."

"Found that out the hard way."

"Care to share? She'll tell me eventually, so you might as well spit it out."

Was this what having a mother-in-law felt like? He chuckled to himself and made a self-deprecating face. "Accepted town gossip without using my head."

"Ah," she nodded with a knowing sigh. "Kelly would never have a baby out of wedlock. Sounds old-fashioned, I know, but that's how she is. Deb wasn't much of a role model but she sure as shit was a great example of what not to do."

He was glad to hear it. Was counting on that attitude in fact because no way was he having a kid without legal protections in place and he certainly had no intention of staying away from her. The damage was done and until a drugstore magically appeared and he could buy a truckload of condoms, the future, as Yoda so succinctly put it, continued to be in motion.

"Can you tell me about the money? And Deb's ongoing relationship with Ward. Help me understand what's been going on."

Ginny unloaded a rapid-fire monologue that pushed a lot of his buttons.

"Here's the four-one-one. We met Deb about a year after she moved to Providence. My Sam is an ex-cop. He bought the town's butcher shop when he took early retirement. Money isn't really an issue for us, so we opted for a simple, country life. There was a minor kerfuffle when it came out that old lady James had an illegitimate heir. There are assholes everywhere, even here, and some thought then and still feel now that they had an unsubstantiated claim to the land." She shrugged. "Deb was what you'd call stand-offish. A recluse. She hated dealing with people. Over time, beyond Sam and me, she isolated her and Kelly. We tried convincing Deb to let the girl go to school, but she was overly paranoid. Little by little she shared her story. How an older, powerful man seduced and abandoned her. I knew right away that my new friend put this man first."

Roman had a hard time not reacting to Ginny's sad face and quick shrug. He knew neither signified indifference.

"Poor Kelly. It didn't require a crystal ball back then to see that her life wasn't going to be easy. Not with a mother who gave all the emotion she had to someone else. Did Kelly tell you what her mother did for her birthday every year?"

"Yes," he answered solemnly.

"Sam and I stepped in when we saw what was going on and made sure Kelly stayed with us. I can't even think about what Deb had done before then. That man was first. Parental responsibility a distant and anemic second, maybe even third or fourth."

The force of his grinding teeth made Roman's jaw lock. He'd sent quite a few to meet their maker. It's funny how that happens in a war. This, however, wasn't a war, but that didn't stop him from entertaining a host of dark thoughts. Two people had to pay for fucking up Kelly's life.

One was already gone. He'd have to be content knowing she died after a miserable, deluded life.

The second though. That piece of shit was currently in the land of the living. A status sure to change sooner than later.

"I didn't know for sure about the money until Kelly found the stash but we always suspected Deb returned from her bi-annual trysts with an envelope of cash. That's when she'd lay in supplies. Kind of obvious, ya' know?"

Oh hell yeah, he knew. That's exactly how she managed to avoid attention. The property taxes were paid by escrow and she supported them with the cash handouts she got for whoring out to that disgusting man.

"As I said, toward the end, the relationship strained. You can imagine, I'm sure, what a hard rural life, punctuated by delusion, depression, and fantasy did to Deb's appearance. And hearing what you said about Liam chopping away at Ward, I'm assuming that was happening around the time Deb became pregnant. She dropped of a massive stroke, did you know?" She was shaking her head. In a soft murmur, she added, "Lots can change between one moment and the next."

Yeah. Tell me about it, he thought.

"Kelly was already in total charge of Matty. She's the only mother figure he's ever known."

His sense of authority and supreme self-confidence were making statements he wasn't in a position to execute, but that didn't stop him. "I'm taking them both away from here."

Ginny sniggered and sat back to eye him with what was best described as pity. "Good luck with that. I think you may discover she has other plans, and if you know anything about her at all," she drawled with eyeball emphasis on his mauled neck, "surely you've figured out that nobody is the boss of Kelly, except Kelly."

He weighed what to tell her. Liam was right to insist on a strict information blackout but all the reasons why were things Kelly and Matty's guardian angels needed to know. Bad actors were everywhere and tended to appear when a previously quiet matter goes public. Being straightforward was part of protecting Kelly.

"Ginny," he started with a good deal of hesitation. "Kelly doesn't realize this yet, but she's a wealthy young lady. Same for Matty once I fill Liam in on the boy's parentage."

"I don't understand," she said. A confused albeit worried frown marred her face.

Roman sighed. Where to start? "When Liam discovered he had a sibling, a trust fund was immediately set up."

"Why would he do that?"

"He did it because as I keep saying, Liam Ashforth is a good man. He had his legal team direct everything he took from Adam Ward into an investment account. An account that will be turned over to her as soon as we clean up her legal status."

"Oh, my word."

He was glad she didn't need further explanation. The money was going to complicate things because he had a growing feeling that Kelly wasn't going to play ball. Not willingly, anyway.

He picked up the rhythmic clicking of an old wall clock as the hands counted off seconds and minutes. Without knowing why, Roman found it the perfect soundtrack to the irregular conversation.

Across the table, Ginny appeared deep in thought. She was picking at the cuff of a sleeve, and there was a pensive glower on her face. He shifted, sat forward and folded his hands on the table in front of him. While considering his next move, he was distracted before she reached across the table and took his hands.

"I can't believe I'm saying this, but I'm going to help you, Roman Bishop. My Sam and I lost our son when he was just a boy. Kelly and Matty are the grandkids we never had."

He didn't ask Ginny about the loss of their son. Hearing her say the words sparked the familiar feeling of loss in his bones that haunted him for years. It sucked that he understood all too well what she probably went through.

In a way, Kelly and Matty were lucky. Sure, the life Deb James provided to her offspring barely resembled anything ordinary, but having the equivalent of an extended family on hand to balance out the bullshit was nothing short of a godsend.

Ginny gripped his hands forcefully and looked at him. She had the expression of someone who knew what she faced wasn't going to be easy.

"Listen to her. Really listen when she speaks. Kelly may be young, but you have no idea how much fortitude that girl carries inside. Disregarding her feelings would be unwise. She has plans and dreams like everyone else, and those dreams are what kept her going. You can't just strip away the past because suddenly the future has more options. Don't be surprised if she tells you which pot to piss in on your way home if you try to force anything."

Fuck. He knew that without her saying it. Whatever the hell was happening in her bedroom—all that equipment and stuff, everywhere—told him she had her shit together.

"But we don't have the luxury of time, do we?" Ginny asked. "If her father is dying and there's even the remotest possibility that he could hurt Kelly from the grave, Matty too, we have to move fast to shield them both."

Roman bowed his head as relief spread through his tension-wracked body. Oh, thank god. Looking up, he grabbed one of her hands and kissed it. "Thank you for understanding. If it was up to me, she could have all the time she needs to come to grips with these changes. But that's not the hand we were dealt."

Plus, he thought silently, Liam was going to be a son-of-a-bitch when Roman briefed him. Just as he had when Rhiann came back into his life, the guy was sure to over fucking react and bring the security hammer crashing down with a vengeance. Unfortunately, Liam had a tendency to overcompensate when it came to people and things he felt passionate about. Discovering a ready-made branch of the family tree was going to throw the guy, big time.

Thinking he was smart and clever, Roman said, "Coaxing her off this land is going to be hard, huh?"

"*Pfft,*" Ginny grunted. "She was going anyway. This is what I mean about listening. The girl has plans, Roman. Don't be a man and hear what you want while disregarding everything else. Sam does that, and it drives me batty."

A jolt of inspiration made his head jerk. "I don't suppose you'd like to come to New York for a, uh…vacation?"

She chuckled. "How the hell did men come to rule the world?" She tut-tutted and tossed around all sorts of grandmotherly shade about silly men until he laughed too. "Scared of a twenty-three-year-old country girl are you? Cheese and crackers! They can't make this stuff up!"

"Shall I take that knee-slapping cackle as a no?"

He couldn't remember the name of the movie, but something happened with the old woman in the blink of an eye that reminded him of a scene where everything is normal one second and then bam! The viewfinder tunnels in rapidly to hyper-focus on a single moment. And those hyper-focused moments are always important.

"Are you sleeping with that girl?"

He started a head-shaking denial and stammered like a first-time petty criminal caught with his pockets full of stolen goods. "Er, uh, what, no, I mean, Ginny. Uh. It's not, no. Uh."

Real smooth, asshole.

"That's what I thought," she scolded. "You work fast."

"Well, actually," he instantly shot back, his voice sounding droll and self-mocking.

Grandma Ginny gave good eyebrow. So good that he felt a hot flush spread across his face. He'd been about to admit that Kelly started what he certainly finished until his determination to protect her, no matter what, stole the words from his mouth.

"Relax. You're not the first macho man to be handed his hat by a girl half his age."

"What?" he barked. "Half my age? Jesus, Ginny. I'm not that fucking old."

She snickered and gave him a pithy, "What's that expression? Thou doth protest too much? But thanks for the confirmation."

Miffed, he blurted out, "I didn't confirm anything."

"And you didn't deny. Here's my point. You and Kelly have to figure this out together. I'm not one for lectures, but I will say this. You're both adults. And you both knew what you did was going to make things more complicated. I'd say that means this one's on you. Will I agree to be on stand-by in case I'm needed? Yes. Yes, Roman. That I will do. I promise. If you hit a speed bump or things go screwy, I'll step in even if it means going to New York."

There wasn't much left to say after that, so they chatted amiably until everyone wandered back to the house. His head was reeling from all the new information on his plate, and he wasn't sure what to do next.

Chapter Thirteen

"That was an excellent story, Matthew."

Kelly glanced over her shoulder and watched Roman close the storybook. He was nodding appreciatively.

"The illustrations are great."

"I know what that means," Matty crowed. "Look."

She turned slightly, wiping her hands on a dish towel, and watched them. Matty took the book, dropped it to the carpet and got on his belly as the pages flipped. Pointing, he turned and looked up at Roman.

"This says who drew the pictures. Kiki told me. And this is the au-thor," he carefully enunciated the way only a small child did.

Roman stretched out alongside Matty, leaning on an elbow as he looked to be closely inspecting the things being pointed out. Feeling a little bit like a forgotten outsider, she'd been reigning in a surge of jealousy ever since Matty decided the stranger in their midst was deserving of all his attention. He took to Roman like, well, like she didn't know like what since Matty never took to anyone.

That's what was baffling. If she hadn't been there and seen with her own two eyes how Matty had reacted, first with a protective outburst, only to wind up being the stranger's new best friend.

And what was she doing while those two bonded over boy things? *Hmph.* She was behaving like a green-eyed twit on one hand while entertaining all sorts of dirty thoughts on the other.

Was this normal? How she felt? How could it be? It didn't seem feasible that a rational person with no interest at all in the opposite sex would suddenly turn into a rapacious sex glutton. But that's how she felt. Roman couldn't move without her eyes darting to his crotch. If he walked across the room, she was eyeing up his junk and wondering all sorts of stuff. Practical stuff like what does it feel like when it starts getting hard or her new favorite thing to ponder…sex or suck? Guys had a thing for blow jobs. Every magazine article, on demand movie and book, made it seem like oral sex was the thing to do. This endless musing led to being caught several times licking her lips while her eyes were glued to his bulge.

Normal? Shit. She had no way of knowing and it didn't help one little bit that she found it so difficult to keep thoughts of her mother out of it. Debbie whored herself out to one man over the entire span of her adult life, and it ended up killing her spirit.

She couldn't help but ask over and over if she was walking down the same path. And then Roman would look at her, and she'd see the intensity in his gaze. This was no passing fancy. If she was wobbling emotionally like a spinning top running out of steam, so was he. Kelly saw it in his expression. This thing hit them both like a bolt of lightning.

Flipping the light off over the sink, she gave the kitchen a final once over and went to join her two guys in the living room. Her foot caught an imaginary dust bunny, and she stumbled awkwardly. Her two guys? Oh my god. Presumptuous much?

Roman looked up first. And then Matty. One pair of eyes she knew like the back of her hand. The other drew her in and made her tummy do summersaults.

Matty had moved and was reclining with his head resting on

Roman's side. He was rambling on about something and wiggling about like any rambunctious preschooler. The big man appeared completely at ease.

He'll make a wonderful father she reflected, and then just as quickly pushed the thought away.

Roman's smile warmed when she approached. He even held up a hand for her to come and sit with him. She sat cross-legged near his head and offered a quick wink. Matty never stopped talking.

"We have a list! Ya' wanna see?" With that, he jumped up and ran to the bookshelf where his storybooks were shoved in haphazard piles.

Roman quirked a brow and looked at her with amusement in his expression. She shrugged her answer. When Matty was a man-on-a-mission, it was easier to just get out of the way.

Kelly's jaw cranked open in surprise when Matty returned and instead of walking around them, tossed stapled pages of paper on the floor and scrambled to climb over Roman as if he was a piece of playground equipment. The boy's instant connection with the unexpected visitor baffled her. People he knew, like the librarian in Fairley, those folks he wouldn't speak to, but this guy? He was all over him like fruit flies on a rotting peach.

An annoying suspicion grew in her head. Didn't he keep insisting that he was more friend than employee to…that other guy? Maybe Roman Bishop was just wired to get along with Matty because of his relationship with…"

Roman was trying to focus on the stack of papers Matty was waving in his face. "Kik says I have to read all these books before I can go to school. She lets me do the checkmark. See?"

Matty couldn't wait to go to school. He'd go right now if he could. She totally got it, because school was something she'd been denied. Getting him ready to learn and make friends was top priority. The book list was her way of keeping Matty moving forward.

The only thing missing from her detailed plans was what the hell to do about the house and land. The Dulbs would take advantage the second she left and not even Sam and Ginny had a decent suggestion for how to handle things.

"Time for your bath," she declared from left field. Suddenly she was tired of thinking. Tired of having her brain overwhelmed with too many changes all at once. "Straighten up this mess," she muttered irritably, "and I'll go fill the tub."

All but running out of the room, she darted into the bathroom and leaned on the sink. She had to think. Get her head straight before…

"What's wrong?"

Two strong hands landed on her shoulders and started a slow, firm massage. Tension rushed from her body. She turned slowly and moved straight into his arms.

"I wish you weren't part of this."

"By this, I'm assuming you mean Liam."

Nodding her head, she hid her face in his chest. He smelled so good, and she liked the way it made her feel to cuddle against him.

She felt his long, deep inhale and exhale under her cheek. He had her firmly around the waist, and his other hand gently smoothed her hair in long strokes.

"I'm overwhelmed." Her voice sounded small, frightened and childlike. Not what she intended, but some things couldn't be helped.

His arm tightened. The rest came out in a pained groan. "And Matty likes you better than me."

He chuckled. She felt his amusement and heard it rumble from deep in his chest. "You have nothing to worry about, Carina. He adores you. The rest? It's a guy thing. A boy needs a man in his life."

She hugged him around his waist and put her chin on his chest. He cocked his head and looked down at her, expectantly. He knew she had something to say.

"Are you that man or are you just standing in until the other one can swoop in?"

"Nobody is swooping in, and I think you know the answer. He's a great kid. You've done a fantastic job."

She didn't say anything right away and ended up being glad for the hesitation when he added, "I'd be honored to help you with him, Kelly. But you're the decider where Matthew is concerned."

Damn straight she was! Snickering, she ended the hug and jostled him with her elbow as she moved away. "Ha! The little shit. He's playing with you. You do know that, right? Making you call him Matthew. The apple didn't fall far."

He enjoyed her tease and let her know by swatting her butt as she sidled by. "Smart ass."

"My mouth or my butt?"

He grabbed her so fast she yelped and crashed into him with a thud. Then he claimed her mouth with his lips and tongue while rubbing her bottom.

"Kiki," a little voice giggled a minute into what ended up being a voracious kiss. "Ewww."

Pushing off with her hands on his chest, she tried to pass off the fact that she'd been giving the big man a throat exam with her tongue.

"It's little boys wearing dinner in their hair and marker ink on their fingers who are 'ewww.' Run and get your jammies and I'll put smelly bubbles in the tub."

"Hey! Roman. Ya' wanna take a bath with me? I've got boats and dinosaurs to play with."

"Sounds awesome big guy, but Kelly is frowning, see?" He was laughing at her! "And besides, I've got to make a phone call. Maybe next time."

She glared at his answer. Matty squealed. "Okay," and off he ran. Roman took her by the neck as soon as he left and pulled her face to his.

"Hey! Carina," he teased using Matty's exact delivery. "Ya' wanna take a bath with me? I've got something you can play with."

If he planned on kissing her he was in for disappointment because she laughed so hard there was a real danger of her peeing herself.

"Oh my god," she whined playfully and with loads of mock

exasperation. "You're impossible. Go make your stupid call and let me get Matty ready for bed."

"I'm still hungry," he growled.

"Yeah? Well, you ate half a cow for dinner. Cut me a break."

"I wasn't talking about food."

"Oh." She swallowed and took a deep breath. "Is this where I say I'm hungry too?"

Roman's knowing leer and sexy eyes almost reduced her to a puddle. "So I figured, Carina. Your eyes have been singeing my dick all night with heat. A little curious, hmm?"

There were questions she wanted to ask. Like, how does that whole oral thing work? After all, he's quite a handful, and her mouth didn't seem like much of a match against an anaconda. And what was the deal with ball fondling? Is it an extra or part of the ground game?

"You make me think dirty thoughts," she laughed. "It's all your fault. Now be good and go away."

"I like this bossy thing you've got going on. We might need to unleash some of that under the covers."

"Roman," she bit out. Crossing her arms, she gave him the look. "I'm serious. Go. Away."

His shit eating, very pleased with his bad self grin was way too cute, and she needed to get him out of the small space before she did something stupid. Popping his sexy balloon was a good place to start.

"Oh, and by the way. You're on the sofa tonight." With a very pointed look, she ended with one word, "Matty."

Yep. That totally threw him. A stunned, disbelieving expression shot onto his face. Her announcement took just enough of his alpha away to give her five seconds of upper hand.

"Now, out. Shoo!" she demanded with a hearty shove. "Don't you have a call to make?"

He was in the hallway, still gaping at her with his mouth open, when Matty dashed down the hallway waving his pajamas.

"Ready," he squealed.

Kelly shut the door on Roman's astonished expression, blowing a kiss at the last second. Matty was chattering on as he ditched his clothes. She sat on the edge of the tub and adjusted the water temperature as a cloud of strawberry scented bubbles grew bigger and bigger.

She glanced at the closed bathroom door and choked off a giggle remembering his face. Did he really think she wasn't going to use him like a jungle gym later? Sheesh. Men!

Roman juggled the phone between his shoulder and chin as he rifled through the ready-bag he always kept stashed in his vehicle. Good thing too, because he had a thing about fresh clothes and man-grooming. Another of his quirks; the result of having spent way too much time at the other end of the spectrum.

He'd grabbed the bag from the truck after being dismissed by a girl younger than him. How the hell did she do that? Wield the upper hand with such ease? He suspected she had no idea of the power at her command. Teaching her a few ways to get maximum benefit and pleasure out of her drill sergeant ways could be hella' fun.

"And of course the motherfucker rallied," he heard Liam grumble through the phone.

The raw anger in his friend's voice didn't bode well for the rest of the conversation. The guy was already on fire and Roman hadn't managed to tell him much.

"Is Rhi there? May I speak to her for a minute?"

Dead silence greeted his request. And then Liam barked, "Are you trying to fucking handle me?"

The outraged, stupefied tone made Roman grimace. And sigh. And rub the back of his neck. "Yes. Now shut up and put her on."

"I should fire your ass," Liam complained.

"Yeah, yeah. Tiny violins. Put the female on the phone, Liam, and nobody gets hurt."

It was just the right amount of levity, enough to get a chuckle from the man on the other end of the call.

"Suck my balls, Bishop."

Two seconds later he heard Rhiann's soft voice come over the wires. "He's being a handful tonight," she chortled as soon as she got on. Liam was griping about something in the background. Roman smiled. "Say it again Mr. Ashforth, and you'll go to bed with no dessert."

More griping and a few of Rhi's eye-rolling sighs later she came back and huffed. "You owe me. He hates being outmaneuvered."

"Sorry," Roman quipped. "No time for deft handling I'm afraid. We've got an issue," he told her with a good deal of hesitation.

"Is it serious?"

He growled. "Fuck, yeah."

"Hang on."

He went back to pulling shit from his bag while halfway listening to Rhiann lower the fiancée hammer on Liam by telling him to scram. Beat it. Be gone. Imagining his boss mumbling and scowling as she dismissed him was pretty funny.

Hmmm. Isn't that what Kelly just did to you, dumbass?

"Okay. I gave him a toy to amuse himself with. It's your dime, Roman. Tell me what's up."

He yanked on the ridiculously long and stretched out phone cord and walked to a spot where he could peer down the hallway. The bathroom door was still closed. Good.

For a few seconds, he took the phone away from his ear and pressed it to his forehead while a jumble of thoughts bounced around in his mind. Liam was going to freak when he learned about Matty. Plus, telling him that he was going to end up with no say whatsoever in how things went from here was not going to be easy. Which is exactly why he wanted to talk to Rhi.

"You might want to sit down," he told her. "Okay. Here goes. We're going to do this like a band-aid. Quickly. Please wait five seconds to react."

"Understood," she murmured.

He took a deep breath. "Kelly has a brother." Rhiann's shocked gasp didn't surprise him. "He's a full brother, Rhi. Not a half."

Five.

Four.

Three

Two.

One.

"Please tell me you're kidding. You're just messing with me, right? Roman? Oh my god. Oh my god. Are you saying what I think you're saying?"

"Yes. Liam has a half-brother too. And Rhi? Brace yourself. He's only four years old."

"Ho-ly shit."

"There's something else. Something that um, Liam isn't going to like. Don't get mad, please."

Rhiann knew him well enough to pick up on the seriousness in his tone.

"What did you do?"

"Um, shit. Rhi, I need you to stay calm, okay? I mean look, I'm freaking out big time, so that should tell you a lot."

"I can't imagine what you could possibly do that warrants such a serious tone."

Fuck. She was in for a surprise.

"Oh god. This is harder than I thought." He cleared his throat. "The girl is, um…what I mean to say is, Kelly? Yeah. She's uh…my responsibility."

"What?"

He sighed.

Rhi asked, "Does she know this?"

"Actually," he drawled, "here's the thing. Kelly James? She makes her own decisions thank you very much, and I'm pretty fucking sure if she heard me claim that she's mine, I'd be wearing her handprint on the side of my head."

"You work fast, Mr. Bishop."

He laughed. "Fuck, Rhi. I'd like to think I was half that smooth but the truth is, she did the claiming and just like with you and Liam, I never stood a chance."

"This is fantastic," she giggled. "I can't wait to meet this girl. And the boy? What's his name? Is he part of the deal too?"

"He's most definitely part of the deal. Kelly has raised him by herself. And in case you cling to doubts, his name is Matthew Liam James."

"No fucking way! For real? Oh my lord."

"So here's my question to you, Ms. Baron-Wilde. Do you want me to tell him or would you rather do the honors?"

"He's going to…"

"Yep. He is."

The bathroom door cracked open, and the sweet scent of strawberry hung in the air.

"Look, I have to go."

"You dick! Is that your way of dumping this on me?" Rhiann was having a good laugh.

"Bingo. I'll owe you one."

"Fuck off."

Roman grinned from ear-to-ear

"Wait," she yelped. "Don't hang up yet. I want a selfie."

"Wouldn't be able to send it. No signal." That sounded reasonable, right?

Rhiann's amused laughter rang out. "Nice try. Take the damn picture, Roman. At some point, maybe at the airport, whatever… you'll have a signal. Fair warning. If you show up here before I get a look at my new sister and brother-in-law, I will kick your Semper Fi butt from here to kingdom come. Got it?"

Rhiann collected selfies the way others gathered smiles. "Yes, ma'am," he chuckled. "Consider it done."

Chapter Fourteen

The warmth of the fire felt good on his front as Roman leaned his hands on the mantle. After Matty had surrendered the tub, there was just enough hot water leftover for him to take the quickest shower on record. He thought of the big tiled stall in his Tribeca loft. The one connected to a tankless water heater that gave him all the hot water he could ever need. Certainly enough for one kid, a small female and him.

That's right. He was thinking in terms of moving Kelly and Matty into his place. Just to start. It was big enough for a small family, and yes, he knew what using that word meant.

After Matty's bath and his shower, the little boy re-appeared in Roman's face, all scrubbed, brushed and tucked neatly into a banging pair of dinosaur pajamas. He grabbed his hand, dragged him over to the kitchen table, and then made him sit at the head of the table. The dad spot.

Roman exchanged awkward glances with Kelly when a chair needed relocating for this honor.

Roman had no choice but to do as instructed when young master Matthew Liam James assigned the seating. So he lowered into the sacred spot while Matty beamed.

Then it was cookies and milk. And more whiplash conversation. Matty was smart. Real smart. He knew a lot about a lot and was eager to share. Roman was half a plate of cookies dunked into ice-cold milk in, when all of a sudden the kid crowed, "Kik! Roman likes goat milk too."

Ah. He thought it tasted somewhat familiar. He assumed fresh dairy from local cows but learning it was goat milk didn't faze him at all. Hell, he'd consumed his fair share and then some during his time in the middle east.

He caught Kelly's tiny nod of approval when he didn't miss a beat in his takedown of the cookie plate. It was easy to say nothing and stuff his face because Matty was full of information that his little kid motor mouth shared without thinking.

That's how he found out that Kelly had never worn a dress. A fact she appeared mortified to hear spoken out loud.

He offered up a blow-by-blow account of Kelly building the goat shed in the backyard. Part of this tale involved pointing out a small jar on a shelf by the window. It was half full of pennies. Each time Kiki said a bad word, a penny was added to the jar. When it reached the top, she had to take him to the ice cream store.

More surprising than finding out Kelly was a prodigious fancier of swear words was learning where this ice cream parlor was. In a town called Fairley…where they went every two weeks to check their mailbox and do other stuff.

So much was starting to make sense. Not only had he been looking for the wrong alias of an alias, it turned out her only interactions in the little town where they lived were to take people's money over a game of pool at Shorty's, use the gas station, and from time to time some of the other small town businesses along the main street.

But it was Matty's detailed lying out of their grand scheme to leave the woods that left him reeling. Not only did they have every intention of moving, but Kiki was also researching schools and looking at small apartments on Craig's List. This thing was further along than he was comfortable with.

Kelly, for her part, said almost nothing as the boy rambled on—only occasionally stepping in with gentle reminders about manners and the right way to pronounce words.

Cookies and milk were followed by story time and for Matty that meant four or five stories. At the boy's insistence, Roman joined them in his little bedroom, sitting on the floor and leaning against the bed, listening to Kelly's exuberant storytelling.

The whole thing reeked of family. No wonder he was mentally moving the two into his home.

He left them after a high five to Matty and a promise to still be there in the morning. It did things to his emotions to see her stretched out on the boy's bed, cradling him in her arms as she kissed his face and hummed a tune to help him drift off.

And now, here he was, hugging the fireplace and waiting somewhat impatiently for her to come to him. They needed a serious discussion about the sleeping arrangements. She had another thing coming for suggesting he cool his jets on the sofa.

Arms slid around his middle from behind. She held on tight and shimmied closer until there wasn't any air between them. Roman covered her small hands with his. He could make out her cheek pressed against his back. Twice, she turned her face and kissed his torso.

When she peeked around his shoulder at the fire, he shifted to give her a better view.

"The heater is on low, so it's okay for this to die down."

She turned him physically and stared up into his face. "Are you okay?" she whispered.

It was killing him that she kept taking on the caretaking role. Believing that as the man, that was his job, it left him feeling out-of-sorts that Kelly was so naturally nurturing. Especially when that nurturing was directed at him. It was easier to hide from his emotions when he was in charge.

He cupped her face in his big hands. "You are uncommonly wonderful Ms. James."

She beamed at his words and offered her lips. The kiss was short and sweet. Just like her.

Putting a finger to her lips, she murmured softly, "Shh," and took his hand. Both of them were only wearing socks, which made tiptoeing silently past Matty's door easier. He caught the faint sound of classical music as they passed.

At her room, she opened the door, flicked on the overhead light, led him inside and then pushed him against the door she noiselessly closed. He expected a kiss at the very least, but she leaned into him and whispered, "No noise. He can hear everything. The walls are paper thin. Nod if you understand."

Roman nodded.

Pushing off of him, she hurried to the bed and waved him over. Without words, she gestured with her hands until he finally understood what she wanted.

In tandem, they lifted the mattress carefully off the creaky bed and lay it on the floor. All the pillows and blankets followed and got hurled into a pile.

An amusing pantomime ensued as each gesture was mined for maximum entertainment value. Before long, they were bouncing around the room doing absurdly exaggerated slapstick moves for the sheer purpose of trying to make each other laugh.

Kelly's silent, belly-holding guffaw could only have been made better if she was dressed as Santa. He opted for the toes turned in shy giggle with a wrinkled nose and two fingers on his lips. They were a regular comedy duo, and he couldn't remember when he'd last had so much fun. Probably something to do with Rhi, but this? Man, this was different.

At some point in their goofing around, they switched to every damsel in distress physical parody they could think of. Kelly on her knees pleading like a silent movie actress while he towered over her twirling his villain's mustache was almost their downfall when not laughing out loud became just too difficult. At the peak of their silliness, she buried her face in his thighs and held on for dear life while muffling a string of giggles that he felt right through his jeans.

Attempting to recover her composure, she sat back on her feet and waved him off with her head down. If she so much as peeked at him, the giggling started again.

Their playful interlude sparked a volley of disjointed thoughts that got his motor running in a surprising way.

Up until this very actual moment, you'd be more likely to find him stripped to the waist covered in sweat, wielding anything from a bullwhip to a leather flogger in some high-class sex dungeon than smiling his ass off with a giggling elf and fighting off a hard-on that was robbing his brain of oxygen.

Jesus Christ. Talk about opposites. It was exhilarating too. Kelly freed him somehow. Being with her was joyful, challenging, and fantastically primal. But instead of feeding his sexual hunger with unrealistic control fantasies big enough for him to hide behind, he found his thoughts and desires going off in a different direction.

She was gathering her hair together and had produced a tie from who knows where. He observed her unhurried actions and chuckled softly when this endeavor ended with her sporting a half-assed mess of a tail. The women he knew tended to be annoyingly concerned with how they looked all the time. The naughty pixie who was captivating his soul didn't appear to give a rat's ass about any of that. He liked that about her. Her default setting wasn't fake.

While he'd been enjoying just looking at her, she'd crawled closer. Close enough to rise up on her knees and attack his belt buckle with sure fingers intent on…

Intent on what?

Pulling the belt through the loops on his pants with deliberate slowness, she played with the leather for a minute and rather audaciously eyed his crotch. Vapor locking was a real possibility when she wound the leather belt around one wrist and looked him straight in the eye.

He knew what she was thinking, but he wasn't having it. Not this soon.

When the belt was tossed aside, and she reached for the button on his jeans, shit got real.

Danger zone! Incoming alert! Pull back!

He took her wrists and gently pushed her back. Kelly's eyes immediately shot to his. Shaking his head, he let her know that her sweet, seductive mouth would have to wait.

She pouted. Actually, god damn pursed lips and frowning. She also sat back on her feet with an angry huff.

The adorably hot way she glowered up at him caused a momentary lapse of reason. Feeding his thumb into her mouth Roman encouraged her with a grunt and then worried for his sanity when she sucked, licked and generally simulated a blowjob with a bit more lusty gusto than his libido could handle. She was quite literally reducing him to a grunting, growling animal when what he'd been trying to do was keep the upper hand.

So what did he do? He grabbed her by the neck in a very predatory and unmistakably commanding way. The soft, warm skin of the dainty column and feeling her heartbeat tested his control in a big way.

This petite young woman was stealing his heart. He was the one who struggled, not her. She went still in his grip, her amazing eyes telling erotic stories he longed to explore.

Well, good, because he had one particular sensual delight in mind and it wasn't going to be what she seemed to be expecting.

He released her and gestured her to remain where she was. The fucking glare from the overhead was harsh and put the shit storm condition of her room in the spotlight. Not exactly romantic. Spying a flexible, gooseneck lamp on her little worktable, he tapped it on and then hit the wall switch, sending the cramped room into blackness broken up into shadows from the small light.

Perfect.

He put out his hand. She took it, and he pulled her to her feet. Leading her to the bed, he maneuvered a spot at the headboard and put her hands on the brass in a silent command to hold on. Then he pulled her feet back until she was stretched out and slightly bent from the waist. She wasn't restrained in any way, but he sure did enjoy the way she responded to the invisible bindings with enthusiasm.

He ran his hand up and down her back. She arched even more. Damn. Maybe what he planned would have to wait.

Forcing his dominant proclivities to stick with the program and not be such a distraction, he kept up the slow stroking, eventually claiming her lovely denim clad ass.

She was starting to quiver, and small, hushed moans kept breaking loose. If staying quiet was on the menu, he'd have to either gag her or keep his tongue down her throat to absorb her cries. Both thoughts held a certain appeal.

Roman grabbed her hips and stepped in close. *Mmm*, nice fit. He eyed up the angle he'd need to take her from behind and moved her around in a practice run that had him grinding his hard bulge into her curves.

Resting his confined cock firmly at the juncture of her legs, he reached around and undid the button of her jeans. The zipper was next. He reached inside her pants and slid his hand in until he was cupping her heated mound.

She shuddered, and his hand detected a flash of heat. It excited him knowing that by the time they got to the main event, her pussy would be dripping.

Sliding the jeans off wasn't a cakewalk, and he wasn't going to win any awards for expertise. Not He got into a hand-to-hand battle between her ass and the tight denim that ended with a mighty grunt when the damn fabric finally gave way.

Dropping down behind her, he helped her lift each foot so he could remove her socks and each pants leg. The view quite frankly was ah-maze-ing. He found her sultry curves and petite stature a huge turn on. Same for the plain cotton panties.

He bit her ass because he could. She hardly complained and, in fact, repeatedly wiggled, offering the other cheek. What was he supposed to do? He sank his teeth in with a deep growl.

Rising to his feet, he ran his fingers up her legs. Goosebumps appeared. This time when he reached around, it was to flick open the buttons on her shirt. His eyes roamed over the charmingly submissive pose she maintained with her hand's white-knuckled grip on the antique brass. It was a damn shame to let her move, but the shirt wasn't coming off until she stood up. And he needed the shirt to join her jeans in a heap on the floor. Kelly had magnificent breasts. Full, deliciously round, and with nipples that begged for his touch.

Taking both big globes into his hands, he pulled her up until she let go of the bed and he smashed her against his chest. She yelped when he bit her earlobe but quickly muffled the sound when he growled low and dangerously.

Massaging the mounds, he marveled at how a bra made for practical purposes was as seductive if not more so than anything Victoria's Secret made He pinched her nipples through the flimsy barely supportive garment that in his mind in no way qualified as lingerie. The practical, bare bones life she led was driven by practicality. It was going to be his pleasure to introduce his sexy paramour to the delights of naughty lingerie.

Momentarily abandoning his gentlemanly seduction, he ripped the unsexy flannel down her arms and grunted with displeasure when he had to stop and unbutton the cuffs.

When she was wearing the plain underwear and nothing else, he used the tangled, messy tail of her hair like a rein and moved her head to the side. He licked her exposed neck. She quivered and whimpered so sweetly that he licked her again.

Her hand covered his as he enjoyed the fullness of her breasts. He started to rip her bra in two but stopped. There was a time and place for underwear torn to shreds. This wasn't one of those times.

Unhooking the worthless bra, her breasts spilled out into his waiting hands. Growling his pleasure into her ear, he massaged, stroked, pinched and squeezed until she was writhing against him.

He guessed she let him call the shots as long as she could and then the feral lioness he tussled with last night took over. She whipped around and frantically tore at his shirt trying to divest him of his clothing with eager, shaking hands.

The smile on his face had a decidedly lecherous feel to it. He was amused by Kelly's inability to control her passions. She was, he concluded, a five minute submissive. An FMS. Why such a snarky thought would make his cock surge confounded him.

Maybe because she was all about the feels. If playing submissive felt sexy, then she was all in. Right now, ripping his shirt off fueled her feels, and he was perfectly fine with it.

There was no mistaking how much she liked his torso. About as much as he liked her curvy ass and stupendous tits. She had wicked fingers. And they were fast too. In no time at all she had his chest mapped and stroked. When her claws came out, he took her hands in his, but that didn't quell her ardor one bit.

Switching gears she went from exploring his chest with her fingers to a thorough GPS-like scan using her nipples. On tip toes, swaying side to side and up and down, the hard nubs tantalized his flesh. Didn't take long for him to be the one quivering.

Because he had control of her hands, he moved them to his pants. It was time for more skin.

She got his jeans off far quicker and a thousand times smoother than his ham-handed exploits, and she would have kept going if he hadn't stopped her. Keeping his briefs on, for now, was an absolute necessity for what he had in mind.

He lay down on his back in the center of the narrow mattress and had her straddle him. Roman closed his eyes and counted back from twenty when the scorching heat from her center settled on his stomach. Kelly stroked his chest. Her eyelids drooped, and she took a shaky breath.

With a hand on her back, he urged her forward until her beautiful boobs swung above his face. He chased a swaying orb and caught her nipple in his mouth. Drawing deeply, he sucked the end of one glorious tit into his mouth and fed their mutual lust with an animalistic offensive.

She was writhing, gasping, and mewling softly. It was beautiful.

The things he did to her tits tested his control. She was receptive and urged him on, so he showed her how to let him know what excited her. There was a moment when he had his hands on her ass as he suckled both nipples going back and forth between them, as Kelly led the action with one globe in each hand, when he took a memory selfie. He wanted to hold the decadently sexy moment in his mind's eye forever.

Holding her still was impossible. Even with his hands firmly on her butt, she managed to hump him with increasing desperation. If he didn't slow her down, she would come before he got into her panties.

Roman lifted her slightly and carefully rolled until she was under him. The kiss that followed was of unparalleled perfection. He wasn't surprised when she got frantic right away, but he was ready for her and slowly took his sweet inexperienced lover on a journey to the type of all-encompassing seduction that promised everything.

She was shaking when he ended the kiss. He rose up and looked at her. If it was possible to swoon lying down, that's what she was doing. He removed her panties. The scrap of white held the fragrant, damp proof of her desire.

Grasping his forearms when he spread her thighs wide, she whimpered as he pushed her legs back. With a gentle push, he silently demanded she hold them up and open.

After her willing but desire-sluggish response, it was his great pleasure to turn all of his attention on worshipping her gorgeous pussy. Despite the dim light, he had no problem finding the silky liquid proof of her desire. Lightly running his finger along her slit, he dipped into the warm wetness and delighted in what he found. She was gushing with arousal.

Roman licked his lips, anticipating the feast to come.

He leaned over her to study her face as he tickled and teased her vulnerable flesh. Each time she gasped, he put his mouth on hers and swallowed the moan that followed.

Her low, feral sounding growl when he pushed a finger deep into her pussy turned his already hard cock to marble.

Shoving his hands under her ass, he lifted her and tilted her pelvis to accept his tongue. The second he licked, she put her fist into her mouth. The desperate attempt to mute her pleasure-wracked grunts was barely successful, but he couldn't think about that right now. Not when her dripping pussy and sweet, swollen clit demanded his attention.

She tasted sweet and warm, like honey mixed with her unique essence. The combination was delicious. He ate her with passionate abandon. His cock swelled when she shook.

Sucking on her sweet nub, she bucked into his mouth and groaned. The more he dished out, the more she quivered. Was anything sexier?

Lashing her pretty clit with his tongue, he slid a single finger slowly forward and swirled it inside the hot wet velvet sheath of her sex. The softness around his finger tightened. He felt her muscles clench and release.

Kissing her clit, he eased back and let his thumb take over, rubbing as he fingered her deeply. Roman liked being close to her pussy when she came. Liked watching what her body went through as he milked a strong, mesmerizing orgasm from her sweet body.

When she barely finished pulsing he removed his finger and parted her pussy lips with both hands. The visual seared his brain. Her hole was pulsing, and a trickle of creamy white nectar dripped out and into the crack of her ass. It was fucking beautiful.

Satisfied that she was sated for the moment, he removed his briefs and crawled near her head. Putting a hand under her neck, he lifted slightly. Her eyes flickered open, and he was taken aback by the fiery lust in her gaze. With his other hand, he fed the tip of his cock between her parted lips. She went from satisfied to voracious in a heartbeat. Opening her mouth, she licked the plump head of his cock and drew it into her mouth with grunts and suckling noises that pushed all his buttons.

He let her suck him for a minute or two and gave in twice when she tried to take more than she should. The sensation when she gagged on his thick shaft was a powerful turn on.

There was only so much he could take. Her eager mouth and wicked tongue would need training, but he knew without a doubt she shared this particular desire.

As quietly as he could Roman growled, "Are you ready to be fucked, Carina? Is your pussy aching for my cock?"

She surrendered his cock and nodded. In the darkness, her eyes sparkled. He liked seeing the fiery lust in her expression.

He moved into position. Her eager hands were everywhere on his body. She took hold of his meaty staff and guided him home. He closed his eyes, and his arms shook from the effort of holding himself up when he felt her fingers spreading her lips open to aid his possession.

Goddamnit. There was no way to ease into her slowly. Or was there? Drawing on every scrap of experience and control he had, Roman entered her with slow motion precision. Her fingers on his cock as he slid deep got his heart thumping. She had a tactile seductiveness that turned his sense to mindless jibber jabber.

When he was fully seated, her fingers remained, teasing his flesh where he stretched her opening. Grunting fiercely, his hips bucked. She pulled her knees back so he could penetrate her as deeply as possible. He tried not to be aggressive, but sometimes he had to.

Sensing she didn't want him to go easy, he withdrew slightly and slammed in deeper with a mighty, grunting thrust. Wet heat scalded his cock as her pussy flooded. She got sopping wet as he stroked in and out. Her hands moved to his ass. On each powerful downward thrust, she whimpered and dug her nails into his flesh.

The carnal pleasure was intoxicating. He really could fuck her forever, and it would never be enough. Her pussy did things to his cock he had never experienced before. It excited the fuck out of him that she responded to his mighty possession with dripping wet surrender.

He leaned close and nuzzled into her neck. Whispering filthy words into her ear, he told her how good her pussy felt, encouraged her to squeeze the shit out of him with her muscles and delivered a crude narration of their fuck that made his cock pulse and led to her pussy spasming with fierce contractions that stole his breath.

He bit her earlobe. "Ah, Carina. My beauty. Yes. Come on my cock sweet love. Fuck me, baby. Fuck me till you're empty."

She did just that. Fucked him. Fiercely. Till the contractions became sweet pulses.

"And now," he whispered hoarsely after a punishing kiss, "now comes your reward. Don't worry baby. It's all yours."

He let loose. Each aggressive thrust caused a lewd sound as he sank into her come-flooded pussy with abandon. She met him stroke for stroke. Passion glazed eyes met his. She made soft grunting sounds on every thrust.

Ecstasy nipped at his heels. All the blood in his big body detoured to his sex. His cock grew impossibly larger. There was no more holding back. His orgasm was loaded and ready to fire off.

The closer he got the more she squeezed his cock with the sexiest grip imaginable. He shook. His body heaved. The sensation of his cock pulsing through a never ending string of explosions that sent his seed spurting into her unprotected womb brought Roman to the brink of consciousness.

She was wriggling under him making desperate circles with her hips, grinding his cock as deep as she could get it. Unless he was hallucinating, another climax rippled through her.

When they finished, and he'd collapsed on top of her, she held him tight and wouldn't let him move away. Roman hated pulling out of her. When he looked down and saw his glistening cock, the sight of their mixed fluids leaking from her body was more erotically satisfying than he was comfortable admitting. Matter of fact, the unsettling emotions had pig-ish overtones. It wasn't okay to feel this arrogantly proud, was it?

Kelly didn't give him time to ponder anything at all except her petite body and delicious curves cuddling into him. He found the corner of a blanket with his fingers and pulled it up and over them. She murmured against his chest as the cover floated down and wrapped them in soft warmth.

"Whatever you're thinking, stop. I'm not a child."

Aw, come on. Seriously? Did the orgasm connection include a channel into his thoughts? That wasn't exactly fair. Not fair at all, because he was fucking baffled more than half the time about what went on in her head.

Tempting as it was in the sated aftermath of their serious love-making to burrow deeper and dial back a post mortem of their unorthodox and risky activities, Roman ignored what he knew from experience was an emotional trap. Not speaking one's truth, no matter how uncomfortable or fucked up at the time, chipped away at a relationship and since he and Kelly were most definitely embarking on an intimate liaison fraught with sober ramifications, holding his tongue wasn't an option.

She felt so good in his arms. He held tighter and kissed the top of her head. "I know you think you know what you're doing, luv, but…"

"What?" she whisper-snapped. "You're older? And wiser? Cut me a break Roman."

When she got pissed off her whole body tightened. It didn't matter how little of the world she knew. Her fire and determination came from within.

The fierceness is strong with this one. Must be a family trait, he thought.

"Don't be upset because I'm worried. About you. These things have consequences. I don't want you hurt in any way, Kelly. You getting hurt is a deal breaker."

She crawled onto his chest and captured his eyes with hers. "I know we're taking chances and I can't explain why, but I'm not afraid. Some things you just know. You have to trust me, fancy man."

No shouted conversation could have shaken him up more than this grim whisper.

"Is that your way of saying shut up and go with the flow?"

"Yep."

Sharp fangs of darkness nipped at his feet. Ugly shadows from the past blew through his mind. He knew what lay in the gloom. Knew that his public persona hid a savage inner core, tested by war, compounded by a black fury, the result of the bastard twins, terror, and loss.

"Kelly."

She smirked. "Give it a rest Roman. We both have shit to deal with. In here," she murmured before dropping a soft kiss over his heart. "And here." Her fingers brushed against his temples. "I'm serious, big guy. You have to trust that I know what's best for me. And Matty. Right now, that's you. What's that obnoxious saying? Borrowing trouble is stupid? Yeah, that."

She cut him off so neatly he was stunned into silence. Trust me. Jesus. Wasn't that supposed to be his line?

Getting into anything right now was counterproductive. Between them, they were juggling several different realities. Remembering that he left Rhiann to drop the Matty bombshell sparked a flurry of random, fragmented thoughts. He knew Liam. Adding a half-brother to the situation was going to stir up the guy's inner demons.

Maybe the best way for him to protect Kelly was with information. Her legal status was a shit show, and Matty? Fuck me, but who the hell knows where that breadcrumb trail would lead. He needed to speak with Cameron Justice. Roman knew Cam dealt with his own background legal bullshit over the years and could probably steer him in the right direction so he could take control of cleaning this shit up.

Yeah. That's what he'd do. He didn't want to hurt Liam any more than he could deal with Kelly being hurt. Or Matty. That sorta' meant it was up to him to keep track of the dozen or so balls up in the air at any given moment.

And right now the ball in the air was his lover's state of mind. She was too fucking wonderful for words, and he was a dick for not showering her with romantic care.

It was clearly important that her autonomy be acknowledged and respected. Not only did he understand, he practically wrote the damn book on the subject. So he gave her what she needed and in doing so felt a peacefulness in his soul that he hadn't been able to access in a very long time.

"I trust you, Carina." He kissed her nose. "But go easy on me, okay? My heart is involved."

She was blushing and the pouty smile making her lips quiver held amusement and delight.

"Did you just tell me to be gentle with you, Mr. Bishop?"

And this ladies and gentlemen, he mentally shouted. This right here is why I'm a fucking goner.

"Nah," he quietly scoffed. "I can take a beating."

"Said my ass to your hand," she giggled.

"Keep it up, Carina," he teased as his hands went on a seek and destroy tickle maneuver that got her wiggling frantically. "And we'll find out just how much your sweet sexy ass can take."

She swatted his hands away and crawled back to lying at his side. A quiet yawn blew across his skin.

"Yeah, yeah. Promises, promises," she murmured with a sleepy sigh and just like that drifted into a deep sleep.

Quieting his thoughts wasn't easy, but somehow he managed to let go of everything and concentrate on the now. It'd been forever since he slept with a woman. Slept. Not fucked. And yet here he was for night two, on a shitty single size mattress on the floor with a sexy wanton elf curled around him. It was just the most perfect moment, he thought, as sleep claimed him too.

Chapter Fifteen

"And poor old Buck," Jimmy said with a good-natured chuckle, "slid right off the road and into a ditch. We had to call for reinforcements to dig him out before the snow swallowed his truck!"

"That shit was wild, I'll give you that," Roman answered.

Tossing him a biscuit, Jimmy's face was transformed with a wry scowl. "Folks around here ain't used to weather like that. The kids had a great time but plowing and digging everyone out sucked donkey dicks. When you vanished into a snow cloud, I just hoped your survival skills were on point, man."

They both snickered for different reasons. Roman because hell yeah his survival skills rocked. He'd taken refuge from the storm. Found warmth inside the seductive body of... shit. Cancel that thought.

Pushing back from the table where he'd shared a late breakfast with his new buddy, he did the obligatory gut smack followed by a rich, full belch that Jimmy easily eclipsed with an impressively overblown burp. His smirk was pure son-of-a-bitch, Marine style.

"I bow to your supremacy," Roman quipped.

"So what now?" his friend asked. "You're taking off I see," he said with a nod directed at the duffle bags on the chair next to him.

He was ready for the question. Had given what he wanted to convey a good deal of thought. He liked this guy. He had a cool backstory. They were interconnected by an oath they'd sworn.

Jimmy was good people, and he wanted to set Kelly's record straight and tell him as much of the truth that he could.

"Back to the big city. Taking Kelly and the boy with."

Jimmy nodded. "Good. She's a smart girl. She'll be fine."

"I need your help, though. She's freaking out about the land. Is her worry about the Dulbs taking over for real?"

"Oh, fuck yeah," Jimmy grated angrily. "Bunch of assholes. Look, I have an idea. Is this move to the big city permanent?"

Roman tried to appear nonchalant. He even gave a lazy shrug. "I imagine so."

"Then what y'all need is a placeholder. Someone to maintain the land. Live in the house. Ya' feel me, right?"

Hmph. Damn. "Great suggestion. Have someone in mind?"

"Bobby Douglas. Regular Army. Got shot up pretty bad over there. He's having a rough time now. Wife. Two kids. Boys. He needs to catch a break. Maybe, oh, I don't know," he muttered. "Caretaker? He's got some issues but nothing that'd prevent him from keeping up the house, the garden, you know."

"I like it," Roman answered. "When life moves us up and on, that's when you reach back and lend a hand."

"I think Kelly might know Bobby. He's a regular in town and has helped out Sam with some handyman work. Maybe the butcher can be a reference."

Roman took Jimmy's hand in a hearty shake and landed a hand on his shoulder. "You rock, man. Is there anything I can do for you?"

The other guy laughed and made a face. "Yelp reviews are always nice." His snicker was drier than the Sahara desert. Yelp reviews for an off the beaten path hole in the wall were about as helpful as a fork with a bowl of soup.

"I'm serious. What've you got going on? Maybe I can help."

"Well," he drawled. "There is the whole custom wood thing me and Lil started. Mostly small stuff. Hand carved boxes. Children's furniture. I make the objects, and she does the most amazing carvings. The internet is a beautiful thing."

"Well shit, Jimmy! A redneck entrepreneur? I fucking love it."

Jimmy laughed. "We love the hick lifestyle, what can I say? The thing is," he said with a shrug, "running a bar ain't enough. But having a business on the side? Fuck. Welcome to the American dream. Me and Lil made enough last year to take care of all sorts of shit and even managed one of those Carnival cruises out of Galveston. You should try it sometime. That there is some good shit."

Roman saw his opening and took it. "That's not a half-bad idea. Kelly would love a cruise, and Matthew? What kid doesn't have a ball in the ocean?"

He expected Jimmy to ask and he wasn't disappointed.

"So…the kid?"

"Matthew. About to turn four, and he's her little brother."

Jimmy's startled whistle about said it all. "She-it Roman. Brother? Damn! That girl is my new hero."

"You and me both."

He headed out not long after that, taking a bunch of business cards and a brochure of Jimmy's side gig with him. He knew exactly who to talk to about giving the guy some pointers on how to grow his woodworking business. Draegyn St. John, also of Justice Brothers fame and another of Roman's tribe of warrior buddies, was a wood artist in a caliber all by himself. What that guy did with a piece of tree was some other level shit.

As he pulled in and parked at his next stop, he did a quick mental rehash of all the things he wanted to say to Sam. Turns out that Roman's initial impression that the curmudgeonly butcher and his know-it-all wife being more than casual friends to Kelly and Matty was on target.

Another thing Liam was going to have to accept. The two siblings came with a ready-made support system in the form of a strong surrogate family. Not only were a brother and sister about to shake up his employer's life, so were an unexpected set of grandparents.

When he entered the store, Sam was helping a customer. He looked at him through the glass case he was behind and gave a perfunctory nod. "Be right with you," he told him.

Roman wandered around and checked the place out. A wall with photos in different sized, mismatched frames caught his eye. He chuckled at several pictures of deer kills with rude comments on sticky notes attached. A photo of Sam wrapped in an apron, holding a trophy next to a huge barbecue smoker was an eye-opener. So was the standard cop in uniform shot showing a much younger version of the man watching his every muscle twitch.

The cord strung with bells hanging from the shop's door tinkled, letting Roman know the customer Sam had helped was leaving. When he turned around, the man was already moving to a small round table by the front window with a coffee pot and two white mugs in his hands.

"Take a load off, son. You look like someone wishing they were anywhere but here. You're safe. For now."

Thank god the conversation went smoothly. It was hard enough managing Kelly's wild mood swings whenever the subject of her future came up. He didn't want to battle the old guy, too.

Sam offered up some sage advice as they shook hands and said goodbye. He'd stayed neutral before now when Roman first presented Kelly with the options before her—as he saw them. After some time to process the changing conditions, he'd told him, the only way forward from Sam's standpoint was for Kelly to ball up and meet with her older brother. Until she did that, anything else was nothing but a stalling tactic.

The problem with that, however, was her belligerent reluctance to take that step. Hell, she still refused to say Liam's name.

"Don't ease up on the gas, my boy. Pedal to the metal. That girl can sniff out uncertainty better than a bloodhound on a trail. If you give an inch, believe me. You're doomed. And whatever you do, don't let her shove you into a corner. It's her best move, by the way. Clueing into weakness in any form and shooting from the corner is how she wins at pool."

"Thanks, Sam," he told the old guy with a warm handshake.

"And if you hurt my girl, I will personally rip off your nuts and shove 'em down your throat."

So much for warm and fuzzy goodbyes.

Message received. He just nodded. That was enough.

He gassed up and took advantage of the public Wi-Fi from the parking lot at the Laundromat. The signal was shit, but he was able to shoot off half a dozen emails and touched base with Liam via text.

His boss reacted to the news about Matty much better than expected. Roman owed Rhi big time for handling that particular microphone drop with her usual aplomb. Somehow she managed to get Liam focused on the future rather than kicking a bunch of dead horses that'd get them all nowhere.

When Liam deferred to Roman's judgment on how best to wind things up in Oklahoma, he was relatively sure Rhiann was also responsible for that. Telling him that he was sleeping with his little sister and was moving them into his home, well, that part Rhiann wisely left unsaid. It was his responsibility to do the right thing on that score.

Driving along the winding road leading to Kelly's home, he took a few deep breaths. Their snowbound fantasy was coming to an end. It was time to get back to the real world.

He sensed the battle waging inside her. She wasn't making it easy and refused to hand over the reins. It was her life she liked to say, and while she reluctantly conceded that a previously unknown sibling was intriguing, she had other things on her plate that were way more important. Kelly's stubborn refusal to acknowledge that the two things were linked was driving him nuts.

So he was going to force the issue. Jimmy handing him a made-to-order solution for keeping control of her land was what he needed to sail over the last hurdle holding her here.

She was coming to New York with him, and that's all there was to it.

The pacing wasn't helping, but she didn't know of another way to burn off energy and anxiety without drawing too much attention. It was making her twitchy that eyes were watching her all the damn time.

Matty, Ginny, Sam, Roman. Even the damn goats looked at her like they thought she was about to unravel right before their eyes. And maybe she was, because right now Kelly was close to jumping out of her skin.

Pushing both fists into the small of her back, she stopped and arched enough to get a good stretch going. Her back was killing her, and she wasn't sure if the ache was from sleeping on the floor, the high-intensity sexual gymnastics, or the non-stop tension she was barely managing.

Pacing resumed, she shook out her hands and willed the wild beating of her heart to settle down. If only it were that simple. A heavy conscience came with a price.

Matty had a particularly awful morning, and she was the reason why. He was picking up on her anxiety. When she snapped at him over nothing, and his little lip quivered, she hated herself.

Angered, she kicked the door jamb with her boot. Deb was a snapping turtle. Non-stop. Having a tart, insensitive attitude was something her mother excelled at, and she didn't want to be like that.

Damn. Poor Matty. She was coming unglued right before his eyes. This morning he asked a simple question about his birthday, and she nearly tore his face off. What was wrong with her? She'd been looking forward to Matty's fourth birthday more than he had.

Wishing she hadn't lost it though was useless. Because she had.

Lost it. And why? Because in the blink of an eye she realized that his birthday was timed to take place somewhere else. Not here. Not in the little house in the woods on the not very big mountain in their little corner of Oklahoma.

That was the moment when panic, real, gut-freezing panic, took hold. And because these feelings were foreign and so out of character, she was having a hard time keeping her shit together.

Without the snow to keep the outside world at bay, their altered reality slowly filtered in. That guy in New York City, Liam? He wanted to meet her. And Matty. There was talk of a trust fund and questions about Matthew's future schooling that made her super uncomfortable.

There was a woman too. Rhiann. She was Liam's fiancée. Kelly spoke with her briefly. Reluctantly. It was only hello, but she got the impression this was a person who was good at ironing out wrinkles and making things go smoothly.

The nagging sense that she was a major wrinkle tore away at her. Was her entire life going to be about other people and how they reacted to her and Matty? Jeez, but she was sick of being the cog in the wheel. Her mother, a father who hated her enough to send a subtle fuck you on every birthday, and now him. Liam. He didn't know her. And what he did know was total bullshit if he thought she was some stupid backwater country girl.

She didn't want to be ironed out. Why the hell would she? To make someone else feel good?

Blech. Her face contorted with disgust.

Where was Roman? She needed him.

A for real guardian angel must have been on stand-by. That's the only way to explain how she missed smacking her head on the coffee table when her feet unexpectedly circled left, and she went crashing to the floor.

Huh? She needed him?

Was she drunk?

Is this a dream?

Needing anything was not her style. She made do. That's how she got this far by herself.

"Oh my god. I need him," she whispered out loud. Staying on the floor seemed safer than pacing, so she scooted until her back hit the sofa. Pulling her legs in she sat cross-legged and slumped. Her hand rubbed and squeezed the back of her neck. How the hell did she end up here?

She let the stillness engulf her. Faint, barely audible sounds of light classical music floated in the air. From the time he was a baby, she'd played music when Matty took his nap. Not long after he was born when she started taking care of him full-time, she'd read every baby book and child development manual the library had. Theories and practices about naptime were a dime a dozen, but she liked the one that focused on teaching a kid how to relax rather than forcing eyes closed. She always told Matty that she didn't care if he slept, as long as he spent the time being quiet and relaxing. It worked. Classical music became Matty's calm down switch. She sometimes wondered what went on in that busy little head of his when things settled and got quiet. He was a deep thinker. Part of that old soul thing, so she hoped he got something positive out of the quiet time.

In the few days they'd been together, she'd discovered that Roman had interesting musical preferences. He knew every single classical song on all three of the CDs she had. And he could sing along to most of the country rock but lost his master of the universe title when the kid songs came on. Who didn't know the wheels on the bus? Sheesh!

She needed him. With him, she felt alive. And safe.

"Am I an idiot?" she asked. The silence held no answer. Just her luck. She was going to have to figure this one out on her own.

Her eyes drifted slowly around the living room. The small house was all she'd ever known. The few modern touches she added, like the cheap CD player, the off brand flat screen, and her very cool laptop, didn't compensate for the elephant in the room.

As long as she dug in and refused to budge, they'd remain

isolated. No longer forgotten but still separate from the rest of the world. And wasn't that exactly what she was trying to change about Matty's future?

Her outsider status had been shoved down her throat a long time ago, but he still had a shot at a different life. She owed it to him to make the best of their strange turn in circumstance.

If she stuck to her guns and put her foot down, maybe, just maybe, the future she so meticulously visualized could still be hers.

A place for her and Matty where he could go to school and they could both find a place in the world. She wanted to grow her brand and make KA James into a real business. And she wanted to stop feeling left out. Invisible. Forgotten. Denied.

Roman certainly didn't make her feel any of those things. Was it insane that she felt the way she did about a man she barely knew?

Oh, hell yeah. But she'd always listened to her gut, and the message coming at her where he was concerned involved a steady, unwavering beam of rock steadiness tied up with a big blue bow of hope. Why blue? Because blue made her smile and the smile she had for Roman Bishop reached into her soul. Reason enough.

All of that was well and good but what about this old house? It wasn't much, but it was hers. She had animals to care for and a huge garden to work. This summer she planned to reinforce the shed and at Matty's insistence was sketching out a brick outdoor fireplace. What would happen if they walked away? She knew damn well it would not take long for the Dulbs to stir up shit. Burt was a smarmy prick with a bad case of girl-humiliation. He'd burn the house to the ground as payback for her being a bigger badass than he could ever be.

Plus there was that other uncomfortable, niggling worry biting her on the ass. She'd almost died of embarrassment when Matty announced to Roman that she'd never worn a dress. Not once. Not ever. Dresses were of no use in her present world. She wore jeans. And flannel. In the summer when it was hot, the jeans were cut-offs and the flannel became t-shirts. Their hats and scarves? She knitted them.

Now, she did have a bathing suit, finally. Got it last year when she picked up an inflatable pool at Walmart. Best summer ever because Matty had been over-the-moon with joy over the water toys. But that was it where her wardrobe was concerned. She picked up her undies from the dollar bin, slept buck naked or in sweats, and when necessary endured picking through boxes of cheap crap at the Payless shoe store.

Who was she kidding? A sophisticated guy like Roman just had to be used to high-class women. Women with dresses and high heels. Women who wore make-up and got their lady parts waxed. It took a fuck-ton of effort to squash the doubts she felt whenever the shitstorm stirrer inside her asked, 'What the hell does he see in me?'

When she imagined moving away from here, it was never to a place like New York. What she envisioned was more suburban, right on the edge of rural, not the busy streets of a major city. Matty would love it, but she wouldn't know what to do. How did she handle going from working sun up to sun down, to doing nothing?

The low growl of an approaching truck roused Kelly from her thorny preoccupation. She was never going to be a girly girl, and that was that. What that meant in the bigger picture where Roman was concerned was a huge kernel of self-doubt that she pushed aside for now.

He found her on the floor and laughed. "What's going on sweet pea?"

Sweet pea. Ha! That one was new. The guy had a world-class vocabulary and was going through every imaginably cute way to call her little without riling her up.

Those doubts she had one minute ago? All gone. Poof. Vanished.

Patting the floor next to her, she scooted over a bit and gave him room to sit down. On his way to planting his spectacular butt on the carpet, he swooped in for a hello kiss.

"Matty's napping? Cool," he joshed with a shoulder shove that nearly toppled her over. "Wanna do it on the floor?"

The playfully fiendish eye waggle and teasing, "Huh? Huh?

Come on! You know you want to," made it impossible to scowl. Even as a joke.

She threw in the towel. There wasn't any other option. Instead of attempting a calm, rational discussion about the future, she said a little prayer and let the winds of change blow through her life.

"To be perfectly honest," she quipped with a saucy smirk, "I'm sort of over the whole sex on the floor thing. I think it might be killing my back."

"There's a solution for that, you know," he chuckled. "Your riding skills are exceptional, love."

"Shut up," she chided. "I was going somewhere with that speech, and so if it's ruined now, it's your fault."

"My bad," he conceded. The smirky nod was one hundred percent Roman.

Pretending exasperation, she drawled, "Anyway…as I was saying. The floor. *Meh*. So yesterday – so over it. Which got me wondering," she paused and took a deep breath, "exactly how big is your bed?"

He almost answered. The matter-of-fact expression on his face told her he missed her point. Then the light bulb went off over his thick man-skull, and she watched as her comment hit the mark. So fast she yelped, he flattened her to the floor and wedged between her thighs.

"Are you saying what I think you're saying, Carina? Don't mess with me, little lady. Is that a white flag you're waving?"

She wrapped her legs around his body and touched his handsome face. "I think I'm ready."

"Kelly," he groaned.

"But I can't do this by myself, and I'm scared." She couldn't believe those words came out of her mouth. His wide-eyed reaction told her he was equally shocked.

"I swear to God, babe. You won't regret this."

She grimaced. "I already regret it, but I know this has to happen."

He took her face in his hands. "You'll call all the shots, honey.

I'll make sure of it. And nobody but you gets a say where Matty is concerned."

His words tore at her heart. He understood, and that was enough for now.

"I need you to be there if this is going to work. Don't leave me, Roman." That's more honest and vulnerable than she could ever remember being.

"Ah, Jesus, Kelly. Leave you? Don't you understand yet? I'm going nowhere that doesn't involve you and Matthew at my side. That's a promise. And before you start imagining I'm only worried about getting you pregnant, let me make this clear. I'm too fucking old for you and keeping you to myself is hella' messed up, but that's the hand I was dealt. So expect the full package. All of it. We're a couple. I take care of you."

She rolled her eyes. He kissed her and continued.

"And you will let me. If you're a bitch about it, then we'll have a heart-to-heart about the spanking scenario you're panting over."

She laughed. "Hello? Did you hear what you just said because unless I'm mistaken, I believe you just gave me permission to be a right royal bitch and reap some super sexy benefits in the deal."

His eyes flared, and then he chuckled too. "Fuck. Can I get a do-over?"

"No, ya' dope, but you can answer the damn question about your bed. Are we talking a hermit's lumpy cot? Maybe an air mattress? Ooh! Or one of those futon things."

He took her hands by the wrist and stretched them above her head. Her legs dropped from his body, and her heels dug into the carpet. Did he have her attention? Oh hell yeah.

"King size…bed and cock. Four posters. Perfect for leather restraints." She held her breath as he spoke. He released her wrists and with one hand stroked the sensitive skin. "Or perhaps satin bindings. Shame to mar your beautiful skin."

As usual when he allowed a glimpse of the things that fueled his sex drive she started melting down. While their lovemaking had been intense and adventurous, she sensed an undercurrent of leashed sensuality that she longed to set free.

"Will a blindfold be made available?" she asked with a breathy moan.

His smile was genuine. And very, very hot. "Really? You're okay with being blindfolded?"

Was she?

The slamming of the bathroom door jolted both of them, and they reacted like the goddamn sex police were about to walk into the room. Quickly disengaging, Roman leaped to his feet and extended a hand to help her up.

When Matty came bounding into the room, they managed to make it seem like they'd been doing nothing more than having a casual conversation.

Chapter Sixteen

Roman lost no time locking down Kelly's startling surrender. Did it concern him that he wore her down and probably forced her change-of-heart? Not in the least.

She was pretending to arrange pillows on the sofa when Matty came into the room. Before buyer's remorse could set in, he wiped out her last escape route.

"Buddy!" Roman hooted. He and the boy high-fived. "Guess what. We're taking a road trip, little dude. Kelly said okay. New York City here we come."

"Hey," Kelly griped. "Slow down. Nobody said anything about a road trip. I've got the house and..."

"Taken care of," he announced. "I'll spare the details now because you'll check with Sam anyhow, but here's the deal."

Roman gave Matty a wink. The kid already recognized the signal and fist bumped him in male solidarity.

"Found a caretaker. You know the guy. Bobby Douglas. Sam says he's cool. You'd be helping a veteran get back on his feet."

Matty's blonde head nodded enthusiastically. "Roman says we should always help a beteran."

Kelly's knee-jerk correction took the wind out of any possible objection.

"It's veteran. V like vanilla. And Roman is right," she assured the boy with a smile.

"Then it's settled," he crowed triumphantly. Shit! He couldn't believe how easy this ended up being.

"New York! New York!" Matty squealed with glee. Skipping around the room he turned into a tiny whirling dervish as the excitement overtook him. "Kiki!" he shouted. "I'm gonna have my birthday at New York!"

Roman saw her face fall. He knew what she was thinking. In her mind New York represented her losing control of their lives. She had plans for Matty's big day. He knew this because he saw a sketch of the fancy homemade cake she planned to construct. A dinosaur of course, and not just that. Somewhere in the mess of crap in her room was a birthday kit of decorations with some balloons, hats, noisemakers, a paper table cloth and cups and plates, and napkins.

It astonished and bothered him what she managed to do with forty dollars. No way was he going to let her be deprived of her plans.

"Dude," Roman drawled. Matty's attention was instantly on him. "Wait till you see what she has planned. I'm totally jealous." He gave her a reassuring smile, and for the first time since they met, he caught a glimpse of something she tried so hard to cover up.

When all was said and done, Kelly James was far too young to take on so much responsibility when you considered that none of what she dealt with was of her making. It was one thing to fuck up with shitty decisions. Not much choice when it came time to own up. But to step into a whirling Bermuda Triangle of poor choices and fucks ups courtesy of someone else and be the one to make things right? Fuck, but that made him mad. Seeing her eyes fill with doubt and anxiety was not his idea of fun.

Matthew Liam James, Mr. Old Soul wearing Oshkosh overalls went to her and wrapped his arms around a thigh. "My Kiki is the best."

She ruffled his hair and smiled down into his adoring eyes.

No matter what, I'm going to do right by these two, he mentally vowed. He'd dropped the ball once before and left too much to chance. Not this time. No way.

"Matthew," he drawled. "I'm feeling Candyland. Why don't you go set up the board and I'll find out what we're having for dinner."

Because kids are so damn easily distracted, he skipped off and left him and Kelly alone for a minute or three.

"Let's make sure we pack his party things. And if you give me a detailed list of what you need for his birthday dinner, I'll take care of laying in supplies."

"You make it sound like we're going on a camping trip, but I bet you've got one of those HGTV kitchens."

Only he would end up with the only female on the planet who would grumble about a state of the art cook's kitchen and do it with a touch of pout that did unbelievable things to his dick.

What could he do to ease her mind? Oh, wait. He had an idea. And it was a good one too.

"Would you feel better if you saw pictures? Of my place, I mean. You might be surprised."

"You have pictures?"

"Well, no," he told her laughingly. "But I can get some pretty quick. I'll text my decorator." He snickered at what that meant. "She'd be happy to snap some pictures."

"You have a decorator?"

The barely concealed wonder in her voice was funny.

"Actually, I have a Rhiann. She's the mastermind behind a lot of what you'll see. No snotty comments about the antlers."

Her disbelief continued. "You have antlers?"

He chuckled and drew her into a hug. "I prefer to think of them as a decorating affectation."

"What the fuck does that mean?"

"Penny jar," Matty hooted.

"It means," he told her with his lips hovering over hers, "that from a visual standpoint they scream, look at me. Hence the affectation inside the decorating focal point."

His kiss swallowed her reaction. When he was sure she'd been silenced, he ended the kiss and swatted her butt playfully.

"The men are hungry," he bellowed with a Tarzan-like chest thump to Matty's grinning delight. "Woman of the house. What's for dinner?"

She whispered in his ear, "Uh, how about your balls on a platter?"

He let rip with a hearty guffaw and swatted her again, this time more forcefully. When she yowled and covered her butt with her hands, he leered suggestively. "No to the platter," he grandiosely declared. "But yes to your mouth."

"I give up," she groused. Throwing her hands up in defeat she marched into the kitchen and started banging pots and pans.

"Kiki," Matty yelled. "Fish sticks and cheesy macaroni. Okay?"

"Well I don't know Matty," she muttered. "I'm not sure fancy men like frozen fish sticks."

As far as digs went, that one was pretty lame.

"Got ketchup?" Roman asked. When both of them nodded yes, he held up his hands. "Then we're good. My mom always gave us ketchup for dipping, so that's how I like them."

Kelly's dark scowl was adorable. He had an answer for everything, and it was getting on her last nerve.

Matty was well on his way to cleaning Roman's clock at Candyland when Kelly called out to them. "It's your job to set the table."

He enjoyed the way her ass rocked a pair of curve-hugging jeans. When she bent over to peer in the oven, he swallowed the primitive grunt that automatically rumbled up from his core. As much as he'd enjoyed their furtive sex life until now, he couldn't wait to bend her sweet little body over the end of his enormous bed and fuck the shit out of her from behind. It'd be even hotter if she let him tie her hands.

Without thinking, he rubbed his hand on the bulge evident in his pants. She turned around at that moment with a hot pan she held by a potholder. She stared at his hand. He stared at her face. Until now he'd managed to keep their shenanigans in the moderately vanilla zone. But it was getting harder and harder to keep things there because his deliciously wanton little lover was pushing for more.

He launched off the sofa and dashed across the room, taking the pan and potholder from her hand before she got burnt. If they were alone, he'd toy with her. Play word games and inflame their passions.

But he was learning to navigate the dad route, and that meant behaving when the kid was around. Well, mostly behaving. He dropped the pan onto the stovetop and glanced back at Matty. He was busy setting the table and wasn't paying them any attention. He took the chance because that's what you did when a clear shot presented itself.

Grasping one of her hands he took her fingers and used his big hand atop hers to fondle his bulge. He bit her earlobe and growled, "Interested?"

He had to give it up for timing because she got quite a handful before they had to break apart.

Roman was one of those guys who happily ate whatever was in front of him. He also knew how to make the most disgusting MRE palatable, and wasn't a stranger to home delivered gourmet. But the pile of crunchy no name fish sticks with the side of gooey mac and cheese was nothing short of bliss on a Melamine plate.

Over dinner, they happily chatted about whatever popped into the conversation.

Kelly shared a truly terrible joke that was so bad even the kid rolled his eyes. Matty informed them that Bob the Builder had a friend named Wendy and for Roman's part, he explained how to power a light bulb using a big potato, pennies, a scrap of copper wire, zinc-plated nails and a nightlight bulb.

It was remarkably family-ish, and he wasn't at all concerned by the thought.

"Are we going to live with you?" Matty asked. He was munching on a fish stick like a bunny eating a carrot.

Roman reached for Kelly's hand and held tight. "Getting a room ready for you right now," he explained. "And you can decorate it any way you want."

"What about Kik? Does she get a room?"

No time like the present. "She'll be staying in my room, with me."

Matty took this news without missing a beat. "She farts in her sleep."

"Matthew James," Kelly shrieked. "Don't tell him that."

Roman had to laugh. From the mouths of babes. "Yeah," he told him in somber agreement. "Found that out. And ya' know what else? She rubs her snotty nose on my shirt."

Matty cracked up with giggles.

"Oh. I see how it's gonna' be." She sat back and fumed at them. "Making fun of the girl."

What came next from this particular babe's mouth?

"I love Kik," Matty gushed. "Don't you, Roman?"

A smart man would have deflected the question, but he wasn't smart. Not anymore. Not since an insatiable sprite shook his world inside out.

"She's easy to love, I'll grant you that."

Their eyes connected but she flushed bright red and looked away.

"Listen," he chatted amiably to the boy. "I have a friend who's going to send some pictures of my place for you to look at. What do you say if we take a selfie to share with her?"

"What's your friend's name?"

"Oh, uh, her name is…" he choked. What would Rhiann be to Matty? Sister-in-law? Shit. That means she's not an aunt. Okay, so first names were called for.

"Rhiann," he said. "I call her Rhi. She's engaged to…"

Kelly's hand slammed onto the table. "That's enough."

Unsure-of-herself Kelly was gone. Don't fuck-with-me Kelly was in da' house.

"Take your picture and then clear the table. Matty, you're on trash duty."

The determined, slightly adversarial tone she used didn't do anything helpful for his raging libido.

They smooshed together for a group shot that nearly got derailed multiple times due to Matty's fascination with Roman's iPhone. It would've been awesome if Kelly made an attempt to smile, but he dashed that thought and instead was grateful she hadn't flipped the bird.

Clean-up was a breeze, and once the boy had the trash ready for the truck, they gathered in the living room, curled up with a bunch of throw blankets, and watched *One Hundred and One Dalmatians*.

Family time. Pieces inside him that he didn't know were crooked fell into place. If he just kept them moving forward, one carefully balanced baby step at a time, they had an unbelievable shot at the sort of homemade happily ever after that he was sure could survive the test of time.

With the phone cord stretched to the max, Roman spoke to Liam while keeping an eye on what was happening in the backyard.

Sam stopped by with Bobby Douglas in tow. The three of them, Matty bouncing by their sides, were going through the backyard step by step. He was damn proud of Kelly. She had a head full of doubts, but she stood by her decision and didn't shrink from what was necessary before they headed out. And that's what he was explaining to his boss.

"Driving will take too long. Why don't you fly?"

Roman sighed. "I told you why. We've got some fairly significant identification issues. The boy still doesn't exist as far as official paperwork goes. A vaccination record isn't enough. We'd get flagged before getting on a plane. And besides, it's too much of a culture shock. Bringing them to New York from the woods of Oklahoma is a big deal. I'd rather ease them into it."

"Where'd you rent the truck? Amarillo? Why can't you drive to

Texas and then grab a private flight from there?"

Because he didn't want to. Because he was looking forward to a week-long road trip with Kelly and Matty. But dammit. Liam wasn't going to back down. He had it all figured out too. They could do the trip in six or seven hours, spend the night in a hotel, and then hire a plane the rest of the way.

It was the only concession he was willing to give at the moment, so he gave in. It was easier than arguing.

"What aren't you saying, Roman? Whatever it is, stop playing me. And low blow you son-of-a-bitch for setting my woman on me. You're a dick."

Hey. No worries, man. I'm fucking your little sister.

And that kid you're so jacked up about? Yeah. About that. Got news for you. Your control position with the boy is pretty far down on the pole.

Oh sure. He couldn't wait to say all of that.

"Can I be straight with you?" Roman pinched the bridge of his nose with one hand and pressed the phone to his ear with the other.

"I don't like the sound of that," Liam grumbled, "but yes, of course. Go ahead."

"We've known each other a long time, and I know better than most how you are. I'm counting on you to remember who you're talking to before you go off on me, alright?"

"Good lord, man. It can't be that bad. Can it?"

Telling the Archduke of Control Freaks that he wasn't going to get a chance to swoop in and take over? Sure, that didn't sound bad. Not.

"As I said Liam, I know how you are."

"I'm a big boy. I can take it. Just spit it out, Bishop. Shit. Beating around the bush isn't your strong suit."

"Bottom line. And please count to ten before you react. This isn't about you and what you want or what you think needs to happen."

"What the…"

He trampled over Liam's angry growl with a reminder, "Ten, nine, eight…"

When the necessary amount of time had passed, the angry growl continued.

"Says who? You? What's going on Roman? Why do I feel like I'm missing something? These people are my siblings goddammit. Family. You can't just tell me to shut up and sit down. That's not how this works."

Ugh. He hated the phone sometimes. This being one of those times. Leaning against the counter at an angle that afforded a view of the backyard goings on, he flipped the phone cord around a trashcan before it pulled the damn thing over.

Matty was hopping around like a jumping bean, going from one snow mound to the next. Sam, Kelly, and Bobby were huddled in conversation. The sun was shining, and the white snow covering the backyard looked almost fake.

And on the other end of this call was his friend. Where Kelly and the boy were concerned, he no longer thought of Liam in boss terms. That part of their relationship came to a screeching halt the second Roman's emotions became involved.

But he couldn't ignore the fact that his friend was also Kelly's brother and that gave Liam some standing.

Rock? Meet hard place. What a tough fucking spot to be in.

"That's not what I'm saying at all. It's just that you don't know Kelly. She's not going to fall in line because you think she should. Right now? She couldn't give two shits and a fart about what you want. Her whole life just blew up in her face. Think about it, man. If I can offer an opinion, I believe you've been cast as the boogeyman in this whole thing. She has nothing to hang her reactions on, Liam. She didn't know her father and shows zero interest in changing that situation. I know you can't wait to make up for everything she was denied, but she has plans. And you should also know that the money isn't a bargaining chip. She really couldn't care less. She didn't go looking for any of this. You need to be ready for what that means."

He felt a bit winded after the long speech and hoped he made his points.

"Be a big brother, is all I'm saying." Roman mentally held his breath and said one last thing. "It's not your job to be the father she didn't have."

Liam grunted. "Shot that one from the hip, didn't you?"

He chuckled. "Dude. Seriously. I'm fucking square dancing as fast as I can. You want to throw money at this to make things right. Rhi wants pictures. Matthew wants whatever Kelly wants, and she wants none of it. Well, almost none of it."

Oh, dear sweet baby Jesus. Mother of God. Did those words just spill out of my stupid fucking mouth? Please don't let him notice. Please.

Wonder of wonders, the comment sailed right over Liam's head.

"Such is my lot in life, Roman," he snorted. There was a considerable amount of amusement in his voice. "Beset with females who aren't impressed with my money. How the hell did that happen?"

"What the hell are you whining about? Imagine the opposite. I can see it now. You being hounded by professional pussy with an eye on your wallet."

They laughed together with Liam drolly adding, "And then there's that."

"So are we good? Can you do the chill-out thing and let me handle this? Please don't make me owe Rhi anything else. The girl is platinum plus when it comes to managing your snarling butt."

"Fuck off you old fart. Stop taking liberties with my fiancée."

"Hey," he chortled. "Just making sure she knows your uptight bullshit isn't her only option."

"If anyone else but you said that, they'd already be on the floor."

"Lucky for you, she likes the pasty-faced, fair-haired thing better than dark and dangerous."

"And what about my sister? Dark and dangerous something she can handle?"

Fuck. My. Life.

"There isn't anything Kelly James can't handle. No lie."

"Point taken. I'll let you go now but one more thing Roman. I'm going to let you handle this. I don't have to tell you how difficult it is to back off, but I will because it's you."

He wanted to shake Liam's hand, but that'd have to wait.

"I don't have a clue what I'm doing, but I'll promise this. No matter what happens, I'm going to try like hell to do what's right for everyone. I want you to have the family you wished for, and I want Kelly to not give up on her dreams."

"Good enough."

When he hung up, part of him felt better. Convincing Liam to trust him wasn't easy so when he conceded control Roman was equal parts relieved and uncomfortable. Relieved for obvious reasons but uncomfortable because he and Kelly were so far over the line with their relationship that he wasn't entirely sure there'd even been a line to begin with.

He heard Matty stomping snow off his boots by the back door and stooped for a better look out the window. Sam, Kelly, and Bobby were shuffling along the walkway to the driveway.

Liam thought it was tough stepping back from afar? Jeez. The guy should try being him for one day. Only in Roman's case, it felt more like being shoved back.

Kelly steadfastly refused to let him help. In any way. Whenever he tried, his ass was neatly returned on a tarnished silver platter. 'I've got this,' was what came out of her mouth about a dozen times a day. He'd never felt so useless. And he didn't like it.

He was boxed in. She wasn't trying to be a bitch, and she wasn't playing a game either. In actuality, she did have it. Shit, she had everything. It was all on her. Help was something she couldn't comprehend. Her standard reaction was to ask bewilderedly why he thought she needed anything at all.

What he did though was do the one thing she allowed which was to step in as a weirdly ironic Mr. Mom and handle the boy. Something he was more than happy to do.

"Hey, Roman!" the kid's energetic voice yelled from the mud room. The sound of struggling with a coat and boots made him chuckle and head down the hallway to lend a hand.

He found Matty sitting on his butt trying to kick off a pair of heavy snow boots. There were tracks of snow and little piles of the white stuff everywhere. Looked to him like the kid tracked in half of the backyard. When it all melted, it'd be a mess.

Swooping in, he picked up a squealing Matty by the waist and slung him backward over his arm, so the kid's face was looking at the floor. His happy laughter rang out. Though he wiggled like a fish out of water, Roman still managed to get the boots off. They landed on the mudroom carpet with a thud.

Brushing off the giggling little boy, he made sure he was presentable and then swung him to his feet at the door to the room.

"Stay there," he told him with a gesture at his socks. "Your feet will get wet."

Then he grabbed a broom and quickly swept the snow out the back door while explaining in kid terms to Matty why.

It was all so damn domestic.

And he loved it.

Pushing Matty down the hallway to the living room he got the rambunctious lad settled with a pile of books and then gave up on trying to mind his own business and went to stick his nose where Kelly apparently thought it didn't belong.

"Don't sweat the details, Kelly."

Sam was so sweet that she worried tears might start.

"Me and Ginny will pack up your personal stuff and handle whatever furniture and equipment Bobby and his family don't need."

"Can't thank you enough, Ms. James. Really. My wife will love your little house, don't you worry none about that."

She offered her new caretaker and tenant her hand. The deal they'd struck was the answer to both of their prayers. Bobby and his family would get the break they deserved, and she got to leave without having to give up her history—no matter how meager it was.

"I'm glad this worked out for both of us, Bobby. I know it's not much," she said with a head bob at the modest home, "but it's a terrific place. You'll have to slog the kids to the school bus stop out where the county route meets Boon's Road, but other than that, you're all set."

Kelly did a double take when Sam puffed up and slapped Bobby on the back. "Ya' never know, boy! This might lead to all sorts of good things."

She wondered what was going on in his mind but shrugged away the thought and made a hasty goodbye. She was freezing her ass off and wanted to get inside. Sam could handle the details. She had enough to deal with just getting Matty and her stuff together for the life-changing journey on which they were about to embark.

She liked thinking about it in grandiose terms. Literary terms that lent a bit of gravitas to something she was barely able to wrap her mind around. So, words like journey and embark flowered her vocabulary.

It was better than every thought beginning with a dark cloud and her mind screaming 'Fuck!'

As she hurried to the back door, she thought about the snow covered rose bushes planted along the side of the house and how she wouldn't be here to see them bloom in the spring.

Did that make her happy or sad? It was hard to tell. A little of both perhaps. It's not like she hadn't been hurrying toward this point for a long time. She always planned to leave and not look back. It was just happening sooner than she planned, and in a manner she'd never dreamed of.

Pulling her boots off in the mudroom, she left them on the boot pan, rubbed her hands together to generate some much-needed warmth, and dashed for the living room to stand in front of the fireplace.

Matty was curled up at the end of the sofa, wrapped in a quilt. An open book was close to sliding off his lap, his head was cocked back and to the side, and his eyes were closed. She smiled at the sight. He had the ability to fall asleep anywhere.

Snatching the book before it fell from his hand, she tilted him just enough that he'd be cat-nap comfortable and ruffled his hair affectionately. His life was going to change big time. This was what she wanted for him. She just didn't know anymore where she fit in or what she wanted.

About the only things she was sure of were her love for Matty and her growing attachment to Roman. Nothing had ever felt so right or been so confusing, but she couldn't work up an ounce of regret. Some things were supposed to happen. It's where it all goes after that that concerned her.

She flipped around at the fireplace and put her hands behind her as she warmed her backside. Signs of Roman's presence were everywhere. Not because he left stuff around but because he had an effortless way of turning chaos into order.

It rankled her at first—the way he walked through a room and like some bizarro-world Mary Poppins left everything in perfect order. Mess and dirt were the enemies, but clutter and piles? A closet or some decent storage would have been nice and solved a lot of problems, but when life hands you muddy water, you boil that shit and use a filter. It's called going with what ya' got and not being a crybaby about it.

When he started organizing stuff, the only thing keeping her from going up one side of him and down the other was the fact that the military made him that way. The whole wartime thing automatically took most of the wind out of her sails. He couldn't help it. Order in the midst of bloody mayhem was understandable. But if he started labeling stuff or folding her underwear, they were gonna need to talk.

Speaking of which, where the hell was he?

She went off in search and ended up at the door to her room where she stumbled to a halt and stared. Roman was sitting on the edge of the bed with one of her sketchbooks open and lying across his lap. He was so engrossed that it took him some time to realize she was there.

Some of her earliest childhood memories were of drawing. She remembered the year Deb let her chalk paint a mural on the shed and the handmade gift tags she labored over with a set of colored pencils that were her most prized possession. Her stuff might be a sloppy mess, but her art wasn't. Hell, she always made sure to empty the pencil sharpener shavings, and heaven forbid if a paint cap wasn't completely shut.

Two silent steps into the room let her see what he found so captivating. It was a pencil drawing of him. Asleep and sprawled on her bed with nothing but a hastily drawn sheet to protect his dignity.

Of course, if he thumbed a dozen pages further he'd also find a detailed study of a particular part of his anatomy. Oh my god! She had to get that book out of his hands, stat!

"Invading my privacy, I see," she teased. "Find my diary yet?"

He slammed the sketchbook shut and put it aside. Relief swamped her body. To her delight and amazement, he reached into his pocket, pulled out his wallet and tossed it to her. She caught it with one hand like a big league shortstop and earned some hearty applause.

"It's hard to snoop when everything is out in the open, but you're right. I didn't realize," he admitted to her with a funny face, "how personal the sketches would be." He gestured to the wallet. "Your turn, lady. Go ahead. Have a look."

She joined him on the bed when he patted the spot next to him and sat facing his side with one foot tucked under her butt and the other on the floor. Going through a man's wallet seemed kind of fiendish in a way, so she proceeded cautiously.

Handling the soft leather warmed from his body heat, she turned it in her hands and gave an unimpressed shrug. "Damn. I expected a mysterious Illuminati symbol stamped in the leather."

Roman shoved her playfully and snorted his amusement.

"Illuminati. Good one."

Opening the plain billfold, she counted the bills first. More than she imagined but less than obnoxious, so she gave him a pass for cash-on-hand.

One by one she pulled credit cards from their slots. A scowl marred her face when she saw that one of them was a business card for the Black Phoenix Group. BPG was Liam Ashforth's kingdom. Shoving it away, she pulled out a blank blood red card with fancy gold-colored edges that showed nothing except a magnetic strip on one side.

"What's this?"

Roman looked at the card, went still and then chuckled softly. "Uh, classified," he muttered.

Interesting reaction. She put the card aside and arched a brow. There was more to it than a one-word answer. She made a mental note and moved on.

Next, she pulled out his driver's license. Her annoyed growl was a reflex. "And of course your picture would be fine. Better than fine, great. Mine? I look like a redneck serial killer."

There were some random business cards shoved into a pocket. She picked out the first one she saw, an engraved card with an interesting logo that looked like three flames.

"Justice? What's that? A superheroes club?"

In a lowered voice she thought sounded awfully mocking, he drawled, "In a manner of speaking, yes."

Smiling, she drank in his cheery reaction and slid the card away. That was when she saw the picture. Pulling the old photo from the jumble of cards, she put the wallet down and stared at what she held in her hands.

It was a picture of a smiling woman taken with the Eiffel Tower in the background. She looked like the rest of the tourists except for the fact that she was obviously pregnant.

Roman was silent. She could hear his ragged breathing. Kelly froze and then turned wide, searching eyes his way.

On a harsh sounding sigh, he told her, "That's Vanessa. My wife."

Her jaw fell open. "W-wife?"

"Yeah. She's uh, dead."

She slapped a hand over her mouth and stared through the tears gathering in her eyes.

He took the picture from her trembling hand, looked at it briefly and then put it back in his wallet.

"That was a long time ago, in a different life."

She hated the flat, slow way he spoke—wanted to know more, but was afraid to ask.

"She was killed in a terror attack. Collateral damage was how the police report read. I was off fighting bad guys. Thought she and the baby would be safe. I was wrong."

No! She couldn't hear another word. While he was fighting the war on terror, his wife gets killed in the same war? No, no, no. Not Roman. Oh my god. It wasn't right.

She swung onto his lap and grabbed his head. "I'm so sorry, so sorry," she mumbled through desperate kisses pressed to his face.

"Kelly," he grated out. "It's okay. Really."

"No it is not okay," she growled forcefully. "Not at all. Did you love her very much?"

She wasn't sure why she asked. The romantic lurking in her heart, perhaps. It was weird but at the moment? She just wanted him to have been happy. To be happy.

He took her hands in his and kissed them. Something skittered up and down her spine when he looked her in the eyes and held her gaze.

"There's a time and a place for everything. We loved the child we made. I hoped that would be enough."

What was the mechanism for swallowing? She couldn't remember, so the big wedge of emotion lodged in her throat stayed uncomfortably put.

Now she understood why he was so adamant about them marrying if she got pregnant. Wow. Did this feel like déjà vu to him?

Another woman he didn't love.

The freakishly painful thought made her chomp down on her lip.

Love. *Pfft.* What was it anyway? Love baffled her, not that she'd had much practice.

Debbie withheld the emotion from her children and let fantasy-love chip away at her life until nothing was left.

She loved Sam and Ginny, so at least there was that. They were family.

But oh, how she loved Matty. Loved him desperately. Until he came along, she'd known nothing but soul-piercing loneliness and an unhappiness that clung to her skin like a damp, wool blanket.

Oh well. Pondering her lack of love and what it meant, if anything, was best left to another time.

"Why aren't you angry?" she asked curiously.

She understood masks and how everyone wore one. What people saw and the reality of her inner life were very different things. The same was true of everyone.

The glimpse behind Roman's mask triggered an unusual response from her. It would be stupid to pretend she didn't like the man. He was easy on the eyes and had a sexual hotness factor that boiled water.

He rubbed her arms up and down. The warmth from his casual touch moved her in a different way than before. As their unexpected relationship played out, she dragged her feet but reached a conclusion none-the-less. She cared for him. The admission meant every simple touch and smile struck chords of emotion hidden away deep inside.

His head ducked for a moment, and then he met her gaze. "There's enough anger in the world without me adding to it."

"I don't know what to say," she told him. "And I just want to…"

Pressing hands to her heated cheeks, she shook her head with frustration when the words failed her.

"What do you want, Kelly? Tell me."

Oh, my. How to explain the jumble of feelings that she didn't fully understand?

"I um," she grimaced slightly. What she had to say wasn't like her at all but the words were clamoring to be said, so she did. "I want to make the sadness go away. I want you to be happy, Roman."

He seemed startled and let out a harsh breath. Undoing her ponytail, he spread his fingers into her hair and shook it out. With his hands buried and holding fast to her head, he pulled her toward him.

"You already have, and I am, Carina. For the first time in forever, I am."

She rushed headlong into the swirling deluge of need his lips inspired when he took her mouth by storm.

Was he saying that she helped his sadness go away? That she brought happiness to his life?

She gave the kiss her all.

He grabbed her hips and held her tight against him. Nothing quite compared to a good man-straddle. Not that she'd straddled any man except the one on whose lap she was gyrating.

They went at it like that for a few minutes before Roman took her hair and gently yanked her back far enough for their mouths to separate. They remained briefly connected through a ribbon of saliva.

"Matty," he ground out. His chest rose and fell with deep, rapid breaths.

Panting and desperate for air, she sucked in a huge lungful of oxygen, held and then blew it out. He kneaded her shoulder softly and pushed her hair away. His smile melted into a knowing smirk.

"Shut up," she said, laughing.

"I didn't say a word," he quipped.

"This parenting thing sucks sometimes."

Shocked eyes met shocked eyes, and then they dissolved into a fit of giggles that she tried to quiet by pressing her face into his neck. His big, solid chest vibrated with laughter.

"Well shit," he eventually croaked. "If I'm up for the role of dad the least the kid could do is let me call him Matty. The Matthew thing is getting old."

She caressed his bearded jaw and chuckled. "You need me to explain this? Really? I mean, after all, I'm just a girl."

"Just a girl? For real? Oh, we're definitely revisiting the spanking thing," he drawled. "So tell me oh wise one, what am I missing?"

She tugged his earlobe. "Think, fancy man. What was the very first thing he said to you?"

Roman scratched his beard and thought. "Uh, he declared himself man of the house."

"Right. So a kid that never spoke to strangers takes one look at you and promptly states his status. He's the m-a-n. Got it yet?"

"Not really."

She jokingly smacked her forehead. "Unbelievable. Okay, big guy. Here goes. He's marking his territory. Isn't that what happens when a new alpha appears? I mean it's obvious the kid likes you. Shit. It's all Roman all the time since you showed up. But he has a responsibility as man of the house, right? Maybe when he's sure, you'll get the pass."

"What's he need to be sure of?"

Only an idiot wouldn't see this for what it was. "That you aren't going to hurt me."

"Ohhh."

Kelly folded onto his broad chest and snuggled close. "We have to tell him what's coming. Sam shooed him away, so he didn't hear us making arrangements with Bobby to take over the land."

It felt so good when he wrapped her in a fierce hug. "The timing is one hundred percent your call, love. I told you. Nothing happens without you being on board. You'll tell him when you're ready."

She heard what he wasn't saying. Roman was a patient man. He was giving her all the time and space she needed to come to grips with everything on her plate. She was his priority and Matty, while important, was secondary.

It occurred to her that a ruthless man would have used Matty to manipulate the reaction he wanted.

This Roman Bishop was…an unusual man.

She made a snap decision.

"I don't want to drag things out. The decision is made. Lingering only creates doubt. And fear."

Very very quietly, he explained what would happen once she gave the go-ahead.

"We'll drive to Amarillo from here and spend the night in a hotel. Liam is arranging a private jet."

"What? Why? No!"

"I know, I know," he groused. "But here's why. Both of you are a security nightmare. Your paperwork is a mess. No fucking way are we getting on a commercial flight without iron-clad identification. And driving will take forever. Matty might like the adventure on day one or two but five or six days in and he'll be bouncing off the walls."

"I don't like it," she snapped. Pursing her lips, she flipped her hair and bit a nail. "The expense makes me uncomfortable."

"I'm sorry babe, but it can't be helped. The bottom line is this. Liam doesn't live in a world of price checks, and once we clean up your legal status, you'll be in the same boat. Resisting facts creates unnecessary struggle."

She huffed out an angry breath and wiggled off his lap. "Why the hell do you always have to make sense?"

He grinned. "Because I'm the m-a-n."

"Oh great," she laughed. "Outnumbered."

"Don't worry," Roman said with a huge smile. "Just wait till you meet Rhiann. Being outnumbered is child's play to her!"

Things were changing at an unbelievably fast pace. Worry unleashed a dull ache in her middle. She arched slightly for relief. More than anything she hoped she didn't disappoint.

This was Matty's chance at a real life. Whatever doubts and fears she clung to had to take a back seat to what was best for him.

Chapter Seventeen

They left three days later. When it was time to drive away from the house, she didn't look back.

Knowing what her limitations were, she asked Sam and Bobby to wait until they'd cleared the county before heading to the property. An emotional farewell with Sam and turning the keys over to Bobby were both things she'd rather not deal with, and she absolutely didn't want Matty to see her break down.

In the end, it was a tense morning made worse by the universe having a laugh at their expense the night before.

Long after Matty was packed and asleep, dreaming of the glorious adventure ahead, she and Roman made love long into the night.

Not the energetic, raunchy fuck-a-thons they were so good at. On that occasion they clung to each other in the darkness, sharing their feelings and emotions. It was beautiful and heartfelt.

Until…until after a particularly draining coupling when she felt like she'd given him everything plus some, Roman was busy being his wonderful self in the aftermath when he lost his shit in spectacular fashion.

After throwing the covers back, he stood up and let loose with a horrified sounding gasp. "Oh my god, Kelly. Look."

She lifted her head and glanced his way. His body looked like a crime scene. Seeing splotches of blood made her shoot up in bed so fast her head swam for a second. Her initial thought was, 'What the?' followed by, 'Oh wait.'

After some quick math, she gave a dismissive, no big deal wave and told him, "Guess I got my period."

His stunned expression was going to stay with her forever. Did he not know about things like periods? Men were so thick. She had no way of backing the thought up, but she was pretty sure there wasn't a female alive who hadn't been awakened unexpectedly by cramps or found herself washing bloody sheets.

For a guy who survived a war, his horrified reaction was all sorts of funny.

It didn't get better from there.

For her, it was a simple practical matter. Clean up and move on. He, on the other hand, was in full male-meltdown within minutes. She had to wonder if he'd ever been around a woman who had her period. He didn't act like a guy with much experience with these things. Mostly he ran around trying to make things better. Jesus. She got her period. She hadn't lost a limb.

And now he was nothing short of a major grump.

"We should stop for lunch," Roman muttered at the same time Matty announced from the back of the extended truck cab that he had to pee.

Looking at Roman, she told him, "I need to dig around in my bag."

"What do you need?" he asked.

"Oh, you know," she answered. "Girl stuff."

"Where's your purse?"

"What? Purse?" She laughed. "Never had one. Don't need to lug around anything that won't fit in a pocket."

A solid wall of uncomfortable silence greeted her remark.

Pulling into a McDonald's, he found a parking spot on the right side of the building and explained in that professorial way he had that all McDonald's bathrooms were always on the right.

Matty, who was just learning the difference between left and right, found this tidbit of information highly illuminating.

"Kiki makes me use the girl's room when we go to the diner."

With an uncomfortable blank expression, he told Matty not to worry, that he'd escort him to the men's room.

She was pawing through her duffle and mumbling to herself when Roman came to her side. A quick look around showed her that Matty was patiently waiting at the door to the fast food place.

"Can I help?" he asked.

"Back off," she snarled.

The more she thought about it, the pissier she got. He'd been a huge dick about what happened, and the only conclusion she could piece together was that he was annoyed that his sex life just got put on hold.

Jerk.

"Hey! What the hell, lady. Lighten up why don't you?"

"Stuff it, fancy man. You've been a horse's ass all morning. I'm sorry that your pussy privileges got yanked but boo fucking hoo. Don't take it out on me and news flash buster. I feel like shit so how 'bout you be the one to lighten up."

He stomped away, took Matty's hand and led him into the restaurant.

She found what she was searching for, shoved it into the pocket of her jeans and followed them.

Not only did she have back cramps and a headache, but she also hated fast food.

Great.

Roman studied his reflection in the restroom mirror. He looked the same but man he sure didn't feel like himself.

Taking Kelly and Matty away from the only life they'd ever known, even though the leaving was inevitable, was harder than he'd thought it'd be. For him. The time he'd spent in the tiny house tucked far from the bustling civilization he was accustomed to ended up transforming his life. He'd been enjoying himself, dammit.

But once the clock ticked all the way down and it was time to leave, it was him who faltered. The weight of everyone else's expectations drove him to his knees.

Liam.

Rhiann.

Kelly.

Matty.

Even Sam and Ginny.

Was he doing the right thing? For her? Maybe Liam was out-of-line for insisting they were family. His family.

That's part of what was bothering him. Even though it made no rational sense at all, Kelly and Matty had become his family. Not Liam's. He wasn't an idiot. This simple fact was going to be something of a problem.

The rest was a matter between him and his conscience. After he had climbed down off the ledge from thinking they were in need of an emergency room visit after being bloodied, he felt the crushing squeeze of disappointment.

The grim face of his reflection was a great indication of significant inner turmoil.

He was disappointed.

Jesus.

Disappointed that a girl who was too young for him, that he'd known for less than a couple of weeks, wasn't pregnant. Wasn't knocked up. Wasn't going to have his kid.

What the hell was wrong with him?

The air dryer was so loud in the small space that he couldn't think and a good thing too because his attention needed to be on Matty. He had to remember that everything they saw and did was new to him.

When they left the men's room and passed through the small dining room, Matty stopped to stare at the big flat screen on the wall playing Sponge Bob cartoons. His interest lasted ten seconds, and then he shrugged and looked at Roman.

Roman shrugged back. "I know, right?"

Kelly was coming from the ladies' room, saw them and walked over. He knew that she wasn't a big fan of TV. Not for Matty. She controlled the boy's screen access with an iron fist that he found easy to applaud.

"I'm hungry, Kik."

Kelly looked at him. He looked at her. He saw an apology in her expression. The same one he was sure she saw on his face. He didn't want to argue or make this any harder for her than it was.

Clearing his throat, he said, "Hamburger okay? I'll go order."

"Yay! Hangaburger," Matty squealed.

"With milk," Kelly chimed in. "No soda."

"What about you," he asked. "Feel like eating?"

She held up her finger and crooked it for him to move closer and catch her whisper. "Um, can you just make the decisions? I'm having a hard time, and…"

He silenced her with a swift, publically acceptable kiss. "Take Matty and grab a booth. Away from the TV. On the other side, near the window. You leave everything to me."

"Thank you."

Her small voice had the unmistakable shakiness of someone near his or her breaking point.

"Beverage preference, Carina?"

"Tea. Do they have tea? Tea would be good."

She was charmingly unsure of herself in the new surroundings. He'd be wise to remember that as they went forward.

They lingered in the booth for a long time. He made no moves to hurry anyone up so they could get back on the road. This wasn't a sprint to the finish line. Slow and steady would win in the end.

"Oh hey, look," he chuckled when it dawned on him that they had Wi-Fi and phone service now. Retrieving his phone, he went to the pictures and brought up the shots Rhi sent of the loft.

"Here's my place. Check it out!"

Matty and Kelly leaned across the table and peered intently at the first photo.

Laughingly, he pointed out the obvious. "Not that you should care about the bathroom, but here ya' go."

"Wooooow," Matty mumbled. "Is that a bathtub?"

"Yep. Rhiann calls it a soaking tub." He rolled his eyes to let them know what he thought of the term. On a quiet aside to Kelly, he added, "Tile shower big enough for two."

She blushed and gave him the cutest stink eye ever.

"Here's the kitchen," he said next.

Matty giggled. "What's in all the cabinets?"

"Stuff," Roman quipped.

The next photo showed the living room and fireplace. "My favorite chair," he pointed out.

"Look at the books Kiki!"

"Matthew. This will be your room. You can decorate it however you want."

Both of them sat forward to inspect the picture. A rectangular room with an enormous high window at one end, it had hardwood floors, and all of the walls were exposed red brick.

He felt like a realtor as he extolled the perfection of the small room. "Plenty of space for a bedroom suite and a desk. And look," he said scrolling quickly to another picture, "I use this as a little den area. We can set this space up with your toys and stuff. Cool, huh?"

"Where's Kiki's room?"

Oh shit. Uh....

He flipped to the shot of the master and looked at Kelly. Her face had the same oh shit expression.

"Well big guy, here's the thing. Only two bedrooms, so Kelly has to bunk with me."

Matty eyed him skeptically. "Lemme see."

Now, in his defense, he only balked for a nanosecond. Not because he was afraid there'd be a flashing neon sign over the bed declaring him an unabashed dominant, but because he wasn't sure how much the kid needed to know. For someone about to turn four he handled himself like an adult, but what the hell could he possibly know about what went on between the sexes?

The kid eyeing the picture acted like an art expert looking for signs of fakery. He studied the four-poster bed and simple furnishings for what seemed like a dog's age. Finally, the boy looked at him and then turned to Kelly.

"The bed looks big enough, Kik. It is, right?"

She was studying the picture too. Did she envision being tied, spread-eagle, to the four posts? God, he hoped so.

"Seems okay," she murmured.

"Hey," Matty blurted out a bit louder than necessary. "Are you Kiki's boyfriend?"

Kelly nearly jumped out of her skin, but he stepped in and settled the whole thing. There weren't going to be any more secrets. Not if he could help it.

"Yep!" he crowed. "Can you believe it?"

"That's so cool. Is that why she's always kissing you? Where'd you learn how, Kik?"

Roman's barking laugh couldn't be helped. The stupefied look on her face was that funny.

"Excuse me," he drawled with an affronted huff. "I taught her. And she's good at it too."

"Roman," Kelly snapped. Her brows bumped together in censure, but he just grinned.

Matty wasn't letting it go. "But I thought boys did the kissing."

Kelly groaned and hid her face in her hands.

"Not if he finds the right girl."

The factual comment earned a kick in the shins that made him jump.

But just like that the kid shifted to an entirely different topic and shut down further conversation.

"May I have a cookie now?"

Roman picked up the single-serve milk and shook it. "Sucked it dry," he exclaimed at the same time that he gave Matty a high five across the table. Then they looked expectantly at Kelly.

Ever the über efficient, practical one, Kelly's forehead puckered as she barked instructions. Jumping through her hoops was fun. He liked the bossy miss thing she had going on. When they were alone, all that energy got channeled into other things. Demanding things without the bossy edge.

Squaring her shoulders, she laid down the law. "You're on restroom duty," she told him. "Face and hands. For real. Not a quick pass under the water."

To Matty, she said, "Potty first and then wash up. Tuck in your shirt, too. I want to see two gentlemen walking to the car. Got it?"

Like it was scripted, he and Matty saluted her in unison before doing as they were told. At the door to the men's room, he held it open so the boy could scamper inside. Roman peered across the open space to Kelly waiting by the trashcan. The look of love on her face tugged at his heart.

For Matty? Absolutely, but holy god did he ever hope that at least some sliver was reserved for him.

The rest of the road trip wasn't nearly as tense. Or silent. When they'd sat down to eat, he'd all but forced her to take an analgesic to ease her discomfort. She'd tried a snotty put-down but he persisted and won in the end. It blew his mind that popping some ibuprofen when she had her period wasn't an automatic. Then he remembered who he was dealing with. Her first aid kit was stocked for major emergencies, not boo boos or aches and pains.

She wasn't chatty, but the go-fuck-yourself vibe wasn't shooting from her eyes like solar flares anymore.

He gave a hasty glance over his shoulder. Matty was conked out in a kid sprawl. His eyes shifted to the female next to him. Kelly scratched her chin and smoothed her hands down the buttons of her shirt. She appeared oblivious to everything, but he knew different.

"Mind if I ask something?" he asked softly.

Fiddling with a button, she murmured, "Sure." The delivery sounded nonchalant, but he knew about these things, and she was anything but.

"Why haven't you told Matty about Liam?"

Her answer was emphatic and immediate. "I have told him."

"Hon, saying there's a friend of mine I want you guys to meet isn't in the same ballpark as saying hello to your older brother."

"I know what I'm doing."

A weatherman needed to whip out the windchill gauge because the frosty blast coming from her side of the truck cab was quite chilling.

"Care to let me in on what it is that you're doing?"

"Can't you just trust me?"

If she needed reassurance, he'd give it, but she had to recognize the flip side of the coin.

"I trust you completely. You know I do. I'm dead serious about turning around if you decide you can't do this. But what about you trusting me? We're on the same side. All I'm saying is don't shut me out. Maybe I can help."

He'd never been this open, this straightforward, or been this fearlessly confident. Being all those things was important.

"I'm a rotten sharer, I know. But being sorry about not knowing how to be a lover or a friend is a waste. I've never had friends. Confiding in someone isn't on my list of things to do because it's not an option. Or it wasn't an option. This stuff is hard for me. I know it shouldn't be, but it is."

"Is that your way of saying it's you and not me?"

"Yes. And because I can't say sorry I have to ask you not to be mad."

"I'm not mad at all, but now that you've explained a little I am going to let you know when it feels like you're shutting me out."

Since reading body language was a big part of an interrogator's skill set he noticed everything. She shifted in her seat and angled her body toward him.

"Oh god," she grunted. "Will there be rules? There will, won't there? The saucy smirk she threw out felt like a gift. A wicked challenge.

"Nice try."

She gave him an innocent look.

"Now that you brought it up, you're damn straight there are going to be rules. But don't distract me. I asked a question."

"Oh fine," she bit out. Plucking imaginary lint off her sleeve, she started spelling it out.

"If I all of a sudden one day pop up and say we've got a brother, he's going to think I knew all along. I don't want his future dragged apart by suspicion. Secrets like that almost torpedoed my life. I can't have that for Matty. So, he gets the truth."

The truth? *Hmm.* What was the truth from her standpoint? He was intrigued.

"He has to be the one. Not me. Let him explain. There's no way I'm taking that on. He knew. We didn't. I'm done being a pawn in anybody's game."

A smile tugged at the corners of his mouth. She was so much like Liam that it was scary. Her temperament was eerily similar, only from a shit-kicking female point-of-view. Rhiann was going to adore this girl.

But not as much as he did.

"We'll be in Amarillo in the next hour. Do you care where we stay?"

She sighed and scrunched up her face. "Remember the part about you making the decisions? Come on. Cut me a break."

"Well in that case," he teased, "no snide remarks from the peanut gallery about what I decide."

"One request though if you don't mind. Please don't put me in a situation that will be uncomfortable."

"Aw, hon. Relax," he told her with grinning authority. "We're road tripping not hanging out at the Four Seasons. You'll see. We'll blend in, and no one will look at us twice."

"Good."

She had more to say. There was hesitation and an unfinished quality to her single word statement. But she held her tongue, and in a way he was glad.

Considering himself a man of the world, he had a pretty clear idea of what was bothering her. Flannel shirts and heavy boots in Oklahoma versus what she imagined New York City was like. And she wasn't all that wrong, but he was counting on Rhiann to step in and handle that whole thing. After all, she had several years in the fashion business under her belt and was the undisputed fashionista of her three equally gorgeous sisters. Easing Kelly from the woods to the concrete jungle of Manhattan was a task she was more than capable of handling.

When the first sign for the Amarillo exits appeared, she sat up straighter and gave the countryside her attention.

"It's so flat," she murmured.

Deciding on a Holiday Inn Express on the outskirts of town, he got them checked into adjoining rooms and had their overnight stuff loaded onto a cart while Kelly woke Matty up and got him situated.

He was all wide-eyed and amazed as they entered the cheerful lobby and made their way to the elevator. When it dinged, and the gleaming stainless steel doors opened, Matty froze.

"It's an elevator," Roman told him. "Come on. It's fun. There's a button you can push." He held out his hand, and Matty cautiously transferred from Kelly to him. He felt like a million god damn dollars when the little boy took his hand.

Shoving the luggage cart in and to one end of the mirrored car, he helped Kelly with a gentlemanly hand and kept Matty close.

"We're on the third floor so push this button young man," he directed with a pointed finger.

The elevator moved smoothly upward. Though Kelly's face was blank and unreadable, she seemed okay. He was so new at this he didn't know what to react to and what to let slide.

Never had a highway hotel been viewed more positively or as enthusiastically as this HI Express. Matty reacted as though their rooms were at the Taj Mahal. Roman didn't know it was possible to say wow that many times.

He led them around the basic room and explained everything. Showed them the nearly hidden refrigerator, pointed out the coffee pot and played around with the hair dryer.

The personal toiletries fascinated Matty, but it didn't prevent him from grumbling about the lack of smelly soap. Kelly sprang into action, ripped apart the largest of their duffles and produced a pump bottle of hand soap carefully secured in a plastic bag. With some adorable flourish, she saved the day, and he was aware yet again that this transition wasn't going to be easy.

Sometimes simplicity is an end rather than a beginning. Having a lot of stuff didn't make a bit of difference at the end of the day. This random thought brought Adam Ward to mind.

Now there was a man with a lot of stuff. He lived for his stuff. The more stuff he had, the happier he was. The man lorded his stuff over everyone like somehow that made him a better man. For men like Ward, stuff was the symbol of his moral lapses. He was the Gollum of stuff. It was all precious and his.

Liam deprived Adam Ward of his stuff. It took time, but there was no argument that when all was said and done, the score was Liam Ashforth twenty-five, as in million, and Ward? He was left with a sum less than one. And he'd taken the man down with cruel disregard coupled with a viciousness that earned Liam a wide berth in the business world.

Kelly, on the other hand, was the queen of anti-stuff. Her whole existence was built on a single point—what is the function of stuff? If the answer wasn't concrete, immediate and practical, she moved on.

Oh, and he'd discovered that persuading her to take another look was a huge waste of time. Once she had her mind made up, that was it.

He pointed out the extra pillows and made a huge production of explaining the entertainment options. Kelly's immediate scowl was as predictable as the hard-on it triggered, so he was ready for her when she tried to shut him down.

In truth, he admired her resolute determination to raise Matty as a real, live boy and not a Nielson audience subject. There was no disputing the advantages of growing up in the natural world. The wonders found along a stream winding through the woods or a tire swing hanging from a tree limb in the yard nourished a curious mind far better than a game controller or an HD movie with surround-sound.

He would know, after all. That's how he and his siblings were raised. It wasn't a mistake or a quirk or a coincidence that he was well-read and a life-long student of philosophy. To him, losing one's self in deep thought had as much benefit if not more than an award-winning documentary. First hand, immersive experiences helped shape him. Matty would be the same.

Completely riding over the objections he saw forming on her lips, he quickly scrolled through the available listings, found what he was looking for, and brought up the on-demand classical music channel. He was about to point out the bottom left where the current selection's information was displayed when a picture of a cloud-shrouded Bavarian castle played on the screen. Matty's wondrous gasp got his attention.

"Oh, Kiki," he softly exclaimed. "Look! It's your castle."

Kelly looked at the TV, smiled and ruffled the boy's hair. "That's a good one," she joshed. "Bet it takes forever to sweep the floors, though, huh?"

They cracked up laughing over the obvious inside joke. This wasn't the first time he'd heard Matty speak of castles and Kelly in the same breath. The boy was obsessed with his Kiki having a castle. Next to dinosaurs and Mickey Mouse? Castles. Not knights or kings and queens—just the building itself.

Unlatching the door connecting their room to his, he hurried next door and did the same on the other side. When both doors were fully open, he made a big deal of the fact that this was how it was going to be from now on. The three of them. Together.

"This way," he announced, "you can curl up in your very own bed while Kelly and I hang out in the other room. Isn't that cool?"

He caught Kelly's curious gaze from the corner of his eye. Didn't require a cheat sheet to tell him that she was thinking about the sleeping arrangements. They'd get to that later. First things first.

"So look guys, I don't know about you, but I'm starving. How about if we do this? Let's take half an hour to get organized and then let's hit up the Applebee's we passed a few miles back. Sound good?"

What he got back were blank stares.

It took a minute for his mind to catch up. Right, right, he thought with a brief nod. Transitions.

"Applebee's is a family restaurant. Great kids' menu," he told them, although he had no fucking idea what he was talking about. "Trust me. You'll like it."

One dark-haired head and the other dirty-blonde bobbed up and down. What did that mean? Were they on board with the suggestion? It was a bitch trying to read these two when everything coming their way was new and unfamiliar.

He lifted the big, heavy duffle Kelly packed and placed it on the luggage stand. The two smaller overnight backpacks he put on the bed. The cookies she kept in an old tin box decorated with Christmas scenes he shoved under his arm.

"I'm keeping these." With a pointed look and a winking smirk, he teased Matty. "She counted them, ya' know. So we can't sneak even one without her knowing."

Matty belly-laughed and hopped up and down on his toes. "Ya' have ta' be good to get a cookie."

"Oh, I can be very good," he growled.

Kelly laugh snorted and then tried to cover up with a large-and-in-charge vibe that always snagged Matty's attention.

"Take your PJs out and lay them on the bed. Then scoot into the bathroom and wash up. Roman's right. I'm starving so let's get a move on." She clapped her hands twice, barked "Chop, chop," and tucked a stray lock of hair behind her ear. "And get the brush, Matty. You have sleepy-head hair."

When he dashed away, Roman reached for her hand, gave a gentle squeeze and tugged her through the connecting door. The need to kiss her, to taste the sweetness that melted his brain, drove him hard.

She got there first when his arms enfolded her into a brutish hug. Thinking he'd hold her close and kiss her senseless, he was taken by pleasant surprise by how swiftly she turned the tables. And she whimpered when begging for his mouth. How fucking cool was that?

It was her kiss from the start, and he was happy to let her lead. Hell, he encouraged her every step of the way. How she went about doing the ravishing was nothing short of hot. The girl knew what she liked, knew what she wanted, and didn't hold back. But he was sharply aware that they had an audience and that there were practical considerations he needed to bear in mind so he did what he could to keep things from spiraling out of control.

Her stomach growled on cue, providing him with the perfect out. She wasn't happy about it but let him end the kiss and gently separate their over-heated bodies. When her head tilted so she could glare at him, he chuckled at the venomous look in her eyes.

"You get scary mean when you're hungry."

He meant the comment to be funny. Her initial expression suggested a total lack of humor and then she broke out a big smile.

"Guilty," she said, her face brightening with amusement. "And in the interest of full disclosure—fair warning. It's worse at certain times of the month. Chalk it up to things you should know."

"Ah," he chuckled. Screwing up his face he chortled, "Thank you for the foot note."

Her eyes sparkled, and she wet her lips. "Anything I should know? Secret toothpaste fetish? Wearing socks to bed?"

The murmured silliness charmed the pants right off him. "Socks in bed? Sacrilege and you already knew the answer. As for hints and hacks for the care and feeding of a Bishop, I suggest starting with the basics."

She giggled quietly and smirked. "Oh god. Bishop basics. Can't wait to hear what's involved."

"Hey now," he teased. "You asked!"

"I know, I know," she chuckled. "It's my own damn fault. Well, go on then. Clue me in on these so-called basics."

He pressed her against the wall with his body and ground his twenty-four-seven erection into her belly. After a quick nip to her earlobe, he whispered on a growl, "Basic number one. Morning hard-on. Heads or tails if you catch my drift."

She instantly colored. Kelly was an enthusiastic, curious and oh-so-very-eager and willing student of the oral arts. They were still on page one but she was an avid and quick learner who he was sure would test his control in a thousand ways.

"You on top though is the A.M. default setting."

"Sounds good," she snickered. "I'm told that exercise first thing in the morning is a good thing. A very good thing."

He heaved back and stuck out his hand. She did a double take, laughed and gave him her hand. They shook as if a billion dollar deal was just struck.

"So we're good then? Once a month I'm to expect a voracious female wanting to tie on the feed bag morning noon and night."

"And I'm to ride the Bishop carousel every morning." She gave him a mock frown. "Something doesn't add up here. A couple of days versus every damn morning?"

He held up his hand. "Now hold up there little lady. There's a protocol around the feed bag scenario."

"Is there?" she asked with an arched brow and a good degree of skepticism.

"Yes, there is, and yes, I'm making this up as I go along. But cut a guy a break, would you? I've got a plan, so don't you worry about that."

She shoved him away and physically turned him around. "Get ready. I'm gonna use the bathroom and check on Matty's progress. Oh, and hey!" she called out. He searched her face. "Is this a date? 'Cause if it is, there are proprieties."

"Proprieties?" he huffed on an amused chuckle.

"Yeah. You heard me."

"Understood. Prepare to be dated, Ms. James. Now shoo."

She danced away with a happy laugh.

Sure, why not? He thought. Makes perfect sense. Reverse was an interesting gear but hey, whatever works. First fuck followed by being spared an oh-shit pregnancy and then comes the dating. Sounds about right.

Chapter Eighteen

She'd eaten way more than normal and would probably still be gorging on loaded potato skins and sweet tea if Roman hadn't distracted her with belly grabbing laughter. All through dinner he kept up a running commentary of the most random stuff—all of it either wildly inappropriate or beyond hilarious—much to her delight and Matty's amusement.

She found out he liked cigars and that his guy friends had, on more than one occasion, subjected him to eyebrow-singeing encounters with exploding stogies. Matty found the story quite funny.

In a particularly enlightening share, he told them about his fondness for holidays and how his parents made those occasions amazing and special, even though they were dirt poor.

He had a serious patriotic streak too. Matty was mesmerized when the man went off on a tangent about 4th of July parades, being grateful for the sacrifices of the armed forces and showing deference to one's elders.

Out of the blue, he started babbling about getting a dog. Had they been debating pets? No. He just shot out with it. Matty, of course, was quickly on board.

The scene felt oddly routine. As though family discussion and decisions about pets were what they did.

She fiddled with the sugar packets and checked out the glossy card with photos of the daily drink specials.

Roman and Matty left the table for another trip to the men's room. Poor Roman, he was a good sport, but Matty was pushing the envelope. It was hard to figure out what the attraction was. Was it a communal bathroom thing? A health problem she should worry about? Or was it merely the novelty of a guy to do things with?

Kelly shifted uncomfortably. It was childish of her and seriously petty, but she wasn't used to sharing Matty's affections, so the boy's fascination with Roman and the male bonding dynamic made her twitchy.

They were hard to miss on their way through the bar to the table where she waited. Roman was so big and solid that even the most casual observer stopped and stared. He was one yummerific specimen of sexy hotness.

Next to him and held by the hand was a hop-skipping-and-jumping Matty.

One of them was big, dark and imposing.

The other was a blonde haired jumping bean that barely came up to the man's waist.

A wild, untamed animosity exploded in her gut when she noticed a booth full of girls around her age who were making no effort to hide the blatant ogling and damn near catcalls that Roman's swaggering virility inspired.

She harrumphed and sat back heavily. Stupid girls. She eyed them, her forehead creased with dislike. Who were they kidding? Having experienced Roman's powerful sexuality first-hand, she highly doubted any of the four flirtatious females had what it took to satisfy the man's appetite.

Perhaps as a group, but that thought set off a firestorm of possessive jealousy that brought out her snippy side.

"Sit down," she grumbled when they got to the table. "You're moldy ass is attracting flies."

Roman looked back at the booth of rowdy women and snickered. "Ooh," he quipped. "Is an ass-kicking about to go down?"

Matty was scrambling into the booth and cracked up at his BFF's snarky comment. "Penny jar!" he crowed.

They decided to share a death-by-chocolate dessert. With three spoons on the attack, the gooey lava cake didn't last long. The chocolate on chocolate on chocolate deliciousness was her undoing. So much so that she let Matty indulge his three-year-old sweet-tooth, something she worried would be a regret later.

On the way back to the hotel, they stopped at a convenience store and ended up leaving with a bag of Texas souvenirs. They also had a sack full of snack foods that boggled her mind. Coming from a life of homemade, the sheer variety and availability of nutritionally empty crap was eye-opening.

Back in their rooms, she produced her bag of Matty tricks, and they settled in for a rousing game of Candyland. If there was ever a Candyland tournament, Matty would clean up in his age group and probably make the adult competitors nervous. He had an uncanny ability to focus for long stretches. Where others his age might start bouncing off the walls after a minute or two, he held a distinct advantage.

Bath time was a full-on production due to the unusually large tub. She loved Matty's boyish enthusiasm and was proud of how well he was handling the changes. Sure, it had only been one day, but he was different already. Now that he talked non-stop to Roman, the floodgates holding back his communication skills opened and a deluge poured out. It was what she hoped would happen when it was time for him to go to school. That he went from purposely mute to a non-stop chatterbox overnight without any effort at all had to be a by-product of his young age. He didn't know how desperate she'd been for him to converse with other people.

"*Sammy and the Dinosaurs*," Matty squealed with delight when she pulled his favorite storybook from the bag. He ran to the sofa and jumped onto the cushions, smacking his hand on the empty spot next to him. She started to take her usual place until Matty asked if Roman could do the reading.

Thwarted yet again by the bond forming between the two she gave in only to end up on one side of Roman as Matty took up the other because although he agreed to narrate the story, Roman insisted she provide the sound effects.

He knew she was having an emotionally hard time. His thoughtfulness touched her.

When the story ended, she pulled a stack of homemade flash cards from her satchel of goodies and tossed them to Roman.

"Can you two boys behave while I shower and change?"

Matty yawned and nodded yes. Roman smirked.

She high tailed it into the privacy of the big tiled bathroom before she made a fool out of herself.

The shower was as fantastic as the tub, and she threw herself into a head to toe scrubbing. Tearing open a package of cheap razors she'd grabbed months ago at the Dollar Store, she sat down on the tile bench at the back of the stall and shaved her legs. Instead of using the shampoo and conditioner she brought with her, she cracked open the hotel stuff and had a grand old time washing her hair.

At that precise moment, life was good. She wasn't worried about whether the hot water would hold out or how long she lingered beneath the spray. And a good thing too, because her lower back was on fire and the cramps making her miserable were driving her to the edge.

Reluctantly and only because she felt like a water pig, Kelly ended the shower and toweled off.

She picked up the plastic bottle of hotel body lotion, flipped the cap and took a sniff. *Mmm*. Almonds and vanilla.

In no time at all the little bottle was empty after being repeatedly slapped against the palm of her hand to get every drop.

Her hair was next. Briskly rubbing the towel on her head to draw off as much water as possible, she used the unfamiliar hair dryer and ended up with a cascade of soft, bouncy curls.

Pulling on a pair of sweats, some pink socks and a baggy sweater, she tidied up and paused for a final glimpse in the mirror. Deciding that what she saw was the best she could do, Kelly flipped off the light and headed back to the room.

Roman and Matty were on the bed by the window, playing a speed round with the flashcards she made. When his phone went off, he looked at her and made an apologetic wince. "Sorry. Do you mind?" He handed her the flashcards and went into the next room to take the call.

It won't be long before I'm carrying a phone too. The sudden thought made her flinch. Things were changing. Fast. Crying about it wasn't going to make one bit of difference so she might as well get with the program.

Concerned by the flat, dry tone Liam was using, Roman had to listen carefully to what wasn't being said as he relayed details for the flight tomorrow. He wasn't looking forward to explaining how Kelly was handling Matty and the subject of their shared DNA, but the guy needed to know.

"I don't think that's such a good idea," he responded when Liam started issuing demands.

"All right," his sometimes boss and all-the-time friend griped. "I've had enough. Somebody better tell me what the fuck is going on before I lose it. When did you become th person in charge, Roman? And what the hell does Rhiann know that I don't?"

Boom. No dancing around—straight to the point. Typical. He was tempted to call Kelly in and say, 'Hey, wanna hear a male version of what you sound like when you're an asshole?'

How should he answer Liam's questions? He just didn't know. Gripping the back of his neck, he went and stood by the window looking out over a whole lot of night time nothing.

They'd always dealt with each other directly and with a minimum of bullshit. It was Roman's requirement when he agreed to take on security for the CEO of BPG. He didn't have time for word games and power plays. Luckily, neither did the man hiring him.

"Okay, look. Bottom line. I'm closer to this situation than you are so I have no problem telling you that being a dick isn't helpful. I can't juggle your butt-hurt and their confusion and worry at the same time, so cut me a fucking break."

He swore he heard Kelly's soft snicker at his little outburst.

"Fuck you, Bishop. That's my goddamn sister and brother you're cock-blocking, and if you don't tell me why I promise you a scene that none of us ever forget. Understood?"

"Yeah," he murmured. "About that. You might want to sit down."

"Ah, Jesus. Come the fuck on man. Now what?"

He had an idea and asked if Rhi was there. Liam's grumbling response was funny.

"What did I tell you about managing me via my fiancée? Cut it the fuck out."

"Yes sir, Mr. Ashforth, sir," he snarkily replied. "Now shut up and put this call on speaker. She needs to hear this too."

There was grumbling, a few pithy 'motherfuckers' uttered, some shuffling, and then Rhi's voice joined in.

"Roman Bishop. What have I told you about riling him up?"

He heard the affection and teasing in her voice and smiled.

"Oh dear lord," he groaned into the phone with long-suffering emphasis. "Will you two please give it a rest? You know damn well he riles himself up, plus he's a playacting baby because you manage him while you're sleeping and his big, bad ego can't handle being pussy whipped."

Liam barked, "I'm going to fucking kill you."

Rhi was snorting with laughter and shrieking, "Bah! Pussy whipped!"

"What the hell is wrong with you, Bishop?" Liam hollered.

"Ah, so much," he answered drily. "So much."

"Boys!" Rhiann chided. "That's enough. Now you hush," he heard her say bitingly to Liam. "Start talking Roman. You know how he gets…"

Just like he would in a mission debrief, he went with an outline of facts and then added supporting detail.

"She's not telling the boy what's going on because, and I quote, she didn't invite this into their lives."

"Meaning?" Liam's hurt outrage rang through.

"Settle down and let me explain. There's an excellent reason behind her decision. Liam, you two are a lot alike. She doesn't suffer fools. At all. And despite her age, she has a steely determination that served her well considering the surroundings. This girl isn't a fool, and she's not like anyone you've ever met. No lie and not joking."

"I like her already," Rhiann snickered.

Liam's only response was a tersely muttered, "I'm listening."

"She's explained that you're my friend and I've mentioned Rhi. For now, that's all he knows. When I asked why, she gave a smart answer. They have a fierce bond, Liam. Let's call it what it is—in every single way that matters, Kelly is the boy's mother. She's raised him and been his only caregiver since he was barely a toddler. He adores her."

"Shit," Rhiann mumbled. "You're making me cry."

"I realize that from the outside looking in she's just a girl, but Kelly Anne James is more badass woman and fiercely so than anyone I've ever met. I'm not in charge, Liam. Not at all. She makes the decisions for her and Matty. And I promised her that wouldn't change."

"You respect her," he heard Liam say with a touch of amazement that Roman shared.

He laughed. "I'm afraid of her."

Rhiann started to giggle. "Oh wait! Let me guess. She doesn't have time for your alpha shit. Am I right?"

He laughed right along with her. "No she does not, and as a matter of fact she remarked earlier that my ass was moldy and therefore drew flies."

Shrieks of laughter came through the phone. "You bring that girl to me right away, Roman!"

"This is a bit off-topic, isn't it? You're supposed to be explaining why the boy is being kept in the dark."

He could tell the other man had had enough.

"The more time I spend with her, the more I understand what she's been through. If you hated Adam Ward before you will have to find a way to hate him even more."

He had to pause and take a breath when an angry red haze filled his brain.

"You had your mother Liam, but Kelly had no one. Debbie put Ward first until her dying breath. Not only that, the manipulative asshole went out of his way to separate mother and child every fucking year on Kelly's birthday."

Rhi gasped. "Oh my god."

"There's so much more, but you get where this is going, right? For Kelly, things like secrets and lies are deal breakers. She's got a well-honed rant about being a pawn that'll make your stomach gurgle."

"She doesn't want to be the one to tell Matthew. I get it," Rhiann murmured. "She's protecting both of them from something she didn't want. Probably still doesn't want. Am I right?"

Here was the hard and crunchy truth in the middle of a hoped for warm and fuzzy. He nodded at Rhiann's take on things even though she couldn't see him.

"She'll get there, you guys. But we have to give her time. And as far as the boy goes, it's quite simple. She won't lie to him, and she won't pretend. If she announces there's a surprise brother, she worries some day Matthew will wonder if she always knew. If he, just like she was, had been purposely kept in the dark. It's not up to her to explain anything at all. Not as far as she's concerned. You're the one that came looking for her. This one's on you, bro."

"She hates me, doesn't she?" Liam asked.

"She doesn't know you. You can't make a happy family happen

because you say so. On the other side, she can't deny that same family because it's inconvenient."

"What exactly am I supposed to do here? Shit!" Liam barked. "Why the fuck do all of Adam Ward's turd bombs fall on me?"

And that right there was his cue to wrap up the conversation.

"Rhi. You got this?"

"On it. Thanks for being honest."

He winced. Rhiann knew there was still a nugget of honesty he wasn't sharing. He also hoped she understood that he had to do that part in person. He owed Liam a face-to-face. It was the right thing to do.

After Matty had fallen asleep, she crept into the adjoining room and found Roman at the desk with an open laptop and a deep frown. He looked so serious.

Walking toward him she quietly asked, "Is something wrong?"

He had the damn reflexes of a jungle cat, reacting so swiftly she was on his lap before her eyes had a chance to blink.

"Nothing now that you're here."

No response possible or necessary when he crushed her to him and took her mouth with a savage thoroughness that left her panting and breathless.

"Is he asleep?"

She nodded when her senses returned. "Out like a light."

Cradling her with extreme gentleness, she curled into him and sighed. He swiveled them back and forth in the desk chair.

"Wanna watch some TV?"

"No. The news just makes me crazy, and I don't know what shows are good. Maybe another time, though, okay?"

She threw in that last part because it occurred to her that maybe he wanted to turn it on and was being polite by asking. Just because she didn't see the purpose in anesthetizing her mind with junk didn't mean she had the right to be a bitch about it.

His chest rose and fell on a chuckle. "You'll get no argument from me. Didn't you notice from my apartment pictures? No television."

She sat up, smiled and searched his face. "You're serious, aren't you?"

"Mostly," he said with a shrug. "There is a TV. A big one. But it's behind the wood panels above the fireplace."

"Why?"

"Did you see the books?" he asked with a laugh. "I'd rather have a personal library than a stack of DVDs. Although I admit, got a whole cabinet full. Mostly classic movies. Black and white stuff. My friend Cam is a serious movie buff. He turned me on to Cary Grant and guys like him."

"Matty nearly shit a canary when he saw your living room library. He didn't notice the ladders, but I did. We might need to child proof your place."

"He's a great kid, Kelly. Smart as fuck and my god with the grown-up vocabulary. I'm going to clear off a low shelf, and we'll fill it with his books, okay?"

She stated a concern and framed it as a question to see how he'd respond.

"Bedroom decorating, promises of dog adoptions, shelves of books. So, I guess we're living together now?"

His answer surprised her. "Did you think I was going to let you go?"

"I don't know what to think," she admitted candidly. "I've never, well…you know."

A hardness came over his face, and his jaw clenched. She touched a nerve.

"I don't go through life defiling virgins. And as incomprehensible as it may seem, I've never been flat-footed by a twenty-three year old innocent before. However," he grated bitingly, "I'm an adult and knew what I was doing. If this makes me sound like a pig, then so be it but I promise on all that's holy that by the time I was inside you? I'd already decided that you were mine and that no one and nothing was going to take you from me."

She searched his face. "Been there, done that?"

"Yes."

Whoa. That was some revealing shit he just shared. Losing his wife, being denied their child? And now, hearing just how determined he was from the beginning to claim her, she understood him now on an even deeper level.

"I can't force you to be with me, Carina." His big, warm hand caressed her back beneath the sweater. "But that doesn't change the fact that I want you. All the time and not just in bed. And not just in a sexual way."

"If you ever feel crowded or," she shook her head and searched for words. "I don't know, taken over, I guess. You'll say something, right? I don't want to be a burden. I can take care of Matty and me just fine."

His whole demeanor changed. He softened and relaxed. "Can you find it in your heart to take care of me too?"

"What are you saying?"

"Fuck if I know," he answered with a wide-eyed snicker. "I just don't want to lose you. Or Matty."

"He's not going to like us being together."

"Who?" he asked. "Matty? Are you kidding? He's thrilled."

"No," she grumbled. "Him. You know."

Roman swallowed his sigh before it hit the air. The raw, worried sound to her voice warned of bumpy roads ahead.

"Are you referring to he who will never ever be called by name?

She narrowed her eyes and made a face. "Okay fine," she huffed. "Liam. Liam isn't going to like that you're doing his sister. Is that what you wanted me to say?"

His hand moved from the gentle back stroking to cupping a breast. He rolled a nipple between his fingers. She leaned slightly into his touch.

"He knows better than to stick his nose into my private life."

"Did your private life ever involve a family member before?"

"No," he bit out. "But…"

He got tongue-tied and zipped up the rest of his stupid word diarrhea before he made an idiot of himself.

"Oh no you don't," she laughed. "But what?"

He sounded like Matty when he didn't get his way. "I saw you first."

She gawked at him. He squirmed and instantly regretted the movement when she shifted on his lap and enflamed his cock even more.

The gawk turned to a squint. "Is this you clowning me? I can't tell because I think you just implied that since you licked it first, it's now yours. Do I have this right?"

Her voice steadily rose until she was on the edge of…something. He wasn't sure what. It seemed like a toss-up between a fiery bitch-fit or thigh-slappingly funny hysteria.

"So your strategy here is to plant your flag, declare yourself master of all, and that's that?"

"Pretty much," he admitted. "It's a guy thing so don't give the details much thought."

"Are you serious?"

It was way too easy to get her going. "Oh, completely," he assured her with a straight face. "But don't get yer' panties twisted in a knot over it, sweet tits," he drawled in a comical twang."

She reacted with incredulous affront. He almost dumped her off his lap when an explosion of laughter threatened.

"Excuse me?"

The biting retort, the way each syllable was lengthened to convey her outrage—he was one fucked up son-of-a-bitch because these things were music to his ears. He was an interrogator. That level of emotion most definitely implied her emotions were engaged. Hot diggity damn!

"It's the same for the ladies," he continued as though this was a normal conversation. Having a tactile field day with the sweet tits he teased her about kind of killed the premise of normal but hey, who was he to quibble over details?

"Why do women hit the head in pairs? What's the deal with the whole damn tribe trailing after? Is there danger in the ladies' room? These are things that mystify men, but you don't see us convening a listening tour to figure it out."

She slapped her hands atop his with the sweater separating them. Okay. Yellow light. Not red and flashing. Something more along the lines of slow down, dangerous curves ahead. Or even better, slippery when wet.

Oh, wait. Scratch that. Bad timing. And besides, he had a better plan of action for their nocturnal activities. Tonight she was getting a dose of what being taken care of really means when all the layers of daily phooey are stripped away.

She arched a delicate brow and cocked her head. "Did it ever occur in that thick skull of yours that you've got this wrong?"

Wait. Huh? Wrong? What the fuck?

He froze and searched her eyes. He saw, wait. What?

She was fucking laughing at him!

"Dude," she snorted on a hearty chuckle. "Sorry to burst your alpha bubble and all but I did the flag planting first. And if you're laboring under the assumption that to protect your ego I'm going to pretend to be some backwoods Barbie with a bad case of the lady swoons for your sorry ass, well…" her scoff was incredibly sexy.

All the worldly experience Roman imagined he had? Yeah. Screw that. The adorable minx turning him inside out and upside down had no time for his shit and he loved every goddamn second of her feisty push backs. Finding her was a miracle and he'd be damned to the blazing fires of hell for eternity if he let her slip through his fingers.

"And as far as he who doesn't know me and frankly gets no say in what I do, well, he'll have to suck it up. I'm letting this unfold because of you Roman. Because I trust you for some insane reason. Not because I give a flying beer fart about some stranger from the big city and his bags of money."

Well goddamn. That was quite a compliment. Earning this little lady's trust was a humbling feat. Oh god, seriously? Were those tears swimming in his eyes?

She wasn't finished shocking him. With a sweet, slow kiss she gently pushed his hands out of her sweater.

"Um, things you should know. Part two."

He waited.

"The girls are a bit tender," she snickered with surprised awareness.

It was time to get her moving off his lap before he took things too far and tested his composure in dangerous ways.

"You feeling okay otherwise? I know it was tough being cooped up in the truck all day."

"I'm not a once-a-month whiney crybaby if that's what you're asking. Do I have cramps and want to punch puppies in the face? Yes. The shower helped."

"You smell delicious."

She brightened like a searchlight at the throwaway compliment. Sniffing her skin as she shoved a sleeve up her arm, Kelly giggled.

"Almond vanilla! You like?"

Hell yeah, he liked. Shit, she overloaded his senses morning, noon and night. He loved it all. The smells of soap and toothpaste or the fruit shit she shampooed her hair with. Even her sweat hit his senses with a sledgehammer. And the mother of all baselines? The scent of Kelly, the woman. Turned him into a drooling, knuckle-dragging, horny man beast with a hard-on that felt like a one-ton weight strapped to his groin.

The corners of her eyes crinkled. Pushing the waterfall of soft dark curls off her shoulders, Roman contemplated his shifting priorities. She was on her way, if not there already, to being the single most precious thing in his life. He liked it when the smile reached her eyes. Seeing her happiness was immensely satisfying.

"I like you."

He shook his head and gave her a scornful snicker. "I was hoping for something a bit more than just like."

"Well, then you're going to have to try harder."

He busted out with a laugh at the same time that she launched out of his grasp and started stalking the room. "Wish I'd thought to bring a book."

"Hey," he blurted out. "You want a book? I've got books. Come here." He put his hand out, she took hold eagerly and followed him to the luggage rack in the corner where his big bag sat open.

"Let's see," he murmured. His hands located the three books at the bottom and pulled them out one by one.

"*Zen and the Art of Motorcycle Maintenance.*"

She glanced at the cover. "An inquiry into values. *Hmph.* That's a little too cerebral. What else ya' got?"

He smiled. Next, he pulled out a weary, dog-eared and beaten up paperback of *Tom Sawyer*.

"Good stuff," he told her. "This baby has been through a war and back. Friends, boyhood rebellion, superstition, fantasy. It's a life manual."

He meant every word. Tom's story embodied so much of how Roman saw his life.

"And finally, *Seinfeldia.*"

"What's that?"

"Seinfeld? No?" he asked. "Ah, yes. Well. How can I explain a cultural phenomenon about nothing?"

"You're losing me," she snorted.

"It's a TV show that ran from 1989 to 1998. I am a Seinfeld geek," he admitted with a hand raised. "We watched episode after episode when I was overseas. Let me tell you, nothing prepares you for life more than long, rambling, completely sober debates about this show."

She handed him an unbelievable gift when she shoved him playfully with her shoulder and said, "If you're nice and supply popcorn, maybe I'll sit through some episodes. Just to check out what you're talking about."

He totally won this round. Shoving the ratty copy of *Tom Sawyer* into her hands, he jerked his thumb at the sofa and said, "Pick your side, plant your butt and get comfy."

"Why? Where are you going?" she asked when he made for the door.

He gave her a thorough once over and grinned like an idiot. "I've decided that what you need is some pampering and I'm just the man to do it."

She rolled her eyes.

"So I'm headed to the lobby. There's a hot beverage station for guests. Sit back, put your feet up and relax. I'll bring you tea and rub your back while you read."

"Ya' know," she laughed. "All that sounded an awful lot like instructions."

He laughed right back. "Got a problem with that, Carina?"

"Nope," she said with a cocky headshake. "Not at all."

"Cream and sugar?" he asked with his hand on the doorknob.

"Surprise me," she said.

Well alrighty then!

Chapter Nineteen

Her eyes kept drifting shut, and the words swam on the page, but she was way too comfy to give in and go to bed. Not when cuddling with her hunky man while they both read turned out to be such lovely fun.

When he returned from what should have been a simple beverage run she nearly fell over laughing.

"What's this?" she'd asked when he wheeled a cart into the room.

"Well," he confessed with a great deal of self-congratulatory aplomb, "the lady at the front desk chatted me up and next thing I knew I'd told her my wife was kind of miserable from being cooped up in a truck all day with cramps. Apparently saying cramps is some universal signal you ladies use to communicate." He was having a jolly laugh that swept her along. "Next thing I knew she hooked me up with a thermos of hot water, tea bags of all sorts, cream, sugar, honey, lemon. Pretty much a little of everything they had. Plus, a plate of pastries—just in case the chocolate coma from earlier wasn't enough sugar for the day."

She'd clapped her hands and giggled. Then, because verbal burps happen when you're least expecting it, she declared, "I love you!"

"Oh Jesus," he'd laughed. "Don't make this too easy, Carina. It's just tea."

The joke was on him because she truly did love him at that moment for not rubbing her nose in what she said and for taking her motor-mouth flub in stride.

They'd been comfortably curled on the sofa for the past hour, silently reading. Most of the time he had his hand under her sweater, pressed to her lower back and occasionally rubbing in small circles that did a lot to ease her discomfort.

Because he seemed to have some mystical awareness of her physical needs, he'd squashed her dissent in quick order and demanded she take another analgesic. It had helped earlier, so she gave in and did what he asked.

The pain relief, his gentle touch, a belly full of warm tea, *Tom Sawyer* and a comfortable shoulder to lean on sent her to bliss town.

A yawn forced her mouth open wide. She rubbed her nose on his soft cotton shirt. He patted her leg and kissed the top of her hair.

"Hey, sleepyhead. Time for bed?"

"No," she grumbled. Burrowing deeper she murmured, "I like it here."

"Tell you what. You go put on whatever you're sleeping in and get ready, and I'll turn down the bed. When you come back, I'll give you a back rub to help you sleep."

"You want me to sleep here? With you? But I thought because..."

"You thought that I'd make you sleep in another room because fucking you into tomorrow isn't on the menu?"

She jerked at his words. "Ouch. That's a bit harsh don't you think?"

"It's what your overactive brain came up with so save the denials. Here's something you need to know. Despite what you pick up from cultural depictions of today's man, I do not always let my dick do the thinking."

"You have a dirty mouth," she answered with a snarky chuckle.

"And your point would be?"

She dropped the book and wrapped him in her arms. "I'm okay with dirty."

"Whew! Good to know I dodged that bullet."

She reacted without thinking, pressing her fingers to his lips. "No, no. Shh. I don't want that in my head."

His gaze softened. He nodded slightly to show he understood. "Sorry. Warrior humor."

"And I'm sorry for being so…out of my depth with you."

"Having a relationship isn't all fuckery all the time."

She had to laugh. He wasn't trying to be funny but damn! "Don't tell me that," she joked. "I was sort of hoping for some, um…options."

"Says the woman who was just dozing off and yawning like crazy."

"Busted," she chuckled.

"How long does this go on?" he asked.

"You mean having my period? It's okay to say the words, Roman. I'm not a delicate flower who cringes at the sight of blood or who can't handle some gritty with my nitty."

"Oh dear god," he cried on a burst of laughter. "Gritty with your nitty. Rhiann is going to love you. Get ready for your first fangirl."

"You like this woman. A lot."

"Indeed. I thought she was unique. One-of-a-kind. And then I met you. Now I'm sure there's a whole tribe out there of bad ass babes who I swear to god were put on earth for the lofty purpose of keeping men's butts in check."

Good answer. She wasn't nearly as resistant to Rhiann as she was to that other person.

"What's she do? Or is she arm candy?"

"Arm candy? Holy mother of god. No! Not at all. Shit, that's funny, though." He offered a winking grin. "Rhiann Wilde is a writer. At least that's what she told me to say if you asked."

"What the hell does that mean?"

"It means, sweetheart, that she had a good job, a career and a secret life. One day those things crashed headlong into each other.

When the dust settled, the career got kicked to the curb and with Liam's love and support she let her secret life out of the bag. Rhiann collects words like a squirrel gathers nuts. Her superpower is a bad mouth…something you have in common."

Another good answer. She'd keep probing, but her internal timer just went off. It was time to hit the snore pads.

He stood, effortlessly, with her cradled in his arms. What was this wonderful feeling? She wanted to freeze the moment in time so that she could replay it over and over.

Carrying her into the gleaming white tiled bathroom, he sat her carefully on the closed toilet. His hand lingered on her face, caressing a cheek and lightly tracing her lips. How could such a big man be so gentle?

"We share everything, Carina. Even the bathroom. Don't try to hide with Matty."

Aw. He was awfully cute. "Uh, okay."

"What would you like to wear to bed? Tell me, and I'll bring it to you."

Hey, she thought. Hold on a minute. This waiting on her hand and foot was all kinds of interesting. She might like letting his bad self be in charge. His manly psyche would certainly like the chance.

"Can I have your t-shirt?"

He did an adorable double-take and scraped his fingers through his hair. "Um, uh…any t-shirt or one in particular?"

She eyed the long sleeve Henley he wore and inclined her head. "What you have on will do."

There was a slight pause, and then he drew in a long breath that made his chest expand. After that, he pulled the shirt from his waistband and hauled it over his head. When he handed it off, her waving hand missed it by a mile because her attention diverted to his mind-blowingly muscular torso.

Laughing, he bent to retrieve the fallen shirt, stood up and pretended to wipe drool off the corner of her mouth then asked with a smirking grin, "Have you ever had a cat?"

A cat? What the hell was he going on about?

"Some will tell you that cats aren't trainable. They're wrong. All you need is a squirt gun. Every time kitty wanders off or gets into mischief, a quick squirt or two brings them right back into line."

Kelly blinked. Seriously. What was he dithering about?

"You give so much away with your face, Carina. I think it's adorable. And hot. But you haven't found your game face yet. The one you'll need when I get you off in a room full of people."

Oh jeez. She got where he was going and started to giggle.

"I'm not into toys all that much. Equipment? Yes. Toys? No," he drawled suggestively.

What the hell did that mean?

"But I think a squirt gun to zap you out of that very sexy trance you fall into might qualify as equipment. What do you think?"

She smacked him on the thigh. "I think if you come at me with a squirt gun all hell will break loose."

"Promise?"

"Oh my god," she wheezed through laughter. "You're even worse than Matty. It really *IS* a guy thing!"

Pushing him away she said, "Get out. I'm good with sharing a bathroom, but no way am I peeing in front of you."

"Thank god," he drawled. "There is such a thing as too much togetherness." He kissed her forehead and exited saying, "Yell if you need anything."

Watching him leave was pure man candy. His front was drool-inducing but his back? Impressive. Broad shoulders, tapered waist and an ass begging for attention.

Aieee!

When she finished up and wandered into the bedroom, she saw right away that he'd moved her bags. He was doing that staking a claim thing again.

In the adjoining room, she found him by the window watching Matty sleep. The way he stood and the vibe he put off was protective and loving. Her gut told her Roman was a wonderful role model for the youngster. Just the little she knew about him made her appreciate all the more how important qualities like compassion with a side of honor would be for Matty as he grew.

Shielding him from comparisons or whispers about his parents, especially what appeared to be a complete douche-canoe for a father, was her new worry.

Roman looked up when she came through the door. He raised a finger to his lips. She nodded her understanding.

Creeping quietly across the room, she knelt by Matty's head. He was sound asleep with a small smile curling his little mouth. She kissed him softly on the cheek and adjusted the blanket.

In all the excitement of the road trip, she hadn't remembered to make sure he said his gratitude prayers. Damn. Keeping him grounded and aware was more important than ever.

Turning the bedside light off, she gently touched his hair. Roman had moved away, so she glanced about and found him playing with the remote control. Classical music, exactly what Matty was used to, floated in the air.

Satisfied, he dropped the controller and looked at her. His hand came out. She gave Matty a final look and then went to her man. Her fingers touched his, and he drew her in. Kelly studied their entwined hands. Without thinking, she chewed her bottom lip.

Tiny explosions of panic fired off inside her. She'd never let anyone in. Hell, there hadn't ever been anyone around to be let in. The lack of friends and peers, years of social isolation, and the belief that she was better off that way clashed with one irrefutable fact—she hadn't ever felt alive or truly connected to the world until she met Roman Bishop.

And admitting that put her in a tenuous spot. It wasn't easy to acknowledge this need. And why? Because wants and needs made her vulnerable. Vulnerability killed her mother.

The taste of blood in her mouth stopped the frantic lip chomp. She pulled it together with one final thought. Her mom's vulnerability also brought Matthew James into her life.

Everything had a good and not-so-good side. Her challenge was to cling tightly to the hope that being vulnerable to Roman was the start of something wonderful and not the first step along the road to hell.

He was up at the ass crack of dawn after a sound night's sleep. And there was a warm, female body wrapped around his in the unfamiliar and slightly uncomfortable bed.

Inhaling deeply, he breathed her in before his eyes cranked open. *Mmm.* Yes. Waking up with a sweet sexy pixie sprawled on his chest was all kinds of awesome.

She'd been restless after finally drifting off. Amazed that sleeping together was as satisfying as the other things they did together in bed, he'd been more than content to hold her close and rub her back until sleep eventually claimed her.

He liked that there weren't previous experiences with men to mess with her head. It made showing her how special this relationship was and how much he cared for her an adventure and not a chore. The truth was it turned out to be quite enjoyable.

Relaxed, happy and oddly at peace, Roman lay there and took the moment in. There was no question in his mind that he'd found her…

What he felt was different from before. Shit, it was worlds different. He'd regret losing Vanessa and their child every day he lived, but what they said was true after all. Life does move on, and if he was going to commit himself to this, it was time to send the past packing. Kelly deserved nothing less than one hundred and ten percent of his attention, so he vowed this would be the last time he'd think about the bad stuff. He'd retain only the sweetness and move on. With Kelly and Matty. As a family. A rather immediate and shocking family, but considering the rest of his unconventional life he had to concede the point, why the hell not?

She stirred slightly but didn't wake up. Good. He liked how it felt to wake up with her even if the surroundings were stripped down and basic. Plus, it gave him more time to think.

Today was going to be busy, and at the end of the day they'd be in New York, at his home, and a new chapter in so many lives would begin.

He'd put his foot down when Liam attempted to badger him into an immediate face-to-face with Kelly as soon as they landed. There was no fucking way he was going to fast-Freddy her. Roman counted it a small victory when he persuaded him to back off and agree to wait until the following day.

Since the very suggestion of a private plane set her off, he'd been tiptoeing around the subject. There wasn't a lot she could offer as a counter-argument when the legal documentation problem came up, but that didn't mean she was happy about being boxed in.

At this point, he was praying she woke up in a good mood and didn't give him too much shit. Matty was going to be enough of a handful.

A low groan came out of her mouth. The warmth of her breath skittered across his skin. His damn cock reacted. Being a somewhat smart guy, he'd wisely slept in his briefs. Temptation and morning erections being strong influences, he'd decided to err on the side of caution. And a good thing too, because one of her legs was wedged between his thighs. All it would take was a slight shift in position, and he could slide inside her.

"*Ergh. Ugh.*"

Uh oh. That did not sound good. Not when her eyes hadn't even opened yet.

All of a sudden she shot up, pushed off him and plopped on her butt where she sat cross-legged and slightly hunched. He immediately got moving and slid to his feet next to the bed.

When she finally looked up, he had to hold back a laugh. She resembled the victim of a hurricane. Her hair was everywhere, and by everywhere he meant everywhere. Some was sticking straight up, but mostly she looked like a cartoon character after putting her finger in an electric socket.

The corners of her lush mouth turned down in a scowling frown. There were dark circles under each eye, and her body language screamed misery.

Grabbing a pillow, she scrunched it up and folded it against her stomach. Then she glared at him and whatever smile he'd been fighting withered under her baleful glower.

The look she spared his way-too-obvious erection almost singed his flesh.

Oookay, then. Hmm. He didn't have a chance to say a thing before she muttered, "Shut up."

Not knowing what the hell to do or say, he opted for silence and waited for whatever came next.

The pillow went sailing through the air when she scooted to the side of the bed and stood up. Yanking the hem of his shirt down, her pursed lips and fierce scowl reminded him of an outraged prude.

"Things you need to know," she whined after an unsuccessful attempt to calm her hair. "Day two sucks."

Then she stomped off toward the bathroom and shut the door.

Well, the good news was that they'd found a way to communicate important stuff. He knew what to do and sprang into action. As he snuck into Matty's room to check on the still sleeping kid, he finally laughed.

Women! Who can figure it out? The comparison was hysterically amusing. After slam fucking for hours, she appeared fresh as a daisy. But this? Roman snickered to himself. His hat was definitely off to the fearsome power of a woman's cycle, 'cause that shit left marks!

She crawled back into bed and pulled the covers over her head. What a lousy time to get taken down by her damn period.

Bloated, uncomfortable and fending off a major case of the bitches, she wanted to curl up and die. Whoever decided that putting women through this shit every thirty days was the way to go needed an ass-kicking.

The only thing she had going for her at the moment was the time. It was barely six thirty, which meant she had a guaranteed hour until reporting for Matty duty.

A hand touched her shoulder, and the bed dipped. "Honey? Here. Sit up a minute, okay?"

She slammed the covers back with a pissed off grunt and snarled. "Don't wanna."

"Now, come on. Don't be difficult." He lifted her upright with an arm around her shoulders.

She couldn't believe how easy it was to pout at him. "Feel like shit."

"Yeah, I got that," he murmured. Putting two tablets in her hand, he motioned with his head. "Upped the ante. Think you can use the extra oomph."

Swallowing the pills took extra effort and half a bottle of water. She looked at him miserably and gathered her fright wig hair into a bunch. "What time do we check out?"

"Couple of hours. Don't worry. It's not like the plane will leave without us. When we get there, we get there."

"Silver lining after all," she muttered harshly.

Roman's deep chuckle and cheery "Now see?" made her even grumpier.

"Matty," she said in a barely audible voice.

"Covered. When he gets up, I'll take him downstairs for breakfast. And whatever you want, I'll bring back to the room."

"He can't have sugary cereal."

"Yeah, I know," he drawled. "Been paying attention. I promise he'll drink milk."

She gave up. What was the point in issuing instructions? He had a damn answer for everything. Snarling "Oh, fine!" she threw herself down on a pillow, assumed the fetal position and hauled the covers back over her head. "I want oatmeal. The lady at the front desk said there'd be oatmeal."

Roman's amused chuckle was audible through the blankets.

"You got it, babe. Oatmeal it is."

If she could kick him in the shins, she would. Just because.

***

If there were a Guinness challenge for the number of times a kid said 'Wow,' Matty would win. Starting with the run-of-the-mill road hotel, free breakfast, through the check-in procedure at the private plane terminal and as they crossed the tarmac was one amazed wow after another.

Liam, being perfectly aware of Roman's preferences, hooked them up with a large-cabin Gulfstream roomy enough for a dozen people. Far from overkill, it was however pretty obvious that it was more plane than three people needed.

The pilot, an affable guy calling himself Captain Nemo, made a huge fuss over Matty. Not only did he present the kid with the standard wing pin, but he also took him into the cockpit and let him say hello over the com system. He also laid down the aviation rules.the aviation rules

No yelling.

No running.

Seatbelt on when instructed.

Matty was awestruck.

Kelly? Not so much.

You're all set folks," he told them after pointing out the galley stocked with their selections and the entertainment options. "Flight time about six hours. It'll be night time when we arrive."

After some more pleasantries, he saluted smartly and went about his business.

Roman got them strapped in and comfortable. Both of them were wide-eyed and nervous, so he started rambling.

"Normally there'd be a flight attendant, but I'm an old hand at this. Know my way around a galley," he assured them.

Matty asked if there was a bathroom. Kelly played with the cuffs on her sweater and said nothing.

Take-off was uneventful. For him. He'd done this too many times, so his reactions were, *meh*. Once they were safely in the air, and at cruising altitude, he started moving around the cabin. In the galley, he unwrapped a charcuterie board, a fruit platter, and a couple of mini-milks that got shoved into an ice bucket. The sight of Bologna folded in tidy logs made him smile. So did the enormous selection of teas in a trendy little burlap bag. He was relieved to learn that his friend had being paying attention. Liam was using his damn head for a change.

Hmm. He paused for a moment and wondered who Liam put in charge of making the arrangements. A quick sweeping glance up and down the length of the cabin and he was more than sure Rhiann wasn't the source person for their flight. If she were, there would be welcome bags and if he knew her at all, cushy slippers for Kelly and the boy. There'd also be cashmere throws draped over the seats. And flowers. Lots of flowers. It hadn't taken her long once she was firmly established in Liam's life to turn a tiny delight into a full blown tour-de-force. It was a Wilde sister quirk. Probably instigated by Charlize, Rhiann's baby sis. She was the resident hippie-girl of the three and forever going on and on about being present and smelling the coffee or in this case, the flowers.

With none of that in evidence, he concluded it was Gardner in charge. He loved Marjorie Gardner in a Bruce Wayne and Alfred kind of way. She was Liam's undisputed right hand at BPG and, just like Roman, had far more personal connection to the man than what you'd expect of an employee.

He tried to imagine the conversation. Liam explaining Kelly and Matty's imminent arrival and that the pair were traveling with Roman and under his wing. Nothing rattled Gardner. He admired the quality. The woman could lead the way through an onslaught of hungry zombies, swatting back each threat with her usual unflappable calm, while consulting a guide for surviving an undead apocalypse without her heart rate increasing one little bit.

They could have used a kickass babe like Marjorie Gardner in the war. She wouldn't take anybody's shit—no matter which team they played for.

As he slid into the leather seat across from Kelly she barely looked up. He wished she didn't look so damn unhappy. It was going to be a long flight.

The sky seemed bluer at thirty thousand feet. And the clouds. They were different, too; floating around the plane in solo white puffs instead of as two-dimensional scenery viewed from the ground.

She liked blue. It was an excellent color with an infinite number of shades to play around with. There was dark blue, sky blue, and baby blue. There was also cerulean and azure. Color words to describe the endless shades were limited only by one's imagination. Periwinkle, teal, indigo and midnight. Blue was perfect for so many things.

A stained glass design formed in her thoughts. Using only her imagination, she built a hinged box from scratch in opalescent glass done in flowing swirls to suggest movement. It would be mid-range in size. Nothing too small and definitely not bulky.

Roman touched her leg. Half-startled that she'd been so far away, Kelly blinked and quickly checked to be sure Matty was behaving.

"I'm not sure you heard a word I said. Where'd you go?"

She crossed her legs and arms. The defensive posture was stiff and ridiculous considering who she was with, where they were, and the innocence of the question.

Overreact much? Sheesh. Damn period hormones.

Lifting her shoulder in a defeated shrug, she gave up and rearranged in the seat one more time. She wasn't used to being inactive. There was a universe of difference between still and sedentary. Living a busy life lacking down-time shaped her habits. When there was nothing to do, she well…she didn't know what to do.

Was the explanation lacking in eloquence and making no sense at all? Yes, but there you have it. The world according to Kelly James. Not knowing what to do when there was nothing to do.

"I was in my workroom. The one in my head. Sorry. What were you saying?"

His mouth twitched. He was holding back a laugh or comment. Was she being that difficult?

"If I don't make any sudden moves, will you please come sit with me?" Patting the leather chair next to his as encouragement, he lifted his tempting mouth into a lopsided smile with eyes hopeful and wide. "Pretty please with whipped cream and a cherry on top?"

She ducked her head for a brief second to hide the amusement and then came back with a response that made him bark with laughter.

"Make it two cherries with extra whipped cream, and I'll take your request under consideration."

"Sprinkles?" he quipped.

"*Ew*, no." She stuck out her tongue and made a face. "Yuck."

"Fudge sauce or caramel?"

She groaned. "Now you're just mean."

He shook his head. "What? How?"

"Things you need to know," she announced snippily with an exaggerated hair flip for shits and grins. "Don't poke the bear."

"Uh," he mock-growled in a warm, teasing voice. "There's a bear?"

She rolled her eyes and lingered with her gaze heavenward as if praying for patience. "Yes, you boob. In this scenario, I am the bear. Would you poke a bear for any reason? No. Not if you're sane. Bear poking when said bear has um, female issues, is suicidal. Waving imaginary ice cream, whipped cream, fudge and cherries in my face is akin to bear poking. Cut it out unless you want to be a eunuch."

"Lady," he snickered in his sexy drawl. "Using words like akin and eunuch in a conversation is practically guaranteed to end with you being bent over the end of the sofa with your panties in my back pocket so I can demonstrate why not castrating me benefits you. Or, if you want to get specific, benefits your pussy. Take your pick."

She smacked his knee, swiftly flew across the space between them, and swung into the chair by his side. He'd raised the armrest making the spot more like a loveseat. "Will you watch your language please?"

He glanced at Matty who was gleefully ignoring them while coloring on a large art pad with a plastic pencil box crammed full of new crayons—a surprise gift from Roman to commemorate his first airplane flight.

The innocent butter-wouldn't-melt-in-his-mouth expression as he put a hand on his chest in faux outrage over her slapping him down was freakin' hilarious.

"I thought you liked dirty talk." He sounded like a kid who just learned the tooth fairy was bullshit.

Well, she sniffed. He had her there.

Once he'd pried open the floodgates to her dammed up sexuality and let the deluge of lust she felt for him run freely, the filthy words he taught her fell quite easily off her tongue.

Bringing every drop of prude she had to her reply was easy considering her current hormonal phase. "Do not be a dick."

She yelped and tried to smack him when he pulled her into a loose headlock with one arm and drew her close to mutter thickly in her ear. "*Mmm*. Pussy and dick in the same conversation. Continue."

"What is wrong with you?" Giggle-snorting, she pushed away from him and sat back in her seat.

"God, so much," he drawled in response. "But not nearly so much since I met you."

"Hey. Don't blame me for your guy problems. The way I recall this thing going down, you were already second hand, dinged, dented, and generally full of shit when you teleported into my life."

The look he gave off came damn close to setting her jeans on fire. She more than liked how he did that. Did it bother her at all that she quite literally met, got bitchy with, touched, and then bedded the hunky stranger who came fully loaded with an agenda?

Eh. Maybe a little bit. Not enough, though. Whatever this thing between them was, to her, it felt right. If he fucked her over in the end, she would have to deal with it.

Still, he didn't give off a threatening vibe and had asked, well, actually…both of them asked the other for a bit of trust. In her estimation, these things were clues to his true character.

There was no denying Roman was in a tough spot. But she was grateful for the effort he put into being on her side. And for not scaring or rushing her. If she couldn't trust that and him, then she wasn't capable of the emotion.

"Why don't you get up and move around? All this sitting has to suck."

Does it show, she wondered? The restless tension. Was it apparent to others?

"No," he murmured quietly. His head shook back and forth. It was freaky and comforting to know he read her so easily.

He took her hand and twined their fingers together. This was another thing she liked. The handholding.

"I know what it's like." He sounded serious.

Kelly felt a pull on her senses. The draw. She shifted closer and turned into him when he started to speak.

"Being in a war is a twenty-four-seven, three-sixty-five deal. When it's happening all around you, there's no such thing as intermission or let up. Me and my crew would take an out-of-country R 'n' R break and end up supersonic with our balls on fire the whole time instead of chillaxing. It took a couple of months for me to downshift and find a new gear."

"But you knew what your other life contained. What it smelled like. How it felt. I just blew up every shred of familiar. None of this is real to me."

"Carina." The slow, lazy drawl claimed her full attention. "We are alike. I see the warrior in you."

All the air caught in her chest. To him, she wasn't invisible or forgotten.

"My time on the battlefield had a beginning and a middle and an end. Fuck, babe. I even knew the date when my service would wrap up. You never knew anything else, and there was no end in sight."

"Until Matty," she hastily reminded him. "Matty changed everything."

"Ah, exactly. The boy. He gave you the confidence to imagine a different life."

Thinking about his words, she stared at their joined hand and welcomed the surge of heat shooting up her arm. He was so right. She did a better job as a single mother than other girls her age that had given birth. The experience wasn't without benefits either. The confidence and determination she nurtured along with Matty had done well by them so far.

And she'd done it all with nothing. Less than nothing.

"Honey. You're showing some serious cojones by taking a shot in the dark. I'm humbled by your strength. Every leap of faith is a judgment call." He raised their joined hands and kissed hers. "I've got your back, Kelly."

It all poured out of her. Every doubt, insecurity, worry, fear, and folly. He listened without censure and never let go of her hand. When she got to the part about how the fish out of water analogy fit and that she felt vulnerable, exposed and naked, he put two fingers on her lips to silence the outburst.

"I'll just say again that nothing will happen without your consent. There's no time frame, no need to rush. We're on your schedule.

However long it takes and whatever you need. I'm there for you."

"What if I hate the city?"

She didn't expect the scoffing snicker. "You won't be the first. The city is a love-hate thing to begin with, so don't beat yourself up about it. Besides, nothing's set in stone."

Relief spread throughout her body. Oh, thank god. She needed to hear that.

"Um, Roman?" Worried Matty might hear she carefully whispered. "What happens when we land? I know you explained all that earlier, but I wasn't paying attention."

"Our body clocks will think it's early evening. Right after dinner. But on east coast time, it'll be around ten. We'll load our stuff into an SUV and go straight to my place. Rhiann sent a text. The refrigerator is packed, and she put a plastic container full of homemade chili in the front, so we don't have to dig for it. That's it. Promise. Plane to apartment and then we shut the door. Tomorrow will take care of itself."

She said one last thing, waited for him to laugh at her, and ended up doing a double, triple take when his reaction was the complete opposite.

Wiggling her hand away from his grip, she got manic in a heartbeat. "I look like a slob. My hair's a mess. Ginny trimmed it for me but still. My wardrobe is nothing but jeans, t-shirts, and hoodies. Hell, Roman, I don't have a purse or a wallet. You heard what Matty said. He wasn't kidding either. I'm almost twenty-four years old and haven't ever worn a dress. My shoes are from the Thrift Store. Buried in the woods, I didn't care about these things. Oh, I knew," she assured him somberly, "that when Matty and I moved I'd have to make some sort of socially acceptable effort. But not at a finger snap. Or overnight."

By the end of her tirade, Kelly was out of breath and felt even more emotional.

The way he looked at her made everything happening around them shift into slow motion. She felt like the center of the universe.

"You are," he breathed heavily, " the most beautiful, alluring, gorgeous female alive on this or any other planet. Truth, honey. I would never set you up with a lie just to spare your feelings. And before you object by cutting me off with a few more of your imagined shortcomings, relax. Did you think I'd put you in a situation where you'd feel… less?"

"It's not you," she persisted. "Nice thought but you don't rule the world."

"I think this is a wrap it up moment, so it's my turn to do the cutting off. Maybe not the smoothest surprise ever but at least I tried. Rhiann got both of you hooked up with a few casual outfits."

Her jaw dropped.

"Master Matthew James will be dressed by Gap for kids. I believe there is even a pack of dinosaur boy-briefs. She wouldn't go into detail, but I know Rhi. Whatever she came up for you with will be casual, low-key and super comfortable."

Swallowing took effort as she tried to wrap her head around this development.

"How much did she spend? I mean, I'm sure I can cover it but, uh…" Oh shit. She sounded ungrateful when all she wanted to do was take care of her own shit.

"Kelly. Hon. I know it's tempting to deny that you're a fairly wealthy young woman, but ignoring the facts won't make them go away. Money is not the issue. Rhiann understands major life changes. She's just trying to be helpful."

"It's not her. I don't want that man's filthy money."

Roman grunted. She knew he understood and was grateful he didn't try to soften her bitchiness.

"By 'that man' I hope you're referring to Adam Ward and not your brother. Liam isn't the bad guy in all this. He's also trying to do the right thing."

"I don't want to talk about it." She shut down like a steel door closing. There was only so much she could take.

He didn't push. Part of her wanted to argue for the sake of

arguing, but he wouldn't engage. By cutting her off at the knees and conceding to her emotional hide-and-seek maneuvers, he drained her denials and arguments of their oomph.

Dick.

She slid her gaze to his handsome profile and amended the thought.

Hot, crazy, sexy, and funny as shit, dick.

Flicking a piece of fuzz off her jeans, she counted the time left in the flight and returned to worrying about everything.

He'd said tomorrow would take care of itself.

She sighed heavily and thought, 'Is it ever that simple?'

Chapter Twenty

A MAN IN A DARK GRAY BUSINESS SUIT MET THEM AT THE airport in New York. She knew the second she spied him from the window, walking across the tarmac on the way to the plane, that it wasn't Liam Ashforth. This guy carried himself in a tense and overly formal way.

Kelly licked her lips, scraped her teeth across her bottom lip and pushed some loose hair behind her ears. It didn't matter who the approaching man was. Not really.

What did matter was one simple thing, something she'd been steeling herself for. Feeling a bit like Dorothy with Toto by her side, the small, scared voice in her head shook when she thought, 'Matty, we aren't in Oklahoma anymore.'

Her life before this moment, Matty's life, all of it was effectively wiped out. When that man came aboard, she'd never be plain Kelly James, a simple country girl from the backwoods, again. From now on she was Adam Ward's bastard daughter. A bastard daughter raising another of the man's bastard children. And she was being publically welcomed with open arms by a brother who was a complete stranger.

People would stare. And judge. With such a salacious backstory, who could blame them? Hell, she'd be staring if it happened to someone else.

Roman, Matty and Captain Nemo were high-fiving, fist bumping and saluting through an amusing dude-pantomime that made her smile. Sam had always been Matty's only male touchstone. She was really, really glad that Roman was a positive male role model.

As she moved to the door of the plane, her feet felt like concrete blocks. Dread and anxiety fought for primacy in her stomach. A small gust of frigid air blew into the cabin from outside.

New York was fuh-reezing in January. *Ugh*. Wishing she had a warmer jacket and thinking about the bulky, practical coat she left back in Oklahoma, Kelly instinctively sought the warmth and security of Roman's physical presence. Coming upon him from the rear, it didn't surprise her when his hand swung back to urge her forward as if he'd seen her coming with eyes in the back of his head.

She took his hand. His grip felt confident. Some of her jitters backed off. There was no hesitation on her part when he brought her to his side. She glanced up when he looked down at her. His expression said, 'I like you at my side.'

Captain Nemo greeted her with a deferential nod. "Well, Ms. James. How'd I do for your first flight? No barf bags needed I hope."

"Barf bags," Matty hooted with childish glee. "That's cool."

The captain pulled open a compartment, shuffled some stuff around and withdrew two of the bags emblazoned with the charter company's logo.

"Here ya' go Matthew. Official vomit containers approved by the FAA. Use them wisely."

Matty's reaction was priceless. His eyes were wide and full of wonder as if he'd been handed Excalibur to look after. A long, amazed, "Wow," filled the cabin.

Roman squeezed her hand and chuckled. The captain looked at her and winked.

Matty was her anchor. She took her cues from him. He liked the comical pilot, and she appreciated his professional manner. With Roman's support as fuel, she extended her hand and smiled.

"Thank you, Captain Nemo. No barfing, no quiet sobbing or screaming in fear. Let's count this as a success."

He shook her hand and chuckled. "Best critique I've ever had. Please feel free to use those exact words on Yelp."

She gave a good laugh.

The captain saluted her and Roman. "Joking of course. But it doesn't hurt to pander, right?"

"Mr. Bishop?"

A new voice joined the conversation. Everyone turned and looked at the same moment. It was the man in the business suit. Matty instantly took a few steps backward until he bumped into them. She put her hand on one shoulder, and Roman covered the other.

The pilot melted away. She studied the man with the formal bearing. He was older than her but not by much. His suit was slightly rumpled, and he had an odd way of standing. Not exactly full attention—it was something more along the lines of fist-clenched rigidness. There was an American flag pin on his lapel. He was looking directly at Roman.

Something clicked, and she knew two things. First, he was either an ex-cop or former military. And second? Roman was either his boss or someone with so much authority that the guy started sweating. She sensed an invisible salute. *Oh, my.*

"Conaway."

She stood stock-still but swung her gaze to Roman when he used an authoritative voice she'd not heard before. He didn't utter another sound, and she almost started to laugh. Power plays were so much fun to watch when it was other people.

"The luggage is handled, sir. When you're ready, the car is across the tarmac."

Roman nodded and patted Matty's shoulder. The business suit guy never broke rank.

A tense few seconds ticked by in silence. Would Roman

introduce them or was this guy too far down the ladder?

"Matthew," Roman started with a gentleness that warmed Kelly's heart. "Let me introduce you. This is John Conaway. Say hello."

Tick tock. An uncomfortable minute passed. She knew what Roman was doing. By introducing Matty first, he declared the boy's status. The gesture was so sweet she wanted to cry.

Finally, her brave little protector took one and a half very tentative steps away from her. With Roman's hand still protectively perched upon his shoulder, he looked up at the big man. Roman nodded and smiled encouragingly.

He didn't offer his hand, I mean, after all, the kid was only three. But he did use his words and in doing so sent waves of proud joy filling her up.

"Hello. I'm Matthew James."

Kelly choked on a coughing laugh. Even an outsider would have to admit that the way the kid wielded his full name was funny as shit. He was the decider, thank you very much, about who was okay and who needed an eye kept on them. She had to talk to him about letting Roman off the hook. He'd more than earned a ticket to the Matty show.

John Conaway answered as formally as she knew he would.

"Good evening, Mr. James."

Then, and only then, did he look at her. She forced her muscles to remain still when he subjected her to a visual once-over that, if they'd were at Shorty's, would end with her smacking him across the face.

Roman's reaction wasn't pretty. And he didn't introduce her. If she wasn't sure what kind of man he was before now, all lingering questions were squashed when he ended the weird encounter with a terse bark of commands.

Snapping his fingers, Roman's hand shot out, palm up. "Keys. You ride with the luggage."

Oh fuck. Kicked to the curb like an old duffle bag. Whoa. Shockingly turned on by this new side to her lover, she admitted that if they were alone and it wasn't the wrong time of the month, she'd be climbing him like a coconut tree.

Matty, who read the tea leaves better than a fake gypsy at the county fair, snickered when the business suit dutifully handed over the keys. The deep red flush on Conaway's face told her he knew how badly he'd fucked up. She didn't have to wonder what the conversation would be like when Roman tore this guy a new one. Whatever was said, it wasn't going to be friendly.

When John Conaway scurried from the plane, Kelly knew they'd seen the last of him.

To his credit, Roman didn't dwell. He had an interesting way of keeping them focused and moving forward. After dropping a few jokes that changed the subject, he shuffled them out of the plane, down the short steps and across the tarmac in a mad dash for the black SUV that roared to life at the click of a button on the key ring Roman clutched.

She scrambled into the passenger seat and shivered like crazy. The cold was bitter and cut straight through her clothes as if they weren't there. Roman got Matty settled in the back seat.

"This is so cool," she heard him murmur. Flipping around to see what was happening she was startled to find him strapped into a very sophisticated looking safety seat. Complete with cup and snack holders.

"Kiki," he cooed with childlike wonder. "Can you get one of these for the Bandit?"

She didn't know how to tell him that the Bandit was a thing of the past. A lump formed in her throat.

After checking to be sure she was adequately seat-belted, Roman joined them, buckled in, adjusted the heat settings, clapped his hands and announced, "Okay M'lady and young Master James. Welcome to New York City. Keep your hands and feet safely inside the vehicle at all times."

Matty cracked up giggling.

"Approximate travel time is who the hell knows, so sit back and enjoy the nighttime view. Next stop, Tribeca. Ready?"

"Ready," Matty shouted enthusiastically from the back seat.

Roman's head swiveled, and he pinned her with a look. "Ready?"

His body language was sending loud signals. With his hands off the wheel and resting on his thighs, he was making a major statement. He kept insisting nothing happened without her consent. Even now he was giving her a choice.

"Ready," she said in a hushed murmur.

His answering smile was filled with admiration. She wasn't so sure she deserved the response. At this point, she was in wing and a prayer territory.

Hearing the low rumble of his growling stomach, Roman gave a comical grimace and a hasty apology.

"Sorry. Us growing boys need a slab of protein every few hours, right Matthew?"

Matty stopped jumping up and down long enough to fix Roman with a serious look. "Kiki says it's up to me."

"What is?" he asked.

"You can call me Matty if ya' want," the precocious youngster informed him and Kelly. His blasé shrug was fucking adorable.

Being waved through to the inner circle by a preschool aged kid was a novel experience. Roman afforded the unexpected compliment all the seriousness it deserved.

"Thank you, Matty," he replied. "I won't let you down."

He wasn't sure why he said that last thing but what can ya' do?

The elevator doors opened. They stepped into the car. After inserting a key card, the lift started upward.

Kelly was shivering from the cold. The five minutes of exposure, when they went from parking to the elevator, gave the bitterly frigid temperatures a chance to grab hold. He had to admit that it was freezing. New Yorkers didn't ordinarily bitch about such things. It was a waste of time, but the extreme cold pushed the city to the limit.

With Matty on one side holding his hand, he swung the other arm around Kelly's shoulder. He liked the feeling of family. This is what was missing from his life. This was what changed his Justice brother friends out in the Arizona desert. This is what transformed Liam Ashforth.

The elevator door swung open, and home filled his view. Familiar sights, sounds and smells welcomed as he ushered them into what for now at least was home base for their new life.

The lights were on. He recognized a tune playing softly in the background. From the small foyer they stepped into the den. A modest flower arrangement in a Mason jar sat on the small round table against the wall that separated the kitchen and dining area on one side of the apartment from the living room on the other.

A sense of pride filled him up. This was his home. He wanted them to like it and be comfortable.

From the kitchen, he smelled the aroma of coffee, and on the far edge of his peripheral vision, he noted that the fireplace was blazing.

He chuckled and wondered how close Rhi cut it. She probably paced back and forth in front of the fire, waiting to hear his plane landed. It would be exactly what he'd expect of her too. To obsess over the details. The fine print.

She understood the importance of a first impression. It was good to know he had a partner in this unusual situation. A partner equally as invested in everyone's happiness as he was.

The nickel tour followed. His apartment wasn't huge. It was larger than most New York condos, but nothing like the modern, spacious penthouse Liam and Rhiann had.

Matty lost his shit when they entered his new room. Emotion clawed at Roman's heart. What greeted them wasn't Rhiann's doing. It was one hundred percent Liam, and he seriously wanted to cry.

Taking advantage of the fourteen-foot ceilings, a jaw-dropping custom bunk bed sitting atop a desk and workspace area with sturdy ladder access and adequate side rails sat on one of the long walls. One end of the wood structure was fashioned into a bookshelf. A bookshelf filled with all sorts of books and dinosaur models. On the red brick wall hung a huge lifelike canvas of some exceptionally friendly-looking dinosaurs. Two low dressers sat end to end with a chair and small ottoman next to the closet doors. It was night, so the shades had been drawn on the huge oversized window at the end of the room.

It was his jaw's turn to hit the floor. Wasn't this every boy's dream room? There was nothing he would do differently if it were up to him.

He quickly calmed Matty down when the kid went off like a firecracker, rapturously expressing his thanks. No way was he taking credit for this.

"Hey," he said with a big laugh to draw the kid's attention. "I'm just as surprised as you. You know what?" he barked. "I bet this was my friend. The guy Kelly told you about. I might have mentioned that you're a dino-buff. He is too."

Roman shrugged and smiled at Matty's astonished expression and Kelly's scowl.

The doorbell chimed. He glanced at his watch.

"That will be our bags. Why don't you two poke around and make yourselves at home? This is your place now, okay?"

He didn't wait for a response. He just put a hand around Kelly's neck and pulled her in for a quick, wet kiss. Then he marched off to activate the security camera, send the elevator down and crossed his fingers hoping that Liam hadn't inadvertently stepped in it.

Who knew a bubble bath could be so…heavenly?

With a long, drawn-out sigh, Kelly scooted lower in the nickel-plated cast-iron soaking tub. She felt decadent. Like a kept woman in a classy bordello.

Laughing at the fanciful thought, she closed her eyes and willed the tenacious tension to take a hike. The water soothed her nerves and let the jumble of thoughts bouncing in her head settle down.

It happened. They left the woods and now here they were in what had to be the most famous of cities, the Big Apple. N-Y-C.

And they hadn't been consumed by flames when they stepped off the plane, held up at gunpoint, or been sold into slavery.

Dramatic? Hell, yeah.

Something she should feel guilty about?

No.

She could do this. Right?

Scooping handfuls of warm water over her shoulders, out loud she murmured, "Maybe."

She thought about Roman mediating a battle of wills that broke out earlier between her and Matty. When she tried calling him out of his room to eat something, he'd dug in his heels, and refused to budge. It was the big man and his stern, no-nonsense swagger that got the unusually belligerent boy in line.

If things got any weirder, well...

There was a light knock as Roman called through the door. She detected warmth and amusement in his voice.

"Honey? Are you in the tub?"

No. She was knitting a sweater! Sheesh. Of course she was in the tub.

"Are there bubbles? Please tell me there are."

She laughed. "Seriously, Roman. What is wrong with you?"

"Yeah, we've covered that already. Back to the bubbles," he chuckled. "May I peek? Please, please, please."

Was he serious? Befuddled, she called back, "Whatever for?"

"Well first of all," he drawled. "This is the first time the tub's been used. I'm a shower guy. And more importantly, there's never been a sexy sprite draped in bubbles sitting in my bathroom before. I'd say that warrants a peek, don't you?"

"Never?"

"Cross my heart. Never. Things you need to know…"

She held her breath.

"There hasn't been anyone seriously in my life since…well, in a very long time. Every step we take, we take together. This is all new to me too."

"Hold on," she answered. "Give me a sec."

Turning the water on full blast and letting some out at the same time, she squirted a huge glob of bubble bath directly into the churning stream and created a poofy cloud of fragrant, glistening suds.

She scooted around, sloshing water almost over the sides and assumed what she hoped was a sexy pose. Only the ambient lights were on, and at one end of the tub alcove, a thick pillar candle flickered from an arched niche in the wall.

A giggle shot from nowhere. Oh my god. She was role-playing her woman in a bordello fantasy. How damn funny was that?

"You can peek now," she purred in a breathy voice.

The soft snick of the doorknob turning upped her excitement level. The anticipation was spine tingling. Slowly, like in a movie, the door swung open. Roman appeared, his large presence filling the space.

He stepped further into the bathroom, staying in the shadows beyond the tub alcove—moving side to side, taking in every angle, and devouring her with his eyes.

"Carina." His voice was smoky and seductive. "If seeing you like this gives me a heart attack, I'm dying a happy man."

She swirled her hands beneath the suds and smiled. Taking a handful of bubbles, she made a production out of draping them across her bobbing breasts.

His sultry growl did funny things to her body when he let out an amused sound. "God damn. I didn't think the tub was worth the expense until now."

Licking her lips led to a little pout that drew his gaze. Ah. Right. His complete fascination with her mouth. *Hmm.* Her mind started clicking. Maybe she could turn his fascination into something.

Waving him closer with a suds-covered hand, she slyly whispered, "Things you need to know."

His eyes flared briefly and held her in place by the strength of his powerful gaze.

"I can't help it."

"Help what?" he asked while stepping even closer to hear her barely audible response.

"Checking out your uh…" she reached for him and caressed the always present bulge with a hand dripping in bubbles.

He swatted her away, took two steps back and growled, "Nope, nope."

"Aw, come on," she pouted. When that didn't work she went straight to whining. "You're being mean to me."

"That is not true, Carina. I'm being sensible. Taking a break every couple of weeks isn't necessarily a bad thing."

"Says you."

He laughed, put his hands at his waist and shook his head. "I am so fucked where you're concerned."

"Well, I'm glad somebody gets fucked in this scenario."

He gasped and acted shocked by her naughty mouth. "Don't make me teach you a lesson."

"Go away now. I'm mad at you."

First he laughed, but when she scowled, and half ignored him, he stopped. "Oh, I see how it is," he snickered. "This is where you do wicked things with your mouth and make me question my sanity."

"Wicked things like what?"

"Like make that damn pouty face. And bite your lip. And show me your tongue. You are either very brave, little one, or foolish."

She had him. What a dope!

"And those things make your sanity an issue?"

"Well, yeah."

"Why?" She made sure to bat her eyelashes innocently. Thank you, Mom, for those trashy old romance books.

"Because when you do those things, I'm not paying attention.

All I can think of is sinking my cock into your mouth. Sliding across your tongue to nudge the back of your throat. Until you gag."

Oh, my. If he thought that would scare her off, he had a wake-up call coming.

"What if I don't gag?"

"Excuse me?"

She swirled her hands some more in the water and struggled not to laugh. "What if I like it?"

"Like what?"

Oh my god. He was so freakin' cute with the puzzled expression and searching questions.

"Sucking your cock. What if I like it? The gagging and everything?"

He gaped at her for the longest time then muttered, "How the hell did I lose control of the conversation?"

She smirked and gave a half shrug. "You came through the door."

"Doomed by my own horniness."

Okay, *hmmm*. She had to think. So the seductive bubble posing didn't work. Change in tactic. She sloshed around and ended up with her arms draped across the edge of the tub with her chin resting on her hands. The pose forced her to peer up at him through lashes she took pains to bat. The angle of her gaze afforded Kelly a quick and adoring pit-stop when his groin came into view.

"Where's my damn squirt gun when I need it?" he quipped.

Her answering smile was slow and deliberately naughty. She had no idea till right now how much fun it was to push his buttons, and she sensed he wasn't used to the insolence. Or the challenge.

She had him pegged pretty quickly. Beneath the well-groomed, cultured gentleman lurked other things. He thought he was keeping all that warrior stuff in a box, but she saw plenty of his errant quirks and warrior behaviors. Some of his needs she assumed grew from those times.

Control wasn't nearly adequate to describe or explain what she felt rolling off him in waves. It was something else that she just couldn't put her finger on. It confused her a little, because the way she read his vibe didn't make sense.

On the one hand, he gave off charming delight at her clumsy naiveté. But then with the other hand, he urged her on to explore and unleash a physical fierceness that took Kelly out of herself.

The innocence turned him on and filled what she presumed was a normal primal need to be a sexual alpha.

But her fierceness turned him into an animal which in turn pushed her higher until the moment of surrender—a surrender she needed to give.

It all confused the hell out of her.

So she did what any girl would do. Right? She returned the favor. After all, men were incredibly easy to confuse.

"Are you working from a step-by-step guide or something? Is that why the oral portion of this learning curve has been denied?"

He didn't even try not to laugh. "What do you mean? Are you asking if there's a manual? Training the Virgin? Something like that?"

Training the virgin. Oh my lord. How could she not love this man?

"Is there?" she asked with saccharin innocence. "There has to be," she drawled in answer to her question. "That's the only explanation that makes sense as to why you keep stopping me every time I put my mouth on you."

"Do you even know what you're talking about?"

He asked the question in his bad man voice. She smirked.

"I'm talking about this," she said with a finger pointed at his crotch, "and this," she taunted as she ran her fingertip across her tongue. "An introduction is in order don't you think?"

"An introduction?" There was disbelief and amusement in his voice.

She giggled.

"Get the fuck out of that tub, lady."

He picked up a towel from the vanity bench and tossed it at her head. "Rub some smelly shit all over that delectable little body and then join me in the bedroom."

"What for?" she answered with a snarky bite.

"So we can explore your gag reflex of course."

She gave him the eye and snickered, "Don't tease."

"Nah, we're good, babe" he drawled. "You want to spend our monthly break time sucking on my dick like a lollipop? Who the fuck am I to object?"

He was laughing and muttering to himself as the door to the bathroom shut, and he left her to get ready.

She was halfway through primping and preparing when guilt struck her like a thunderbolt. Biting her lip as she gasped, all she could think of was that not once in any of what just happened had she asked about Matty.

A moment of remorse, and then she relaxed. She and Matty were safe in Roman's care. He wouldn't have sought her out during bath time if he hadn't gotten Matty tucked in and asleep in his fancy new digs.

Oddly enough, she had no reservations co-parenting with him. In fact, it came as something of a relief to finally have enough trust in someone to allow it.

Whatever.

She wasn't going to suddenly start questioning every little thing when her gut had never guided her wrong before.

She trusted Roman.

This was what she was supposed to do. Where she was supposed to be. With him.

All the other stuff? The brother and dying father? Background noise.

She was focused on the full orchestra, the emotional percussion, and the freedom of letting the music flow through organically.

Her future and Matty's were part of the symphony. So was Roman's. A sobering thought. One that reminded her that it wasn't all about the Kelly and Matty show. Roman played a major role. She wanted him to be happy too.

Figuring out how to make all those things work was her challenge.

Water dripped off his eyelashes as he scowled at the gleaming tile wall in his king size shower. Every goddamn bell and stupid whistle available in a modern bath were at his disposal. Except for one thing.

Stabbing his finger on the wall, he muttered, "Right here."

Yep. Right here there needed to be a fucking gauge to let him know how much water he was wasting while he stood there and imagined the shower was somehow magically going to wash away his mortification from the scene he'd just made in the bedroom.

He didn't know what to make out of any of it.

Was he losing his touch? Getting old? Addled? Is that what just caused him to embarrass the holy fuck out of himself?

Slowly turning around so the hot water could cascade down the back of his head and pound away the tension in his back, he wiped a hand across his face and groaned.

After Kelly finally drove him nuts with her insatiable curiosity, and he figured there'd be no harm in letting her have a taste of what was sure to come, he gave in but didn't consider the part where he went off like a green fourteen-year-old getting his first blow job.

It started off so perfectly when she pranced out of the bathroom in nothing but a perfectly respectable pair of pink panties with her fantastic tits swaying and bobbing. As usual, she gave new meaning to the word eager.

A more rehearsed woman would have approached him with a seductive dance, but not Kelly. Hell to the no. She bounced out of the bathroom and ran to him like a kid hitting the playground after a long morning of being cooped up.

Her enthusiasm scrambled his thoughts and short-circuited the control he normally had over his body.

There'd been loads of kissing. That part was all kinds of hot. Just when he was sure he'd kissed her into submission, she pulled the rug out, climbed him like a tree, and took control. The girl had a wicked tongue, and she wasn't shy about using it.

He wanted her to undress him. Seemed like a cool lesson. But she wasn't having it and dropped to her knees to watch while he did his best Magic Mike as his clothes became a pile.

Looking back, that was probably when he shoulda' realized how tenuous his control was. She asked questions. Anatomy questions, and expected demonstrations. Her knowledge was health class basic coupled with dirty book flair. She was the perfect combination of sweet and innocent wrapped in fucktacular wanton. He liked it.

Another mistake, he realized belatedly, was imagining he was all big and bad. A monster dick was just a monster dick if a guy couldn't keep his shit together. A fact he found out the hard way.

The very hard way.

There was something about watching his beautiful woman on her knees conducting a tactile love fest on an erection that took his ego to an eleven. The things her small hands did to his body blew him away.

And that was before she took him in her mouth.

Thinking about it made his jaw clench. "*Aargh.*" His loud pained grunt bounced off the tile walls.

When she got handsy with his balls and purred like a turned-on jungle cat, he snapped. The lewd demands couched as instructions that she took extra care to follow ended up being his undoing.

And shit. He was just kidding himself if he allowed for one second any suggestion that he lasted longer than a minute once her mouth joined the party.

Any clue what her gag response actually was? None, because he was lust blind and grunting within seconds. Roman vaguely remembered grabbing her head, and he may or may not have explored her throat. What he did remember was her groaning and the way his cock expanded, shuddered, and then exploded in a rush of spasms that left him weak.

She looked nothing short of stunned after he emptied in her mouth. He was pretty sure it was safe to say neither of them expected what happened.

Was it sexy and memorable?

Fuck no.

He lost control and came like an untried kid, not an experienced Dom. His membership in the Master of the Month Club should be immediately revoked.

Mortified and disappointed by his embarrassing performance, he'd been a total chicken shit right after and run off to the privacy of the shower where he could hang his head and be a pussy about it.

No shit, man. He didn't get it. Him. Látigo. The Whip Master. He wasn't a stranger to public scenes. Either viewing or participating. There was a time when he could be persuaded to do a bullwhip demonstration in the private studio at the club. The high-class, very exclusive, extremely expensive gathering place for those involved in the lifestyle, which he was part owner of. Those sessions, always intense, generally ended with a hearty face fuck. He had experience controlling his response and orgasm.

But Kelly played a new card in the deck. Her card had to do with pushing boundaries. His.

The primal response she drew out of him, the feelings she inspired. It was more than greedy lust keeping him hard all the time. She was his equal. They were the same. He needed her with a passion stretching far beyond the bedroom.

She fascinated him, and that fascination robbed him of all his bad boy skills. With her, he was just a man. A man driven by animalistic desires so far removed from anything he'd experienced before that his world was shaking.

Uncertain what to do, she sat cross-legged in the middle of the big four-poster bed and stared at the hallway to the master bath.

Maybe she'd done it wrong. That's the only explanation for why he ran off.

Chewing on a thumbnail, her leg started to shake nervously. The temptation to Google blowjob techniques had been there since losing her virginity to Roman. She stopped herself because more than anything Kelly needed their time together to be real. Not a re-creation of something she'd seen or read. There had been enough smoke and mirrors in her life.

Her eyes took in the surroundings. Roman's bedroom. The sweet tingles racing along her nerves didn't allow for anything other than pleasure. Pleasure in his beautiful home, pleasure in his company, pleasure everywhere.

The high ceilings, exposed red brick and masculine vibe fascinated Kelly. So did the enormous bed. The head and footboard featured laddered spindles. She glanced up at the four-poster frame high above her head.

Dirty fantasies provided plenty of fodder for her overactive imagination. She'd seen pictures of women in scanty lingerie tied spread eagle to all sorts of things. Something that resembled an X, the ceiling, and quite a few beds. Her heart started pounding. Being trussed up like that had to be freakin' hot.

Whoa. Being tied up was hot? She shivered.

Oh. Um. Well, damn. Her mind took off on a hundred yard sprint. Did she want to be tied up? The idea of being helpless scared the bejeebers out of her.

But …

Kelly placed a palm against her chest as her heart beat wildly. She wasn't fantasizing about being helpless in a crisis. No. She imagined being rendered defenseless before Roman's powerful sexuality. Huge difference.

She didn't doubt he'd take full advantage of her vulnerable state and wondered if that might explain why he bolted from the room like a deer racing through the woods. He'd been in the vulnerable seat and didn't like it.

Oh, he liked the mechanics of what happened, but she knew the second he lost control that something had pushed him over the edge.

She just wished she knew what.

He was coming back…she heard him leave the bathroom. Tension, sweet, drugging sexual tension, overtook Kelly's body.

When he swaggered into view wearing black Dolce Gabbana briefs her eyes fixed on the sight of his powerfully muscled thighs. Chewing on her lip, she tried to calm her erratic breathing.

He came straight to the side of the bed, stopped, and stared at her. She stared back.

Something passed between them. His eyes challenged hers. The spreading heat from a blush crept slowly up her neck and onto her face. Whatever vulnerability her clumsy attempt to seduce him orally had uncovered was gone. The man ravishing her with his gaze was in complete control.

Not being able to fuck his brains out was a serious bummer.

In a voice she'd not heard before he captured every bit of her attention. Snapping his fingers, he pointed to the floor and demanded she stand at the end of the bed.

Shaking like a leaf from spine-tingling excitement, she quickly complied, eager to do his bidding. Scrambling off the wide bed, she dropped to her feet and moved to the spot he was pointing at.

His finger spun in the air. "Turn around. Face the wall. Don't move."

He remained where he was as she moved into position. Glancing at him, she gasped. His face wore a fierce-looking mask of desire.

After a minute he left her peripheral vision. She could still sense him nearby, but he was moving around the room. Her breathing did not calm down at all. Anticipation clawed at her composure.

When he returned, she was light-headed and panting. A

thud on the floor to her left got Kelly's head swinging toward the sound. He'd dropped a worn, leather duffle bag on the hardwood. Crouching next to it, he ripped open the zipper and yanked apart both sides of the bag for access.

She watched intently, wondering what the hell he was up to.

Roman glanced up at her. His gaze scorched her skin as he inspected every inch of her body. Then he reached into the bag.

He issued more orders, which made it difficult to see what he pulled from the mystery bag.

"Hands clasped behind your head. Feet spread." She felt his breath on her skin. "In other words, kitten, assume the position."

Kitten? Oh my god. She trembled from head to toe. His joke about treating her like a cat needing training suddenly took on a very, very sexy meaning. Without realizing it, she purred. His eyes turned smoky.

He knelt at her side. His hand slid slowly up her leg. He touched the inch or so of pink cotton between her legs. The subtle caress made her moan.

Something wrapped around her ankle. She tried to look down. In the span of time it took her brain to register what was going on, he'd bound an ankle to a bed post.

Then he moved to the other side. She was shaking uncontrollably and whimpering softly when he finished. At one point she wondered why he just happened to have special, soft rope. And a lot of it.

He stood up and stroked her butt through the panties.

What he did next would be seared into her brain forever.

Taking a length of thick, white rope, he expertly tossed an end in the air. It looped over the bedframe and fell back into his hand. In the time it took to make a cup of tea, he had her bound with arms stretched wide and wrists tied firmly above her head to the bedframe.

He turned down all the lights in the room. For the first time, she realized there was a door on the other side of the bed that opened onto a private patio. She watched him lower the blinds on the tall windows to ensure their kinky privacy.

Walking behind her he moved in close and breathed deeply, but didn't touch her at all. Then with the agility of a jungle cat, he leaped on the bed and scooted back until he was reclining against the headboard like a desert scoundrel inspecting his latest harem captive.

He crossed his legs at the ankle and relaxed. The wicked leer on his face ignited a firestorm in her center.

"Very pretty," he murmured with a chuckle. "And so obedient. Kitten," he growled, "you surprise me."

Surely not that much of a surprise. "Obedience or reading my mind?" she asked with a naughty leer of her own.

His grin became huge. Like, really huge. "Just trying to level the playing field, pet."

She liked how that sounded even though in reality she had no idea what he meant.

He left her hanging there…literally, while he occasionally rubbed his cock and stared at her. She started squirming against the bindings. Heat poured from her core, and her nipples became so stiff, they ached.

The amused grin grew lascivious. He even licked his lips and made sound effects. When she broke down and cried his name, shit got real.

"Roman."

He was off the bed in a flash. "I think you're sufficiently warmed up."

Gathering all her hair into a raggedy tail, he wound one of her elastic bands around it. He pulled her head back. The yank on her scalp was as pleasurable as his mouth between her legs. She was confused but incredibly turned on.

Directing her head with a fierce grip, he ran a single finger down her back making goose bumps break out.

"I meant what I said – nothing happens without your consent."
She shuddered.

"So tell me quickly, Carina. Is this okay?"

No kitten. No pet. Carina. He was asking her permission. She couldn't love him more if she tried.

"Oh god, yes," she moaned.

He bit her earlobe and grunted. "I'm glad. Now let's find out how much stroking my naughty and very sexy kitten can take."

Letting go of her hair, he plastered against her from behind and put both hands on her waist. His lips started doing crazy things to her neck. Writhing and whimpering, she melted under the spine-tingling assault.

With intoxicating slowness, his hands moved to her stomach, caressed her waist for a bit and then climbed, palm down, up her ribcage. Instead of covering her aching breasts, they stopped and remained a scintilla of space away.

Kelly gasped, fought against the bindings and softly groaned when he licked her from shoulder to ear. His breath, hot and sweet so close to her ear, got her trembling before he spoke.

"Your sexy kitten tongue made me lose it earlier. My apologies."

Apologies? Oh no, no.

"Roman," she gurgled when a shudder of desire wracked her body. "I loved it. And I promise," she wailed quietly. "I'll do better next time."

His big, warm hand carefully took control of her neck. She relaxed against him.

"Brought down by a voluptuous, decadently sexy elf."

She wiggled her ass into the bulge pressed against her from behind.

"You did just fine, pet. More than fine. Blind lust took me by surprise. Next time, I'll do better."

Beneath his powerful grip, the wicked laugh shooting from her mouth vibrated in her throat.

He gently caressed the fragile column of her neck, and there was nothing she could do but melt.

Then, he swatted her ass. She wasn't expecting it and yelped.

"Purr for me, kitten. Let me hear your pleasure."

Every spot he touched became an erogenous zone. She responded with mindless grunting, bucking and mewling.

He mauled her neck and shoulders while doing all sorts of things to her breasts. One minute he would tease and tantalize. The next she was in the grip of a feral beast.

Not being able to move her legs drove her lust-mad. When his hand moved between her legs and cupped her mound with a firm grip, she almost came.

His teeth were in her neck, two fingers rolled a hard nipple, and his hand ground mercilessly. She didn't stand a chance.

The climax when it hit was intense and terrifying. She went wild, struggling against the bindings, shaking with a passion that emptied her brain, screaming, crying, panting. A mess.

The more she shook, the harder he bit and squeezed. Blackness gathered at the edges of consciousness. She went limp.

With two quick moves, her wrists were freed, and she collapsed in a slump over the edge of the bed. Her chest heaved as she grappled for oxygen. He yanked her panties down. They wouldn't go far because of how her legs were restrained. It didn't seem to matter. She mewled and whimpered when he caressed her ass.

She turned her face, tilted her head and caught sight of him. He was stroking his cock and her ass with an expression on his face that made her feel like a goddess. Watching as he came on her skin was more deeply satisfying and balls out erotic than she thought possible.

When he threw back his head and grunted, she joined in to create an animalistic chorus that filled the bedroom.

She was barely conscious when he untied her ankles, pulled her panties up, kissed her ass before gently biting it, and then lifted her in his arms. He walked around the bed and placed her on it. Kissing her cheek softly as he pulled the covers up he asked, "Need anything?"

"Just you," she answered.

He quickly joined her beneath the covers and pulled her close.

"I like this," he growled.

She shifted and peered into his face with a question on hers.

"I like that you're wearing my come on your skin and that you smell like a satisfied woman."

"Silver-tongued devil," she snickered before placing a soft kiss on his chest, curling into his big body with a contented purr and falling into a deep sleep.

Chapter Twenty-One

A LIGHT TAP ON THE DOOR INTERRUPTED HER THOUGHTS. "Honey? They'll be here soon. Are you okay?"

She honestly had no idea how to respond.

Sighing deeply, she gave her reflection a final cursory glance, flipped off the lights and left the bathroom. He was on the other side of the door with a worried frown and some anxious sounding sighs.

"Where's Matty?" she quietly asked.

He blocked her movements with his bulk. She didn't push him aside like she normally would. Unfamiliar feelings and concerns clogged her system. It wasn't so much impending doom as it was pins and needles.

Why couldn't they lock the door and go back to bed?

Roman brushed a lock of her hair from the side of her face, caressed her cheek and smiled. "He's doing a puzzle in the den, which by the way we will now be calling the family room. He likes that term better."

"He's got family on the brain," she murmured almost to herself.

"So do I."

She raised her eyes to his. What possible bargain could she make with God for everything else except this to go away?

"You look beautiful," he told her with a wink and a smile.

She couldn't resist messing with him so a hip was cocked and she planted a hand on her waist. "Are you reading from a script?'

He shook his head and did a comically perplexed double take. "A script? I don't understand."

"Yeah, you know," she sniped. "The be nice to keep her calm script."

Watching him blink, scowl and then bark with laughter was a balm for her frazzled nerves.

"Ah," he drawled lazily. "So the secret is out?" He held up his hands in a surrender plea.

"I have to thank Rhiann for this," she told him with a wave at her clothes. "Love the Uggs."

He smirked.

"What?" she asked.

"I specifically asked her not to get you those fugly boots."

She didn't understand. "Why? They're so warm and comfy."

The conflict raging on his face struck her funny bone. She slapped him kiddingly on the arm. "Oh my god! Are you playing dress up Barbie with me?"

"I believe my wisest move is a hasty tactical retreat." He laughed and slung and arm around her waist to draw her close. A drugging kiss followed. "Wear what you want."

Kelly giggled and kissed him fiercely. "As long as from time to time it's thigh high boots and sexy lingerie?"

"*Grrr*," he playfully growled.

She wrapped her arms around his waist and cuddled close. He needed to know she wasn't worried about what was coming. He felt everything so deeply and was adamant that a line in the sand with Liam Ashforth was drawn. No matter what happened, his decision was made. He was with her. Even if it meant leaving his job.

"Kelly," he murmured into her hair. "We're okay, aren't we?"

Tell him, her inner voice screamed.

Rising on her toes, she slid her arms upward and took his handsome face in her hands. "I'm here because of you, Roman. I didn't come to New York for any other reason. I'm not ignoring the grizzly bear lurking in the corner," she was quick to assure when he seemed about to say something. "I'm meeting with...' she had to suck in a deep breath before continuing, "I'm meeting Liam because you asked me to."

The guy's name did not roll easily off her tongue. She didn't give a shit that she was being unreasonable. She was only human dammit, and that was how she felt.

"Everything will work out. You'll see. He's not the bad guy, honey, and he's suffered as much as you and Matty from the actions of Adam Ward."

"I understand that," she replied. "But he's not responsible for that horrible man's mistakes."

"You're not a mistake."

"You know what I mean," she bit back. "He owes me nothing. And I don't want anything."

"Maybe this is more about the receiving than the giving. Liam's already dealt with his demons. The money means less than nothing to him. Every penny he has, he made through incredibly hard work. Starting from nothing. Was he fueled by rage? Yes. But honey, so are you. You're more alike than you know."

He kissed her.

"You're not invisible anymore, and Matty will grow up as a normal, happy kid. A family is forming here. Can't you feel it? Give Liam a chance. You two need each other."

In the background, the chime for the elevator sounded. She knew Rhiann had access, so there wasn't any need for Roman to unlock the lift.

He picked up her hand and kissed it. "Together," he murmured.

"Thank you."

He started to say something and cut himself off. "What?" she asked.

"Don't freak."

"Things you need to know," she laughed. "What time of the month is it? Don't freak? Bah!"

"I'm falling in love with you."

Awww. He was so cute. Kelly shrugged and laughed happily. "I know." She squeezed his big bicep. "It's okay. I promise to go easy on you."

Heading down the hallway in front of him, she turned around just before stepping into the so-called family room and looked at Roman. He was gaping at her and looked like he froze in mid-step.

"Are you just going to stand there? We've got company."

She put out her hand. He started forward, stopped, and then came straight to her. Their hands slid together perfectly.

"Don't let go," she told him.

He squeezed and then the two of them strode into the future, together.

It would be a miracle if he didn't drop of a heart attack, that's how tied in knots he was. Several minutes had elapsed since the elevator was called. At any moment the door would swoosh open, and seconds later Rhiann and Liam would be there.

Kelly appeared calm, but she had a death grip on his hand.

"Matty," she called softly with a quick glance behind where they stood. "Come here. We've got company."

"Roman made me brush my hair."

She smiled at him. "You look very handsome."

A fearsome instinct to protect these two people made Roman take a step forward. He kept hold of her hand but effectively blocked both of them but from what he wasn't sure.

He tracked familiar sounds. The elevator ping when the car arrived. The nearly inaudible swoosh of the doors opening. Rhiann's heels tapping on the floor.

She appeared first, a sure sign that Liam was struggling. It wasn't like him to show any vulnerability. Roman's heart ached for his friend.

Rhiann's bright smile was genuine. He instantly relaxed. Liam followed, and Roman was sure he saw him straighten his shoulders before stepping forward.

He took the lead. "Liam," he said. "You look like shit, man."

They shook hands as a tiny voice giggled and said, "Penny jar."

Liam's startled expression and Rhiann's amused chuckle made it easier not to hyperventilate and hit the floor.

Roman watched as Liam searched the empty air until Matty peeked around Kelly's leg.

"Matthew," Roman said gently. "Come here, little dude. There's someone you need to meet."

Kelly squeezed his hand but remained safely behind his shoulder. He squeezed back.

Matty crept from the shadows and stared at Liam. Emotional electricity crackled in the air around them while the two brothers faced each other for the first time.

A wide range of feelings clogged Roman's throat when Liam took a knee to be on the boy's level and held out his hand.

"Hi, Matthew. My name is Liam."

The whole room got silent, and he swore the air became thicker. For long seconds Matty said nothing. And he didn't move. He simply stared.

And then his little hand came out, and he shook Liam's much bigger one. "You have Kiki's eyes," the little boy muttered.

Every adult in the room gasped.

Matty let go of Liam's hand and looked at Kelly. "He has your eyes."

Roman cleared his throat and put a hand on the boy's shoulder. He looked up at him with wide, uncertain eyes.

"He has her eyes because she's his sister."

Kelly let go of his hand and knelt down, pulling Matty to her.

"Isn't that cool? A brother! And he's a friend of Roman's."

He never felt more proud of anyone as he did of the two of them. Kelly's calm, sweet graciousness blew him away.

She stood and put her hand out. "Hi. I'm Kelly."

Liam's awkwardness lasted all of about five seconds before the polite handshake became a tentative but heartfelt hug. The second they separated Rhiann rushed forward and enveloped Kelly in a fierce hug.

"I'm Rhiann, but you probably figured that out."

She was beaming at Kelly and then looking at him. "Roman Bishop. We need to talk!" she laughed.

Kelly pointed to Rhiann and said to Matty, "Sweetie, this pretty lady's name is Rhiann. She's going to marry Liam. Isn't that fun?"

Roman looked at Liam and found him staring a hole through his head. He could see the reality of his and Kelly's situation starting to dawn on him, knew what was coming and let it happen.

"You son of a bitch," Liam suddenly hollered right before he lunged and connected with an impressive right hook that hurt like hell and knocked him on his ass.

The shit then promptly hit the fan.

There was yelling. Rhiann flipped out and pulled Liam off him when he continued the smackdown from his knees. Kelly jumped in front of Roman with her arms out. Matty stood nearby with his eyes bugging out of his head.

As far as happy family gatherings go, this one was a category five shit storm of epic proportions.

"Don't you touch him," Kelly shrieked at Liam.

He couldn't believe the fierce roar of his protective little lioness as she fended off his attacker.

It was all kinds of fucked up that he'd never been more turned on. Ever. Watching her go toe-to-toe with Liam was pretty god damn funny. And sexy as fuck.

That's when brother and sister started yelling at each other.

"He stepped over the line," Liam barked.

"I don't recall giving you a vote on who I sleep with," Kelly responded.

The pained groan filling the air? That was him. The last thing they needed was these two going off on each other.

"You're my goddamn sister," Liam bit back.

Roman struggled to his feet because he knew Liam was gearing up for one hell of a verbal tirade.

"Oh, and what?" Kelly shot back. "I thought you two were friends, at least that's what Roman keeps saying. So which is it? Is he not allowed to fall in love? Or do I have to ask your permission?"

"In love? What?" Liam was approaching Def Con status. "Is that what he told you? Kelly, do you have any idea what floats this asshole's boat?"

Okay. That was it.

"Shut up Liam."

"Fuck off Bishop."

Next stop? Clash of the alpha titans. Roman had a burst of belligerence that manifested in a shove which Liam returned with an uppercut. An instant piling on happened next. While he and Liam slapped each other around and made asses out of themselves, Rhiann, Kelly and even Matty jumped into the fray.

With Rhi on Liam's back like a monkey trying to pull him away and Kelly frantically yanking on Roman's belt, also to break things up, Matty suddenly hollered "Kick him Kik," as Kelly's fugly Ugg reeled back and shot forward, smacking Liam in the shin so hard he and Rhi fell into the sofa with a loud, pained grunt.

The moment was so ridiculous and over-the-top, fall down funny, that he started to laugh.

After Liam and Rhi tumbled, Kelly pushed him into a chair across the room. She crossed her arms and glared at him and Liam. Rhiann and Matty joined her in the center of the room.

Rhi spoke first.

"Sweetie," she murmured with quiet gentleness. "He's in love with her."

Liam glared at him. "For real?"

He nodded.

"Okay then," Rhi gleefully quipped. She looked at Matty. "So, Matthew," she said. "I hear you have an awesome new bed. Wanna' show me?"

The kid didn't seem like he was going to fall for the obvious redirect, so Kelly chimed in. "Good idea," she told him.

Matty's baleful sneer at him and Liam was a perfect reminder that he had competition where Kelly was concerned. The only side the boy would ever take in a dispute was Kelly's. Even if she was a thousand percent wrong.

Snickering and nodding in unison with Rhiann he bit back a chuckle when Kelly added, "Don't worry about these two. They're in time out."

Well! Things he now knew…time out was the universal sign for bad behavior because Matty instantly brightened. He also ran to Roman, and like the energetic kid he'd come to love, balanced and bounced on his big thigh like a playground jungle gym as he rather soberly told him, "She'll make you say sorry." He leaned in, his feet dangling off the floor, and whispered, "Don't laugh. Kiki doesn't think laughing is pro-pree-it in time out."

They fist bumped. "Thanks, dude. Anything else I should know?"

Matty giggled and whispered, "He's just like Kiki. It's funny when they yell."

Roman looked up, caught Kelly's eye and then looked to Liam. Once again Matty the old soul went straight to the heart of the matter.

Rhiann held out her hand. Matty slapped her a five and ran ahead into the hallway on the way to his room. Halfway there he turned around and yelled, "Hey! Do you like dinosaurs?" Rhiann's soft, amused chuckle hung in the air and then they were gone. It was just the three of them now. Him. Kelly. Liam.

He gulped.

Across the room, Liam was massaging his jaw. He made a slightly pained noise that drew Kelly's attention. She marched over to him, grabbed her older brother by the chin and swung his head right, then left.

"*Pfft*," she sniped. "You're fine, you big baby."

Then she stomped over to him, but instead of a short, clipped, dismissive assessment, she went into full Nancy Nurse mode.

Her fingers gently explored his face. She gasped harshly a few times and made a point to shoot Liam the occasional dirty look. The way she was going on you'd think he'd barely escaped death. At one point he met Liam's dumbfounded gaze and behind her back gave him the finger.

When she was eventually satisfied he wasn't permanently disfigured, she surprised the holy hell out of him by pushing his legs around until a proper landing for her ass was in place. And then she sat down and turned her attention to Liam.

Was she staking a claim?

Absolutely.

He sat back and smiled. So, this is what master of the fucking universe felt like.

"Are you two finished acting like idiots?"

This one was on Liam. He'd have to accept that for once, something wasn't all about him, or he and Kelly would never find common ground.

There was a brief, uncomfortable silence and then to his great relief, Liam shook his head like he couldn't believe what was happening and chuckled.

The man Rhiann helped loosen up came out, and just like that, rigid, stick-up-his-ass Liam took a hike. He smiled. An actual, eye-rolling smile, and said, "Yes Ma'am," in a hilariously contrite voice.

When Kelly turned her head to look down at him for his reply, Roman caught Liam making rude hand gestures and sticking out his tongue. His spirit lifted. Even if his business relationship with Liam was on slippery ground, their friendship remained intact.

For shits and grins, he responded like a petulant child. "Well, he started it!"

She patted him on the cheek and offered a pitying sigh. "You poor thing. He started it? Is that like saying I started it? You're beginning to sound like a broken record."

Liam's roaring guffaw at the 'fuck-you-chip' she just handed him with that little nugget of inside information grated on his ego.

"All right. Look," she bit out. Her ass tightened on his thigh. He sat back and enjoyed the Kelly in charge show and fantasized about fucking her into next week the minute she gave the all clear.

"If I make nice and give this sister thing a chance, will you two shake hands and do that bro hug thing? I um," she stammered. A quick push of some hair behind her ear and some back stiffening and she finished the thought. "I need you both."

Impressed, encouraged, humbled. All these things swirled inside him. Her admitting to needing anything at all was huger than huge.

Liam rose and showed them the true measure of the man he was. Speaking directly to her, he said, "I was out of line. I'm sorry. Can we start over? I'd like that, Kelly. You're…family. My family."

Since she was nothing but a younger, female version of Liam, Kelly didn't immediately roll over. She had a few specifics of her own to lay down before they moved forward.

With a hand on Roman's shoulder, she spoke distinctly and clearly so there'd be no misinterpreting what she said.

"Roman is family."

It was a challenge and a promise wrapped up in one neat little package.

Liam snickered. "Us rolling around on the floor throwing punches? That's the stuff brothers do so no worry there. This motherfucker," he drawled with a nod, "was already seated at the family table and not just because my fiancée wouldn't have it any other way."

Their eyes met, and they both smiled. Truth.

"Good," Kelly replied. "Now let's discuss Matty."

Liam waved her off. "Not necessary, sis. I get it. It's gonna be fucking weird and an interesting legal kerfuffle, but I do get it."

Roman finally spoke. He pointed to each of them and stated

their titles. "Brother," he declared with great care. "Kiki is the mom," he said with a gesture at Kelly. "And, whatever the fuck he wants to call me, but essentially, the dad."

Everyone nodded and then he quickly added, "Oh, and Kelly is the decider. She made me promise."

He stood up and helped Kelly slide to her feet.

With the self-assurance and kick-ass snarl of a drill sergeant, she told them what to do. "Now shake you two and say sorry."

Liam, the dumb fuck, was quick to point out that he'd said sorry first. Kelly walked up to him and tugged on his ear. "What did I say?"

Her brother's startled yelp and pissy, "Ow," was music to Roman's ears. These two were going to be a party in the years ahead. He wished Rhi could see this because a grumpy, pouty Liam Ashforth was front-row, comedy gold.

Kelly looked around at the big empty walk-in wardrobe and shrugged at Rhiann. They were sitting cross-legged on the floor in the middle of the big closet, picking at a plate of nachos on the carpet between them.

"Seems like overkill to me. Who needs so many clothes?"

Rhiann Baron-Wilde's easy, amused laugh rang out. Sticking out one leg she wagged her foot. "I don't need these suede pumps, but they look bangin' with jeans and quite frankly, heels do amazing things to a woman's posterior."

"Roman hates the Uggs," she sniggered.

Catching a glob of gooey cheese with her tongue as she held up a chip loaded with nacho toppings, Rhiann chuckled and made a face. "He told you that, did he? Idiot."

Kelly nodded and laughed.

"I am one of three sisters," she explained, "so relationship advice comes naturally to me. You can tell me to shut up if you want but when it comes to hacks and hints for the care and feeding of today's modern, alpha shithead, I'm your girl. You think Liam's a handful? Bah!" she chortled. "Wait till you meet Brynn's husband and Charlie's hunk of burning love."

This was fun. She'd never ever hung out with a friend and shot the shit about men and shoes. She could get used to this.

"I'm all ears."

Rhiann re-arranged her position and laughed happily. "First, don't let him get his way all the time."

She barked with laughter. "Oh shit. No worries there. Half the time I have no idea what to do with him! He acts like a knuckle-dragging caveman when I don't ask him to open every damn lid with his manly muscles. Seriously, Rhiann. Do guys think all we do is sit around and wait for them to handle everything?"

"It's in the alpha code of conduct. But you'll get the hang of it. Every time he pounds his chest and plays the manly-man card? That's generally when you have the upper hand."

She had to give it some thought, but she was beginning to see the point. When Roman was knee deep in testosterone? She could bat her eyes, chew on a lip and pretty much get anything she wanted out of him. Men, or at least her man, was easy that way.

"The Uggs are a reminder to his bad self that a, you don't give a shit what he thinks when your feet are cold and besides, he ain't the boss of you."

She arched a brow.

"Ah," Rhiann chuckled. "I see Roman's bad boy ways have already corrupted you."

"I kind of like that bossy, domineering thing he's got going on."

"Good lord," Rhi bawled with laughter. "Don't ever tell him that! Keep him guessing and always on his toes. You'll thank me later."

"Can I ask you a question?"

"Sweetie, I have very few filters. Sisters, remember? Ask whatever you want but just know that I will answer whether you like it or not."

"Fair enough," she quipped. "Rhiann, you know Roman pretty well, right?"

"I know that he's an extraordinary man and that I trust him with my life. And Liam's."

She nodded and chewed a lip as she gathered her thoughts. "Do you think I'm crazy? I mean, we're moving awfully fast. One minute we were snarling and spitting at each other and then…"

Rhiann leaned against the wall, stretched her legs out in front of her and crossed them at the ankles.

"I met Liam just out of high school and let me tell you something. Ya' think he's a handful now? Back then, he was a grad student with a chip on his shoulder the size of Plymouth Rock, and he had a conservative stick rammed up his butt. I remember thinking he was so tight that a quarter would bounce off his forehead."

"Wow."

"By then his demons were gearing up for battle, and there was a menacing intensity about him that I didn't understand. Adam Ward did a lot of damage to a lot of people."

"So, what happened?"

"We had a brief, wild fling. Very secret. I was far too young, and he was not in a headspace for a real relationship. And then almost as soon as it started, we were over. He pulled the plug."

"You broke up?"

"I'm not sure that breaking up was part of what happened. We snuck around like naughty kids so it's not like we were a couple to begin with. Even though I was monumentally stupid and in over my head, I didn't regret any of it. That was almost a decade ago."

"How long have you been back together?"

"Roughly?" she asked with a nonchalant shrug. "About a year. Give or take. He bought me."

"He what?"

Rhiann laughed, smirked, and rolled her eyes. "You heard me. He bought the fashion magazine I worked for. Out of the damn blue. Hadn't heard a peep from him in forever but in his crazy mind being my boss was somehow going to be a good thing." She snicker-snorted and looked at Kelly. "I mean, honestly! Really? Men are so dumb."

"Is this when you met Roman?"

"Yes, indeed. A long story best shared over a few bottles of wine. Our tale has everything. Drama. Intrigue. Danger. A crazed stalker. Bullets. Kidnapping."

Kelly whistled and murmured, "Wow. Wild…but explains a lot."

"I've never had a brother," she murmured. "Roman would take a bullet for Liam and me, and I know this first-hand. He's a great guy, Kelly. And he needs a good woman in his life."

Lots to think about, that's for sure.

"So, when you ask if I think you're crazy, consider what I just shared. Is it possible for two souls to meet and instantly join? Yes, and I believe that with all my heart. In my case the bond weakened but never broke. When the time was right and each of us ready, the universe, as my hippy-dippy sister would say, brought us into the same space. What we did after that was all on us. Thankfully the love survived and now look."

She waved a pretty sparkler in Kelly's face. "We're getting married in June. I can't wait to have it be official so we can start making some bay-bays."

Marriage and babies. Hmmm. She blurted out what shot into her thoughts. "He um, sort of demanded that I marry him. Uh, a technical malfunction. But, well…Mother Nature must not have been impressed by our antics because the problem never materialized."

Rhiann's jaw was hanging open.

"And since, well, the subject hasn't come up."

"Oh my god," she muttered. "Do not let your brother know any of that. He'd have Roman neutered in a heartbeat."

"Newsflash," she drawled sardonically. "What happened? I didn't exactly give him much choice."

"I knew I was going to like you, Snow."

"Snow?"

Rhiann laughed merrily. "Yeah. He described you as Snow White when I demanded he send a selfie. I can't believe that old fart found himself a Disney princess to salivate over and that's exactly how I'm describing you to my sisters."

"Well, thank you for the compliment, but I'm not so sure me and my crappy second-hand jeans qualify for admittance to the romantic heroine show."

Oh, Sweetie! Did you think I wasn't going to do a Baron-Wilde makeover on you? We're going shopping!" she merrily declared. "And I have the best hair and make-up people. You just let me handle that part of things."

"I have a confession," she muttered.

"Unless you're secretly a dude, nothing you say could shock me."

"Roman told me you have a mouth," she giggled. "You must scare the snot out of those guys."

"Serves them right. Now spill. What kind of secret?"

"Yikes," she exclaimed. "I can't believe these words are coming out of my mouth, but here goes. I, um…well, I've never worn a dress."

Rhiann's brows bumped together, and furrows of frown lines marred her face. "Huh?"

"Yeah, I know," she sniggered when Rhiann's stunned expression froze on her face. "Pathetic, right? And it gets worse."

"I can't see how."

Kelly studied Rhiann's super sexy shoes and then pulled a face. "I roll for comfort. And practicality. Farm life isn't a fashion parade. Never have I ever…worn heels."

Rhiann gasped and clutched her chest. "Say it isn't so!"

She held up her hands in defeat. "My undies? Whichever five pack is on sale at Walmart or whatever looked halfway decent at the Thrift Store."

Rhiann started fanning herself while she pursed her lips, shook her head and muttered over and over, "Nope. Unacceptable. Not on my watch."

"Look at this place," she lamented with a dramatic wave. "Roman is so damn sophisticated and worldly. What's he doing with a girl in work boots and ratty jeans?"

"From where I'm sitting, he looks to me like a man finding out at long last that he's worthy of love. Being loved and showing love. Some wounds take a long time to heal."

"I know," she murmured with quiet anguish. "He told me."

Rhiann looked genuinely surprised. "Really?"

"Yeah. He has a picture in his wallet. That was more than a little sobering for me. Seeing his pregnant wife."

Kelly wasn't sure what was happening when Rhiann seemed to struggle, and her face went ashen for a moment. "He suffered greatly," she quietly murmured.

"It's because of what happened to Vanessa that he does personal security. Isn't it?"

"He knows he can't change what happened, Kelly. That's not what motivates him. I'm sure you know his background and understand that it's hardly a stretch when highly trained soldiers leave the military and take what they learned to the private sector. For Roman, security is a real, tangible thing. Unfortunately, all of his efforts to keep his family from harm's path didn't mean a damn thing in the face of evil. He isn't trying to atone. He just doesn't want anyone else to go through what he did."

"He has control issues."

"Don't we all?"

Excellent point.

"Will Liam forgive him?"

"He forgave him the second you used the word love."

"Don't be upset with me, Rhiann, but I'm not sure about your fiancée."

They both sighed.

"I know, and it's okay," Rhiann assured her. "None of us except perhaps Roman truly understands what this must be like for you. And Matthew. Leaving your lives behind. Going someplace that has to be scary. All these people sticking their noses into your business. You're my new hero, Kelly Anne James."

She gave a half shrug and dug around the nacho plate. "My whole life I've been someone else's pawn. And I didn't even know it. Not all of it, anyway. Then some snot-bag guy claiming to be an older brother who has some delusion about fixing my life comes along. I don't like it."

"You have it all wrong. He's not trying to fix you, Kelly. Is he trying to clean up Adam Ward's mess? Yes. But you're not a problem. Not you and not Matthew. I think you may find when the emotional blowback finally clears and the dust settles that having an older brother who puts family far above anything else will heal inner hurts you might not realize exist."

Rhiann rolled to her knees and crawled over, sat down next to her and put an arm loosely around her shoulders. "You're not on your own anymore. I will do everything I can to tamp down Liam's enthusiasm, but you need to understand that to him, finding out he has siblings is a gift. His upbringing left him feeling he was unworthy of a family. He'll stand on his head to make sure you're happy."

The idea made her chuckle. "Poor Roman."

"I know, right?" Rhiann laughed and hugged her tighter. "Shall we go see what the boys are up to? Guaranteed they're talking sports. Or cars."

"Or dinosaurs. Matty has a way of commandeering every conversation and steering it to his interests."

"Just like his older brother," Rhiann chuckled.

Kelly started to get up and then stopped and looked at Rhiann. "Oh god. Really?"

"Welcome to the tilt-a-whirl," Rhiann laughed. "Mr. King of All He Surveys has a mini-me."

They had a good laugh, stood up, rearranged their clothes, did some hair smoothing and grabbed the almost empty nacho platter.

"I can't wait to set Roman's credit card on fire."

Kelly sneered, "I have my own money."

Rhiann looped her arm through hers and led them from the big wardrobe. "As do I, but Kelly darling, practically rule number one with these alpha types is let them do the spoiling. It's easier than resisting. Roman will shit a bag of rocks if you make this a point of contention. Choose your alpha battles, my dear. And choose them wisely unless you don't ever want to sit down again."

"Rhiann," she gasped. "Are you saying what I think you're saying?"

They stopped walking, and Rhiann smirked at her. "Seriously?"

"What is it with guys and the spanking thing? I don't get it."

Rhiann's delighted sounding laugh rang out. "Well, clearly Mr. Bishop has yet to put you over his knee."

"He keeps threatening," she drawled.

"Well, sweetie, when he does? Relax and enjoy it. And then pout prettily and make some noise about your bottom being sore. The rest will take care of itself."

"No fucking way! Are you serious? Season tickets? Who the hell did you have to blow to score those?"

"Remember the creepy hipster dude with the mad computer skills? I brought him up from the IT department to look at that hacking issue we talked about. He mentioned that his grandfather gave him the tickets for Christmas. Next thing I knew he'd admitted to giving less than a crap about sports of any kind and said he planned to Craig's List the stuff and see what he could get. You can imagine how it went after that."

Roman snickered and held his beer aloft. "Only you, man."

"Hey. What can I say? Season tickets, dude. Center ice, fifth row."

"I bet Rhi is thrilled," he said with lots of sarcasm.

Liam grinned from ear-to-ear and Roman perked up. What had he done now?

"Hooked her bad ass up with VIP passes to half a dozen of her favorite designers at this year's fashion week. Not much she could say after that."

A belly laugh rumbled from Roman's mouth. "That's going to cost you a shit-ton. Rhiann and New York Fashion Week? Oh my god."

"Right?"

"So who are you taking to the Rangers? Are these business comps?"

"Fuck no," Liam howled. "I thought you and I…"

"Are you asking me on a date?"

Liam stammered to a halt and scowled despite the amusement pouring from his expression. "Tell me again why I put up with your fucking bullshit."

He finished off his beer, slammed the empty on the table, let out a belch and snickered. "Because I'm not eyeing up your pasty white ass for some butt fucking."

"Jesus lord, Roman," Rhiann screeched when she and Kelly came around the corner into the living room. "Have you a screw loose?"

"Whaaaat?' he teased. "No good? But I thought you knew the bears down in the parking garage, and a bunch of the dominatrix gals from payroll have a betting pool going on for who brings the lube and who does the honors."

Kelly stepped forward wearing the stern-nanny expression he enjoyed so much and gave him a major dose of shade. "Matty better not be anywhere in this room while you two are discussing butt lube."

"He's sawing wood in his bedroom. The kid dropped like a rock mid-afternoon and fell right asleep. Sorry," he added. "His naptimes are a bit off. The time change, ya' know?"

He searched her face for clues. She'd been gone a long time. After Rhiann took over and swept her off to discuss wardrobes and god only knows what else he'd had a hard time not charging after her.

"So," she asked with a snide smile that was a mirror-image of something Liam did. "Did you two kiss and make up?"

"Sis," Liam chortled. "It's all good as long as you realize I'm girlfriend numero uno."

Kelly looked to a grinning Rhiann and gave a long-suffering

sigh. "My competition thinks he's a comedian."

"Wait till Fantasy Football starts. We might as well book a cruise because these two enter some macho fugue state when the NFL fires up."

Liam didn't deny it and added a detail that somehow wiggled right past Roman's normally astute scrutiny.

"You'll note please, that our wedding is scheduled between play-off seasons."

"Sadly, he isn't kidding," Rhi muttered.

He and Kelly laughed.

"So what happens now?" she asked the group.

Nobody pretended not to know what she referred to.

Liam took the lead. "When you're ready, there are some legalities you need to handle. My lawyers will handle the heavy lifting, but you're in charge of the details. My hulking friend here," he said with a thumb jerked in his direction, "made something of a big deal out of me telling you that from time to time. So there you have it. You're in charge."

"What kind of details?" she asked.

Roman took the opportunity to draw her close and pulled Kelly onto his lap. "Mostly identity stuff. And your brother found a way to handle the Oklahoma property in a way that protects you and Matty from local encroachment or challenge."

"How?"

"It's too complicated to discuss right now. We'll sit down with Liam's legal team and go over everything."

"She needs a phone," Rhiann interjected. "And a driver. You're on that, right Roman?"

Kelly reacted to this comment with expected anxiety. He had about five seconds to clarify unless he wanted to get into a royal verbal skirmish with her later.

"Non-negotiable," he told her. "You and Matty will be assigned an assistant to handle logistics and security."

"What the fuck does that mean?" she immediately bit out. "Are you talking about a bodyguard?"

She started to get up, but he held her around the waist to cut off an angry retreat.

"Rhi?" he asked with a slight tinge of desperation.

"Choose your battles, Kelly. This one is unwinnable, so it's better not even to get started."

"I don't understand," Kelly griped.

"You know I was kidnapped, right? People are crazy. What can I say? Before that harrowing experience, I thought an assistant was complete and utter bougie bullshit…until I didn't. Almost getting killed has a way of making things simple. You're in New York City. Let them do this, Kelly. It's important, okay?"

Kelly gave him such a malicious look he was tempted to put both hands over his privates in case she nut-punched him. He read her expression. She was sick and tired of him continuously getting his way. There wasn't a lot he could do about that at the moment. Until she found her footing away from Oklahoma, he was in the driver's seat.

Roman knew the second she'd had enough. He was so damn proud of how she handled Liam and their first meeting, but he saw her starting to flag.

"Matty's birthday is next week."

He hated the small, frightened, emotionally exhausted tinge in her voice. "I'll be needing some things."

"His birthday?" Liam hooted. "That's fantastic. What do you need? I can get a moon bounce and rock climbing wall."

"No!" she cried. "No stuff. Just let me handle this. Roman?"

He thought of the big shopping bag full of party crap that they'd hauled with them and Kelly's sketch of a dinosaur cake she wanted to make and knew exactly what to do.

"Dinner with the whole family or just cake and ice cream. You're calling the shots, honey. What are you thinking?"

She bit her lip and looked all sorts of conflicted. "I guess dinner would be nice. Matty will like that. But no presents," she grumbled with a snarky glance in Liam's direction.

"Maybe just one?" Rhiann asked hopefully.

Roman gently caressed Kelly's back. She was done. He could sense it. Now wasn't the time to push this particular issue.

"Let's leave this for another time, hmm?" He directed his attention to Liam. "As for tomorrow, nothing before lunch, okay? They're still adjusting to the time change."

"No sweat," he answered drily. "Legal will do what they're told when they're told."

His little lover continued to surprise him when she became the perfect hostess and said all the right things as Liam and Rhiann gathered their coats and strolled toward the elevator vestibule.

They held hands as they walked along.

"I'm glad we did this," she told them. "Matty found the fight club detour quite amusing."

Liam groaned. "God, sorry about that."

There was more friendly banter, and then Kelly got in a parting shot. He very nearly fucked her brains out while pinning her to the wall when her ballsy inner bitch had the last word.

Offering her hand, she fixed her older brother with a classic Kelly James sneer and said, "Nice meeting you. I think you're a dick."

Rhiann burst out laughing, and Liam shook his sister's hand with comical vigor. "I *AM* a dick! Thank god we got that out of the way straight off."

The elevator came and as their company started taking their leave Roman began laughing.

"What's so funny dickhead?" Liam's asked with an arched brow sneer.

He snorted, offered Kelly a wink and then gave Liam a healthy dose of cheeky snarkasm. "Ever use that fancy pool table you've got?"

"Not really," Liam replied.

"He has a pool table? Kelly asked with a real laugh.

"That he does," Roman answered.

"Aw, this is gonna be great," Kelly chuckled.

As the elevator doors whooshed shut, Liam said, "Why do I feel like I'm being set up for something?"

He and Kelly laughed like hell and went arm in arm back to the apartment.

Chapter Twenty-Two

The dinger went off, and she dashed to the massive industrial looking gas stove to open the oven door. The aroma of warm vanilla and cinnamon filled the air. She'd made one of Matty's favorite things, monkey bread, and by the looks of the bubbling confection, had held her own in the modern kitchen.

Wiping her hands on a towel, she grabbed the list on the counter and checked off the monkey bread. Next up—meatball chili, but she had a few hours before getting started.

Laughter rang out from the living room. Happy laughter. She smiled.

Matty's birthday had been more than memorable. Roman put his personal spin on the occasion and arranged for Sam and Ginny to fly in for the big day. He even put them up in a fancy five-star hotel. For the past several days they'd all been running ragged around the city, taking in every imaginable tourist stop. Roman thought of everything, including an eye-opening, behind-the-scenes private tour of the dinosaur exhibit at the American Museum of Natural History. The boys, including Sam, enjoyed the day-long nerd adventure while the ladies tagged along and feigned enthusiasm.

To Kelly, if you've seen one stack of dinosaur bones, you've seen them all.

A particular highlight found her, Ginny and Rhiann experiencing the deep indulgence of a VIP spa day at the Mandarin Oriental. All in all, she was exhausted and happier than she'd ever been.

Their week together was coming to an end. She'd be sad to see her friends go but she had something extra cool to look forward to.

Roman was taking her on an actual date. For Valentine's Day! And she had a sexy black lace dress for the occasion, courtesy of Rhiann, plus a pair of shoes she was secretly practicing walking in.

Today, though, they were doing nothing except hanging out, much to Matty's delight. He'd grown so much in the last few weeks. Ever since that fateful moment when he stepped forward and challenged a big stranger in their midst, her sweet Matty was changing. Right before her excited eyes, he became what she always hoped for. Just a normal kid.

"Need any help?" a deep voice asked from the doorway.

She turned toward the sound with a ready smile. Roman. She sighed. If the man got any sexier, she was going to need an intervention because her one constant thought morning, noon, and night was making love with the man.

They went through an embarrassing number of condoms and talked about other forms of birth control. Because they didn't limit their sexy times to just the bedroom, that made the condom procedure a challenge at times.

"What did you have in mind?" she purred.

He yanked her flush against him. Exactly what she expected when she turned the flame to simmer with her growls.

"Five minutes in the pantry with the door shut."

She smirked and wagged her tongue. "Will there be fucking involved?"

"Most definitely. A quickie though. No time for a full course meal."

She studied his face to see if he was serious. The glittering gleam from his eyes told her that yeah, he was serious.

"What's everybody doing?"

She couldn't believe that she was crazy enough to consider his raunchy suggestion, but she was.

"They've set up camp in Matty's room. Candyland followed by Connect Four. It's a tournament I think. And unless I miss my guess, Sam is headed for a short nap. Bet you're glad now that we put a recliner in his room."

She chuckled and smacked his chest. "Best story time equipment ever invented!"

"All right little madam. Stop stalling. Anything need to be turned off in here?" he asked with a sharp glance at the stove.

She was dancing toward the pantry with her hands flapping in the air. "Safety first? We're good, fancy man. Now you stop stalling and get your sexy ass in there." She'd stopped, grabbed the pantry's door knob, and was waving him on.

"Yes, Ma'am," he snickered as he slid by.

She took one last look around, didn't see or hear anyone, and quietly pulled the door shut.

When she turned around Roman's pants were down around his ankles, and he was casually handling his impressively rigid cock.

"My, my," she purred. "You're a very big boy, aren't you?"

"You've proven you can handle it," he drawled.

She tapped a nail on her chin and eyed him up with undisguised hunger. "How do you see this going?"

"Well, it's your lucky day, kitten. Rhi thought I'd lost my mind for putting a carpet in here. I hate cold wood floors on my delicate feet."

"Let me guess," she cooed as she came toward him. "All fours?"

His wicked leer got her engine running. "You know me so well."

Eager to get his lovely fat cock inside her, she ripped off her stretchy yoga pants, shimmied like a stripper out of a scrap from the naughty lingerie Rhiann loaded her up with, and dropped to the carpet.

"Face down and that sexy ass up. Spread your thighs. A little more," he growled after a moment.

She heard the sound of a condom wrapper being ripped open. A second later his fingers were exploring her opening. His pleased growl made her pussy quiver. She was ready and becoming wetter and more aroused by the moment. She loved when it was like this. No foreplay. Just animal lust. Pure, nasty, fucking.

He moved into position and spread her ass apart as his hard shaft began to penetrate her. Almost immediately she started to pant. Just thinking about him inside her was enough to make the juices flow and her body respond to the promise of an orgasm.

The sensation as he stretched her and his fat cock pushed deeper was amazing. They both groaned at the same time when he was fully seated.

He shifted and pushed her one knee out. A gush of arousal greeted the head of his beautiful cock as the slight change in angle sent him just that much deeper. Sweet tingles crawled slowly along her nerves.

"Give me your hands," he demanded in a harsh, guttural growl.

Right away she started melting down. He knew she got an extra thrill out of having her hands restrained.

Crossing her wrists low on her back, he grabbed them and held tight. His grip and the control it gave him served as an anchor as he got serious about the fucking.

With her face on the carpet, she bucked into him and rolled her ass. The circular movement made his cock feel enormous. Holding tight to her wrists, he pulled back and almost out of her and then slammed home with a violent thrust. She came immediately.

Her leg shook. She shoved a fist in her mouth as a screaming climax took her under. She was barely finished when he bent down and bit her shoulder. "Count it down, kitten. A dozen should do it."

Oh god. He was killing her. And she loved it.

"Twelve," she grunted.

"Hard or easy, baby?"

"Hard. Please, Roman."

His chuckle had a dirty vibe. "Yes, Ma'am."

He pounded into her as she counted down with each mind-emptying stroke. By the count of eight, she was almost incoherent. He slapped her ass. "Count kitten. I want you to know when I come."

Three quick, brutal thrusts sent her spiraling.

She was gasping for air as Roman paused, caressed her ass with one hand and squeezed her wrists with the other.

"How many left?"

Unf. She struggled to answer. "F-four."

He grunted. Two hypnotically slow strokes followed. She whimpered when his cock swelled, and he yanked on her wrists. She arched as much as possible and went with him as he came.

When he pulled out a minute or so later, he bent and kissed her ass. She loved this part too. Roman enjoyed this position. So did she. He said he liked watching her ass when he fucked her. There wasn't a lot of doubt in Kelly's mind that one day he'd be claiming a different sort of virginity.

He dealt with the condom and helped her up. She got quite a thrill when he knelt in front of her to help put on the ridiculously skimpy panties.

"Let me say again how much I like this." He leaned in and dropped a wet kiss real low and breathed her in.

During their spa adventure, she let Rhiann persuade her to give waxing a try. Ginny thought the whole thing hilarious. She would have done it too except she declared that her downstairs situation was currently in tiptop shape.

Refusing even to consider one of those Brazilian numbers where every hair was ripped out, she opted for something called a sweetheart trim. When it was over her out-of-control garden was a delightfully neat and pretty hedge with the suggestion of some heart shaped lady-scaping clearly visible. Roman lost his shit the first time he saw it. Since then he'd taken to licking her pussy every chance he got.

With a cheeky smirk, she answered. "Well, once you explained how much careful trimming and man-mowing goes into your uh, presentation," she silkily teased, "it seemed the least I could do."

She quickly pulled on her stretch pants and suggested he hurry the hell up and do the same. When they cracked the door a minute later and peeked their heads out, she breathed a sigh of relief to find they'd pulled off some pantry hanky panky while there were people around.

Dashing into the kitchen, she washed her hands and made a small production out of consulting her list. Roman went straight to the refrigerator, pulled out a bottle of that disgusting Yoohoo shit he loved so much and guzzled the whole container.

That's what they were still doing a good minute later when Matty came busting in.

"Hey!" he hollered. Boyish excitement was bouncing off him. "Can we have a puppy? Gigi says we need a dog."

"Oh she does, does she?" Kelly drawled at the exact second Ginny appeared.

"I'm so sorry, you two," she half-apologized, and half laughed. "I wasn't paying attention. You know how it is."

Everyone but Matty nodded in agreement.

"He mentioned a puppy, said Roman was on board, and before I could think it through I said it was a great idea."

"What's a great idea?" a new voice asked.

She turned toward the other end of the kitchen in time to see Rhiann and a casually dressed Liam striding toward them.

She didn't say it out loud, but her expression certainly revealed her thoughts. *This place is like Grand Central Station.*

Roman chuckled, kissed her forehead and went to welcome the rest of the family. For someone who spent her whole life in solitary confinement, this near-constant ebb and flow of person-to-person contact proved a challenge. She was getting better at it though, and had even softened a bit toward Liam.

Not long after their arrival in the city, Adam Ward finally died. It was a non-event. She didn't feel a thing, and if Liam did, he kept it to himself.

While their interactions were politely pleasant and at times oddly close, they were still dancing around each other. Matty, on the other hand, got sucked right into having men around. The one and only time things got obviously weird was when Liam presented Matty with a small gift bag containing two DVDs.

She'd been so proud of his big boy reaction. Politely accepting the gift with the appropriate thanks, he then handed the bag off to her and informed Liam that, "Kiki doesn't let me watch TV without… um."

"Permission," she explained.

Liam looked horrified by his gaffe. Roman quickly explained that they were determined to raise the boy without an overdose of technology. Especially mindless TV watching.

Since then, Liam went out of his way to interact with her on what she'd come to think of as the parenting portion of the program. He was genuinely curious to learn how she'd managed when Matty was a baby and asked smart, open-minded questions about her parenting philosophy.

She assumed this was because he and Rhiann wanted to start a family. The whole clueless husband-to-be thing was adorable and cute.

A long time later after a family style meal of meatball chili, Roman's favorite homemade cornbread and a big salad, they were lounging around the living room when out of the damn blue Ginny said, "Are you two planning on raising the boy here in the city?"

"We're exploring other options," Roman told her.

"Tell Gigi about the house," Matty insisted with an emphasizing karate chop.

It was Liam who did the explaining. Kelly looked at Rhiann whose face was positively beaming as he laid it out.

"My lovely bride and I are looking for a family house that we can move into after the wedding. There are a few new developments we're looking at. One is outside the city, and the other is in Connecticut."

Roman offered his opinion. "I like the Connecticut house. The development is secure, and it's in a great school district."

"That sounds to me like you're in the market too," Ginny observed.

Sam chimed in. "What are we talking about here? Big family houses?"

"Oh no," Rhiann was quick to say. "Not at all. The development Roman refers to has about forty homes. It's gated and is just four blocks from a huge park. The houses aren't cookie cutter. There are sprawling colonials and single story ranch style."

"We sound like a realtor brochure," Liam said with a chuckle. "Do I hear the sounds of my future wife making a decision? Can it be?"

"Maybe we should both buy in the same community."

Kelly's head whipped around at Roman's comment.

"Now, hold on," Sam interjected. "Me and the missus might want to get in on this too."

"What?" she stammered. Were they in an alternate reality? What was going on?

Ginny rubbed her husband's shoulder. "Providence isn't the same without you," she said with a warm smile.

Matty launched into her arms. "I love my Gigi."

"You know we think of Kelly and Matty as family," Sam said. "I've been thinking about giving Bobby a chance to take over the butcher shop. And asking Jimmy to manage my stuff if we leave. Bet he'd be happy to be your property manager too, hon."

She was stunned. They had it all figured out. She jumped up and ran to Sam, folding him in a hearty hug. Ginny joined in. Matty too.

Then Roman squeezed in and before long so did Liam and Rhiann. They were group hugging and laughing at the same time.

Her whole being filled with light.

This is what love is, she thought.

Sam and Ginny. She loved them as the grandparents she never had.

Matty was more son than brother and her devotion to him was

without question.

Rhiann's welcoming inclusion left her feeling like one of the Baron-Wilde sisters. It was an amazing and special thing.

Even Liam. She loved him. How could she not? He was practically her twin in manner and temperament. Heaven help all of them if they ever truly tangled. His arrogance and her take-no-shit personality were a recipe for disaster.

And then there was Roman. The love she felt for him was different. It scared her a little because of how fast and completely she fell for him. But he'd been the most amazing gentleman despite their raunchy proclivities, and not ever for a single moment in all of this had she wondered if he was for real or if he truly did have her back.

He was, simply put, the best man on the planet. No competition. None. End stop as far as she was concerned. She loved him with her full heart and intended to follow him to the ends of the Earth if she had to. And surprise, surprise. She didn't care one little bit if they were married or not.

"So I guess this means we're all moving to Connecticut." Sam was having a good hearty laugh that quickly caught on.

"And I'm getting a puppy!"

Everyone stopped, looked at Matty as he did some herky-jerky touchdown dance, and then cracked up laughing even harder.

"I think this calls for champagne," her sexy lover declared before dashing into the kitchen.

There must be a committee meeting, she thought when Liam and Sam followed.

That left the ladies and a still bouncing Matty alone in the living room.

"Can anyone tell me what just happened here?" she asked.

Rhiann, dear sweet Rhiann, put one arm around Ginny and the other around Kelly.

"I'll tell you what happened. The past just got put to rest. You, Ms. James, have gained one hell of a guy and a brother who thinks you're the tits and the balls."

Ginny boomed with laughter.

"And the love of my life and undisputed all around good guy not only gained a sister and a brother, he seems to have picked up a set of grandparents along the way."

"Truth," Ginny sweetly declared.

"We cooked up a goddamn family ladies! I'd say that makes us the shit. And if our men want to buy us pretty shiny things, and by that I mean custom houses, why resist?"

She wasn't sure what to say or how to react. Everything was too perfect.

"And one more thing," Rhiann happily chirped. "You," she said to her with a wink. "Bridesmaid. You and Charlie. My big sister Brynn is doing Matron of Honor duties. And Matty can be the ring bearer. Is that okay Kelly? Will you both please be in our wedding?"

"Oh my god, Rhiann," she cried. "Are you kidding? Matty!" she cried. "Did you hear that? We're gonna be in a wedding!"

"Yay!" Matty yelled. "Liam's getting married!"

"And Ginny," Rhiann said. "I want you and Sam there too. On Liam's side. As his family. Is that okay?"

That's when the flood of tears started. Lots of them. The tissues were being passed around when the men came back into the room carrying the champagne and glasses.

"Kelly?" Roman's concern touched her heart. He was just so damn sweet.

"Relax, Bishop," Rhiann quipped. "Happy tears, every one."

Liam took care of popping the champagne and handing out the glasses while Roman cracked open a ginger ale and poured some into a smaller glass for Matty.

The most unexpected and unique family she ever could have imagined gathered in the living room of her new home and raised their glasses.

Sam made a simple toast that with a few choice words covered a world of emotions.

"To family. The one that stands the test of time. Salud, children!"

"Salud," they all cheered.

"I want to say something," Kelly said after a sip or two.

Everyone looked at her and the emotion clogged up her throat.

"I'm grateful that you cared enough to stick around," she told Sam and Ginny.

"I'm glad you went digging," she told Liam and Rhiann.

To Roman, she said, "Thank you."

"Why?" he asked in a gentle voice.

"I love you."

"Me too," Matty boasted. "Me and Kiki love you Roman. Can we get married too?"

"What?" Roman stammered.

"Matty," Kelly murmured. "Not now."

"No, wait," Roman said. "He's right. This is perfect!" He high-fived Matty and said, "Thanks, little dude. I owe you a big one."

Then he slugged back the rest of his champagne and took the flute from her unfeeling grip and put the two aside. When he got on one knee she mumbled, "What's happening?"

"Kelly," he began. "Things you need to know. I fucking adore you."

Matty put a hand to his mouth and side-muttered a snarky and very comical, "Penny jar."

"And I hate those damn Uggs."

She giggled and gave him her hand when he asked for it.

"Will you marry me and make me nucking futz for the rest of my sorry life?"

"Well, I don't know," she teased. "Does this proposal come with a ring?"

There was no way she expected him to whip some bling out of his pocket but that didn't mean he wasn't a fast and creative thinker.

"Who's got a pen? Find me a pen!"

Everyone scrambled.

"Found one!" Rhiann yelled.

"Me too," Sam said.

He took the blue pen because it was her color and made a silly production out of drawing a diamond ring on her finger.

"How's that? Good?"

His cheeky grin sealed her fate.

"I want you to wear a wedding band."

"Is that the Kelly James way of saying yes?"

The sneaky devil.

She looked at Matty. His face was full of rapturous joy.

"Because you asked this time instead of issuing a demand, then yes. Yes. I will marry you and drive you as crazy as I can. For all the days of our lives."

He leaped to his feet and kissed her with such passion and emotion that she started to cry. Tears flowed like rain down her cheeks.

What started as an unwelcome incursion into her life had turned into the greatest joy imaginable. She wasn't the forgotten invisible girl anymore, and she and Matty were surrounded by an embarrassment of love and support.

Not only were all her hopes and dreams for the future assured, but she also found the love of a lifetime in the deal.

It was the happiest happily ever after of all time.

THE END

A Note from the Author

Bringing you Roman Bishop's happily ever after has been a true pleasure.
His story connects the Justice saga and the Wilde Women series in fun and surprising ways!
I hope you enjoyed Bishop's Pawn.

Wonder what happens next in Roman's story?
Pick up the thread in the next Family Justice Novel!

~ Everlasting ~
A Family Justice Novel
Spring 2017

Acknowledgments

Ella Fox
We're Cooking With Gas, Now!

The Sb's Of My Abs
You Know Who You Are And What You've Done.

My *Halliday Ever After* Family
Okay, Okay. Who Licked Him First?

*D*A*
Nothing Quite Compares To The Support Of Like Minds

OTHER BOOKS BY SUZANNE HALLIDAY

The Justice Brothers
Broken Justice
Fixing Justice
Redeeming Justice
Sanctuary

Family Justice
Always
Desert Angel
Sanctuary
Unchained
Unforgettable

Wilde Women
Wilde Forever
Wilde Heart
Wilde Magic

The Gideon Affair
The Wedding Affair

ABOUT THE AUTHOR

Suzanne Halliday writes what she knows and what she loves – sexy contemporary romance featuring strong men and spirited women. Her love of creating short stories for friends and family developed into a passion for writing romantic fiction with a sensual edge. She finds the world of digital, self-publishing to be the perfect platform for sharing her stories and also for what she enjoys most of all – reading. When she's not on a deadline you'll find her loading up on books to devour.

No longer wandering because the desert southwest finally claimed her, these days instead of digging out from a snowstorm you can still find Suzanne with 80's hair band music playing in the background, kids running in and out, laptop on with way too many screens open, something awesome in the oven, and a mug of hot tea clutched in one hand.

Social Media

Website: authorsuzannehalliday.com

Facebook: www.facebook.com/SuzanneHallidayAuthor

Twitter@suzannehalliday

Made in the USA
San Bernardino, CA
11 May 2017